Praise for
Gameboard of the Gods

"This brilliant book is a miracle. Think *American Gods* with the romantic heart of *Vampire Academy*. What's the point of world building if you aren't building something and someone to love? I'm in love with every character in this book. How do I know? When I got to the last page I turned to the first and started again, thinking this is why I read."
—Margaret Stohl, *New York Times* bestselling author of *Icons*

"A genuinely interesting, well-written, entertaining story. . . . Justin and Mae have real chemistry." —Tor.com

"This book is fast-paced and suspenseful . . . a promising first book in a projected series." —*Booklist*

"Provocative and dark—*Gameboard of the Gods* is epic in scale and impossible to put down."
—Kami Garcia, #1 *New York Times* bestselling coauthor of the Beautiful Creatures series

"It's dark, it's fantastical, and the chemistry is just wow!"
—*USA Today*

"After years of YA, [Mead] has finally returned to her adult roots with an ambitious (and sexy!) sci-fi outing."
—*Entertainment Weekly*

"*Gameboard of the Gods* has a fascinating and well-thought-out setting, thorny and complex problems, and top-notch characters." —Fantasy Book Critic

"Fantasy and science fiction elements merge in an enticing mix, creating . . . a unique world that continues to get stronger and more vivid as you read. Endearing characters forged from steel and strength push this book forward in a way that presents several avenues for action and suspense. . . . *Gameboard of the Gods* is an exceptional read and the first of what promises to be a compelling series." —Fresh Fiction

continued . . .

More Praise for Richelle Mead and Her Novels

"Writing this good tempts me to believe in angels . . . or deals with the devil."
—Rachel Caine, *New York Times* bestselling author of the Morganville Vampires series

"Great characters, dark worlds, and just the right touch of humor."
—Patricia Briggs, *New York Times* bestselling author of the Mercy Thompson series

"As storytellers go, they don't get better than Mead!"
—*RT Book Reviews*

"Mead doesn't go halfway on anything. Her characters are raw, the emotions are deep, and sometimes you want to hit her main characters so hard they'll see stars."
—*USA Today*

"An engaging read with an unusually tangible, believable, living story world, featuring a protagonist of unexpected depth and sympathy."
—Jim Butcher, #1 *New York Times* bestselling author of the Dresden Files

"Absorbing . . . blends an intricately detailed fantasy with a contemporary setting . . . and a diverse . . . cast of supporting characters."
—*Booklist*

"Mead's storytelling improves with each installment, as she keeps readers on the edge of their seats while adding a few unexpected twists."
—The Associated Press

"Exciting, empowering, and un-put-down-able."
—Hollywood Crush, MTV.com

RICHELLE MEAD

GAMEBOARD

OF THE

GODS

AGE OF X

A SIGNET BOOK

SIGNET
Published by the Penguin Group
Penguin Group (USA) LLC, 375 Hudson Street,
New York, New York 10014

USA ! Canada I UK I Ireland I Australia I New Zealand I India I South Africa I China
penguin.com
A Penguin Random House Company

Published by Signet, an imprint of New American Library, a division of Penguin
Group (USA) LLC. Previously published in a Dutton edition.

First Signet Printing, June 2014

 REGISTERED TRADEMARK—MARCA REGISTRADA

ISBN 978-0-451-46799-7

Printed in the United States of America
10 9 8 7 6 5 4 3 2 1

FOR JAY,

THIS ONE WAS WAITING FOR YOU.

As the main body of troops in Rome they were the emperor's instrument to discourage plotting and rebellion and to crush unrest. The emperor's most immediate line of defence; they could also, on occasion, be his most deadly enemies.

—*The Prætorian Guard*, by Boris Rankov

At the nuptials of Peleus and Thetis all the gods were invited with the exception of Eris, or Discord. Enraged at her exclusion, the goddess threw a golden apple among the guests, with the inscription, "For the fairest." Thereupon Juno, Venus, and Minerva each claimed the apple. Jupiter, not willing to decide in so delicate a matter, sent the goddesses to Mount Ida, where the beautiful shepherd Paris was tending his flocks, and to him was committed the decision. The goddesses accordingly appeared before him. Juno promised him power and riches, Minerva glory and renown in war, and Venus the fairest of women for his wife, each attempting to bias his decision in her own favour. Paris decided in favour of Venus and gave her the golden apple, thus making the two other goddesses his enemies.

—*Bulfinch's Mythology*, by Thomas Bulfinch

CHAPTER 1

SHE USUALLY WEARS BLACK

Mae dealt out death regularly. It really wasn't a problem.

Death was clean on the battlefield, and there was no reason to dwell on what it meant. The kills were just mission objectives, and the people weren't really people at all. It was you or them. And when the fight was done, you could just walk away.

But today? There was no walking away. Today, she was walking *toward* death, and that scared the hell out of her. Not much else did these days.

With a deep breath, she leaned her cheek against the living room mirror, closing her eyes and taking comfort in the way the glass cooled her skin. She repeated the soldier's creed over and over in her head, using the familiar words to steady herself: *I am a soldier of the Republic. I do not serve my own will but that of my country. I am its tool and will gladly lay down my life to further this nation's glory. I am a soldier of the Republic. I do not serve my own will but that of my country. . . .*

A knock at the door startled her out of her mantra, and she straightened up. Another deep breath calmed the shaking of her hands, and she pushed her emotions into a far compartment in her mind. Locked away, those feelings could not touch her. They were powerless, and she was free. She double-checked her face in the mirror, but it gave nothing away. It was blank. Empty. In control.

Dag and Val were at the door, as she'd known they'd be. They greeted her with forced smiles that were a far cry from their usual happy-go-lucky selves. Both wore uniforms identical to hers: a mandarin-collared black jacket over black pants with black boots. Black everywhere. Even the buttons were black. The only color came from a scarlet pip on the collar, standing out like a drop of blood. To the inexperienced eye, these uniforms looked no different from the ones the prætorians usually wore into battle. To Mae, who could see and feel the dressy fabric of their formal attire, the uniform seemed flimsy and brought back her earlier fears of vulnerability. Being weaponless wasn't helping matters.

"Here to babysit me?" she asked.

"Who said anything about babysitters?" Dag was always quick with a smile, though his eyes betrayed him that morning. "We're just a bunch of friends going out together."

"You make it sound like we're going to a bar," Mae said. She walked back to the mirror and examined the braided bun she'd so painstakingly worked on. Grimacing, she pulled out the hairpins and began unraveling it all.

Val made herself comfortable on the arm of the couch, lazy and limber as a cat, even under these circumstances. "What are you doing?"

"It's messy," Mae said.

"There wasn't a hair out of place," protested Val.

Mae didn't answer. In the mirror, she saw her friends exchange troubled glances behind her. *It's worse than I thought,* Val seemed to be saying. Dag's expression said he was in agreement but didn't entirely know how to handle it. Snapping a neck, lifting weights, doughnut-eating contests. Those were in his comfort zone. Therapy? Less so.

It wasn't part of Val's skill set either. Neither knew quite what to do with Mae, and she certainly wasn't going to help them out—because she didn't want them to do anything. She wanted them to treat her in their usual flippant way. And what she wanted most was for this day to be over, so that life could return to normal.

"How many times have you braided it today?" Val's voice was uncharacteristically gentle.

"It's not right," Mae said, dodging the question. This was

actually the eighth time she'd braided her hair. She kept pulling so tightly that her scalp had started to turn red, though the tiny metal implant in her arm dutifully dulled the pain. "You wouldn't understand."

Neither Val nor Dag ever had hair problems. Dag always kept his dark hair closely shaved, and Val wore hers in a pixie cut that suited her diminutive frame. *I should cut mine,* Mae thought. She'd considered it a hundred times but could never bring herself to do it.

"It's okay, you know. Grief is a normal part of the, um, process." Dag had apparently been reading self-help books before coming over. "You can even cry."

"Why would I do that?" Mae pulled so hard on a strand of hair that she winced.

"Because that's what people do when they lose someone they care about," said Val. "You're so tightly wound up that you'll explode if you don't relax. And do *not* undo that. It's fine."

Mae had just finished her hair again, neatly wrapping the braid into a perfect knot above the back of her neck. She really was on the verge of pulling it out again when Val grabbed her arm. "Enough, Mae. We're going to be late."

It was another bad sign, Val's using her real name instead of her pet name, Finn. But Mae couldn't deny her friend's point. It was time to go. With one last glance in the mirror, she let them lead her outside to the subway entrance across the street. They took the blue line out to the base, earning a number of startled looks from other passengers. Prætorians weren't that common outside of military and federal centers. A group of them was especially unusual. The passengers kept their distance and glanced around the train uneasily, wondering if they should expect a terrorist attack.

The threesome ended up reaching the base early, but plenty of other prætorians were already entering the ceremonial hall. And here Mae faltered, stopping just outside the entrance. The spring sunshine was far too bright and cheery for a day like today. Dag touched her arm. "You okay?"

"You don't have to go," Val told her.

Mae saluted the flag overhead and continued forward to the hand scanner. "Everything's fine."

Neat rows of chairs filled the hall, which was nearly packed with prætorians. The news had come in less than a week ago, and it would have taken a fair amount of scrambling to pull so many of the guard back in from their scattered assignments. Some wouldn't be here, of course. It was the nature of the job. But the death of a prætorian was so monumental that their superiors would've certainly done whatever they could to ensure a good showing.

Although there was no official seating chart, the prætorians were gathering in cohorts. Val waved at someone across the room. The Scarlets had already taken a middle position and were beckoning them over. Val and Dag started to head in that direction, but Mae stopped again, allowing her eyes to focus on the front of the hall.

There'd been no body to recover, but they'd still set out a casket made of a dark, gleaming wood. Prætorian black. A swath of indigo silk covered it, with the RUNA's flag draped over that. Piles of gardenias sat on either side, their softness contrasting with the clean lines of the casket.

Not caring whether Val and Dag followed her or not, Mae turned toward the center aisle, which led straight to the shrine. A bubble of emotion—sorrow and panic combined—began to rise within her, and she staunchly pushed it down. Throwing back her shoulders, holding her chin high, she began the impossibly long walk toward the front of the room. People stepped aside for her, and those who hadn't noticed her before now stopped to stare. She ignored those looks, along with the whispers that soon followed. She kept her gaze fixed firmly ahead, silently repeating the creed: *I am a soldier of the Republic. I do not serve my own will but that of my country.* Those words were echoed by her mother's, spoken so many years ago: *You can ignore the rest because you're better than them. Empty yourself of all feeling, because if they can't see it, then they can't use it against you.*

Those standing near the front also parted for her, moving away from the casket. Nearby conversation fell silent. There was a golden plate affixed to the dark wood, just under the flag. PORFIRIO ALDAYA, INDIGO COHORT. His dates of service were listed below, along with a Latin inscription that probably mentioned honor and duty. Mae ran her fingertips over his name, and suddenly the scent of the gardenias became cloying and oppressive. The world spun, and she closed her eyes.

Porfirio is dead. It didn't seem possible that someone so full of life, someone who burned with passion and energy, could truly be gone from this world. She couldn't bring herself to mull over what had happened to him after death. Had his consciousness ceased to exist? Or was he in some paradise that religious zealots preached about?

"You killed him, you know."

Mae opened her eyes at the familiar voice and slowly turned around. Drusilla Kavi stood there, hands on her hips, her dark eyes flashing with a mix of grief and rage that mirrored Mae's own feelings. Kavi was half a foot shorter than Mae, and Mae had no difficulty keeping her face still and flat in the path of that anger. Other prætorians standing nearby watched intently.

"You killed him," Kavi repeated. The indigo pip on her collar was an echo of Porfirio's. "You might as well have set the bomb yourself, you fucking castal bitch. He wouldn't have gone if it wasn't for you."

Mae had been called worse and had learned to ignore that kind of thing long ago. "Porfirio made his own choices. No one could make him do anything." She refused to be baited and tried to step around the other woman. *Be calm. Be superior.* "Excuse me, I need to return to my cohort."

"Don't walk away from me!" yelled Kavi. Her voice rang through the hall, and anyone who hadn't been aware of the unfolding drama now was. Kavi grabbed Mae's arm. "Do you even feel anything? Did you even care when he died? How can you be so cold?"

Mae jerked her arm back and felt the first kindling of anger. "Don't touch me again. And don't insult him by making a scene." Mae turned around and saw that Val and Dag were standing nearby, as were a number of other Scarlets. Behind Kavi, several Indigos had also gathered. Backup. All of their faces were tense and hard as they braced to defend their own. The prætorians had a remarkable history of dangerous encounters, but brawling at a funeral probably wasn't in the books.

"Is that what happens to the men you fuck? You kill them?" Kavi caught hold of Mae again and spun her around. "I told you not to walk away from me! *You killed him!*"

"And I told you not to touch me."

That was when everything snapped. Kavi hadn't just shattered the tight reins of Mae's discipline; she'd also opened up all those boxes that Mae had used to lock up her feelings. All the grief, all the fury, all the guilt . . . every emotion that Mae had carefully packed and filed away since she'd learned of Porfirio's death came pouring out. The floodgates burst, and Kavi was in their path.

Prætorians were fast, their reflexes surpassing those of ordinary soldiers. It was what defined them and was what the implant enhanced. When Mae struck out and punched Kavi in the face, Kavi should have at least seen it coming. Maybe she wouldn't have had a chance to react fully, but she should've had warning. It was clear from the widening of her eyes as she flew backward into a row of chairs that she'd been completely unprepared for the attack.

Once the action started, though, her reflexes kicked in. She jumped up with little delay, but Mae was already on her again. Kavi made a few attempts to land a hit, but Mae dodged each time. A leap to the side, as perfect as anything she'd ever done in the *canne* combat of her youth, gave Mae the opportunity to shove the other woman backward. Kavi hit the ground, much more ungracefully than any prætorian should have. They were usually like cats, but Kavi had trouble righting herself. Her response was still fast by other people's standards—but it took a couple of seconds too long by theirs. There was no chance for her to defend herself when Mae shot forward and kicked her in the stomach. It was immediately followed by a hit to the knee. Mae heard a *crack*, and Kavi screamed as she fell to the ground.

Battle mode kicked in so automatically that Mae was barely aware of what she did, only that she had to keep fighting and make sure Kavi stayed down. Endorphins and neurotransmitters surged within Mae, making her stronger and faster—but there was something else enhancing them today, a strange darkness flooding her senses and urging her to destroy. It overshadowed her like a cloak, an outside power that insidiously crept its way into her, letting her revel in the joy of violence and pain. Panic briefly seized Mae as she recognized the unwelcome sensation: *No, not again.* But her mental protests were soon swallowed in the haze of battle.

Kavi struggled a little, vainly trying to get up, but Mae kept her foe pinned down as she punched again and again. Mae became dimly aware of blood on the other woman's face and the sound of shouts growing louder and louder around them. And all the while, Mae just kept thinking, *Porfirio is dead, Porfirio is dead* . . .

She didn't know how much time passed before strong arms pulled her up and away. Her vision was tinged with red, and adrenaline, urged on by the implant, churned furiously within her. And then slowly, agonizingly, the world came into focus again. That grief-driven rage faded, and more important, the dark power that had descended upon her lifted. She saw regular gray-and-maroon-clad soldiers coming into the room, along with military police. None of them touched her, though. Two prætorians restrained her, the only ones who could hold her in full fight-or-flight mode.

"Easy, Finn. Easy." Mae realized one of her captors was Dag. "You won. It's over."

That was when Mae finally dared to look down to the ground. Kavi wasn't dead, though her breathing came raggedly, her eyes mere slits. One of her legs was bent at an unnatural angle, and blood covered her swollen face. It looked as though her nose had been broken. Mae stared in horror, unable to believe what she'd done. Prætorians fought among themselves more often than anyone liked to admit. When you had a group of people who were so physical and so chemically driven, it was hard for altercations not to break out. Usually, opponents were evenly matched. Sure, there would be a victor, but the fights were rarely all-or-nothing.

But this? It was nothing. Kavi was nothing. She'd never got-

ten in a hit. As Mae's implant continued to wind down and metabolize the excess adrenaline, she tried to make sense of what
had happened. The prætorians holding her finally deemed her
calm enough to release to the MPs hovering nervously nearby.
Mae offered no resistance. She allowed them to lead her out,
but not before giving Kavi one last, disbelieving look.

They left Mae in a cell all day, which gave her a lot of time
to analyze what had happened. There was no denying it: She'd
cracked. She'd been weak and allowed her emotions to get the
better of her. Even acknowledging that point to herself was humiliating. A little jabbing from Kavi, and Mae's armor had
crumbled.

But more than Kavi's barbs had gotten through. Even now,
Mae felt cold and nauseated as she remembered the dark force
that had filled her as she fought, a force she was certain had
nothing to do with her implant or sorrow. *It keeps happening,*
she thought frantically. Mae's life was focused on being the
master of her body, and the idea of something else taking control shattered everything she fought for. It had to be some trick
of her mind . . . because what else could it be? *I should tell
someone. I should see a doctor.* But that thought was nearly as
frightening. Prætorians who saw psychiatrists usually didn't
stay prætorians for long. No one was going to pair mental insta-
bility with a performance-enhancing implant.

One other question burned in Mae's mind as she waited out
the day. Why had Kavi been so slow to react? Or had Mae just
been that fast? No, the more she thought about it, the more Mae
was certain there had been nothing out of the ordinary about the
way she'd fought. Yes, she'd been more emotional than usual,
but that shouldn't have affected anything. Even the rush of that
dark power couldn't create that kind of disparity.

Why had Kavi been so slow?

Mae had no answer by the time the MPs came to take her
away again. They escorted her to a conference room, where she
found General Gan sitting at the end of a long table. He wore
the regular military's uniform now, all gray, save for the jacket's
upper half, which was maroon. It was bedecked with the medals
of his rank and a black stripe on the collar that showed he'd

once been a prætorian. More silver laced his dark hair than when she'd first met him years ago, but the constant intensity and purpose in his eyes never changed.

Mae's stomach sank further. She'd hoped someone else would be there to chastise her, maybe one of his many underlings. It wasn't his rank she feared so much as the thought of disappointing him. He gave a small nod to the MPs, and they left, shutting the door behind them. Silence fell in the long room.

"Sit," said Gan at last. He pointed to a chair about halfway down the table. Mae obeyed.

"So. I hear there was an incident today." Gan was a master of understatement.

Mae stared straight ahead. She had never shirked responsibility and wasn't about to now. "I was out of line, sir. I will gladly accept any punishment you see fit to give me." *Suspension,* she thought bleakly. *They'll suspend me for sure, unless they just kick me out altogether.*

He shrugged. "It was a rough day. It's understandable that emotions would run high, especially in the wake of losing a friend."

Gan knew perfectly well that Porfirio had been more than a friend, and his sympathy bothered Mae as much as Val and Dag's. She would've preferred to be yelled at and told how completely disgraceful and inappropriate her actions were— because they had been. She decided to remind him of this, because obviously, his fondness was clouding his judgment.

"What I did was unacceptable, sir. Unforgivable."

That brought a small smile to the general's mouth, thought it didn't soften the lines of his face. "I've seen worse, and half your cohort's been in to tell me about how wronged you were. Valeria Jardin and Linus Dagsson have made particular nuisances of themselves." Yes, they most certainly would. "That doesn't mean we can ignore what happened, of course. The incident will be noted in your record, and you'll be suspended from regular duty."

Suspended from regular duty. She'd expected it, but it was still tough to swallow.

"Don't worry. You won't be locked away or confined to a desk." He snorted. "I can't imagine giving one of you a desk job. I can't even imagine one of you sitting still for very long. Prætorians are too valuable to waste, and I have a task for you."

"I'll do anything you require of me, sir."

He drummed his fingers against the table, momentarily lost in thought. "It's a strange errand, but a necessary one—one that unexpectedly just came up and may be a good opportunity for you to . . . adjust to recent events. We wouldn't ask it of you if it wasn't important, of course."

"Of course, sir." His use of "task" and "errand" didn't reassure her any, but Mae still hoped she might be sent to some volatile location. It'd be no more than she deserved, and maybe in glorious battle, she'd redeem herself.

"I need you to go to Panama City. Have you ever been there?"

It took Mae a few moments to answer. Panama City? There'd be no glorious battle there. The RUNA had no conflict with that region. In fact, she'd heard there were tentative trading negotiations in the works. Panama was still provincial, of course, filled with unchecked religion, a gangster-run government, and old and new aristocracies vying for power. Tame compared to other places.

"No, sir. I've never been there."

"Well, you're going there now. I'll have the mission details sent to you, and we can meet again once you've read them over."

"Of course, sir." She hesitated over her next words. She had no business asking questions in light of what she'd done. Obedience was her only path. Yet, no matter how much she denied it around others, she knew she was one of Gan's favorites. He'd let her ask. "Sir . . . how is Prætorian Kavi?"

"She's fine—well, considering the circumstances, that is. She'll be hospitalized for a while and then be off duty as she recovers. You did a neat job of breaking her leg."

Mae winced, and an image of Kavi's bloody face flashed through her mind. Prætorians were difficult to hurt. *And even more difficult to kill, but it happened to Porfirio.* "I'm sorry, sir. I should visit her and apologize."

Gan chuckled. "I wouldn't recommend that. I don't think she'll want to see you anytime soon. I'd avoid the Indigo cohort in general, if I were you." He studied Mae carefully, weighing her with those knowing eyes. "Go ahead. Ask your next question."

"Sir . . ." She had to look away from that gaze. "Kavi was slow. She should've reacted more quickly, but she didn't. Why? Why did she react so badly? What was wrong?"

Gan's answer took a long time, and Mae dared a look up. "Maybe there was nothing wrong with her. Maybe you're just that good."

Mae knew she *was* good, but she was certain there was more to it than that. It nagged at her, but contradicting the general was unacceptable, so she let the matter go. He dismissed her, and as she neared the door, a final question popped into her head. "Sir, will I have my implant deactivated as part of my punishment?" It had been known to happen, and it scared her almost as much as full suspension or inactivity.

Gan actually looked surprised, which didn't happen very often. "What? Of course not. I'd hardly send you to the provinces unprotected. And you'll hold your rank and title too. Although . . ."

Mae froze. She didn't know what was coming, but there was something in the tone of his voice that contradicted his casual demeanor. That, and all of this had been too easy.

"It's a small thing. You won't be allowed to wear a prætorian uniform until further notice. This mission won't require a uniform at all, really, but if the situation arises for some other reason, you'll have to wear gray."

He was right. It was such a small, small thing, but his words hit Mae with the same force as a prison sentence would have. *No black.* Until that moment, she hadn't realized how big a role the uniform played in defining who she was. The implant and the title were part of it too, but the black lent a power of its own. It separated her from others who were less worthy. She looked down at what she wore, the dress uniform she'd been so contemptuous of earlier. Now she would have given anything to keep it on. *How long until I can wear black again?*

Gan tilted his head and gave her a puzzled look. "I assume there's no problem with that?"

"No, sir. Of course not." She swallowed. No black. "I'm a soldier of the Republic."

CHAPTER 2

A BEGGAR AT THE DOOR

The ravens saw her before Justin did. For figments of his imagination, they were remarkably observant.

Hot, said Horatio. He was the blunt one.

She usually wears black, added Magnus. His commentary tended to be a little more esoteric. He reminded Justin of a guy he'd known in college who'd pretty much been high for four straight years. He'd somehow graduated with top honors.

Even if the bird was an annoying voice in Justin's head, Horatio was right. The woman was a knockout, and it was a wonder the whole party didn't come to a standstill for her. She paused in the doorway, scanning the tightly packed room. She had to be meeting a date, he decided. Or maybe she was just looking for the bar. Justin had already started his third drink and wasn't sure that was going to be enough tonight. This was the sixth party he'd had to go to in just as many days, and he was tired of smiling.

The woman took a few steps forward, still searching through the haze of smoke. There was something in the way she moved that he couldn't quite put his finger on. Graceful, but not a dancer. Her stride was too purposeful, and she held her head up in a way that bespoke confidence and possibly some superiority. An athlete maybe? That didn't feel right either, but he wouldn't rule it out.

Her hair is like winter sunlight, said Magnus, almost sounding lovesick as he whispered in Justin's mind. Still, it wasn't a bad comparison. Not quite gold, not quite platinum. She wore it in a charmingly old-fashioned way that still managed to be stylish, pulled back and folded into itself at the back of her head. It revealed an elegant neck, which Justin rather liked.

"Justin!"

The booming voice was his only warning before a powerful hand slapped him on the back, causing him to stumble into the craps table and spill part of his drink. With one last look at the blonde, he put on the smile he knew was expected and turned his attention back to the game.

"Are you going to bet or not?" Cristobal Martinez, the party's host and—more important—Justin's benefactor, grinned down at him with teeth so white they glowed. Literally. It was a trendy new UV treatment. They tended toward the extreme here in Panama. "You're not out of money—yet." His tone implied that he knew how this night was going to end.

"Sure, sure." Justin set his money on the line and then glanced back toward the doorway. The blond woman was gone.

By the bar, said Horatio.

Sure enough, there she was, accepting a drink from the bar's automated dispenser. Justin touched Cristobal's arm and nodded toward her. "Do you know who she is?"

Cristobal shifted his gaze toward the woman, a small frown appearing on his face. Half of it was covered by a stylized tattoo of flames, the mark of his gang. "Never seen her. One of my prettier party crashers." He studied her a few moments longer and then promptly lost interest in that fickle way of his. He turned back to the action, whooping when someone rolled a seven.

"She's military, whoever she is," said Huan, standing on Justin's other side.

Justin did a double take. "Her? No. No way."

"Takes one to know one. It's in the way she stands." Huan gave her one more scrutinizing look before returning to the game. "She's one of us too," he added. "EA or RUNA." He was from the EA, somewhere Justin would've run to in an instant, if he could've. Unfortunately, the Eastern Alliance honored its sister country's policy toward exiles.

"How do you know that?"

"The dress. Next bet."

Justin obligingly set down more money and pondered Huan's words. He had a point. The woman's dress was a deep plum crepe de chine, with no sleeves and a high neckline.

Who in the world knows what crepe de chine is? asked Horatio.

I had to learn that stuff a long time ago, Justin said.

The dress's slim fit hugged her body and hit just above the knee. To Justin's eyes, it was suggestive but elegant—and completely boring by local standards. Panamanian fashion favored garish colors and excessive embellishment these days, along with necklines that displayed a lot of skin and very little taste.

Too refined to be from around here, Magnus said in agreement. At least he appreciated Justin's fashion analysis. *A woman among women. Can't you see the stars and flowers?*

Stars and flowers. Those were words Justin hadn't heard in a long time—ones he wasn't sure he was ready to hear. A nudge from Huan put the rumination on hold. "Your turn to roll."

Justin did, earning groans when he turned up a three. He yielded his bet and tried to spot the woman again, but she had disappeared.

"Why do you play this?" asked Huan. "You always lose. You could make a killing over at the poker tables, you know."

Justin did know. Cristobal often asked the same thing, but Justin couldn't quite explain to either man how addictive the idea of random chance was. Too much of his life was spent reading faces and other social cues. He observed too much, deduced too much. Sometimes he just needed a casual throw of the dice to dictate his future.

To Huan, he simply said, "Too easy."

Huan chuckled and shook his head. He had an easygoing nature that Justin liked. Justin also liked that Huan was from the EA. He had the same sort of mixed heritage that Justin did, though Huan's features favored Asian ancestry a little more than Caucasian. The RUNA's slang term for that mix was "plebeian," and seeing it reminded Justin of home, as did the fact that Huan was probably the only other civilized person in the room. A large part of their friendship was based on discussing how much Panama sucked. The difference between them was that Huan always got to leave when he concluded his embassy's business here. Justin was stuck.

"Cristobal, there you are!"

A woman pushed her way in between Justin and Cristobal. Justin tried not to wince as he watched her smile up at Cristobal. Well, she tried to smile but had a little difficulty with all the wrinkle injections that had numbed her face. Magenta eye shadow reached all the way up to her brows, and the shiny gold dress she wore was at least one size too small for her plump figure.

"I had to come tell you what an amazing party this is," she exclaimed, cozying up to the big man.

"This?" Cristobal attempted a modest look but failed miserably. "This is just a little thing I threw together. Barely a gathering."

Justin recognized an opening for flattery. "Oh, no. This is definitely your best one yet. I don't know how you keep doing it. I've never seen anything like that band."

That was the truth. Cristobal had dredged up some popular local group whose claim to fame was that they handled snakes while performing. It didn't seem like that difficult of a feat, considering how limp the snakes were. The terrible music had probably killed them long ago. But they were in vogue, so Cristobal had had to have them. They made Justin want to gouge his ears out.

Cristobal laughed. "Save your charm. It doesn't work on me."

But it did. Cristobal was more than happy to give out cash and lodging, so long as Justin continued to smile and show up at parties. There were enough people still charmed by the idea of a mysterious Gemman exile to ensure Justin's position was secure, but he had a feeling that someday Cristobal would get bored of him and find some other novelty to show off. So, stroking his patron's ego seemed like good insurance.

The woman turned toward Justin, her eyes widening in a way that didn't help her appearance any. His accent had tipped her off. "Is this your Gemman? I've never met one before."

"Justin, this lovely creature is Ana Santiago," Cristobal said. "Her husband is a dear friend and associate of mine."

"You should be ashamed of yourself," Justin told him, shaking her hand. " 'Lovely' doesn't even come close to describing her."

Another truth, but not in the way Ana interpreted it.

Cristobal laughed uproariously at the "compliment" and reached around her to slap Justin on the back again. At least this time, he saw it coming.

"Now, now, she's married." Cristobal winked at Ana. "I'll leave you two to chat. Be careful, though. He's trouble." He collected his winnings and wandered off to find his next distraction.

Ana actually batted her eyelashes, which were decorated with multicolored crystals. That was excessive, even by the hideous standards around here. She was most certainly "New Money" if she was at a party like this. And if her husband was Cristobal's "associate," he'd probably amassed wealth through some questionable means. In the cutthroat world of Panama City, people rose through the ranks however they could. Ana had the feel of someone who'd been raised in the lower classes and was trying to compensate now.

With Cristobal gone, she slid over to Justin. The smile on his face was starting to hurt, but he knew that Cristobal's guest had to be entertained. "Cristobal didn't have to tell me you were trouble," she said with a purr. "A little voice in my head told me that right away."

Justin perked up. "You hear voices in your head?"

She looked surprised. "I mean, not literally. You'd have to be crazy for that."

"Right," said Justin flatly. "Of course."

Ana tried smiling again and had the same trouble as before. "Not many Gemmans come here."

"Well, they're missing out. Believe me, their women don't even compare to the ones here." Justin knocked back the rest of his drink, looking down at the empty glass with dismay.

She giggled in a way that was completely inappropriate for a woman her age. "Aren't you sweet. And just as cute as Blanca said."

Justin's smile almost slipped. Almost. "Blanca Jessup?" he asked carefully.

Ana nodded. "She's a good friend of mine. She told me so much about you."

Wonderful. Justin's last encounter with Blanca had involved bad judgment and even worse tequila. Definitely not one of his finer moments. At least Blanca wasn't married, but her brothers bore the same obsessively protective—and occasionally violent—attitude toward their women that was so common among the Old Money upper classes. He wondered what exactly "so much" entailed and whether Ana was hoping for a similar experience. This party didn't have enough alcohol for that.

He cleared his throat and groped for a subject change. "This is Huan Korokov. He's from the EA."

Huan wasn't a bad-looking guy, and Justin hoped she might shift her attention. No such luck. She gave Huan the barest of glances and murmured a polite greeting before turning back to Justin. Out of the corner of his eye, he could see Huan working to keep a straight face. This was probably the highlight of his trip.

She leaned forward on the table, giving her cleavage amplification that it most certainly didn't need. "Blanca said you were some kind of witch hunter?"

He heard that a lot around here. Sometimes they called him a "priest killer." "Nothing so exciting. I used to investigate religious groups for the government. Had to make sure they weren't dangerous."

"Doesn't the RUNA think all religions are dangerous?" she asked.

Ha, maybe she's not as vapid as she seems, said Horatio.

If you were of any use to me, you'd magically appear and get me another drink, Justin told him.

She'd be happy to get you a drink back at your place, said Magnus helpfully.

Justin placed another bet, noticing that his stack of money was growing smaller and smaller. "It's a little more complicated than that. Do you know the Gemman charter?" No, of course she didn't. " 'Belief in fictitious entities is a threat to the fabric of society and must be assessed and regulated for the well-being of all citizens.' " He could recite it in his sleep.

I almost believe you, Horatio said.

"I'd love to hear more," Ana cooed. She moved even closer. "Perhaps we could go somewhere quieter to talk."

Not on your life, Justin thought. Huan came to the rescue.

"Justin doesn't like to talk about his past," he said, looking award-winningly grave. "Too many painful memories. Justin, you should tell her the story of why you left."

A few players standing nearby perked up. Cristobal's pet Gemman was a topic of great interest around here, as was his shadowy exile.

Justin averted his eyes and put on the tortured look he'd perfected for this story. "I don't know. It's hard for me to discuss. . . . Besides, I don't want to burden you with my personal drama."

"I'm sure Señora Santiago wouldn't mind. She seems like a great listener." Huan was playing a good supporting role. Maybe Justin could work him into the act more often.

"I am," she said, nodding eagerly.

"I can tell." Justin gave her a small smile. "It's in your eyes, you know. That kind of understanding and kindness . . . it shines out from the soul." Huan cleared his throat and had to look away.

"People say that all the time," Ana replied, moving even closer. "Now, please. Tell me what happened."

Justin took a deep breath. "Not much to tell. You see . . . there was this girl. . . ."

"I thought so." Ana squeezed his hand with hers. It was sweaty. "As soon as I saw you, I thought, 'He's a hopeless romantic.'"

"People say that all the time," he said, echoing her.

I'm impressed you said that with a straight face, Horatio remarked.

Shut up, Justin told him.

"Anyway, when I met her, it was love at first sight. I'm sure it was the same way for you and your husband."

Ana's face suggested otherwise. "What was her name?"

"Phoebe," he said promptly.

"I thought it was Pamela," Huan interrupted.

Justin shot him a warning look. "*Phoebe.* I've never felt so connected to another person. It was like we were made for each other, perfectly matched in every way. Every moment with her was like living in a dream. I knew we had to be together forever, so I finally proposed to her on a beach at sunset. There were doves flying in the sky. I can still see the way her face glowed in the light when she said yes."

"What happened next?" Ana asked breathlessly.

He sighed and looked down again, fully aware that half the table was listening now. "Oh, the usual. We began making plans for the wedding. It was going to be in this amazing arbor. The greenest place you've ever seen, filled with flowers and butterflies. We were going to have a cellist and a choir of children to sing wedding songs."

"Don't forget the horse," said Huan. "Pamela was going to ride in on a horse."

"Phoebe was going to ride in on a horse," Justin corrected.

"A white one?" asked Ana.

"Yes, of course." He never mentioned the horse's color when he told this story, but women always guessed white. "Everything was perfect. Then, a few days before the ceremony, we had our compatibility test. You know what that is?"

"They force you to do it to get married," she said promptly.

That wasn't exactly true, not anymore, but he'd found it was a common belief in the provinces. It carried more mystique and romantic intrigue. They loved that out here.

"Well, we weren't a match—not by their standards, at least."

Ana gasped. "So you weren't allowed to get married."

"Oh, we could, but there were . . . penalties." He left it at that. Her imagination would do far more than his storytelling skills could do. "We didn't care, of course. We still went forward with the wedding and planned to leave the country afterward, before they could come after us. Only when the day came . . . she didn't show up."

"They . . . they got to her first?"

He shook his head. "Worse. She backed out. She was too afraid of what would happen. She wasn't brave enough to be with me. And so, after that . . . well, how could I stay in the country that had torn us apart? It was too painful. I had to leave."

So help him, Ana actually had tears in her eyes. She squeezed his hand even tighter. "You poor thing." He hoped she wouldn't try to "comfort" him later. It happened sometimes when he told the story. Sometimes that was actually his goal but certainly not this time. "I can't imagine what you must have gone through."

"It certainly seems unreal, doesn't it?" asked Huan. "It's impossible to believe anyone could endure a tragedy like that. You're out."

Justin looked down. His pile was gone. "Shit." He hadn't been paying attention while talking. There went his stipend for the week.

Huan shook his head in mock sympathy. "Tragedy just follows you around, doesn't it?"

"Aren't you going home soon?" Justin asked pointedly.

"Tonight, actually." Huan waved his hand when the bet came around to him and gathered up his winnings into a large pile. "In fact, I should go right now. The plane's probably waiting on me."

The news hit Justin harder than it should have. Current diplomatic dealings with Panama had put Huan and his delegation in town longer than usual for this trip. Justin had gotten used to having his friend around and suddenly felt as though he was about to be swallowed up into darkness.

"Hey!"

Ana's snarl snapped Justin out of his self-pity. A passing group of men had bumped into a waitress, in turn knocking her into Ana. It was a sign of the girl's poise that she recovered herself quickly and managed to right her tray without spilling any drinks. Still, the motion had startled Ana, and she fixed a nasty glare on the waitress.

"Watch where you're going, you little bitch. Get one drop on me, and I'll have Cristobal kick you out on the streets like that." Ana tried to snap her fingers for effect, failed, and succeeded on the second try. "You can crawl back to whatever hole you live in and fuck your landlord for rent."

Classy, said Horatio.

Justin knew the waitress. After four years, he knew every single person who worked for Cristobal. Her name was Sara, and she was half Ana's age and size. Sara had a good head on her shoulders and a pretty face too, and in a sea of women like Ana Santiago, Sara was someone Justin wouldn't have minded getting to know better. Sara was too smart to get involved with any of her boss's party friends, though, and had made it abundantly clear her sole purpose in putting up with drunken gangsters and would-be socialites was to feed the two small children she had at home. Justin respected that. There was something in her that reminded him charmingly—and painfully—of his sister.

Even now, Sara was too savvy to offer a word of protest. She accepted the rebuke meekly, offering a soft apology as she delivered the table's drinks. Justin handed her one of Huan's larger chips as a tip, earning a nod of thanks.

Ana watched her go in triumph, apparently feeling proud of her ability to demean someone who was already at a much lower station in life. "I get that Cristobal wants easy ass around, but I don't know how he puts up with the incompetence. She's lucky she didn't ruin this dress. It's a Gemman import, you know." That was directed toward Justin, as though he should be impressed. "Not that you'd expect trash like her to understand that."

"Trash? She's from the same place you are," said Justin. He spoke quietly, but everyone at the table heard.

Ana's eyes widened. "I live over on the west shore."

Huan made a low noise of warning in his throat, but something in Justin snapped. He was so, so tired of this place. Tired of the games, tired of women like Ana, tired of dancing for Cristobal's entertainment. The ravens often spoke of greatness and divine plans that lay in store for him, but Justin saw no greatness in his future. There would be no end to this place, and it made Justin angry, angrier still that Huan would get to leave it.

"But you grew up in San Garcia," Justin told Ana. He rushed forward when she started to shake her head in denial. "It's in the way you slur your *S*'s and use expressions like 'easy ass.' All the money and power in the world aren't going to change where you came from, and trying to hide it with piles of fake jewelry isn't going to work either."

Ana flushed. "These are real!"

"The hell they are. I can see the brass tarnishing from here. And that dress is *not* Gemman—unless you managed to visit a post-Feriae costume clearance sale. That fabric's just some flammable castoff from Guatemala. I know, because I saw it in stock at that tailor down on Flores Street, which is the same place I get my shitty knockoffs." Justin paused to take a drink, then remembered he was out. "You can put on as many airs as you want, but in the end, that dress is the same as you: an old, cheap design dressed up to look like it's worth more than it is."

The table collectively held its breath, and then Ana, face furious, flung her wineglass at Justin, leaving a bloody stain on his shirt. "Looks like it's time for another shitty knockoff." She stormed away, probably straight to Cristobal, Justin thought bleakly.

Huan caught hold of Justin's arm and steered him from the table. "Okay. Let's go get a cigarette, Little Miss Charisma."

"You don't smoke," Justin said, letting himself be led.

"It's not for me. Here." Huan took off his coat and handed it over. "You don't want the world thinking you were shot. Unless you want to play dead when her husband comes seeking revenge."

Huan must've come from some work meeting because he had one of the official coats he wore in his diplomatic dealings. It was navy, double-breasted, with the EA's flag embroidered on the pocket and a series of colors edging the collar that correlated to his rank and position. Wearing it felt weird to Justin, but not as weird as walking around in a wine-stained shirt.

"Will this get me out of the country?" Justin asked ruefully.

Huan gave him a sympathetic smile as an answer and opened a door that led out to a back alley. Even with the heat and humidity, the outdoor air felt light and refreshing compared to the haze and crush of bodies inside. The sound of night insects buzzed around them, and above, clouds chased one another across the sky. In the distance, he thought he heard the low rumble of thunder, and the trees on the other side of the building were beginning to sway. Storms had a tendency to blow up fast and furious around here.

Justin groaned. "I don't know why I put up with this."

"Because Cristobal lets you live like a king," said Huan, giving him a comforting pat on the back. "When you aren't insulting his guests."

"I'd rather be a beggar at the RUNA's door than king of this nightmare," Justin replied.

"If it makes you feel better, you did a great job with the story tonight. One of your best performances—even though I'm pretty sure it gets you a little closer to hell each time you tell it."

"I don't believe in hell, so it's okay."

Silence fell around them, and Huan spoke his next words hesitatingly. "I was just in your old stomping grounds, though." His expression almost became compassionate. He knew these conversations tormented Justin . . . but he also knew Justin yearned for them. "Had a meeting in Vancouver."

Justin jerked his head up. Vancouver! The very word had power. "How . . . how was it?"

"The same as always. Beautiful and perfect. The jewel of the world."

"The jewel of the world," Justin repeated. He raised his unlit cigarette in a toast. The same ache welled up in his chest, the longing he felt whenever anyone talked about the RUNA. All the drinking and drugs and other vices in Panama City could never make the pain go away.

"I'm sorry," said Huan.

"It is what it is. It has been for a while."

A hint of Huan's old smile returned. "I don't suppose you'll ever tell me the real reason you left?"

"Nah. I know how much you like the Penelope story. Wouldn't want to ruin it for you."

"I thought it was Phoebe. Or Pamela."

Justin waved it off. "Doesn't matter. She's a shameless whore."

"Right. You're better off without her."

"Exactly."

Huan chuckled and held out his hand. "You going to be okay if I go?"

Justin shook it. "Depends if I can keep the coat."

"Sure. I've got lots more where that came from." Huan moved to the door. "Until next time."

"Until next time," Justin repeated, watching the other man go. Party noise flared briefly as the door opened and then faded once more. A dark mood settled on Justin, and he welcomed the solitude as he lit up.

Smoking outside was a habit from the RUNA. No one cared what or where you smoked here, but there were strict laws back home. He took a deep drag on the cigarette, feeling a pleasant buzz that enhanced the alcohol, which had already made him light-headed. He wouldn't have been able to smoke cigarettes like these back home either. The RUNA was conscientious of its citizens' health. Of course, seeing as the RUNA had stopped caring about him, he figured he was welcome to whatever self-destructive behaviors he wanted. Huan's words replayed in his mind.

Beautiful and perfect. The jewel of the world.

"Goddamn it," Justin muttered.

Which god? asked Horatio.

Whichever one sent me here, Justin answered.

Judging from Magnus's reply, the ravens were back in insolent mode: *You sent yourself here. The gods merely helped.* When they weren't criticizing his life, the ravens were always talking about gods.

Quiet, Justin told them. *I'm trying to have a moment.*

Watch out, said Horatio.

Six hulking figures suddenly loomed out of the darkness off to Justin's right. Moonlight shone off Paolo Jessup's shaved head, along with the many gaudy earrings he wore. Beside him was his brother Miguel, and Justin soon recognized the other thugs as Jessup-family cronies. He had a sinking feeling that he might be closer to Huan's hell than he'd realized.

"Hey, Paolo, how's it going?" Justin managed a smile and wondered what the odds were that this wasn't about Blanca.

"Don't fucking waste my time. Did you think you could get away with that? You think you could just take advantage of my sister like that?"

The odds, it would seem, were not good.

Tell him she wasn't that unwilling, Horatio suggested. Justin ignored him.

"There's some mistake," he told Paolo. "I'd never do anything to Blanca."

"That's not what she told Dora Ramirez," growled Miguel.

Dora? And Ana? How many people had Blanca talked to? Justin at least hoped she'd been complimentary about that night.

He also wondered where the hell Cristobal's security was. The outsides of his establishments were usually crawling with henchmen, and Justin speculated on whether the Jessup brothers had bribed them. He couldn't imagine Cristobal would be happy about the untimely demise of his favorite houseguest . . . or would he? Cristobal would certainly get a lot of mileage out of the tragic tale. Justin could practically hear the big man already: *He was like a brother to me. . . .*

Miguel took a few menacing steps forward, snarling like one of Cristobal's badly trained dogs. He kind of smelled like one too. "I'm going to rip you apart!" he yelled.

I don't think Blanca was worth it, Horatio told him. *She wasn't even that good.*

Magnus's comment was more enigmatic: *Your Valkyrie.*

Miguel's advance was put on hold as the door opened and a woman stepped outside. Not just any woman. Her. The blonde from earlier. Everyone froze for the space of a heartbeat, and then, with impossible speed, she suddenly put herself between Justin and the Jessups, her stance protective and dangerous. A fighter's stance. Huan's words came back to him: *She's military, whoever she is.* She made no other moves, but there was a tension in her that said she was a lioness that could strike at any moment.

You know, remarked Magnus conversationally, *lionesses do all the work while lions sit around.*

"Stay back," she told Justin, her words verifying that she was indeed Gemman. There were only a few inches between them, and he became acutely aware of the neck and shoulders he'd admired earlier, as well as the way the silk wrapped her body. A few wayward strands of hair blew around her face, and the faintest whiff of what smelled like apple blossoms drifted over him.

The Jessups recovered themselves, and Paolo smirked. "Nice trade," he said. "You fucked one of our women—now we'll get one of yours. If you're lucky, we'll leave you conscious to watch."

The others laughed, and Paolo, with death in his eyes, took two steps forward. Unfortunately for him, he never got any farther.

CHAPTER 3

A FEW LESS PROBLEMS

Whatever lingering hopes Mae had clung to of finding glory in Panama had been shattered when Gan had explained her assignment in detail. She wasn't going to thwart an assassination attempt. She wasn't even going to cause an assassination. Instead, all of her elite training and military technology would be used to accompany a couple of bureaucrats from the Ministry of Internal Security on their trip to retrieve an exiled servitor.

Neither of them had impressed Mae very much. The woman, with the unfortunate name of Cornelia Kimora, was a supervisor in Internal Security's SCI division: Sect and Cult Investigation. She was in her fifties, with bobbed hair dyed an orange-ish color that bore a disturbing resemblance to an apricot. Every accessory and article of clothing Cornelia wore was beige, and she had one of the coldest personalities Mae had ever encountered—which was saying something, in light of Mae's upbringing. At least in the Nordic caste, that kind of cool and supercilious attitude was usually paired with the ability to put on a smiling face and act like you cared. Cornelia possessed no such niceties and made her indifference clear to the world.

Her companion, Francis Kyle, was her opposite. He was similar in age but had a scattered and much sunnier—almost overwhelmingly so—attitude. That enthusiasm especially seemed to grate on Cornelia, but he held a higher title than her in Internal Security, meaning there wasn't much she could do but grind her teeth. His bubbliness *was* a little over-the-top, but at least he was always polite to Mae.

Cornelia and Francis also held wildly different views of their task, which made for a long nine-hour flight. Cornelia thought the trip was a waste of time and was clearly opposed to their objective. Francis, on the other hand, could barely contain his excitement as they drew closer and closer to their destination.

"I'm so looking forward to this," he told Cornelia at one point. She looked up from her reader with a grimace and waited impatiently for him to continue. "I've wanted to meet Dr. March for such a long time now. His work is outstanding."

"*Was* outstanding," corrected Cornelia. "And don't confuse the work with the man."

Francis looked pleasantly surprised at the clarification. "Oh? I'd think they're one and the same."

"Hardly." Cornelia snorted unattractively. "Just wait until you meet him."

"He's brilliant," Francis insisted.

"Yes." Her words came grudgingly, and she held up a hand to enumerate points on her fingers. "Also arrogant, impertinent, and manipulative."

Francis remained undaunted. "Those aren't necessarily bad things in his line of work."

"They're annoying things that he tries to spin as charm. And let's not forget his addictive personality." This required Cornelia's other hand. "Stimulants, alcohol, gambling, women . . . if there's excess to drown in, he'll find it. He probably fits in beautifully in Panama. Won't want to leave."

Francis's cheerful disposition turned wry. "I sincerely doubt that. Besides, we need him. You know we do. No one else has his . . . perspective."

"That's exactly my problem. I don't know that we really do need his perspective." Cornelia's tone was grim, and both fell silent for a while.

Mae didn't know what that perspective was or what was so crucial that it would require Internal Security traveling to the provinces. From Cornelia's description of Dr. March, he sounded like he embodied everything Mae hated in a guy, and she hoped she wouldn't have to talk to him on the trip back. Although . . . she couldn't deny her curiosity about his exile.

What in the world would someone have to do to be exiled from the RUNA? If he'd committed a crime, why not imprison him? And most important, if he'd done something bad enough to be kicked out, then why would they want to bring him back?

Those were answers beyond Mae's pay grade, ones that had little to do with her role here. She and the four gray-clad soldiers accompanying Cornelia and Francis were simply muscle. It was inglorious work, but Mae reminded herself that it was no less than she deserved for her breakdown at the funeral. *One trip to the provinces,* she told herself. *One trip to get SCI's brilliantly arrogant servitor, and then I'm back to regular duty—and my uniform.*

Panama required no uniform—at least not a military one. Bizarrely, Mae had been instructed to bring formal wear. Once their group arrived and was settled in what was dubiously considered Panama City's safest hotel, she was a little astonished to learn what exactly her dress would be used for.

"You want me to . . . deliver a letter?"

"Yes." Prætorians didn't intimidate Cornelia, and her small frown showed how displeased she was that Mae would actually ask a question. "He's staying with a local gangster down here—Cristobal Martinez. Martinez owns all sorts of clubs and housing, and it's impossible to know where exactly March is in that mess. Martinez should be easy enough to find. He's a flamboyant man who's always throwing parties. All you have to do is make yourself pretty, show up, be discreet, and give this to him." She handed Mae an envelope with *Justin March* handwritten across the outside. "Shouldn't be too difficult for you and your formidable skill set."

Mae put on a look as polite and deferential as any she would give Gan, though inside, she was seething. *All you have to do is make yourself pretty.* The sneer on Cornelia's lips and contempt in her voice suggested she didn't like castals, but it was probably even more basic than that. She was just someone threatened by a younger woman, period—regardless of whether that person was one of the most feared soldiers in the RUNA.

And there was also the small fact that Mae would go where no one else in their entourage would. Both Cornelia and Francis made it perfectly clear they had no intention of setting one foot outside their hotel until they were headed back to the airport. For all their airs, the provinces terrified the two, which Mae took a little grim amusement out of.

But she kept all of those thoughts to herself, remembering that she was a soldier, one who was being punished. She accepted Cornelia's condescension without complaint, only stopping to ask, "Do you want me to wait around and bring Dr. March back myself?"

"No. There's no telling when Martinez will get around to finding him, and there are instructions on where we're staying in the envelope. When March reads it, he'll come, believe me." Cornelia's sneer returned. "And no need to escort him. If he's managed this long on the streets of Panama, he can survive a little longer on his own." It was probably Cornelia's last effort to thwart the plan she was already against. Maybe she hoped he'd be gunned down on his way to the hotel.

And so, Mae found herself in her own room later that evening, in makeup and a mauve cocktail dress, arranging her hair into a Gibson tuck. Old-fashioned styles like that were trendy in the castes now, and no matter how far she'd strayed from her upbringing, it was hard not to fall back on old habits. *Make yourself pretty.* Maybe she shouldn't have been so contemptuous of Cornelia's attitude, because Mae suddenly had a weird flashback to her sixteen-year-old self, primped and polished to the same level of glamour, ready to be set out on display.

I am not that girl, Mae reminded herself, with one last look in the mirror. *I am a soldier of the Republic.*

A prætorian might not have had any fear on the streets of Panama, but a lone woman—especially a blond, foreign one in a short dress—certainly attracted attention. It was a flaw in Internal Security's plan. If they'd really wanted a discreet message sent, they should have brought a male prætorian. Of course, they probably didn't have any men in enough disgrace right now to deserve such a mundane mission.

Mae almost hoped one of the locals would start something. Her emotions were still in enough turmoil from the funeral that she would've welcomed the physical outlet. But although she received a few bold looks and dirty comments in Spanish, the tattooed teenage gangsters lingering outside her hotel left her alone. Most of her trip across town to Cristobal Martinez's club was by hired car, and although the driver made no attempt to hide his leer, he too kept his distance.

In fact, the most significant encounter she had was with someone who wasn't interested in her body so much as her soul. About half a block from the club's entrance stood a man with a shaved head and ragged coat. He was beseeching everyone who walked past, waving crudely drawn pamphlets at them. Mae didn't speak Spanish, but she did pick out words like "*dios*" and "*salvación*." She didn't know if he was peddling an old religion or one of the many newer ones that had popped up after the Decline, but it didn't matter. They all ran rampant and unrestrained out here in the provinces, and one was as bad as another. She had no use for any of them and made that clear when the man ignored her polite refusals. After a harsh shove into the wall, he decided to keep his salvation to himself.

Women met little resistance at the door, much like at the nightclubs of her homeland. Unlike any Gemman establishment, however, this one had a gun check. It boggled the mind. The RUNA saw absolutely no reason for civilians to carry guns, and Mae watched incredulously as poshly dressed playboys and call girls strolled up to the guards and surrendered weapons as casually as their coats.

Inside the club, high-powered air-conditioning vied for control with the heat generated by so many people packed together. The latter was winning. Equally oppressive was the smell, body odor mixed with smoke from cigarettes and other substances. It created a haze in the dim room that made her eyes water. Between all of that and the deafening music, Mae's senses were in overdrive. It might have been a party, but it was a dangerous one, and her wariness woke the implant up.

She didn't entirely understand the intricacies of Panamanian gender roles, though she knew they were tied to class. There was an aristocratic demographic that kept its women out of the public eye, as well as a newer upper class emerging that was looser in its rules for the sexes. That latter group made up the majority of the club's guests tonight, though there were also a number of less affluent women around who had no qualms about making themselves available to men of greater means. Being alone suggested to others that Mae was in that group, so she was eager to complete her task before anyone decided to test the theory.

As it turned out, she was hit on five times before finally finding Cristobal Martinez. Only one of her "suitors" turned hostile at her rejection, but a sharp look from a passing security guard saved Mae the trouble of standing up for herself. It was just as well, for the sake of discretion, though her increasingly darkening mood was still trolling for a fight.

She located Cristobal near an automated bartending machine, an antiquated one with poor voice recognition that gave Mae tequila when she asked for rum. Cristobal was a big, gregarious man who was energetically telling a story to his friends. When he noticed Mae standing near him, his face lit up.

"My pretty party crasher," he said in English. He spread his hands out expansively. "Welcome to my humble home. Well, one of them."

"Thank you for your hospitality." Mae smiled as though they were having tea on the Nordic land grant. "I was wondering if you could give a message to Justin March."

"You can give it to him yourself. He's right over . . ." Cristobal turned and scanned the part of the room that held gaming tables. "Well, he was over there. No telling where he's gone now. Probably in someone's bed." He looked apologetic about that. "But it's hard to say. You might not be too late if you want him."

Mae tightened her smile. "I just need to get this to him." She produced the envelope from her purse. "Can you help me?"

"Of course." He slipped the envelope into his pocket as deftly as a magician making coins disappear in his fingers. "Now, what else can I do for you? Name it, and it's yours." His show of generosity was as much for the onlookers as for her. "I like you Gemmans. I want to encourage more of you to come visit me."

Mae nearly mentioned the rum but instead gave him a head-shake and another polite smile. "That's more than enough. I have to go—but thank you for your help in delivering that to Dr. March." She felt the need to mention it again because Cristobal's personality seemed a little distractible.

He clasped his hands over his heart in mock pain. "So cruel, you Gemman women. No wonder Justin left. I hope you'll at least make the rounds before you break my heart further. There's food in the room over there, and I have an ash dealer around here somewhere—he's got the real deal. Not that crap that gets smuggled into the RUNA. And the band absolutely *cannot* be missed."

He was right about that. It was impossible to ignore them, no matter how much she tried. She thanked Cristobal again, hoped he'd remember the envelope, and then started to turn toward the door she'd come in. A group of men had just entered, all from the same gang, judging from the matching tattoos. They were dressed in the flashy attire of questionable taste that passed as high fashion around here and had the self-satisfied swagger of those on the prowl. Not wanting anything to do with them, Mae abruptly changed course and headed toward the doors she could just barely make out in the back of the room.

It took her a couple of tries to find one she wanted. One led to a room of people snorting some mysterious powder off a round glass table. Another looked like a storage room, though an enterprising couple had decided to turn it into a bedroom. At last, she found an exit and stepped gratefully outside to an alley—and into a fight.

The adrenaline shot up in her system as soon as she recognized the signs of an altercation, even though she knew none of its context. Six thugs with more of those face tattoos were shouting in Spanish and advancing on a lone man. She recognized the markings on his jacket as an EA diplomat's, and within seconds, she was in motion. Loyalty to the RUNA's sister country kicked in, as did a simple dislike of seeing someone facing such overwhelming odds.

The odds weren't that overwhelming for her. They were kind of pathetic, really, but an easy fight was still better than no fight. She needed this outlet, and at least here, there were no morals about disrupting a funeral. Plus, if she took care of this quickly and quietly, she might still get away with being "discreet."

She strode forward and put herself in front of the EA man, who looked understandably startled to see her. "Stay back," she warned him.

The Panamanians looked equally surprised, but then that soon changed to mockery. One of them said something that made the others laugh, though that ended abruptly when she shot forward and punched him in the face. He flew backward into the opposite brick wall, hitting with a *thump* and sliding dazed to the ground. A sharp kick made sure he stayed down, and then she turned on one of his stunned friends. None of them had any real training. They got by on intimidation and brute force, which wasn't enough to overpower her. Mae's greatest challenge came from the fifth and largest guy she fought, simply because of his size. He outweighed her, but her implant-enhanced speed and strength still prevailed. As soon as she managed to get him on the ground, it was easy enough to cling to him and bear down on his windpipe until he passed out.

When she stood up, she saw the last of the gangsters had bypassed her as she fought and had gone after the initial victim. The EA man was on the ground, holding up a warding hand at his attacker. In a flash, Mae was at their sides. She caught hold of the Panamanian kid—because really, that was all he was—and swung his head at the wall, knocking him out in one blow. Barely a minute, and the whole fight was over. Endorphins churned through her, making her high and giddy. That dark *otherness* that had seized her at the funeral swirled within her as well and then slowly lifted.

She looked down at the Easterner, who was looking back up at her with amazement. "Are you okay?" She held out a hand that he took after a few moments of hesitation.

"I—yes." He got to his feet without much difficulty and stared around at the scene. "You were . . . amazing. And slightly terrifying. But mostly amazing." He spoke English exactly as she did, with no discernible EA accent, but that wasn't too surprising. Gemman children learned Mandarin in school, Easterners learned English, and diplomats from either country would especially have to excel at the other's language.

She grinned, feeling high from both the fight and a sudden and unexpected physical attraction. Every man she'd met today paled beside this one.

"We have to stick together, right?" She nodded toward his jacket.

"Together . . ." He looked down, as though noticing his coat for the first time, and then finally recovered himself. "Yes, of course. Of course." He turned his attention back to her and smiled, his confidence growing by leaps and bounds. "Do I get to know your name? Or are you going to vanish into the night and just leave me with a sweet memory?"

His smile was nice. Really nice. After growing up almost exclusively around blond hair and pale complexions, Mae had grown to love and crave darker looks. This man had typically plebeian tanned skin and black hair and the kind of features that came from three generations of ethnic mixing. A shadow of facial hair covered his jaw, giving him a sort of roguish appeal. It could have been from neglecting shaving, but there was a meticulousness to the rest of him that made her think it was probably there by design. A flush of new endorphins swept her as she took all of him in . . . the knowing eyes, the chiseled features. He was already dangerous enough, and that smile just sealed the deal.

She held out her hand. "Mae Koskinen."

He took it and then hesitated. "I'm . . . Huan Korokov." His hand was warm, and he continued holding hers as his dark gaze wrapped around her, in a way that was both intimate and provocative. "Nordic?"

She couldn't hide her surprise. It was hard enough for Gemmans to distinguish her caste from all the other blond ones, and the EA had no comparable frame of reference. "How'd you know?"

He seemed very pleased with himself. "I know a Valkyrie when I see one." He finally released her hand but stayed close. "What I don't know is how a beautiful one came to save me. Are you military? Or just an avid self-defense fan?"

"Both." She chose not to mention she was a prætorian. It unnerved people, even Gemmans and Easterners, and she didn't want to undo the mood that had settled around them. Simply admitting to being a castal woman in the military was already odd enough, and she tried to gloss it over with the first moderately plausible story she could think of that would diminish her role. "I'm just here for a little while as research support to our military attaché."

Too late, she realized acknowledging a connection to Gemman diplomats might not have been a good idea. If he was part of an EA delegation, he could have connections that would undo her lie. She tensed, waiting for him to ask whether she knew so-and-so, but he let the matter go and simply said, "They're training support staff pretty well these days."

"They wouldn't send us to the provinces if they didn't," she pointed out.

He gave the unconscious men one last curious look and then seemed to accept her story—or at least not feel like questioning it. Before he could say anything else, a streak of lightning cut the sky, followed instantly by deafening thunder and a downpour. Both of them moved toward the doorway and the shelter of the building, not that it did much good. Within seconds, Mae's hair and dress were soaked. He glanced at the door and grimaced.

"You want to go somewhere else and get a drink? By which I mean, my place," he added quickly. "No more of these dives. I'm sure you've had a lot of fun dodging fumbling provincial advances."

"Sure," she said. Maybe going off with a guy she'd just met would have been dangerous for most women, but Mae wasn't most women. Besides, her gut told her he was safe, or at least safer than anyone else she was likely to run into tonight, and Cornelia had told her to take as long as she needed to deliver the message.

He led Mae back through the crowded club and out to the street. Those lined up to get inside were huddled against the building, trying to protect their party clothes as best they could from the rain. The sprawling apartment she was led to was only a few blocks away and was actually above another of Cristobal's nightclubs. That club was in full swing too, and they could faintly hear music below them when they entered the apartment. The music faded to a dull beat as her companion shut the door.

"Sorry," he said. "It's one of the downsides of this place. I can put on something else to cover it—unless you play." He gestured toward a dusty piano on the far side of the living room and took off his coat, revealing a wine-stained shirt underneath.

Mae walked over to the piano. "You don't?"

"Nope. Came with the place. Be right back."

He disappeared down a hallway, and Mae sat down at the bench. She played a few lines of *Danse Macabre* and then let her hand drop as it began to shake from the implant's metabolism. Her brief experience with Panamanian décor, at both the hotel and the club, hadn't been pleasant, but this place was decorated almost as tastefully as something she'd find back home. Neutral colors. Fabrics that looked expensive without being gaudy.

He returned wearing a clean shirt and tossed her a towel. She did what she could to pat herself dry and then moved over to the living room's brown leather couch. Two empty wineglasses sat on the coffee table, and he knelt in front of a nearby cabinet. "All I've got are Argentinian reds," he told her. "They drink that stuff like water here, but it's pretty good."

"That's fine." The wine made no difference. The implant regarded alcohol as a toxin and metabolized it quickly, making it nearly impossible for prætorians to get drunk.

He filled their glasses and then settled beside her on the couch, wincing slightly as he shifted. "Another glamorous day in Panama. Nothing broken, at least."

"Why were they after you?" she asked. Her hands were still trembling, and she kept them tucked into her lap to avoid attention.

"I beat them at poker," he said quickly. "Not that it matters. Those young ones have so much to prove around here that it doesn't take much. If you see where they come from, you can almost understand and feel bad for them. Almost."

He didn't elaborate on what work had brought him to Panama, and she assumed it was something government related that was none of her business. In fact, as the evening progressed, he spoke very little about the EA at all. He had plenty of funny Panamanian stories to share but seemed most interested in hearing her talk about the RUNA.

"You could just visit, you know," she teased at one point, after he'd quizzed her extensively about the latest happenings in Vancouver. They were more than halfway through the wine. "Find me, and I'll show you around."

"Ever been out to Vancouver Island?" He looked astonished when she shook her head. "It's gorgeous. And in the middle, there's this observatory from before the Decline. They've restored it, and you can go out there and stand on the hill and feel like you're in the center of the galaxy." He spread his hands out. "Stars everywhere. And so quiet. Not many places are that quiet anymore."

Mae wasn't one for fantasies, but she could suddenly picture it and found herself taken with the idea of some starry escapade with a guy she'd just met. "Then you'll have to show me."

He gave her that heart-pounding smile, though it was tinged with a little wistfulness. "I'd like that, but . . . I'm pretty busy here. I don't get home—or anywhere—very often."

"Diplomacy's hard work, huh?" She nodded toward the jacket he'd tossed aside.

"I suppose," he said in amusement. "I don't really think of what I do as diplomacy, though. Mostly I read people and figure out puzzles."

"Are you any good at it?" He was right about the wine. It was excellent. Too bad she couldn't experience the full effect.

"Well, I'd be fired if you were part of my job. You're not so easy to read." When she didn't say anything, he gave a low chuckle. "But you like that I said that, which starts to tell me something after all."

She lifted her eyes from the wineglass. "Like what?"

His eyes held her once more as he pondered for a few seconds. "That your whole life is—and has been—about different images. What people think you are. What people want you to be. What you want yourself to be. You don't like people making assumptions about you, but you don't want to show them the truth either."

"And what truth is that?" She tried to sound joking but couldn't quite manage it. His words hit too close to home. Again, he took a long time to answer.

"That you're sad, for one thing." He reached out and brushed messy, damp hair from her face. It was a gentle gesture, but it sent a spark of electricity through her. "What does a devastatingly beautiful Nordic woman who can throw grown men around and play piano arrangements of Saint-Saëns have to be sad about?"

Something in Mae tightened, and she suddenly had to fight an overwhelming urge to tell this handsome stranger about everything: her father, Porfirio, the prætorians, the recurring sense of an inexplicable force controlling her. . . . Instead, she smiled at something he'd said. "You know Saint-Saëns."

"Of *course* I know Saint-Saëns." The tone of his voice implied it would be ludicrous if he didn't. "You're trying to dodge answering."

"Will you answer the same question? Why are *you* sad?"

Because he was. She hadn't noticed it right away, not until he'd called her out. He'd been all charisma and wit tonight, and that disarming smile and the rest of his looks had done a good job at keeping her distracted by what was outside rather than within. But she could see it now as he studied her so intently: a melancholy inside him that resonated with her own. She expected him to respond with a quip, but he answered in all seriousness.

"I'm sad because you remind me of home." He dropped his hand from her and sighed. "Because you're beautiful and bright and dynamic and a whole lot of other things I haven't seen for a long time . . . and won't see again anytime soon."

Mae rested her hand on his. She felt an ache in her chest for the pain she sensed, even as the touch of his skin on hers again sent heat through her body. They'd barely known each other for two hours, but there was something about this man, who flipped effortlessly between charming and brooding, that drew her in. Mae had been adrift in her own life for the last few months, and being with him was the first steady moment she'd had in a very long time.

And yes, she wasn't going to lie to herself about the effect he had on her physically. It was more than those dark good looks—not that those weren't working too. It was his attitude, she decided. It was in the way he looked at her and flirted, with a confidence that was magnetic all on its own. *Men like him get that self-assured because they know they're good in bed,* she thought. The chemicals of desire weren't all that different from the ones that governed battle, and the implant, sensing the change in her, "helpfully" began increasing her body's response. Maybe it was fitting. Sex and battle were each dangerous in their own ways.

"You're talking like I'm already gone," she told him at last.

"You will be," he said.

"But I'm not."

Mae leaned forward and found him already moving toward her. Their lips met and parted, and with that one kiss alone, she was lost. She couldn't fix all of his problems any more than he could fix hers, but as she wrapped her arms around him and let him pull her body against his, she hoped that maybe when the night was done, they'd each have a few less problems weighing them down.

CHAPTER 4

EACH OTHER'S UNDOING

She was a dream made flesh, with a body even more exquisite than the fantasies his mind had conjured earlier. Her skin was alabaster and felt like silk, a soft contrast to the strong muscles he could feel when he ran his hand over one of her long, sleek legs. His athlete assessment hadn't been far off. She was definitely someone who trained her body hard, but it hadn't been at the cost of sensuality or femininity. She was still slim and lovely, with curves that he couldn't keep his hands off of, and blue eyes that flirted with green.

Her hair, dry and unbound now, cascaded around her face like some golden veil, and her beauty made his chest hurt—which made it surprising when she turned off the lights in the bedroom. Someone like her was meant to be gazed upon while making love, worshipped even. But he didn't question it. He was too lost in the taste of her wine-sweet lips, intoxicated by the scent of sweat and apple blossoms.

He entered her slowly, almost reverently, exulting in the way she felt around him. She was so wet, her body soft and yielding. She arched it up against his, murmuring softly in Finnish, as he began to move more forcefully. He lost himself in her, and everything in the world vanished, except an urgency to drive his body into union with hers. Her nails dug into his back, and then, without warning, she pushed up and rolled him over. Her hips straddled his, and she rode him into ecstatic oblivion, until at last, he couldn't hold out against the mounting pleasure. He came with a great cry, finding release in that glorious body.

Slowly, they both stilled, staying as they were and holding on to the weight of the moment. She was only a dark silhouette in the doorway's scant light as she looked down upon him, but for the space of a heartbeat, he could see her crowned in stars and flowers. It left him breathless for an entirely unexpected set of reasons.

Sated, she shifted off of him and curled up at his side. He wrapped an arm around her, drawing her close as both of them breathed raggedly. They lay like that for a long time, and then he reluctantly disentangled himself to go get the wine. At least it gave him the chance to turn the lights back on and take her all in when he returned. There was a faint sheen of sweat on her brow, and her cheeks were flushed from her own climax. Her disheveled hair spilled over his pillow, and he thought she looked more beautiful now than she had primped and polished for the party. She accepted a glass of wine with trembling hands.

He regarded her fondly for long moments, amazed at how she completely undid him. It wasn't just the stunning looks either. He'd meant what he said: She reminded him of home. That, and she was a tangle of intriguing contradictions. A castal princess. An avenging Valkyrie. That kind of puzzle was what he lived for, a turn-on in and of itself.

From the long, languid smile she gave Justin, he knew he wasn't the only one captivated here. They were each other's undoing. "Why does a devastatingly beautiful woman like you have sex with the lights off?" he asked. "I've known women who need to do that. You aren't one of them."

"I just like it, that's all."

He touched her lips gently with his fingertips and had the satisfaction of seeing her shiver with desire. They'd taken their time, but the night was still young. "You really have walls within walls around you, don't you?" His fingers moved down her neck and then on to trace the curve of one of her breasts. "What are you afraid I'll see with the lights on?"

"Everything," she said simply.

"You like to be in control," he guessed. "And you're afraid for me—or anyone—to see you lose it. To see your emotions unbound. To see your soul."

Her smile grew. "You believe in souls?"

"I believe the next time we do it, the lights are staying on."

"You sure have a high opinion of yourself, thinking it's going to happen again."

"Well, why not? You didn't seem to have that bad of a time. Besides, you got anywhere else to be?"

She hesitated. "No. I don't think so."

"Then it's settled." He rested back against the headboard. "We'll have a nice wine break, and then—lights on."

That earned him an outright laugh. "You'll have to fight me for the lights."

"Gladly."

"I don't think you'd win."

He set the wineglass on the bedside table and leaned toward her. "Then I'll tie you up and keep you down."

She seemed even more amused by that—but also intrigued. Her pupils were dark and dilated with desire. She could do it again right now, he realized. "Hope you tie a good knot."

"I tie an excellent knot. And then I'll drag things out as long as I want, do whatever I want. You don't beg much, do you? But you will. . . . You will, and you'll love it." He trailed his lips along her cheek, and his arousal had returned. He was already imagining her face when she came with him inside her. "And all the while, I'll look at you as much as I want with the lights on—your body, your face when you come . . . all those emotions you won't let anyone see. . . ."

Mae's breath came fast, and the wineglass slipped from her hand, spilling onto the floor. He didn't care. His lips found hers again, and all that mattered was his burning need to possess her again and—

A soft chiming sound that he barely heard made Mae sit upright and pull away. With more of that remarkable speed, she sprinted from the bed and out the door. She returned moments later, more slowly, looking at something in the palm of her hand. At first, Justin was too transfixed by the sight of her naked body to notice much else. Then he realized she was holding an ego.

Careful, said Horatio. *Dashing Eastern Alliance diplomat Huan Korokov wouldn't even blink an eye at that.*

I know, I know, Justin said.

He wished he could get a better look but knew Horatio was right. Telecommunications were sketchy around here, and it was hard enough getting a good portable phone, let alone anything as sophisticated as an ego. It governed a Gemman's life. It made calls, provided unlimited access to the stream, managed money, verified identity. . . . Being without one for four years had been a huge adjustment for Justin. He'd grown up with people and information instantly accessible, and that lack had only increased his feeling of isolation in exile.

Mae sighed and looked up from the ego's screen. "I have to go. I took too long." She began hunting around for her dress. "I'm sorry."

"Don't be," he said. His words were gallant, but there was a sinking feeling welling up in him, not unlike when Huan had announced his departure. "I'm honored to have even had such a brief moment of a Valkyrie's time."

She gave him a wry smile as she tugged the dress up. "You already had me in bed. You don't have to keep laying on the charm."

"I don't know how to stop it."

That got him a bigger smile. He found a robe and walked her to the door. She opened it and then lingered in the doorway, looking at him in a way that managed to be both bold and shy at the same time. "I hope you find something to make you happy."

"I already did," he assured her.

"It really doesn't stop with you." She gave him a long kiss good-bye, one even she was reluctant to break. "If I ever get back here, I'll look you up again."

He smiled. "I look forward to it."

Won't that be a nice surprise for Huan the next time he's in town, said Horatio.

Justin watched her walk away, feeling both light and weighted down at the same time.

The bargain is complete, said Magnus. *You've claimed the crowned woman.*

That startled Justin out of his melancholy. *What? No. Not her.*

You saw the crown of stars and flowers, insisted the raven.

Panic suddenly seized Justin as he remembered that moment, in the throes of postorgasmic bliss, when he had indeed had a brief vision of Mae crowned in glory. A conversation from long ago, with a figure in shadows, replayed in his head. Justin knew the words by heart: *You'll know her by a crown of stars and flowers, and then when you take her to your bed and claim her, you will swear your loyalty to me.*

After a bit of analysis, he relaxed.

No, he told the ravens. *I didn't claim or take the crowned woman to bed.*

Really? Horatio was incredulous. *You were most definitely in bed with her. And there was a lot of claiming going on.*

No. The deal was that I would know *her by the crown and then* claim her. *Key word: then. The woman I took to bed was a lovely Nordic. I didn't see the crown until afterward. So, therefore I didn't claim her when I recognized her.*

The ravens were silent for long moments, and Justin held his breath, more terrified than he was willing to admit of the precipice he stood on. It was a tenuous argument, but he had a feeling their master appreciated such subtleties. In fact, he wondered if they were conferring with him now. Finally, Horatio admitted grudgingly, *You're right. You're a slippery bastard, which is why he likes you.*

But you know her now, Magnus warned him. *You've seen the crown. You know who she is. No more excuses. The next time you make love to her, the deal is done, and you must fulfill your part and swear loyalty. Do you understand?*

Yes, Justin told him smugly, amazed he'd gotten away with this. *And I also understand I'll never see her again.*

Just then, one of Cristobal's henchmen rounded the corner and approached. Justin sighed, unhappy at this intrusion on his afterglow. "Are you here to break my knees for pissing off Señora Santiago?"

"Nah." The guy fished an envelope out of his pocket. "I'm just supposed to deliver this to you."

Justin took the envelope, nearly dropping it when he saw its seal. The RUNA rarely used paper for correspondence, but when it did, there was a type of sticker used to ensure the envelope's security. It was a metallic square that showed the country's seal in glowing blue. As soon as the edges of the sticker were lifted even a little, the seal went dark.

"Where the hell did you get this?" Justin demanded.

"I don't know. Someone gave it to Cristobal." The guy waited expectantly, and Justin realized he wanted a tip.

"I'm out of money. Hit me up next week."

"You spend it on the blonde I just passed?"

"Didn't need to."

Justin shut the door without another word and moved toward the couch like a sleepwalker, unable to take his eyes off the seal. He sat down, took a deep breath, and then opened the envelope. It contained a small piece of paper reading: *Perhaps there are supernatural forces in the world we can't rule out after all. — CK.* Below that was the address of a hotel across town and a room number. Justin felt his mouth go dry. He closed his eyes. This had to be a trick. There was no way—not after four years—that this could be real.

One way to find out, said Magnus.

Justin opened his eyes and sprang up from the couch. He made the effort to find dry clothes but did little else to improve his disheveled state. Five minutes and two shots of courage bourbon later, he was out the door, on his way to the hotel in the note.

He knew the place. It was owned by one of the older families, one that held a fairly neutral position. That was a nice perk for guests not wanting to be woken by or shot in middle-of-the-night raids. The downstairs lobby and bar still held plenty of vices, prostitutes and dealers available to make visits that much more enjoyable.

The room in question was on the third floor. The part of Justin that was still certain this must be some kind of joke or death trap fell silent when he cleared the stairs and saw uniformed Gemman soldiers in gray and maroon standing at attention outside a cluster of doors. He came to a halt, wondering if perhaps he shouldn't rule out a death trap after all. But none of them shot at or even assaulted him, though their eyes followed his every move. He reached the door in the note, hesitating in front of the soldier.

"I'm Justin March, here to see . . . Cornelia Kimora." Surely there was no other CK the note could've been referring to. The soldier gave a curt nod and knocked. Someone called an invitation to enter from within. He disappeared inside for a few seconds and then returned to wave Justin in.

With no more hesitation, Justin plunged forward, ready to face whatever it was that waited for him. He stepped past the soldier and found whom he'd both hoped and dreaded to see: Cornelia Kimora, his old boss, complete with boring clothing and a bad dye job. She looked exactly the same as she had the day she'd told him his last report was unacceptable and that she was "sorry things have to end this way." His military escort had arrived soon thereafter.

They were in the living room of a suite, and she rose from her chair with a smile Justin knew with absolute certainty was faked.

"Justin," she said. "I'm so happy to see you again." That too was a lie, and he returned it in kind as he kissed her cheek.

"Likewise." His brain was screaming with a thousand questions, and he had to fight down the urge to grab hold of her and demand an explanation for what had happened to his life. Instead, he put on the same pleasant face he'd have worn if they were friends catching up after a few months apart. It was the same face he used to interrogate cults and learn their inner workings. "You're just as lovely as always. Do you want to get out and see some sights? I'd be happy to show you around."

Her smile tightened, showing how unfunny she found him. "Just as droll as ever. Please, have a seat so we can talk." No pleasantries here. It was nice to know some things hadn't changed. She glanced over at the soldier who'd let Justin in. "Go fetch the others."

Justin took the offered chair, which was one of four set up at a round wooden table. A wall near it displayed a large portable screen Cornelia's entourage had brought along. Justin felt the same pang of longing for it as he had Mae's ego. It was thin and light, with crystal-clear visuals and all of its hardware contained within itself. No need for a separate computer. The Panamanians had no technology to match that. Their computers always seemed clumsy and unwieldy to Justin, not to mention slow and unreliable.

Dents in the carpet showed the table had been moved to this position, which provided optimal viewing of the screen. Justin wondered whether there was a presentation in his future. Cornelia wasn't offering any guidance. She'd sat down again as well, crossed her legs, and seemed content to wait until "the others" showed before casting light on this situation. He had to give her points for staying true to herself. There was no awkwardness on her part, no gruff "sorry about the exile; you know how it is" or "glad you're still alive." Cornelia probably hadn't lost any sleep over her decisions and wasn't going to pretend otherwise now.

The door burst open, and a tall, gangly man entered. He was close to Cornelia's age and had thinning gray hair. Upon seeing Justin, the man's face lit up. He sprinted across the room, and Justin managed to get to his feet just in time for a frenzied handshake.

"Dr. March! At last! I am so, so, so happy to meet you. You have no idea. I'm such a huge fan of your work."

I wonder which work that is, mused Horatio.

Me too, said Justin.

But again, Justin played it cordial and unassuming. "Why, thank you. That's very kind of you to say, Mr. . . . ?"

"This is Director Francis Kyle, from Internal Security," said Cornelia.

Just Internal Security. When no one assigned you a subdepartment, it meant you were high up. Very high up. Certainly higher than Cornelia, who was having a difficult time hiding her dislike for her superior.

"Please, please, just call me Francis. I want this little gathering to be as friendly as possible."

At least someone does, Justin thought, casting another look at Cornelia. The circumstances of this meeting were still a total mystery, but one thing Justin knew at a glance was that Francis wanted to be here and Cornelia did not.

"We should order drinks, then," Justin told him. "I'm sure they have some sort of room service to—"

The words died on his lips as another person slipped into the room.

It was her.

She wasn't naked or even in a mauve dress, but there was no mistaking Mae. She was dressed simply in blue-gray linen pants and a white cotton T-shirt. From the way her hands hastily tied her hair back in a ponytail as she walked, she'd probably only just finished taking a blow dryer to it. The makeup was gone too, not that her complexion had really needed it. She looked brisk and efficient in her sportier attire, though still devastatingly beautiful.

Also, devastatingly surprised.

She came to an abrupt halt in the middle of the room when she saw Justin. Her hands dropped to her sides, and her eyes widened. Justin felt his own face mirror her shock as he lost control of his casual façade. For a few seconds, he was almost able to grasp at some sort of explanation. She was support staff for a Gemman military attaché, so perhaps it wouldn't be that unreasonable that she would be here for a—

"Ah, Prætorian Koskinen," said Francis, beaming at her. "You're back. How splendid. This is Dr. March."

Mae gave a weak nod, her eyes never leaving Justin.

The words hit Justin like a slap to the face. "Prætorian?" His sluggish mind suddenly started working again as a terrible thought popped up. "Are you . . . are you here to kill me?"

After several more moments, she seemed to regain her own control too. Her astonishment vanished, replaced by a cool and composed face that was much frostier than the one Justin had gotten to know earlier that night. "Dr. March," she said calmly, "if I wanted you dead, you already would be."

CHAPTER 5

A BURNING BRIDGE

Even Cornelia seemed to find that comment funny, probably because it was something she wished had actually happened.

"She's joking, Dr. March," said Francis, taking a seat beside Cornelia.

Justin, studying Mae's face, wasn't so sure. *Prætorian.* His blood ran cold. He'd been such an idiot. He prided himself on his powers of observation and ability to draw out the truth of a situation from the finest details. How had he really let himself believe that someone's "research support" had taken out the Jessup thugs back in the alley in so short a time? In heels and a dress? He hadn't been able to watch the fight as it happened, thanks to Miguel, but even so, anyone looking at the carnage Mae had left behind should've been able to deduce that something wasn't normal there.

You weren't looking at the carnage, said Horatio.

Justin couldn't deny the accusation. He'd been dazed on alcohol and ash, high on the idea that a pretty Gemman woman was charmed by him. With a distraction like her, who could pay attention to details or ask uncomfortable questions about his impending death?

Francis glanced back and forth between them. "Did you deliver the message personally?" he asked Mae. "You must've been at the party around the same time."

"No. We missed each other," she said.

"She must've been tied up," added Justin, deadpan.

Mae gave him a sharp look that made him wonder if baiting

a prætorian was such a smart idea. A prætorian. He'd slept with a fucking prætorian. Who did that? And who lived to tell the tale? That beautiful exterior took on a sinister edge as he allowed himself to contemplate all that she was capable of. Why had she lied? Her initial shock upon seeing him suggested this turn of events had caught her off guard too, but Justin suddenly wasn't so sure. Had she sought him out at the party and lied about her identity to get close? Was this part of Cornelia's larger scheme? For all he knew, they'd orchestrated the Jessup assault to conveniently give Mae a reason to "save" him. It sounded far-fetched, but Justin had learned long ago never to underestimate the RUNA's government.

Forget all of that, said Magnus. *And just remember your deal.*

Oh, I remember it, said Justin, realizing the new danger this reunion presented. *And I will never touch her again.*

"Well, we're all here now," said Francis, cheerful and unassuming. "Let's get on with this. We have very exciting business ahead."

Justin took his seat again, and after several seconds, Mae reluctantly sat as well, positioning herself as far from him as possible.

Cornelia looked relieved to be done with all the unnecessary and wasteful parts of the meeting, like introductions. She gave a curt nod to the uniformed soldiers, and they left the room. Clearing her throat, she turned to face her tablemates. "Yes. Let's get this settled. Justin . . . I'm here to give you a chance to be a servitor again."

Justin's heart nearly stopped, but he refused to let that show, especially since Cornelia's admission seemed to cause her a lot of discomfort. "They don't need servitors in Panama. You can buy salvation on the streets."

Francis chuckled. *He finds everything you say delightful,* observed Horatio. Judging from her scowl, Cornelia didn't share the sentiment. "Not here. *There.*"

There was no need to elaborate on where "there" was. The RUNA. Some inner voice of wisdom that wasn't the ravens cautioned him to dial back the snark.

"You're offering me my citizenship back," he said.

"I'm offering you your job back," Cornelia clarified. "Our country doesn't give citizenship lightly."

"Yes," he said bitterly, "but it sure doesn't have any problems taking it away."

Her eyes narrowed. "Are you interested or not?"

Hell yes, Justin was interested. He wanted to get up and walk onto a plane right then and there. But the situation was still too strange, and there were too many unknown variables for him to jump in blindly. He'd already had one moment of carelessness tonight, and that had landed him in bed with a dangerous woman.

"Why?" he asked. "Why now? You've got hundreds of bright-eyed graduates who could do what I used to do, for less money and with more ambition."

"Some people," said Cornelia, in a tone stating she was not one of them, "feel you have certain qualifications that make you a valuable asset for a particular situation that's arisen. We can't elaborate on any other details until you've agreed to return."

Francis looked ready to burst with excitement. "Oh, Cornelia, just show him the offer."

She grimaced at having her rehearsed presentation interrupted, but after a few moments, she produced an ego and told it, "Bring up the Justin March offer." She handed the device to Justin.

For a moment, he was more taken with the ego than its display, now that he could actually hold one. They were smaller and lighter than when he'd left, and voice commands had apparently improved significantly. Reminding himself there was an incredible chance he might be surrounded by all this technology once again, he focused back on the ego's screen, which detailed a very generous employment package. It cited a salary much higher than his previous one, as well as other perks, such as "luxury accommodations" in Vancouver. The offer also mentioned that he'd return with a visa of unspecified length, which he didn't find reassuring.

"How much are you authorized to go up to?" Justin asked, handing the ego back to Cornelia.

"I beg your pardon?" she asked.

"This is an offer. You're coming in as a bargainer, meaning there's room to negotiate on this. Whatever max salary Internal Security's authorized you to go up to, I want it."

Cornelia's antagonistic expression and reluctant nod told him two things. One was that this was real, that they wanted him back—wanted him back very, very badly. And that led to his second conclusion, that he had more power here than she wanted to admit.

"Fine," she said. "So we're settled?"

"No. If I'm going to take up the mantle again, I want a few other things."

None of them said anything. They were probably too astonished that he wasn't down on his hands and knees begging to be taken back. He was kind of astonished himself.

"I want arrangements for my sister."

"Your . . . your sister?" Cornelia was too baffled by the request to be scornful.

"I'm guessing she's still stuck in Anchorage. Get her out of there. Bring her to Vancouver, and give her a place as nice as mine. Somewhere in the suburbs."

The more this continued, the more Justin was getting a feel for the group dynamics and who was in what role. Francis, with his rank, undoubtedly held the most power and authorization, but Cornelia was the one charged with negotiation. Judging from Francis's lack of involvement thus far, Justin hadn't made any outlandish requests yet. After all, if they were already willing to spend so much on him, how much more would it cost to relocate one woman and her son? Meanwhile, Mae wore an excellent poker face, but she was watching everything so avidly that it was clear she wasn't privy to SCI's bartering. Maybe she was along for the ride simply to ensure their safe travels. Or maybe she had been ordered to kill him if he refused.

"Fine," repeated Cornelia. "We'll take care of your sister. Now, let's—"

"One more thing," Justin interrupted. Even doting Francis looked a little amazed at the audacity. It was time to see just how badly the RUNA wanted its servitor back.

Be careful, said Horatio. *Even they have limits.*

I know. But I have to ask. You know I do.

"There are some people here . . . a family. I want them to get visas too. The guy used to have business relations with us, so it shouldn't be that big of a deal."

"You want some Panamanian family allowed into the RUNA?" asked Cornelia incredulously.

"Yeah. There's only . . ." Justin started counting out on his fingers. "One . . . two . . . guess we've got to bring her. Probably the in-laws too. Nine. There are nine of them."

"No." Cornelia didn't hesitate. "There is absolutely no way we can bring in nine Panamanian nationals."

Justin ignored her and looked at Francis expectantly, assuming this required clearance from a higher tier. Conflict filled the older man's features. It was obviously hard for him to deny Justin anything, but as Horatio had said, even they had limits.

"I'm sorry," Francis said. "We can't get that many visas, unless they're defectors with some kind of critical information about the Panamanian government. Which I'm guessing they aren't."

He was right. Panama wasn't a big enough blip on the radar to be worth much of the RUNA's effort, nor did it have a government stable enough to seek intelligence on. Justin had known it was a long shot, but his heart sank anyway. *I promised him,* he thought. *I promised Sergio I'd make this happen.* Inspiration hit.

"What about one? Can you get one visa? A student visa. Perfectly harmless."

"You want to bring a kid back with you?" asked Cornelia.

"Girl," he corrected. "Tessa—er, Teresa Cruz. She's sixteen. A real prodigy."

"A sixteen-year-old?" She couldn't keep the accusation out of her voice.

"It's nothing like that," Justin snapped, losing a little of his composure. "She's practically like another sister, except she doesn't nag me as much as my real one." Silence met him, and he pushed forward. "Come on, it's nothing. One little visa. They issue a handful of student ones each year. Do that for me, and I'm yours."

He regretted his choice of wording in that last bit, but there was nothing to be done for it now. He'd made his play. If it panned out, he could very well have his life back. Of course, there was still the teeny-tiny fact that the reason they wanted him was still unknown, but surely it would be worth what he was getting in return.

"Done," said Francis firmly. "I'll make it happen." He held out his hand to Justin. With only a breath of hesitation, Justin shook the offered hand.

Cornelia updated her file to reflect the new concessions and then had Justin sign the screen. Along with all the perks, there was a fair amount of legalese in the employment agreement that probably detailed imprisonment or a return to exile at their discretion. He signed anyway and had to fight to keep his hand from shaking.

He was going home. How had this happened? How could a night that started with a garish Panamanian woman throwing wine on his shirt end with his returning to his homeland in glory?

Don't get carried away, said Horatio. *You aren't there yet.*

And don't forget everything else that happened tonight, said Magnus, almost sounding offended.

Justin lifted his eyes to Mae. No, he certainly hadn't forgotten about that part.

Although Cornelia wasn't a fan of accommodating Justin or even taking him back, she seemed more at ease once the paperwork was in order. After all, she was now his boss again, which meant she could exert a little more control and feel entitled to her condescension. Francis was elated and appeared to be on the verge of starting the Justin March Fan Club.

Mae remained the enigma here. She was still doing a good job of keeping her expression neutral, which wasn't surprising from someone who'd gone through a castal upbringing and prætorian training. It was her body language that gave her away, especially when Cornelia jumped to the next order of business: revealing what the burning reason behind Justin's return was. Mae leaned forward to look at the screen, anticipation crackling through her.

She doesn't know why she's here, he thought. *She doesn't know why I'm here. It's possible what happened earlier was a complete coincidence and not part of any larger machination. Maybe.*

"So. Now that all that unpleasantness is out of the way, you're probably wondering why we've taken you back," said Cornelia.

"I figured you thought I'd learned my lesson," he said cheerfully. Maybe he should've been a bit more humble, but his exuberance over this change of fortune was running strong.

"No," she said with no humor at all. "I don't believe that for an instant. Which is part of the reasoning for this unorthodox decision."

Justin's cockiness faded. All was not forgotten and forgiven.

"Now," continued Cornelia, "I'm sure you're familiar with the patrician murders, which have been all over the news." She paused and then gave a contrived laugh that was supposed to sound embarrassed. "But of course you wouldn't be. I don't imagine much Gemman news makes it to Panama, does it?"

"Depends on if the homing pigeons are up and running," he replied.

Cornelia didn't blink, but in his periphery, he saw a smile play at the edge of Mae's lips. She caught it quickly, apparently remembering she was angry, and her business mask slipped back into place.

"Bring up the patrician murder records," Cornelia ordered the screen.

The screen came to life, displaying a list of five bolded names. Under each one were four bulleted items: age, caste name, location of death, and date of death. Justin forgot all about Cornelia's attitude and the strange circumstances of his homecoming. Seeing the list, this set of data, snapped him into a mode he hadn't been in for a very long time. Immediately, his brain wanted to make sense of the information. There was *always* a pattern to the world, and even with no other background on this list, he immediately began summarizing it.

Each person belonged to a different caste: Erinian, Lakota, Nordic, Welsh, and Nipponese. All of them were twenty-seven or twenty-eight and had been killed within the borders of their respective castal land grants. The murder dates extended over the last six months, with the most recent being a few days ago.

"These have been highly publicized," said Cornelia. "Despite the wide ethnic spread, the cases share some similarities, leading us to believe they were all committed by the same person. The age similarity, as well as the identical nature of their deaths."

"Which was . . . ?"

"Stabbed through the heart with a silver dagger. During a full moon. Quite brutal." Cornelia almost, *almost* sounded like she actually had some emotion behind the words. "The prevailing theory is that it's a plebeian with antipatrician sentiments."

"Obviously," said Justin. He leaned forward, propping his elbows on the table and never taking his eyes off the screen. A rush of pleasure ran through him at finally having something substantial to use his brainpower on. "A plebeian with remarkable access, since they all happened on land grants." The castes kept the borders of their lands closed. Federal officials could enter at any time, of course, and other patricians had limited visiting rights. Average plebeians were only allowed entry if they had special permission, such as a friend's sponsorship or something business related.

Cornelia gave a nondescript grunt that could have been either impressed or disappointed. "What also makes them remarkable is that they all took place within homes or offices that showed no sign of entry, ones that were even locked from the inside."

"Then they were invited in. Or are just cleverer than you think." Justin spun through the possibilities. "You're probably looking for a delivery person, a plebeian who'd have reason to visit all of those castes. Someone strong enough to wield a dagger like that. Probably male."

"Yes," said Cornelia. "Police have also come to the same conclusions."

Justin finally looked back at her. "Then what exactly does this have to do with me? This is a police matter, and apparently they've already figured out what I have—probably not as quickly as me, but still."

"What this has to do with you," said Cornelia, ignoring his self-compliment, "is that forensics has shown the weapon used was made of an antiquated silver mix and had a nonmanufactured blade—an unusual choice that could have many ritualistic and spiritual associations. As could the fact that all of the murders happened during full moons."

"And that's why we're involved. You think some religious group is responsible." It wouldn't be the first time religions had been tied to crimes, forcing servitors to work with local law enforcement. "This is still the kind of work any servitor could do."

Wait for it, said Magnus.

Francis, grinning from ear to ear, finally couldn't take it anymore. "There's one more piece of evidence! Something uniquely suited to you and your expertise. No one else is capable."

Cornelia frowned at the outburst. "Most of the victims had security cameras inside and out. All of those were cut, so we have no footage of the crimes—with one exception. This last victim, the Erinian, had a secret camera that wasn't wired into the rest of her security. It seems she didn't trust her cleaning staff. She thought they were stealing her jewelry."

"I haven't heard anything about this," said Mae, speaking up for the first time.

"It's been kept out of the news," exclaimed Francis. "It's too incredible."

"Show us the Madigan footage," Cornelia told the screen.

A video immediately started. The camera appeared to be mounted into a corner of the ceiling and looked down into a sumptuous bedroom. The dark windows indicated it was nighttime. A red-haired woman stepped into frame and paused to examine herself in a dresser mirror. After a few moments, she took off her shoes and began unfastening her earrings, silver hoops of Celtic knot work. She had just moved on to a similarly stylized bird necklace when a black shadow flashed across the screen, coming from the right. The entire thing took only a few seconds. As the shadow entered, it had no form. It simply looked like a nebulous cloud of smoke, save that no smoke could move that fast. When that dark mass reached the woman, it suddenly took on a human shape. There was the brief motion of an arm pulling back and thrusting toward the woman's chest. Her mouth opened, and before she even hit the ground, the figure had darted out of frame.

Justin was on his feet. "What was that?"

"That," said Cornelia, "is exactly what we need you to find out."

"Show it again," he demanded.

Cornelia played it once more at normal speed and then again slowed down.

"Again," said Justin. By then, he'd walked right up to the screen. When he requested a fifth viewing, Cornelia refused.

"No matter how many times you watch it, it's not going to change."

"It's a trick," he said. "It's been manipulated."

"We've had our best people examine it," explained Francis, seeming to love this. "There's no sign of any modification. The type of camera used would make it difficult to hide it anyway."

"Then they obviously weren't your best." Justin finally returned to his seat. "Give me a copy of this. I've got a guy—or will have him, when I'm back—who'll find out what happened to it in five minutes."

"You may have it examined however you like," said Cornelia crisply. "And I can assure you, I'd like nothing better than to resolve this fraud."

"If it's a fraud," said Francis, eyes still shining.

Mae's face was full of confusion as she turned to him. "What else would it be?"

Cornelia carried on as though Mae hadn't spoken. "While you have the video analyzed as you see fit, you will have the freedom and resources to investigate the murders and hopefully uncover whatever group is responsible for this."

"And," added Francis, a meaningful gleam in his eye, "*your* expertise in particular may be what breaks this case."

And that was when Justin knew. He knew why they wanted him back, and he also knew that Cornelia and Francis had very, very different views on both the case and his involvement. Francis was the one who thought Justin truly had something to offer. Someone at Francis's level would've been allowed to read that last, dangerous report, and something in it had struck him. Word had probably gotten to him as well of the unofficial reports, the things whispered at high levels that Justin had refused to commit to writing, the things that had gotten him sent here.

They know what you've seen, said Magnus.

I bet you never thought things would pan out like this, mused Horatio.

No, Justin certainly hadn't. It also occurred to him that they weren't explicitly spelling out what part of his "expertise" was of use here. They weren't enlightening Mae about the secrets he'd unwillingly become enmeshed in, which again made him curious about why she was here.

"How much will you need to know about my methods?" he asked carefully. He already knew who to talk to and that it was a conversation that should be had off the record.

Cornelia and Francis exchanged looks in a rare moment of solidarity. "We need this taken care of as soon as possible," she said. "It's drawing too much attention, too much panic. And if word gets out that there's a murderous cult behind this, everything our country was founded on will be on the line."

"So," said Justin, reading the subtext, "the results are more important than the methods."

Their silence on the matter answered for them, and Cornelia shifted the topic to logistics, telling him what to expect when they returned to Vancouver. Justin only half listened. *Vancouver. I'm going to Vancouver!* He would've been ecstatic over the RUNA's humblest town, let alone its dazzling capital.

"You're probably not in any significant danger from investigating the cold cases." Justin couldn't be certain, but Cornelia almost sounded disappointed about that. "But one can never predict what some of these zealots will do. Since they may be, uh, uncooperative, we feel you should have more security than usual."

"After that group tried to set me on fire, I don't really have a problem with enhanced security," he told her. "Add as many people as you want."

Cornelia shook her head. "I'm sure Prætorian Koskinen will be more than sufficient by herself."

"What?" asked Justin and Mae in unison.

"Didn't General Gan explain the nature of this mission?" asked Cornelia, sounding legitimately puzzled.

"No," said Mae, visibly trying to bury her shock again. "He simply told me to accompany you here."

"For which we are very grateful, my dear." Francis smiled at her as if she were a favorite granddaughter. "And now you'll be Dr. March's bodyguard as he travels and completes this assignment."

"A bodyguard," said Mae flatly. "I'm going to be a bodyguard."

Boring work for a Valkyrie, said Magnus. *If you want her in bed again, piss off someone dangerous so that she has something interesting to do.*

"It may also be useful to have a patrician around," added Francis. "It might get you a friendly reception if you go to the land grants. You know how they are—no offense."

"None taken," Mae murmured. She still looked stunned, and it seemed legitimate to Justin, reducing the odds that she was here to kill him. "Do you know how long I'll be assigned to him?"

Cornelia looked irritated that this meeting was still going on, now that the essentials were covered. "We need this solved in a little less than four weeks."

"Why four weeks?" asked Mae.

"The next full moon," said Justin. His high came crashing to the ground.

"He's so smart," said Francis, grinning.

Cornelia rolled her eyes. "Yes. Brilliant."

"And what happens if I don't solve it in four weeks?" Justin asked quietly.

She fixed him with a cold gaze. "Well. We'll cross that bridge when we come to it, won't we?"

Justin attempted a smile, but all he could think was that said bridge would probably be on fire, with him stuck in the middle and alligators circling below.

Mae's obvious disappointment at this turn of events irritated Justin. She certainly hadn't seemed that miserable around him in bed. "I'm sure it won't be that unbearable, prætorian. I'm really not that bad once you get underneath everything."

Her eyes looked more blue than green in this lighting, and he saw a flash of anger in them. It reminded him of the passion he'd seen earlier. *I wish she wasn't so hot,* he thought wistfully.

You have to help her, said Magnus. *She has gods swarming around her and no way to stop them.*

No, Justin said. *Don't bring up gods anymore. This isn't the time. Not when we're on the verge of getting my life back.*

It's always the time, said Magnus. *Besides, what do you think you're going to be dealing with when you return?*

Mae said nothing to Justin's comment and directed her attention to the others as she stood up. "Do you need anything else from me tonight?"

"No, no," said Francis, stifling a yawn. "You've done more than enough, my dear. Get some sleep. We're leaving early." He paused and laughed. "Ah, you don't sleep, do you? Well, then, do whatever you want. You're young. Maybe you can find some dashing, exotic fling."

Mae didn't even blink. "I'll just stay in my room, sir. There's no one worth my time in this place."

She turned with military precision, but her air was all castal, displaying an attitude that refused to acknowledge those people—or rather, the one person—she considered beneath her. As Justin watched her go, he barely heard Francis dismissing him as well and telling him to go fetch his "provincial girl."

A haughty, lethal bodyguard. An assignment involving shadowy phantoms. This homecoming was starting to accrue a hefty price tag.

You still want to pay it? asked Horatio.

Absolutely.

CHAPTER 6

GENIUS, CON ARTIST

Tessa wasn't asleep when someone pounded on the front door.

She wasn't supposed to be awake. Her mother would kill her if she found out, but Tessa couldn't help herself. Her father had acquired a reader from the Eastern Alliance and given it to her this morning. She knew it was old technology for them. Everything that trickled into Panama was. But to her, it was a miracle: a small, lightweight device that contained hundreds of books. Some were old; some were current. Most were written in Mandarin, which she couldn't read. There were still enough from the RUNA to keep her busy, and she could read English as well as she could Spanish. Her father had made sure of that.

The reader became irrelevant when she heard the noise, however. She froze where she sat, tense and wide-eyed. It had been years since gangs regularly raided the houses of their rivals, and her father wasn't even involved in anything that would attract attention or retaliation. Still, the drills her parents had made her and her sisters practice over and over were still fresh in her mind. *Go to the tunnel, bring nothing.* All it would take was one shout from the bodyguards, and Tessa would be out of her room in a flash.

But no shouts came. Whoever was there banged on the door again, and several moments later, she could hear loud voices engaged in some sort of argument. No shouts of alarm. No stomping of feet. No gunfire.

Tessa waited a little bit longer, but when the noise didn't stop, her curiosity got the better of her. It was a problem she often had. Slipping out of bed, she found her robe and tied it tightly over her floor-length nightgown. Out of habit, she nearly pulled up her hair but then decided to leave it down to save time. She moved quietly and slowly as she left the room, still cautious of any possible threat, and prayed the old wooden floor wouldn't creak. The closer she came to the staircase leading down, the more she relaxed. She recognized the voices. There would be no raid tonight.

She made it downstairs and paused just outside the doorway to the foyer, keeping out of sight but still managing a good view. Her mother stood there in a similar robe, arms crossed, but she'd taken the time to pull up her hair. Marta Cruz would never be seen with her hair down, not even in the middle of the night. Tessa's father stood nearby, and his clothing suggested he hadn't even gone to bed yet. Two of the family's bodyguards were also on hand, looking more confused than concerned.

But none of them really caught Tessa's attention. It was the sight of Justin March, standing in front of the door, that made Tessa take notice.

She hadn't seen Justin in a long time. After her mother had insisted he move out, Justin had been by only a few times to visit her father. Most of their outings were now to restaurants and clubs, places that were inaccessible to Tessa. She'd never met anyone like him and missed having him around. Justin seemed glamorous and worldly to her, and most important, he never talked down to her. He always spoke in a frank, open way and wasn't afraid to discuss the topics no one else would. "He has no sense of propriety," her mother had once told Tessa. "But what can you expect from such godless people?"

Justin certainly didn't seem so glamorous tonight. His clothing was soaked from the rain, and the hair he usually kept so carefully styled was equally wet and disheveled. There was a bright, almost fervent look in his eyes that even Tessa recognized. He was drunk or high—maybe both.

"Slow down," Tessa's father was saying. "You aren't making any sense."

"I'm making perfect sense," Justin insisted. He raked a hand through his wet hair and began pacing back and forth, a habit she recalled from when he was engaged in some intense mental exercise. "This is her out, Sergio. This is *my* out. Don't be a fool and waste this chance. It'll never happen again."

"Mr. March, you are out of line." Tessa's mother always refused to call Justin "Dr." and was driving home her disapproval now by using the Voice. It was the one she reserved for lectures that usually resulted in Tessa being confined to her room. "If you truly have something important to say, please return in the morning when you are in a more presentable state." Her tone implied that she sincerely doubted there was anything important here at all.

Justin completely ignored her and focused his attention on Tessa's father. "I'm not screwing around here! We have to—" His eyes flicked to the far side of the room, toward the doorway, and Tessa realized she'd been spotted. "There you are! Come here. Your life's about to change forever. You can thank me later."

Tessa hesitated for a few seconds but then realized she might as well take the plunge. There was no more hiding. She stepped forward, and her mother nearly passed out.

"Teresa! What do you think you're doing? Return to your room this instant!"

Belatedly, Tessa realized that maybe she should've pulled up her hair after all. It was bad enough for a non–family member to see her in her robe, even if it did completely cover her nightgown. Wearing loose hair, at her age, wasn't something that women of her status did. It was the kind of thing you'd find in New Money or the lower classes, in women who worked beside men or ventured out alone.

"No, no," said Justin, taking a few steps forward. He didn't go too much farther. Drunk or not, even he knew getting closer to a girl in her nightgown might spur the bodyguards to action. They knew him and liked him—and had won a lot of money from him—but some lines still weren't meant to be crossed. "Let her stay. This is important."

"I don't even know what 'this' is," her father said, looking weary.

Justin took a deep breath, seeming to finally realize he needed to approach the matter in a calmer way. "I'm going home, Sergio. Back to the RUNA."

Her father lit up. "You got your citizenship back?" Tessa noticed her mother looked happy too, but probably because she thought they'd be getting rid of Justin once and for all.

"Not exactly." Justin's enthusiasm dimmed for a moment. "It doesn't matter, though. I'm going back and talked them into making a visa exception."

Tessa's father's forehead wrinkled in confusion as he tried to parse the words. Then, suddenly, his face transformed. Never, never, had she seen such joy within him. "You did it," he breathed. "You're bringing us back."

Justin shifted and looked uncomfortable. "Um, not all of you."

That radiant joy went away. "But you always said—"

"I know, I know. And I tried, but the borders are too tight. They can't allow a group that big in, but . . ." Justin took a deep breath. "I can bring Tessa back with me."

Tessa hadn't seen her mother look so horrified since the time Tessa had worn black shoes to Donna Carlos's spring tea. "Why on earth would you do that?"

"Why do you think?" exclaimed Justin. "To get her out of here! I can only take one of you, and she's the obvious choice. You can't abandon your family, but she can strike out into her own future. She can get a student visa. She can study there—get a real education." He stepped forward, catching hold of Tessa's father's arm. "Sergio, can you imagine it? Tessa in the RUNA, getting a Gemman degree. It's the kind of thing that could get her citizenship, you know. I've seen it happen. And from there, it might open the door to the rest of you."

Her father caught his breath, his eyes going wide. Justin knew exactly how to get to him, exactly what words would make Sergio Cruz's world come to a complete standstill. Tessa had seen Justin work that magic on others before.

Her great-grandparents had left the RUNA years ago, back in the days of the first genetic mandates. In the beginning, the RUNA and EA had forcibly swapped large amounts of their population in order to create optimal genetic mixing. Those

who tried having "nonoptimal" children were fined and impris-
oned. Eventually, mandatory contraceptive implants ensured
the government's control. Her refugee great-grandparents had
had to scrape and crawl their way to the top of Panamanian society, and they'd believed it to be a worthy sacrifice in order to
be together and have their own children. But that hadn't stopped
them from singing the praises of their homeland, instilling a
worship of the RUNA that had been passed down to their children and their children's children and so on. The RUNA had
almost become a mythical fairyland to Tessa, which was why
Justin had always seemed so larger-than-life.

Her father was especially obsessed with the RUNA. His adoration of all things Gemman had increased when he'd been
allowed a couple of trading trips there. He'd come back star-
struck, full of stories about the country's technology and the
luxuriant way its citizens lived. People could walk the streets
safely, and everything was clean and bright and perfect. It was
where he'd met Justin and why Justin had been allowed to stay
with them when he'd first come to Panama City.

"It's impossible," her father said at last, though she could tell
from the faraway look in his eyes that he was already imagining
this fantasy.

"It's completely possible," Justin said, looking just as excited.

Tessa's father seemed to return to reality. "Why are they letting you go back?"

Justin shrugged. "They want me to resume my old job. I was
good, you know. One of the best. You saw the way I lived. I had
access to all sorts of connections and opportunities—things that
Tessa could be a part of. She could live like a queen."

There it was again, the wonder in her father's eyes. Tessa
had always believed Justin was a genius, but her mother had
said he was a con artist. When Tessa had asked her father which
was true, he'd said Justin was both.

Her mother reminded the two men of her presence. "Sergio!
You aren't actually considering this, are you? She's sixteen.
You can't just let her go off and live with some man, especially
one like him." Even while outraged, she couldn't bring herself

to use any improper language to clarify what she meant by "one like him."

"Oh, she wouldn't live with me," Justin said quickly. "She'd live with my sister. She's a, uh, real lady. She'd look out for Tessa. She'd totally make sure Tessa's protected and behaving properly. And well fed. Besides, let's be honest here. What are you really going to do with her if she stays?"

"She'll do what all young ladies do," she said. "She'll finish her education and then marry someone appropriate."

Justin shook his head. " 'Education,' huh? You mean more homeschooling with insipid reading and remedial math? And do you actually believe it's going to be that easy to marry her off?" He glanced over at Tessa. "No offense, sweetie." To her parents, he said, "She sits out at dances. She says things she shouldn't—in public. And worst of all, she's *smart*. She's cute enough that you'd eventually get someone. It'd be worth it for some up-and-coming guy just to connect to your family. She'd hate it, though. And you'd spend a fortune waiting for that someone."

Tessa wasn't sure whether she'd been insulted or complimented, but both of her parents fell silent. Even her mother couldn't deny what Justin had said. Putting girls out on the marriage market was expensive. It required a lot of parties, a lot of clothes, and a lot of gift giving. Tessa's oldest sister, Laurentia, was stunning. She'd been engaged within a month. Her next-oldest sister, Regina, was pretty too, but for whatever reason, it had taken her almost a year to make a match. Their family was well-off, but that year had strained their finances.

Justin knew he was making progress. "You've got two more after her. Business is good . . . but is it that good?"

"How do we even know any of this is true?" exclaimed her mother. "This could all be one big story so that he can take advantage of her."

"Justin wouldn't do that," snapped Tessa's father. Maybe he wasn't sure about this offer, but he was confident of Justin's character. He always had been.

Tessa's mother wasn't convinced. "I don't like it. It's completely unheard of, and I won't allow it."

Silence fell. Justin was watching Tessa's father so, so closely. *Justin knows,* Tessa thought. *He knows he's got Papa.* No other offer would've been so tempting unless Justin actually could've relocated their entire family. It was her father's greatest desire. His grandparents had always hoped the mandates would lighten and allow their family to go back. Those mandates had indeed shifted. There were only small fines now for nonoptimal children, and those who followed the old ways were compensated generously. That didn't change the strict Gemman policy toward immigrants, however. Still, Tessa's father had clung to the family dream that some miracle might bring them back. Here it was, and there might never be a chance like this again.

"She can go," he said at last. His face hardened. "But you have to look after her. Swear to me you will."

Justin held up his hand. "As though she were my own daughter."

"No!" cried her mother. "Absolutely not. I won't allow this."

Tessa's father put on the fiercest look she'd ever seen from him. "I *will* allow it."

Tension hung between them, so thick that Tessa could practically see it.

"Let Tessa decide," said Justin. He sounded very reasonable and diplomatic.

All eyes turned on her, and Tessa took a step back. She'd kind of liked it when everyone had forgotten about her.

"That's fair," her father said, ignoring her gaping mother. "It's up to you."

There was a knowing look in Justin's eyes. She understood now why he'd so gallantly offered the choice to her. *He thinks he's already got me because he always gets what he wants.* Well, aside from the exile none of them understood.

"Go ahead," he told her. "You're going to piss off someone no matter what you decide. Might as well do what you want."

"I don't know if I want to go to the RUNA," she said haltingly.

Justin's smile faltered, but she'd spoken the truth. She was just as fascinated by that glittering, mythical country as the rest of her family, but completely relocating to a society so unlike her own was terrifying. Maybe she didn't always like the way hers worked, but she knew it. It was comfortable. It was safe. Kind of.

Then she thought about the reader, that beautiful and miraculous device. What would it be like to be surrounded by things like that? What would it be like to go wherever she wanted? What would it be like to make her own decisions? Of course, that was presuming Justin's sister would let her. Tessa wasn't entirely sure how strict she would be.

"But I don't know if I want to stay here either." Her mother made some kind of strangled noise, and Tessa took a deep breath. "So . . . I'll go."

Justin smacked his hands together and whooped with joy. "You won't regret it. None of you will. This is going to change your life."

Tessa nodded weakly, unsure of what she'd just agreed to. Judging from her mother's glare and red face, she suspected her parents would be continuing this conversation in private later. Her father would win out, of course. That was the way it was around here; the men governed the household. *But not in the RUNA,* she thought.

Her father, face jubilant, looked Justin over and beckoned him forward. "Come in and dry off. Get something to eat—and some water. You can spend the night, and I'll have my driver take you back to Cristobal's in the morning."

That was too much for Tessa's mother, and she stormed out of the room in a rage. Tessa quietly followed the men into the kitchen, mostly because no one seemed to notice she was still there. Her father walked on, but she daringly caught hold of Justin's sleeve. He glanced down at her and grinned, still dashing even when wet and intoxicated.

"You made the right choice," he told her. "As soon as you're there, you'll never want to come back."

"But why would you do it? Whatever happened, I know you must have put up a fight to get me in. Why? Why would you do this for me?"

A little of that pride faded, and she saw a faraway look in his eyes. "Because your dad took me in when no one else would. And when he did, I was so sure of myself—and so desperate—that I swore I'd get back home someday. I promised him I'd get him back too—all of you. He took a big chance on me and would've done it without any payback. But I owed him. I still owe him. I couldn't deliver all of what I promised, but I can get you in. That has to be enough for now."

Tessa had never known any of this. "But why *me* instead of one of the others?"

That upbeat attitude was back. "Because you deserve it and can make the most of it. You're smart—smarter than even you realize. You notice things no one else does, and I only know one other person that observant."

"You?" Tessa guessed. Dashing, yes, and also confident to the point of arrogance.

"Exactly. See? That's what I'm talking about. Keep watching the world, and you'll go far. You couldn't do that here, and I hate to see waste."

Tessa studied him a few moments more. Maybe she really was as observant as he said, because she suddenly knew there was more. "What other reason? Why else would you try to lift me up?"

He smiled, probably at having his assessment of her confirmed further. "Because someone once did it for me."

CHAPTER 7

FAIRYLAND

Tessa had never flown on a plane, and as she and Justin walked across the runway the next morning, she wondered if she could actually bring herself to do this. She hadn't been able to sleep last night, and now, coming face-to-face with her transportation to Fairyland, her nervousness shifted to complete and total fear.

Justin, however, had other concerns.

"Do you know how primitive this is, actually walking across the tarmac?" He was smoking a cigarette, and despite his complaints, there was a swagger to his step. He'd woken up hangover free this morning, something her mother said could only have been accomplished through a deal with the devil. "You'll see when we get home. There are Jetways to all the planes, and the airports don't look like shantytowns."

Tessa nodded. He'd been "enlightening" her all morning with tales of the RUNA, which he was already calling home again. She'd listened to his stories for the last few years, but there was something different about them now. Before, he'd been wistful, describing something distant and unattainable—almost exactly the same way her father spoke of the RUNA. Now Justin was already acting as though he'd never left and Panama was just some layover, rather than the place he'd called home for four years.

Two armed soldiers in gray-and-maroon uniforms stood stiffly at attention outside of the plane, but Tessa didn't find them nearly as intimidating as the plane itself. Everyone in this city walked around with guns; she'd seen them her entire life.

Nothing new there. The woman who emerged from the plane, however, made Tessa do a double take.

"Prætorian Koskinen," Justin called, giving her a mock salute. "Good morning."

"Dr. March," she returned, crossing her arms. Her expression was calm and unreadable, like a marble statue's. "So nice to see you again."

Justin stopped and put his arm around Tessa. "First test," he whispered. "Is she telling the truth?"

"No," said Tessa.

"I didn't think so." More loudly, he said, "Tessa, this is Mae. Mae, Tessa. She's the prodigy I told you about. She's super good at this stuff. Almost as good as me. You'll be impressed. Just wait."

"Wow, almost as good as you?" asked Mae dryly. "Is that even possible?"

Tessa regarded Mae with apprehension. She wasn't in uniform but still radiated strength and dignity. Justin had spent a considerable amount of time describing her this morning as he analyzed how a Nordic woman had ended up in the military's highest ranks. Occasionally, he'd gotten sidetracked and expounded on her hair and eyes. Tessa, however, had stopped paying attention to his discourse after he'd said the word "prætorian." Prætorians. The monsters of the RUNA. She'd heard about them, of course. *Everyone* had, and even if this blond woman didn't look like a killing machine, Tessa vowed not to say anything that might test that observation. She simply gave a polite nod as she walked up the steps.

The wry expression Mae had reserved for Justin transformed into a smile as Tessa passed. "Prodigy or not, I'm very glad to meet you. You'll love the RUNA."

Tessa blushed and nodded again, overwhelmed at such kindness from a woman who managed to be both glamorous and dangerous at the same time. Justin lingered on the ground and dropped his cigarette onto the tarmac. He gave it a fond look before stamping it out. "The only thing I'll miss from around here. I'm quitting here and now. Nothing that good back home anyway—well, at least nothing legal that's that good." He shifted his messenger bag on his shoulder and headed up after Tessa. It was his only luggage, since he'd claimed he had nothing here that was worth taking back. Tessa was starting to wonder why he'd ever come to Panama at all if he hated it so much.

"Mae was telling the truth about me," she murmured to Justin, once they'd stepped inside the plane.

"About what?" he asked.

"About being glad to meet me."

"Show-off."

The rest of the Gemman delegation responded with varying degrees of politeness and directed her and Justin toward the back of the jet. Along with the soldiers and Internal Security officials, there was a young woman named Candace who appeared to be some type of assistant. She jumped whenever any of her higher-ups spoke to her. When she looked at Justin, however, Candace would flush and smile.

Tessa had seen women behave that way near him before and couldn't understand being stupid around a guy, even handsome ones. Her mother had had plenty to say about Justin's appearance. *Too good-looking,* she'd said. *Make sure you marry a plain man, Tessa. They won't stray, and they'll never have power over you.* Tessa wondered what that said about her father.

No matter how much Justin kept poetically painting it as "soaring off into a new life," she found flying absolutely terrifying from the instant they left the ground. The jet's interior felt too small and the sky too big. As the plane bounced along air currents, it seemed impossible that the engines would keep them up. Tessa expected to come crashing to the ground at any moment. She wished now that she'd worn her rosary but had packed it at the last minute. Gemman attitudes toward religion were no secret, and she hadn't wanted to attract attention.

She squeezed her eyes shut and felt Justin put his hand over hers. "Breathe, sweetie. You're okay. This is completely safe."

Tessa forced her eyes open, seeing rare compassion on his face. "How long is this going to take?"

"Nine hours. We'll probably stop to refuel once we're back in RUNA airspace. This is a small plane for a trip like this." He grinned. "I guess I wasn't worth first class." His eyes drifted forward, focusing on Mae as she spoke to the orange-haired woman from Internal Security.

Tessa closed her eyes again and tried to distract herself from her imminent death. "Why are you obsessed with her?"

"She's my boss. My life is in her hands."

"Not her. Mae."

"I suppose there's an argument that my life's in her hands too. But I'm not obsessed. I don't even know her." His tone was too casual, even for him, and his eyes constantly strayed to her when he thought no one saw. Mae never looked at Justin, and it seemed to Tessa that the avoidance was too adamant to be a coincidence.

Tessa eventually tried to sleep, with no luck. She wasn't sure how much time passed before she heard Mae join them. Each minute felt like a lifetime. The plane had steadied a little, and with a great effort, Tessa opened her eyes. Mae was watching her, her face kind.

"Do you need anything?"

"I could use a drink," Justin said.

Mae turned toward him with an exasperated look. "I wasn't talking to you."

She called for some water, and Candace came scurrying back with a glass. "Thank you," Justin told her. It was only two words, but the way he smiled completely bedazzled Candace. She tripped as she returned to her seat.

Mae shot Candace a look of contempt and turned back to Tessa with concern, making Tessa feel even more backward than when she'd first boarded. She'd been an idiot to think she could slip off to this glittering world that her father dreamed about and Justin embodied. Her mother had been right, and this plane ride was probably some sort of divine punishment.

"Do you want something to watch or read?" Mae asked her.

Tessa shook her head. "I've got a reader."

"You do?" Even Justin seemed surprised at that.

Tessa leaned over to her suitcase, welcoming the small distraction. She pulled out the beloved reader and handed it to Justin.

"EA tech," Justin said, examining it. Even Mae leaned in for a closer look. "Where'd you get it?"

"Someone gave it to Papa," said Tessa.

Mae sat back in her seat, no longer interested. "It's out-of-date. Very out-of-date. They fold up now without hurting the screen. Can probably hold about three times as many books."

Justin looked up from the device. "Voice commands?"

"On the newer models. About as good as the egos."

"I don't even think they bothered with voice on these." He handed it back to Tessa, his expression as dismissive as Mae's.

Tessa snatched it back, surprised at how irritated she suddenly felt. "You make it sound like it's a stone tablet."

"Not far off," said Justin. He patted her arm. "We'll get you a new one, a better one. You don't need an EA castoff."

"I like this one," she insisted. She slipped it back in the suitcase, half-afraid Justin would throw it away right then.

"Because you don't know any better," he said.

A spot of turbulence suddenly made the plane lurch. It soon righted itself, but Tessa gasped and forgot all about readers. Justin nudged her arm. "Here, take this."

When Tessa looked down, she saw he was holding out a tiny white pill to her in one hand. "What is it?"

"Something that'll make you feel better. Just let it dissolve." He shook a second pill out of the bottle. "Might as well take two. I won't be able to bring them through customs anyway."

Tessa took them without question. Mae looked disapproving, but it seemed to be more over Justin's offering them, not Tessa's accepting them. Mae tossed her long hair over one shoulder and returned to the front of the plane.

"Did you see that?" Justin grumbled. "That hair flip? Pretty sure castal girls have to learn that in school."

"You're obsessed." It was the last thing Tessa managed to say before the pills suddenly seized hold and black curtains closed across her vision. . . .

*   *   *

Someone was shaking her and saying her name. "Time to wake up. Come on, sweetie."

Tessa blinked the world into focus, which was hard since it felt like someone had scraped her eyes with sandpaper. The wheels of her mind turned sluggishly, and for a few moments, she had no idea where she was. Slowly, she recalled the god-forsaken airplane and saw that it was Justin who was waking her up.

"Is it time to refuel?" she asked. Her own voice sounded husky and far away.

"Been there, done that. You slept through it. Vancouver's right outside your window."

Tessa felt the plane tilt, and when she looked out, she could see that they were slowly circling over a body of blue-gray water. The sun was low, the sky dotted with a few stray clouds. A cluster of tall, shining buildings clung to the coast, like sentries of the water. They were pretty but not that different from some of the skyscrapers in Panama City—except for the fact that most of those Panamanian buildings had been abandoned and fallen into disrepair in the Decline.

From the way Justin stared at the city's skyline, you would've thought they were flying to some golden city in the clouds that was populated by angels and unicorns. There was an emotion she'd never seen in his eyes, an ache that was radically different from the cynical air that usually followed him around.

Her teeth rattled when the plane landed, but it didn't matter. She was on the ground again, back where she belonged. She'd never fly again if she could help it—unless, of course, she returned home. Maybe she could take a boat.

"Civilian airport," Justin observed.

Mae heard him as she waited for them near the plane's exit. "You need to go here to get your visa straightened out—and to get her authorized for chipping."

Tessa jerked her head toward Justin. "I don't want a chip."

She knew about Gemman chipping, of course. It was one of their laws. Citizens were all tagged in their hands, allowing their government to keep track of their every move. Her mother said it was the mark of the beast and a sign of their pact with hell. It had never occurred to Tessa that she would have to get one too. Seeing her panic, Justin told her to worry about it later.

"You have plenty of other things to deal with first," he said when they were disembarking down the Jetway that led inside the airport. Windows in the tunnel showed a constant flurry of planes landing and taking off. "What's the biggest number of people you've ever been around?"

"I don't know," she asked, a little taken aback. "Why do you want to—"

They emerged into the airport, and Tessa came to a halt and even tried to back up. She'd never seen a crowd like the one that faced her now, not even when her family had traveled downtown. She was adrift in a sea of bodies. Men, women, and children of all ages, all of them in motion. And everything was *bright*. Huge lights in the ceiling bathed everything in a cold, white glow that reflected off the abundance of metal in the room. There were monitors everywhere, thinner and crisper than anything she had ever seen before, with information constantly flashing and scrolling. All those people and machines created a roar of noise that beeped and buzzed so loudly, she could barely hear herself think. The room began to sway, and she couldn't breathe.

Justin tightened his hold. "Need to sit down?"

Tessa swallowed and shook her head. She could do this. She'd be okay as long as she stayed close to Justin. He wouldn't let her get lost. She clung to his hand, barely aware as Cornelia Kimora and Francis Kyle made their farewells, with promises to be in touch later. They and the uniformed soldiers soon walked off toward a line with an overhead monitor that read MILITARY/GOVERNMENT. Tessa noticed now that although the room felt chaotic, most of the people were arranged into several similar lines filtering through checkpoints. Each one had a monitor. Directly above her, Tessa saw a sign hanging from the ceiling that read REPUBLIC OF UNITED NORTH AMERICA—CUSTOMS AND IMMIGRATION.

"Well," said Mae, glancing at her ego, "you're in my hands

now. I'll get you guys settled in." She gave Tessa a sympathetic pat on the shoulder. "Hang in there. I know there's a lot of new stuff to get used to. You'll be home soon."

No, Tessa thought. Home was a very long way away.

"I think she can deal with the tech better than she can the crowd," Justin said. "I used to make a lot of jokes about pampered castal girls before I left. Never again. You should see the way the Old Money sequester their women."

Mae nodded in understanding and pointed. "We're just going right to that line, Tessa. Straight ahead. Easy."

Tessa nodded obediently, using Justin for support. They reached a line labeled CITIZENS and came to a halt to wait their turn. Despite standing in the thick of the mob, Tessa felt a little better. The line offered order, and she had Justin and Mae flanking her, creating a sort of protective barrier. She calmed down enough that she was able to study a little of her surroundings. Most of the people she saw had the same plebeian features Justin had, tanned skin and dark hair and eyes. Some of their faces showed a nondescript heritage. Others leaned slightly toward a more dominant gene pool—African, Caucasian, or Asian—but nothing *too* pronounced. Scattered among them were those who displayed a much more distinct lineage. There were fair-skinned people like Mae and others whose skin was nearly black. Almond eyes, round eyes, blue eyes, brown eyes. And yet, with more study, she could see it wasn't all so cut-and-dried. She saw tanned skin paired with red or blond hair. Some of it was obviously dyed, but others were harder to deduce. She knew recessive genes could still pop up, even after a few generations of aggressive mixing, but wasn't sure how to identify whether something was natural or not.

"How can you tell the difference between plebeians and cast—" She caught herself, remembering enough of Gemman history to know the slang terms Justin used weren't polite in front of someone like Mae. "Er, between plebeians and patricians?"

"The attitude," said Justin promptly.

Tessa looked back at the crowd, trying to figure out what he meant. All of them seemed purposeful and confident, men and women alike, no matter their physical appearance. No one openly carried weapons, which felt strange, but then, no one appeared as though they were about to start a fight either. Women who looked to be affluent moved around without chaperones, dressed in pants like Mae or short skirts, with hair worn down or up or even cut astonishingly short.

Justin didn't say anything more about plebeians and patricians, but as they moved forward, he whispered to Tessa, "Pay attention to the screen. You can learn a lot about a person."

She didn't know what he meant until they reached the customs agent. Mae immediately set her hand, palm down, on a rectangular glass box. Beside the agent, a large screen suddenly flared to life. There was a head shot of Mae staring straight ahead, with a cool and calm look in her eyes. Beside the picture, in large letters, was her name: *Koskinen, Mae Eris.* Underneath it, in smaller print, was: *Koskinen, Maj Erja (Nordic Patriarchy).* Other lines of info detailed Mae's citizenship, profession, address, age, and more. Tessa couldn't quite follow it all. There was also a section for general notes. Hers read: *Authorization to carry arms.*

The agent looked surprised at what popped up and shot her a quick, nervous look. He had a smaller screen in front of him that they couldn't see, which he began to tap notes on. After a few more seconds, the agent looked back up at Mae. "Do you have weapons to declare?"

Mae removed a gun from her purse and laid it on a nearby table. Then she took out a smaller gun that had been at her waist, hidden by the knee-length jacket she'd put on in the plane. Lastly, she pulled out a knife from her boot.

"Really?" asked Justin. "Who keeps a knife in their boot?"

"No one ever expects the knife," she said.

The table had a glass cover shielding it. The agent flipped a switch, and a light came on for a few seconds. He nodded and told Mae she could take the weapons back. He started to wave her through, but she said, "I have visas for them."

Justin rested his hand on the scanner, and once more, it filled with a flood of data. The first thing Tessa saw was that his citizenship space read: *None.* She also saw something she hadn't paid attention to on Mae's, a field marked "Genetic Resistance." The number nine was filled in beside it. Perhaps the most striking part of his screen was the notes section, which was written in flashing red letters: *No authorization to enter RUNA territories. Detain immediately and contact authorities.*

"Some homecoming," he said.

The agent looked as though he was indeed about to call authorities, and Mae quickly handed over her ego, that device that Justin had been enthralled with on the trip here. The agent ran the ego over the palm scanner, and a shimmering, holographic image of the RUNA's seal appeared briefly in the air. A few seconds later, the red-lettered warning went away, replaced by a much more subdued *Provisional Visa, Ministry of Internal Security.* The agent scanned Justin's small bag and then cleared him for entry.

When Mae showed him Tessa's documentation, the agent issued her a thin, plastic card and told her to keep it until she was chipped. It displayed the RUNA's seal shining on the surface, along with her name, citizenship, a long string of numbers, and *Provisional Visa, Student.*

"One more scan," Justin told Tessa once the agent waved them on.

"It's not easy getting in," she said, starting to feel dazed again.

"No," he agreed. "A lot easier getting out."

They crossed that last checkpoint and finally entered the airport's crowded lobby. There were no lines here. People moved in every direction, all going their own ways. A wall of glass doors shone before them, lit by the early-evening sun. Hanging over them was the RUNA's flag, half maroon and half dark purple, with a golden circle of laurel leaves in the center. Written under the circle, also in gold, was *Gemma mundi.* The jewel of the world. The motto that had eventually given name to its citizens, the Gemmans.

Tessa felt Justin come to a halt beside her. His eyes were fixed on the flag, his expression reminding her of when their plane had descended into the city. She saw that ache and longing again—and more. There was joy in his eyes. And relief. And awe. And disbelief.

Until this moment, he never actually thought he'd make it back, she thought.

Mae had stopped as well and watched as Justin gazed at the flag. For the first time today, Mae didn't regard him with exasperation. There was a softness in her expression, something fleetingly affectionate, that took Tessa totally by surprise.

"Welcome home," Mae said.

CHAPTER 8

NOT COOL

He didn't believe in Huan's hell, but as Justin stepped into the RUNA, he could almost believe in a heaven.

It was everything he remembered. Bright. Orderly. Efficient. Clean. And *advanced*. No armed thugs or dilapidated buildings. The lack in provincial technology had always been apparent in his exile, but it didn't really hit him until he was surrounded by modernity again. The chip readers. The monitors. The egos. Here was the world as it should be, the country that had survived the Decline to emerge more brilliantly than it had started. His homeland. Where he belonged.

Stop drooling, snapped Horatio. *The girl's going to pass out.*

Justin glanced over at Tessa and saw that the raven wasn't that far off from the truth. She was still pale and anxious. He squeezed her hand.

"You're okay. Stay with me here."

She was having a hard time, but Justin stood by his decision to bring Tessa here. She was capable, and she deserved this. Sergio had taken Justin in without question when he'd shown up penniless in Panama. Marta Cruz had always believed Justin was a freeloader, but he had strong convictions about paying his debts. Choosing where to go in exile had been the biggest gamble Justin had ever made, with his life as the wager. Gemman authorities had escorted him from his office straight to the nearest airport, telling him he could go "anywhere but here." He'd had only minutes to make a decision. Central and South America were the obvious options. Their populations had been diverse enough to help them weather the Decline better than other places, and they were more stable than most provinces.

And you see yourself in her, Horatio said.

Justin didn't deny it because it was true. For a moment, Tessa's face dissolved, and he saw another one in his mind, an older face that had seemed beautiful to his ten-year-old self. The noise and smells of the Anchorage market had surrounded them, and his boss had been yelling for him to return. *How did you do that?* the beautiful woman had asked. *It's easy,* Justin had replied. *You just have to look at their faces.* And with those words, his life had changed.

Studying Tessa now, he was struck by how painfully out of place she looked. With her ankle-length skirt and thick hair, she could've been a time traveler from another century. She attracted a lot of stares, so it was probably just as well that her eyes were kind of glazed over. Walking next to Mae, so perfect and polished in her tailored outfit, didn't help Tessa's appearance, though it occasionally allowed Justin to see flashes of compassion on Mae's face when she didn't think anyone was looking. Killer soldier, haughty castal, bitter one-night stand . . . Whatever she was, Mae had a soft spot for frightened provincial girls.

"Can't we take a car?" he asked her when he realized they were headed toward the airport's entrance to the subway.

Mae shook her head. "We need her chipped, and this way's faster to the Citizens' Ministry."

"I don't want a chip," Tessa repeated, abandoning one fear for another.

"It's easy," he said. "And it'll make your life a lot easier."

She looked skeptical, probably because her crackpot mother had filled her with all sorts of idiocy about chips sealing Gemmans to the devil.

Proving his point, Tessa triggered an alarm when she passed through the transit entrance. The guard waved them on once Mae stopped to show him Tessa's documentation and card, though Justin was pretty sure Mae could've achieved the same effect by flashing a gun, that ridiculous knife, or the look she'd given Justin last night upon learning he wasn't Huan Korokov.

"That'll happen every time you go through a checkpoint if you don't have a chip," Justin told Tessa. "Sensors like this are scattered around the city."

"Tracking us," she said darkly.

"It's not recorded. Most are just scanning to make sure everyone's got an authentic chip—or the paperwork to explain why they don't. The chip will send its person's name to the scanner, but that's only to match it against outstanding warrants. Most of the time, the names are dumped after that."

"Most?" Tessa asked. Smart girl, picking up on the one-word nuances he loved.

"Most," he affirmed. They came to a halt near the yellow-line train's platform. "High-security spots—like this airport—will have scanners synched to the National Registry. All the people going through are checked against that to make sure they have a matching official record."

"Still sounds like tracking to me. No one can go anywhere unnoticed." At least ruminating over conspiracy theories distracted Tessa from the tightly packed subway tunnel. "And doesn't the registry control names?"

He thought about it. " 'Control' isn't the right word. It's just a way to strengthen national unity." Per RUNA policy, all citizens had to have a name of Greek or Latin origin to be in the National Registry database. Castals could call one another whatever ethnic names they wanted on their grants, but in the eyes of their country, their names had to meet the same criteria as those of plebeians. "Besides, there are thousands of choices."

"It's still a limitation."

"Whatever you say, *Teresa*. Your dad isn't stupid. He gave all of you RUNA-friendly names in a continuing insurance plan in case you ended up back here."

Tessa looked dumbstruck at this revelation, then almost appeared offended that she'd been put into a preexisting system without her consent or knowledge. It kept her quiet as they rode the train through the city, and although she caught her breath when they emerged out onto the high light-rail platform, she didn't have a meltdown, which Justin took as a promising sign of her ability to adapt. She'd be part of this world in no time.

Once they were off the train and walking outside at ground level, Justin found he was the one dazzled and overwhelmed. The soaring buildings glittered in the setting sun, casting shadows on the earthbound pedestrians moving below. The light-rail track curved between buildings, while below it, automated traffic flowed smoothly and efficiently. Screens with ever-changing images filled shop and restaurant windows. Other, larger screens were mounted on buildings, running the latest headlines, political profiles, and ads for every good and service imaginable. It was a far cry from the dirty streets of Panama City, with its hodgepodge of shady pedestrians, gas-powered cars, cart vendors, and, at times, horses.

Their subway stop was two blocks from Hale Square. The square was a wide, grassy park flanked by three federal buildings, resplendent in marble and pillars: the Citizens' Ministry, the Ministry of Internal Security, and the Ministry of Diplomacy. A Gemman flag hung on each building, and there were no advertisements or screens of any kind. The Citizens' Ministry was the department that oversaw chips and the National Registry, and as they approached it, Justin paused to glance over at Internal Security. That was the building the servitors worked out of, where his old office had been. It seemed a lifetime ago since he'd strode into work each morning, confident in being at the top of his career. He'd had the world in his hands, never once dreaming it'd be ripped out from under him.

A few people were walking away from Internal Security, carrying signs he couldn't read. "What's going on?" he asked Mae.

"There's a lot of buzz about religious freedom lately," she explained. "Protesters hang out here every day."

"You can't be serious." There were a few core principles that had never changed since the RUNA's inception. The danger of religion and belief in the supernatural was one of them.

"Nothing's going to come of it. They're just making a lot of noise."

It was after hours, and the foyer of the Citizens' Ministry was empty, save for two regular military guards standing watch. They saluted Mae when she identified herself, but she barely spared them a glance as she strode off toward the elevator bank.

Aside from one technician who cringed around Mae, the chipping office was empty. Tessa seemed calmed by the quiet setting and made no more protests about chips. The technician led her to a chair beside a monitor and stainless steel table, and she gave Justin a brave smile as she sat down.

He sat nearby, close enough to reassure Tessa but far enough to let the technician work. Mae took a seat beside him and immediately began jotting out messages on her ego, probably requisitioning more guns and knives or whatever it was prætorians did in their free time to defend the country. Justin kept an eye on Tessa, watching as her profile slowly assembled on the screen.

"Six," he said in approval once her genetic score appeared. "Good for a provincial." Mae's attention was still on the ego, and he added, "Not as good as a nine, like some people have." He'd memorized every single detail on her screen, back in customs.

This made her look up. "So?"

He nodded toward Tessa. "So, a five or six is exactly what you'd expect from her. But from a cas—patrician? I'd say anywhere from two to four. Maybe, *maybe* a five in a rare case." He paused for effect. "Not a nine. That's a plebeian rating."

"Apparently not," Mae said.

"It's too high. I have a nine."

"Do you feel threatened by that?"

"Of course not. It's just weird, that's all. Doesn't it seem weird to you?"

"Not really," she said. "I've had it my whole life."

He tilted his head, studying the flawless skin and hair with new appreciation. "You haven't had any work done, have you? Not a trace of Cain."

"Nope." She looked back down at the ego.

When the Mephistopheles virus had swept the world and taken out half its population during the Decline, it had caused reproductive damage to many of its survivors, passing along a mutation that resulted in poor fertility, asthma, and damaged skin and hair. The mutation had a long, complex scientific name, but zealots who already believed Mephistopheles was some divine punishment called its mutation the Mark of Cain.

The name had stuck. Until a vaccine for Mephistopheles had been created, the RUNA and EA's diverse genetic breeding program had offered resistance to the virus, which tended to attack those of homogeneous backgrounds. Heterogeneous genes had also helped weed out Cain, and it almost never appeared in plebeians anymore. Castals, with their narrower breeding pool, still suffered from it, though there were plenty of cosmetic procedures to cover up the external signs. There wasn't much to be done for the asthma or infertility. Judging from the way she'd behaved in bed, Mae didn't seem to have any breathing or stamina issues.

No fertility issues either, said Horatio helpfully. *Worried? You didn't really take any precautions.*

No. Civilized women in the military get vaccines and contraceptive implants.

Justin lowered his voice. "Are we going to talk about what happened?"

Mae didn't look up, but he knew with certainty she was no longer focused on the ego. "A lot of things have happened, Dr. March."

"I'm talking about the one that happened last night, the one where you and I were in bed and I—"

"—pretended to be an EA diplomat in order to seduce me? Is that what you're referring to?"

He scowled. "It didn't take *that* much seduction. And it wasn't like I did it as part of some greater scheme. It just kind of . . . happened by accident."

Now, at least, he warranted more attention than the ego. "How can you have on a fake diplomatic uniform and give a fake name by accident?"

"Neither of them was faked," he argued. "Huan's a real guy."

"I'm not sure that makes it any better." Those sea-colored eyes narrowed in thought. "In fact, I'm pretty sure that makes it worse."

"Hey, you made the mistake of assuming I was something I wasn't, and I ended up just kind of going with it. Besides . . ." He still had a trump card here. "I brought a military aide back to my place, not a prætorian."

She at least had the grace to look embarrassed about that. "*Would* you have brought back a prætorian?" Shaking her head, she pushed forward without waiting for an answer. "Yes, of course. Of course you would have."

"What's that supposed to mean?"

"It means I know all about you. I heard plenty of it from Cornelia on the trip down."

Fucking wonderful. Cornelia Kimora was being used as his character reference.

Mae's lovely face was full of scorn as she continued. "I know all about how well you can play people and how fast you go through women—"

"It wasn't that fast—"

"—and if your goal was to bag a patrician soldier through lying and manipulation, well, then, congratulations. I'll obey my orders to protect you. No one'll lay a hand on you. But what happened in Panama is done and gone. It's never happening again. Not. Ever."

Justin was rendered speechless for a few reasons. One was that he was usually the person doing the breaking up. The other was that this conversation wasn't going as expected. He'd wanted to make sure things were cut off, in order to reduce future temptation—but not this way. He wasn't used to rejection. Hearing her so adamantly refusing *him* was a blow to his pride and made him want to bring her back to him.

I can't, he reminded himself. *If she is the one, I can't risk finding out just how binding the bargain is. I'm not going to be able to dodge it again.* It was time to deliver the killing blow. If she was pissed off at him, so much the better. He put on what he hoped was a rakish expression.

"Of course it won't happen again," he said loftily. "I don't go out on second dates—although 'date' is kind of a generous term for last night. I didn't have to buy you dinner. Or even ask."

She didn't blink. "I don't go out on *first* dates with plebeians. You're so curious about Nordic nines? They don't give a second thought to fast backwoods flings."

"It wasn't that fast," he repeated. "Unless you count how fast your clothes came off." Her condescending tone and haughty expression were textbook castal debutante, triggering unexpected anger in him. She acted as though she'd been wronged by his deception, but he, of all people, was the one who'd been tricked. The charm, the grace, the wit . . . even that poignant sadness he thought he'd seen. It had been an act, a game for this bitchy ice princess to play with a plebeian.

"And," Mae added, voice prim, "if you try to brag about this, no one's going to believe you. No one will believe someone like me would sleep with someone like you."

That was the gut punch. It was also the last word, because he couldn't muster another response. If he'd wanted to make sure they never even held hands again, then he'd accomplished that mission brilliantly.

The technician finished Tessa's profile and synched it to both a chip and the National Registry. Justin dragged his gaze from Mae and tried to make his spinning brain focus on the screen. It was about what he'd expected, containing Tessa's citizenship, basic info, and visa details. After that, there was nothing left to do but insert the chip into the space between the thumb and forefinger of her left hand. Tessa winced as though it hurt, but he had a feeling it was more psychological than anything else. She flexed her fingers afterward and seemed surprised they still worked.

"Welcome to the civilized world," Justin told her cheerfully. He gave no indication that he was bothered or even cared about his stinging conversation with Mae. After all, he had a nation of civilized—and far more reasonable—women at his fingertips now.

Mae was no longer hostile and had switched into what he was beginning to believe was her normal mode, formal and emotionless. "Well, then. It's time for all of us to get home."

She thanked the tech for working late and then headed for the door, assuming Justin and Tessa would follow. He did without question, suddenly feeling tired. The initial high of his return had faded, and the lack of sleep yesterday combined with today's travel was starting to take its toll. Tessa was practically asleep on her feet, though that could have been lingering effects of the sedative he'd given her earlier as much as fatigue from the journey.

Mae led them back out to the subway, and the three rode in silence. Tessa leaned her head against Justin's shoulder and slept while he looked out the window and tried not to openly study Mae. She was engrossed in reading something on her ego. He could tell it wasn't faked this time because she was absent-mindedly winding a strand of that marvelous pale gold hair around one finger. People who faked ignoring you didn't display subconscious habits like that.

Well, said Horatio with a heavy sigh. *You really messed that up.*

Justin ignored the bird and forced himself to start thinking of the assignment that had bought him this ticket home: patrician murders and Cornelia's shadow assassin. His mind was already spinning with ideas on how to solve the case. He knew what pertinent data to request and what questions to ask when he made on-site visits. Getting the footage to Leo was key. Proving the video had been altered would remove a good part of the mystery surrounding this.

If it is fake, they might not need your "unique perspective" anymore, Horatio warned him. At least he wasn't harping on Mae anymore.

Yes, I know. But for now, I'm more concerned about the four-week deadline.

The train slowed at a station, and that was when Justin truly looked outside at their surroundings. They were in the suburbs. "Why are we here?"

Mae gave a vague answer as she led them off the train and hired a car at the station. The distance they ended up driving was actually pretty short and probably could've been walked, but Mae thought a car would be easier on Tessa. In reality, it just ended up freaking out the girl when she saw there was no driver. It dropped them off at an elegant house in what was clearly an affluent neighborhood. Scattered streetlights lit the darkness in a way that felt safe but wasn't obtrusive to those trying to sleep. Well-established trees canopied the street, and Tessa looked much more at ease here as she took in the quiet homes and wide green lawns. It was only when they were walking up to the door that Justin finally gave up on the night's mysteries and focused on what they were doing.

"Why are we here?" he asked again as Mae knocked on the door.

It opened almost immediately. Justin had only half a second to register his sister's face before she backhanded him and sent him staggering back a couple of steps.

"You have a lot of nerve!" she yelled, advancing menacingly forward. Justin hastily retreated, bitterly wondering what had happened to Mae not allowing anyone to lay a hand on him.

"What exactly did I do?" he asked. Looking back on their lives together, it probably could've been any number of things.

Cynthia didn't answer. The rage on her face vanished, and suddenly, she looked as though she was going to burst into tears. She flung herself into his arms. "I thought you were dead."

He patted her awkwardly on the back. "Not yet. Let's, uh, go inside."

The house's interior was as beautiful as the exterior, decorated at a level even he approved of, but he had little time to admire it. By the time they made it to the kitchen, Cynthia's rage had returned. Justin had grown up disguising his emotions and manipulating others'. Cynthia played no such games. Her feelings were always out in the open. "What the hell did you think you were doing?" she demanded. "Having them bring me here?"

Last night's negotiations came back to Justin, and all of this began to make more sense. He had to admit, they'd really come through when he'd requested nice accommodations for her. And they hadn't wasted any time. "What's wrong with it? This place is great. Don't tell me you were living anywhere like this in Anchorage. You *were* still in Anchorage, right?"

Cynthia put her hands on her hips. "A group of soldiers came and abducted me from work! No warning. No time to get ready. They just said I had to come with them. Do you know how humiliating that was?"

It echoed too closely to what Justin had experienced when he'd been exiled. He gave Mae a curious glance. "What happened?"

She leaned against the counter, perfectly at ease. "You said you wanted her here immediately."

"So they took me literally?"

"How else were they supposed to take you?"

Cynthia glanced back and forth between them, her eyes widening when she noticed Tessa. "Who are these people?"

"This is Prætorian Mae Koskinen," he said. Cynthia didn't even have time to be shocked by that before he really played his trump card. "And this is Tessa Cruz. She's from Panama."

"Panama?" Judging from Cynthia's face, Justin might as well have said Tessa was from the moon.

"That's where I've been," he explained, like he'd been on an extended vacation. "I brought Tessa back to study here."

Cynthia frowned as she took it all in, and then a look of horror crossed her face. "You guys aren't—"

"*No,*" he said in exasperation. From Tessa's innocent expression, she thankfully hadn't picked up on the insinuation. "Why does everyone keep thinking that?"

"Probably because they know how you are," Cynthia retorted.

"I've got limits," he grumbled, trying to ignore Mae's *I told you so* look. "Tessa's father is a friend of mine, and I'm helping them out. She's going to stay here with you."

Cynthia's face went still. "I see. And I don't suppose you thought to check with me first? Just like you didn't bother to check when you had me degraded in front of my coworkers?"

"What the fuck is the problem?" This reunion wasn't going at all like he'd expected. "You should be grateful. This place is like a palace."

"Grateful? *Grateful?*" Justin worried Cynthia might slap him again, and if past events were any indication, his great protector was just going to keep leaning against the counter. "Justin, I was on the verge of a post-prime grant to go back to school. My interview was today!"

He relaxed a little. "So? You don't need the grant now. I'll cover it. The universities are better here anyway."

Some of the anger faded out of Cynthia. She looked tired, and just a little sad. "You really don't get it, do you? You're the

same as ever, still heavy-handed and so goddamned sure that—"
She stopped as her eyes focused on something behind Justin.
He turned and saw a boy standing in the kitchen's doorway.

"Quentin," said Justin, surprised at how much his nephew
had grown. What was he now? Eight. "Do you remember me?"

Quentin's face said he didn't. "This is your uncle Justin,"
Cynthia explained.

Recognition lit the boy's features. "The arrogant bastard
who ran out on us."

"That's the one," she said. She looked quite proud of her
son's excellent memory.

Justin scoffed. "No question that you're part of this family,
huh?"

Really, though, Quentin's features said more than enough
about which family he belonged to. He looked just like Cynthia,
from the high cheekbones to the almond-shaped eyes. They
were hazel flecked with green, an unusual recessive variation.
His hair was all plebeian, though: the dark, almost black shade
of brown that Justin, Cynthia, and their mother all shared.

"I should go," said Mae. "It looks like you've got a few
things to sort out." She managed to keep a straight face as she
delivered that understatement.

"When will I hear from you?" he asked.

She straightened up, displaying that exquisite posture she'd
acquired in her caste or the military, or maybe some mix of
both. "Whenever SCI gets things started. It was very nice to
meet you. All of you."

Mae had taken two steps toward the door when Justin realized something. "Wait. Where am *I* staying?"

Mae's face was perfectly neutral. "Here, I suppose. This was
the only address they gave me."

"Here?" He looked around, feeling like he was seeing it for
the first time. "This is Cynthia's place. Cornelia promised me a
place of my own."

"Hey, don't look at me. I didn't set this up." Mae turned pensive as she mulled things over. "You asked for a nice place. And
you asked for a nice place for your sister. You didn't specify
that they be different."

She's right, said Horatio. *And that's an interpretation Cornelia would love exploiting.*

Justin couldn't formulate a response right away. "But I . . . No! I can't live with my sister. Do you know how not cool that is? I can't live in the suburbs. I'm supposed to have a place in the city."

Mae wasn't sympathetic at all, and despite having her poker face back, he was pretty sure she was laughing at him on the inside. "You should've been clearer. Besides, it's an easy commute on the purple line."

"You should be grateful. This place is like a palace," said Cynthia, mimicking him from earlier. Judging from her look of glee, she actually liked this turn of events far more than his actual return. After a week of living together, she'd probably have a very different opinion.

"Talk to someone in Internal Security when you're back up and running," Mae told him. "I'm sure you can be persistent enough to get this fixed."

Justin nodded in acceptance, knowing there was nothing she could do anyway. He could lay other grievances at her feet, but not this one. Maybe it was just as well that this hiccup had occurred. He could choose his own place instead of having some administrative assistant do it. Without further complaint, he gave Mae a reluctant thank-you and let her leave. He watched her walk away and then quickly turned when he realized he was admiring her legs.

"I kind of like her," said Cynthia after they heard the front door close.

"She's castal," he said, knowing Cynthia wouldn't like that. He glanced over and saw Tessa practically swaying. "Oh, sweetie." He put an arm around her. "She's got to get to bed, Cyn." An alarming thought occurred to him. "Is this place furnished?" The living room they'd passed seemed to be, but after the other zany events surrounding his accommodations, he couldn't presume anything.

"To the smallest detail," Cynthia said. Her expression turned kind as she regarded Tessa. She could be brash and uncouth at times, but Cynthia had been a mother for eight years, and that nature permeated a lot of her actions. She picked up Tessa's suitcase. "Come on, I've got the perfect room for you." To Justin, she said sharply, "Don't go anywhere." Like he had a choice.

"I'll check on you once you're settled," he told Tessa.

The two women disappeared, leaving Justin awkwardly alone with Quentin. "There's wine in that cupboard by the pantry," Quentin said.

"What makes you think I want it?" Justin asked. In truth, it sounded like a great idea, and he headed right to the door.

"Because when Mom was opening all the cupboards, she saw it and said, 'Well, I guess we're prepared if any of the family drunks stop by.'"

Justin pulled out a bottle at random. It was a Syrah. "Your mom's a classy lady."

"Why do I have a feeling 'classy' wasn't the first word that came to mind?" Cynthia said as she returned to the kitchen and promptly found him a glass and corkscrew.

"Because everyone in our family is brilliant and astute." Justin filled the glass up as far as he could. "That was fast."

A smile twisted Cynthia's lips. "Poor kid just went straight to the bed and fell asleep." She nodded to Quentin. "Go to your room. I need to talk to your uncle." He looked reluctant to miss the unfolding family drama, but a sharper command sent him scurrying.

Justin held up the wine bottle. "Want some?"

"Wouldn't want to deprive you." She rested her elbows on the kitchen's island and leaned forward. "I'm glad you're back, you know. I almost missed you. But I'm still mad at you."

"I know," he said. "I missed you too." Until that moment, he hadn't realized how true those words were. Cynthia infuriated him sometimes, but she always kept him honest. She'd been his first, best friend, and being away from her for so long had left a hole inside him. He set the wine down and wrapped his arms around her, finally allowing himself a moment of vulnerability. Too much had happened between them for him to put up his usual façade. "And I'm sorry. I know what a bad position you were left in."

She rested her head against his chest. "I should be used to that by now. But, Justin . . . why did you go? Why on earth were you in Panama? Do you know how weird it is for you to show up after four years with a prætorian and a provincial girl?"

"Yeah," he said, finally releasing her. "Believe me, I'm fully aware of how weird it is."

"You didn't answer my question about why you left."

"Because I can't tell you, Cyn." He could guess her next question. "I'm serious—it's a security thing. And I can't tell you why I'm back. But I'm going to get things in order right away. Your name's going to go on everything I've got, all my accounts. You won't be screwed over again."

Her eyebrows knit together. "Are you leaving again?"

Justin wished he knew. Francis certainly seemed to think the RUNA couldn't get on without Justin, but Magnus had been right about Justin's value possibly decreasing if he found the video's modification. And of course, if he didn't find anything in four weeks, it would all be for nothing. Nonetheless, Justin mustered a smile for his sister and topped off his glass. "Of course not."

Inside his head, he heard Horatio tsk. *Don't make promises you can't keep.*

CHAPTER 9

THE DEADLY WARRIORS
THAT KEEP US SAFE

Prætorians didn't sleep, but Mae felt mentally exhausted as she rode the train back into the city. Her brief visit to the March household had been both comical and heartbreaking, and she couldn't even imagine what else would unfold there tonight.

Their family drama was squashed by the much larger issue weighing on Mae: Justin himself. Her stomach still sank each time she thought of that terrible moment when she'd walked into Cornelia's hotel suite and realized her breathtaking, exotic lover was a guy who got inside other people's heads for a living and made an art of seducing women. It had taken every bit of self-control she possessed to stay calm and pay attention to the briefing.

She'd almost hoped he might convince her that last night had meant something, but all he'd done at the ministry was reaffirm everything Cornelia had said about his arrogance and callous treatment of women. Mae wanted to think she'd transcended her Nordic upbringing, but she knew she hadn't entirely shaken that sense of superiority her family had instilled. She'd been adored and led to believe she was special. She knew now that it wasn't true, that it was just patrician arrogance. But enough men still fawned over her that she'd grown used to it and was therefore blindsided at being used by one of them. Too many people had tried to use her for various reasons in her life, and she thought she'd learned to spot them. Apparently not.

He was so convincing, she thought wistfully. Underneath all his charms, she'd been so sure she'd seen pain in him and even a legitimate sense of understanding for her own melancholy. But was it legitimate? Or was it an act? Mae no longer knew. All she knew was that her pride had been hurt and that it had felt good putting on the façade of a haughty Nordic debutante to hurt him back. And yet, even in the middle of arguing with him, her body had been so, so aware of his. Anger could flip to passion in a heartbeat.

It was a weakness. The best course now was to write him and that night off. She had an assignment—an unorthodox, bizarre assignment far from the field of battle—that they both needed to focus on now.

There was certainly more to the murders than the sensational news coverage had led her to believe. And she couldn't ignore the feeling that there was more to it still. There'd been something big and unspoken hovering between Justin, Cornelia, and Francis. But what else could there be? Strange or not, the facts of the mission itself had been cut-and-dried. The potentially ritualistic nature of the murders required intervention from the servitors' office, which would be able to examine things with a more global and religious-focused lens. And if there was a zealous murderer running around, increased security was absolutely necessary, thus explaining her presence.

They certainly seemed to have a high opinion of Justin's skills—well, Francis Kyle did, at least. The guy had looked like he'd wanted Justin's autograph. She *almost* couldn't blame him. Justin's reaction to the video and his analysis of the murder stats had been fascinating. There'd been no womanizing addict there. He'd been so intent, so completely consumed by just this brief introduction to the case, that she'd found it easy to believe he was the star servitor Francis and even reluctant Cornelia had claimed.

Mae's ruminations were interrupted when she reached her stop in the theater district. Here, the night was brilliant and alive, a far cry from sedated suburbia. Streetlamps and bright screens painted everything with flickering, colored light outside, chasing away the evening's darkness. Even on a weeknight, this area stayed busy with theatergoers and those seeking nightlife in the many restaurants and clubs. Mae navigated through the crowds and crossed the street on a sky bridge a few blocks away, which led her to a bar whose window screen proclaimed that lavender martinis were on special tonight.

She had tried to act like she was conducting important business on her ego earlier, but really, she'd been arranging a bar meet-up. Her eyes easily adjusted as she entered the dark establishment, which had no overhead lights. All the illumination came from purple neon underneath the tables and bar's edge. It cast a ghostly glow on the trendy customers as they sat at high glass-topped tables, chatting among themselves while also scoping out newcomers. It was one of those see-and-be-seen places. Watching the bartenders scurry and make drinks reminded her of Panama and the antiquated drink machine. They'd been popular in the RUNA once, but "real people" were in vogue now.

Val and Dag were already there, having taken over a table by the front window. They were in casual mode, jeans and T-shirts, which earned them a couple of disapproving looks from the more elegantly dressed patrons. At least they hadn't worn their uniforms—which they did on occasion, simply to create a scene and disconcert those around them. The last time they'd done it, their waitress had been so intimidated that she'd dropped a tray of drinks—twice. Mae had felt obligated to leave a generous tip by way of apology.

Dag whistled when he saw her. "Look at you," he said. "Going to the country club?"

"They wear dresses to country clubs," chastised Val, as though she were some kind of expert. "Our girl looks more like she's been giving boardroom presentations."

"You're both wrong." Mae sat down and immediately brought up the table's touch-screen menu and ordered a mojito without even checking out anything else.

"Well?" asked Val. Both she and Dag were watching Mae expectantly. They hadn't seen her since the funeral. "Where *have* you been? Not in detainment, obviously. We thought maybe they'd lent you out to the police. Or had you giving tours of the military museum."

"Well, that may be yet to come," Mae said. "But this week I've been in the provinces."

Her friends looked impressed. "You were in action already?" asked Dag.

Mae decided beating up those backwoods thugs didn't really count as action. "I was, uh, running an errand in Panama."

A waiter came by with her mojito, as well as another round for Val and Dag. They were only social drinking tonight, or else they would've had at least ten drinks in front of them. If you could take down several drinks within a couple of minutes, you could briefly keep ahead of the implant's quick ability to metabolize alcohol. It achieved a very, very short-lived buzz that was usually over in ten minutes. Prætorians called it "slamming the implant."

Justin and Tessa's presence in the RUNA wasn't something that could be kept secret, so Mae gave them a quick—and extremely edited—rundown of her Panamanian adventures and glossed over the murders, simply saying she was working as Justin's bodyguard. Judging from her friends' faces, Mae wasn't the only one who found those events bizarre.

"What the fuck did he do that was bad enough to get exiled?" asked Dag.

Val traced the rim of her glass, dark eyes lost in thought. "And yet apparently wasn't bad enough to keep him from coming back."

"They don't tell me stuff like that," Mae said, trying to act like it didn't bother her. "I'm just the messenger."

Dag brightened. "Still, a lot more exciting than monument duty. Not as honorable, of course."

That caught Mae by surprise. "Monument duty? What are you watching?"

"The National Gardens," Val said. She knocked back half her drink. Maybe she wasn't slamming the implant, but she wasn't really holding back either. Mae was tempted herself, after drinking that Panamanian swill.

"Both of you are in the gardens?" she asked. Her friends nodded together.

"There are a bunch of Scarlets there right now." Val ticked them off on her fingers. "Whitetree, Mason, Chow, Makarova . . ."

"Lucky," muttered Mae, not voicing what the others were thinking.

If they'd assigned a Scarlet team to the capital, she might have been in it—if not for recent events, of course. The most celebrated prætorian posts were in places with active fighting, like the provinces and borderlands. Those were around-the-clock missions and also the ones prætorians died in. Prætorians were also rotated through the capital, however, to guard senators and important national monuments and buildings. It was relatively sedate work for soldiers like them, but there was power in it. The prætorians were a symbol of the RUNA's strength and perfection. Putting prætorians on display in Vancouver reassured citizens of their country's superiority, even if it also sometimes frightened them. Maybe that wasn't a bad thing, though. Capital duty had shifts like ordinary jobs, meaning prætorians received a lot of time off. Having a significant amount of one's cohort on hand was an unusual perk since they were normally split and scattered around the world.

Val and Dag were fully aware that they'd landed a very sweet assignment, but Dag diplomatically tried to make Mae feel better. "I'm sure you'll see cool stuff with a servitor. Maybe you'll get to take down some crazy cult. I saw this one on the news that was sacrificing animals and having naked moonlight dances." He turned wistful. "I wouldn't mind a little of that. The naked part, that is. Not the animal part. I heard they tried to stone the servitor."

Mae gave him a smile for his effort. "Cults usually get taken down with paperwork instead of brute force. They only show the sensational ones on TV."

"Well, just remember, it could've been a lot worse for you." Val's voice was light, but there was a warning note in it. Nobody was mentioning the funeral, but they were all thinking about it. "And hey, how crazy is it that you'll be with a mysterious exile and a provincial girl? That's drama right there. You can't make that stuff up."

"No," agreed Mae, thinking back on what she'd seen. "You really can't."

"Is he cute?" asked Val, with a look Mae knew all too well.

"Don't get any ideas." Mae wasn't going to breathe a word about what had happened with Justin. There'd be no living with Val or Dag then. "I don't need you showing up at his door."

Val's eyes lit up. "Ah, he *is* cute."

Dag shook his head. "Ignore her. She hasn't been laid in, like, a week. It's a wonder she's still alive."

He was joking, although prætorians did tend to have particularly active sex lives. It was another side effect of the natural physical responses that the implant kicked into overdrive. Justin had been Mae's first sex in almost six months, an astonishingly long span for prætorians, but after Porfirio, she hadn't really felt up to it right away.

Val elbowed Dag for the joke, but at least Mae had the answer to a question she'd wondered about. Val and Dag were constantly on-and-off-again, making it hard to keep track of their current status. Apparently they were off right now. That always made Mae a little sad, but at least the two stayed friendly.

She glanced at the time and finished her drink. As much as she loved her friends, she suddenly longed for some downtime. "I've got to go, guys. I'll give you a drama report the next time I see you—unless you see us on TV first."

"Where're you off to?" asked Val. "Hot date? Wouldn't hurt you to get laid either, you know." If only Val knew the truth. "You're cycling back to that castal stiffness of yours."

"That never goes away," Dag said. "But you do need to relax, Finn."

Dag had started calling her that back when they'd first been assigned to their cohort and begun prætorian training. He'd never been able to remember her last name, but he could remember that she was Nordic, hence the nickname he and eventually Val had both started using. Everyone could tell she was castal, which had made for some rough adjustments in the military. Val and Dag had bonded with her immediately and unquestioningly, maybe because they needed her as the straight man for all their jokes.

"I can't relax," said Mae, standing up and swiping her ego to pay for the drink. "I'm not the one on vacation. I mean, monument duty."

"Ha-ha," said Val. She rolled her eyes but was obviously relieved at the turn of events, and Mae felt a small pang of guilt for not getting in touch with them sooner. They'd had no idea what had happened to her after the funeral and had probably assumed the worst. They were closer to her than her biological family.

"Hey . . ." Mae hesitated and rested her hands on the back of her chair. "Do you guys know how Kavi's doing?"

"Still hospitalized," said Dag, sobering. "Well, that's what the rumors say. The Indigos aren't really talking to us."

That queasy feeling Mae got whenever she thought about Kavi returned. "I guess that's normal. It hasn't been that long."

Prætorians were hard to hurt, but for most injuries, they healed like ordinary people. There were always whispers of stem cell treatments or other biological breakthroughs to facilitate prætorian recovery, but the RUNA's policies against biological and genetic manipulation were still too harsh, even for its prize soldiers. Medical research was one thing, but no one wanted to risk abuse that could lead to another virus-caused Decline.

Val stood up and hugged her. "It's not your fault."

"I broke her leg," Mae pointed out. "If it's not my fault, whose is it?"

"She was asking for it," said Dag loyally. He rose too and gave Mae a crushing hug of his own.

"She was just upset about Porfirio." Saying his name brought about that familiar pain in Mae's chest. "We all were."

"Holy shit," said Val. "Did you hear that, Dag? I think she acknowledged having some human emotions."

Mae wished she had the courage to ask them the burning question that still lingered in her mind: *Why was Kavi so slow?* But she knew they'd have no answers. They'd reiterate what Gan had said about her simply being better than Kavi, except they'd use more profanity.

"Let's head out too," Val told Dag. She finished her drink in a gulp. "That Amber party should be starting."

That was one thing you could count on with prætorians in the city: There was always a party going on somewhere. Val and Dag invited her to join them, but Mae declined. Her ambiguous status had left her glum. She wasn't active in combat, nor was she really part of the ceremonial prætorians. It felt weird to go out with them, and she didn't want to be reminded that she'd missed a chance to be assigned with other Scarlets.

Val and Dag's party was on the way to the subway station, and the three of them set off into the crowded streets. In the short time since Mae had been out earlier, the partiers and pleasure seekers had nearly doubled. Some were only starting their adventures, while others had just left the theaters and restaurants and were calling it a night. The three eventually parted ways, and Mae had the good fortune of having her train pull up right when she reached the platform.

When she reached the stop a few blocks from her home, she emerged and found a much quieter scene than the theater district. Although it was still very urban, there were no flashing screens in this residential neighborhood. Live oaks had been strategically planted to complement the neat brick town houses lining the street, interspersed with ornate streetlamps that cast dim light and created new shadows. When she was nearly to her door, she sensed a presence near a tree and spun around, gun in hand.

"Damn, you really are fast." A man stepped out of the shadows, holding his hands up in a placating gesture. "Easy."

Mae didn't lower the gun as she took him in. He was no one she'd seen before. Blond-haired and blue-eyed, he appeared close to her age and to also belong to some northwestern-European caste. He might very well have been Nordic, but it was difficult to make out too many regional specifics in the dim lighting. Despite his ostensibly nonthreatening attitude, there was something about him that set her on edge.

"Who are you?" she demanded.

He stuffed his hands in his pockets and smiled, perfectly at ease. "You can call me Emil, prætorian."

Mae didn't blink or ask how he knew who she was. "And? What do you want?"

"You," he said bluntly. "You had to have known we'd send someone eventually."

"Oh, yeah? Are you some kind of bounty hunter sent by my mother to drag me home?"

"Somehow, I don't think that would be too easy a task." He chuckled. "But it's funny you mention your family, because I do have something that might be of interest to you—something that's a sign of our goodwill and desire to welcome you."

Adrenaline flooded her. She kept her face perfectly still, refusing to let on that she was completely clueless about the context of this visit, seeing as he seemed to think she should know it. Revealing her ignorance would be a weakness.

Emil reached toward his pocket, and Mae's finger tensed on the trigger. "See if this looks familiar." He produced an ego and casually scrolled through until he found a picture. Holding it up, he showed it to Mae.

Again, she made sure her expression gave away nothing, though this time, keeping that control was much harder. "I've never seen her before."

The girl in the picture was about eight years old, wearing a bizarre, homespun dress made of a drab brown fabric. A white kerchief covered her head, but wisps of sunny blond hair escaped it. She stood outside in a grassy area that had no other identifying features. *She looks exactly like Claudia,* Mae thought. *Well, a prettier version, which would make sense.*

"Would you like to?" he asked, slipping the ego back into his pocket. "We have the resources to help you."

And that was when Mae knew. Her breath caught. The Brödern, at long last. She'd tried getting information from them for years, but the Swedish mafia wasn't all that eager to help someone in the military. She never thought they'd finally come through. "Tell me where she is."

Emil shook his head, still wearing that condescending expression. "I can't give it away so easily."

Of course he couldn't, but Mae was prepared for that. She'd had to be, with the kind of sordid contacts she'd made in this quest. "How much will it cost? I have Eastern currency."

"Money, bah. We have plenty. What we don't have is the influence and access of an enterprising young woman in one of the military's most elite units."

The insinuation was ludicrous. "I'm not going to use my position to help your group with whatever plots you've got going."

"You should've joined us a long time ago," he said ominously. "It's your birthright."

She wasn't surprised by that attitude. Organizations like the Brödern tended to have separatist inclinations even more extreme than those of regular patricians. Pointing out that she had more Finnish than Swedish blood, by Nordic ranking, probably wouldn't make a difference.

"Sorry. I'm not interested in joining up."

He tapped the pocket that his ego had disappeared into. "But you're interested in this."

"It could be a fake. It could be anyone."

"Perhaps," Emil conceded. He reached for his pocket again and this time pulled out a tiny, sealed plastic bag. He handed it to Mae and after several moments of hesitation, she took it with her left hand. A lock of golden hair was inside. "But this could only belong to one person."

"You're lying."

He shrugged. "Get it tested and see. Maybe then you'll show a little more respect for doing your duty."

She had to force herself not to study the hair. "You still haven't really explained what it is specifically you want in return."

"It'll depend on how we need to use you."

"You think I'm going to trade some open favor?"

From his face, that was exactly what he thought. "It's a small thing compared to all we've done for you and all we can do." He nodded toward the hair. "Get it tested. Then we'll talk."

He began to walk away, and she toyed with the idea of shooting or at least tackling him. But he hadn't technically done anything wrong. And so, Mae stayed where she was, watching until the darkness completely swallowed him. Only then did she put the gun away and slowly walk toward her town house, clutching the bag he'd given her.

CHAPTER 10

MASTER AND APPRENTICE

Justin's first week flew by like some kind of dream. Part of it was spent getting up to speed with SCI and his upcoming case-load. He essentially had to be rehired, so there were countless authorization hoops to jump through and reams of the paper-work so ubiquitous in government. The delay gave him a lot of free time, allowing him to immerse himself back in the world he'd longed for these past four years.

He spent long days in the city, rebuilding his wardrobe—no more flammable knockoffs—and exploring old haunts. There was no difficulty in resuming his old vices. Sure, the stuff you could score around here wasn't as lethal as Panama's never-ending supply of drugs, but debauchery was one thing you could always count on, no matter the region, and it was easy enough finding dealers and shady doctors to give him the stim-ulants he used during the day and the more euphoric things he used to unwind.

One thing he hadn't expected was a technological learning curve. People often said that if not for the Decline, mankind would've been off into the stars by now. Progress had stalled and even regressed in the chaos of the Decline, especially in other parts of the world. In the last decade or so, the RUNA—stabilized by its triumph over Mephistopheles—had rapidly made up for lost time. His time away had proved no exception. Justin saw progress in more than just the egos, and at times, it was a little embarrassing to have to learn something that was second nature to Quentin.

Of course, Justin had nowhere near the adjustment that Tessa had. She made admirable strides that first week, and though she was hesitant to travel into the city as much as he did, she became obsessed with the media stream and would spend hours in front of the screen, watching anything she could get her hands on. TV, news, instructional videos . . . she took it all in, trying to become an expert in Gemman culture from the safety of their living room.

But he wasn't convinced that was good enough. He hadn't brought Tessa back to the RUNA so that she could hide away at home. She could've stayed in Panama for that. And so, the night before SCI finally told him it was time to get to work, Justin sacrificed a debauched send-off for himself to take his family out to dinner in the city. It was good for his relationship with Cynthia too. Despite living together, each had been preoccupied with adjusting to his or her new life and they hadn't had nearly as much contact as they should've after a four-year separation.

Tessa gazed with wide eyes around the restaurant Justin had chosen. It served some of the best Thai food in Vancouver but had exploited its popularity by pretty much covering every square inch of wall space with advertising screens. Even Justin, who'd grown up with constant media exposure, had to admit the constantly changing images were a little distracting. But after being denied any real Asian cuisine in Panama, he found he could tolerate the media blasting.

"There's so much . . . stuff," Tessa said. "That's the fifth ad I've seen for ego cases. Do you really need different ones to coordinate with your clothing?"

"Yes," said Justin.

"Sometimes," said Cynthia.

Justin didn't pay much attention to Tessa's dubious look because he decided the particular case she'd just pointed out would work perfectly with a suit he'd picked up yesterday. He held up his own ego, snapped a shot of the ad, and had an order placed in seconds.

Cynthia frowned in disapproval. "That's so overpriced. You could get a cheaper one just like that at that store down on Market Street."

"This one's a Bloomfield," he argued.

She still didn't approve. "Label whore."

He smiled at her. Life was still too good for him to be upset about much of anything. He had his life; he had his family; he had his job. The only thing that could've made his situation better was having citizenship in the National Registry.

And the guarantee that you're not going to get sent away, said Horatio.

And Mae not hating you, added Magnus.

Why are you guys such buzzkills? Justin asked them.

But both were valid points, especially the former. As much as he'd enjoyed his mini-vacation, SCI's bureaucratic delay had eaten up days he really couldn't afford to waste. At least they'd reinstated his database access, so the time hadn't been completely wasted. He'd been able to check current servitor records against what he remembered of cults that might have silver and moon connections, creating a list of groups worth visiting. He still wasn't sure whether cracking the case would ensure or harm his ability to stay, but there was no use worrying about it tonight.

A server delivered several dishes to their table, all of which earned wary looks from Tessa—at least until the rice showed up. Her expression brightened at that and then almost comically plummeted again when she saw the chopsticks. Justin requested a fork for her but warned her that she needed to try everything.

"So this is what parenting's like," he murmured to Cynthia. Quentin had eagerly jumped in to teach Tessa how to use the chopsticks, just as he'd also volunteered to be her media guide. With his simpler explanations, Quentin actually did a pretty good job and seemed to have a crush on her to boot.

Cynthia shook her head. "You don't know anything about parenting. Thankfully. It's a lot harder than you think. Speaking of which . . . I don't suppose you've told Mom you're back?"

Justin nodded his thanks as a glass of bourbon arrived. Not the greatest complement to curry, but he felt he deserved something before returning to the grind tomorrow. "I don't even think she realized I was gone. Besides, if she finds out about our living situation, she'll want in on it too. Do you want to risk that?"

Cynthia answered with a grimace. No matter how different the siblings had become, there were certain things they were still of one mind on.

"Oh," Tessa breathed with pleasure, looking up from her pad Thai.

Justin followed her gaze to a commercial showing a model in a fuchsia party dress. "Look at that," he said. "You're a real girl after all. You want it?"

She shook her head. "I don't know how it would look." Her Gemman wardrobe thus far had been ordered straight off the stream, consisting of everyday items in sensible colors. To everyone's surprise, she'd taken to jeans right away, something Justin had been worried about after her lifetime of ankle-length skirts. He squinted at the address at the ad's bottom.

"That's right around the corner," he said. "We can stop by after dinner."

"No way," said Cynthia. "I don't want to go into that store. All those girls are half my age. It makes me feel like I'm clutching desperately at my youth."

"Whatever you say, old lady. I'll go with Tessa."

"Yeah, because that's not creepy at all."

In the end, they decided to split up. Cynthia returned home with Quentin, and Justin took Tessa shopping. His sister wasn't entirely off about the weirdness of being a thirtysomething guy in a teen girls' clothing store, but it wasn't like he was trying things on with her. He turned her over to a capable saleswoman, who was more than happy to show Tessa to the advertised dress . . . and many more.

Justin made himself comfortable on a purple bench near the dressing rooms. A screen on the wall flashed the day's news stories. *Cyn is wrong. Parenting's not that hard as long as you have an open wallet,* he told the ravens.

Horatio didn't agree. *Thank the gods you haven't yet impregnated anyone.*

I told you not to bring up any gods now that we're back. I'm in enough trouble.

Not talking about something won't make it go away, Horatio warned him.

His mental conversation was interrupted by the sight of a familiar face on the screen. His jaw nearly hit the floor. "Is that Lucian?" he asked aloud. The question was rhetorical, but a hovering saleswoman heard him.

"Lucian Darling? Of course it is."

The volume was off, but a headline on the screen read: *Consular Candidates Make Campaign Stops.* Justin had to read it twice. "He's . . . running for consul?"

The saleswoman, who'd seemed quite charmed by Justin when he came in, now looked at him like he was crazy. "How can you not know that?"

"Even I know that," said Tessa, timidly stepping out in the pink dress.

"You live in front of the screen," he said. He glanced back at the beaming senator as he shook hands with a crowd. "What the hell did he do to his hair? Are those highlights?"

"They're hot," said the saleswoman.

Justin didn't dignify that with a response and instead tried to focus on Tessa and the dress. The bold color contrasted with her nervousness, but overall, the look transformed her. She looked like a typical Gemman girl.

"It's cute," he told her fondly. Tessa blushed with pleasure.

"Where would I wear this?" she asked.

"We'll find a place," he assured her. "Maybe the Feriae—the summer holidays."

Or maybe a date, suggested Horatio slyly. *Only a matter of time before boys come calling. Time to get a taste of your own medicine.*

Shut up, Justin told him.

In the end, at Justin's urging, Tessa ended up with two dresses. As the saleswoman wrapped them up, Justin asked Tessa, "Tell me about Lucian, media expert. Why is he running for consul?"

She looked startled but proved to be a diligent reporter. "Because he wants to run the country? I don't know. But he's on the news every day. He's one of the most popular candidates. They make a lot of jokes about his name, and his big thing is that it's time to progress into the next phase. He says the Age of Decline is over and that the Age of Renewal should be too, that it's time for something bigger and greater. His campaign slogan is 'Ushering in the New Age.'"

"Catchy. I knew that outstanding memory of yours would come in handy," he told her.

Tessa smiled at him as she accepted the bag from the saleswoman. "His opponents give him a hard time about it not being specific enough. They call it 'Darling's Unknown Age' and 'Age of X.' Do you know him?"

"He was my college roommate," Justin said, still unable to believe this development. He'd always thought Lucian had gone into politics only to get wined and dined by lobbyists, a theory backed by Lucian's having been on the most brainless senate committees available. How did one go from that to consul?

"You guys have the same smile, you know," said Tessa after several moments of thought. "Did you guys practice with each other?"

Justin headed for the door. "He stole it from me."

His first task for SCI actually wasn't a visit to the murder sites or even the religious groups he'd tagged as possible culprits. He'd meant what he said to Cornelia: He had someone he was certain could crack the video. If it really was faked. The problem was, his contact was being annoyingly uncooperative. Leo Chan was the best biotech engineer Justin had ever met, one Justin had eventually used exclusively because everyone else looked like an amateur in comparison. Apparently in the last four years, though, Leo had given up his government job for the private sector and relocated to Portland. Leo had been wary when Justin called, and refused the invitation to come up to Vancouver. That meant Justin had to go to Portland, since he wasn't allowed to send that dangerous video through the stream. It had to be delivered in person.

The morning of the trip, Justin got up early to go jogging. It had sort of become a mandatory practice after resuming his Exerzol habit. Exerzol was a hundred times better than caffeine when it came to focus and alertness, though not nearly as powerful as a similar one he'd found in Panama. Unlike that sketchy drug, however, Exerzol was much less likely to give him a heart attack. It always hit him with a jolt in the mornings, providing a burst of nervous energy that had immediately been apparent to Cynthia. "Do not hang around this house high," she warned him the first time she'd noticed the rush. There'd been a look in her eyes he knew all too well, one that only a fool would cross.

And so, jogging became his way of dealing with Exerzol's exuberant entrance. An hour loop through their sedate suburb usually brought him back down to a reasonable energy level, and the exercise wasn't a bad thing anyway. Living in a world of bodyguards and constant threats in Panama had encouraged him to stay in good shape, and he didn't want to lose that now.

As he returned to the house that morning, he found Mae approaching. He didn't really think his trip to Leo required a bodyguard, but SCI had been adamant that she be his shadow whenever he conducted any official business.

"What's that look for?" he asked her.

Mae crossed her arms, face impassive. He always took inventory of her clothes, and she was casual today in a damask patterned blouse and jeans that did incredible things for her legs. It was fitting, seeing as her legs could do incredible things. "What look?"

"The one that says you can't believe I do anything physical." He opened the front door and gestured her inside.

"Oh, no," she said with icy pleasantness. "I believe you do all sorts of physical things. I just assumed they involved rolling dice and helping women out of their clothes."

"*And* I jog," he added. He ran a hand over his forehead and grimaced. The downside of these morning runs, aside from having to look at identical lawns, was the sweat. "I'm going to hit the shower, and then we can head out to the train station. Tessa's going with us."

Mae looked startled. "On an assignment?"

"No assignment today. Not exactly. It's a trip to visit an old friend." He frowned as he glanced toward the living room, where Quentin was explaining to Tessa the TV social media feature that allowed viewers to see scrolling commentary from others watching the same show or movie. Tessa was intrigued but also baffled by what she simply viewed as people's need to see themselves talk. "She should get out more, especially since she's starting school in a couple days."

The scathing expression Mae reserved for him faded as she watched Tessa. In their occasional encounters this week, he'd seen Mae's frosty exterior warm up to genuine affection whenever she interacted with Tessa. It reminded him of the woman who'd shared his wine and bed in Panama.

"How do you think she'll do?" Mae asked.

"She'll be okay," he said with more confidence than he felt. "Once she's thrown into the thick of things, she'll adjust."

Thrown to the wolves, you mean, noted Horatio.

Justin ignored the raven and headed off to shower. He returned an hour later and found that Mae had joined Tessa and Quentin as they discussed scrolling commentary on movies. "You'll have to ponder the mysteries of media exhibitionism another day," Justin told them. "It's time to go."

Tessa's face fell. "I really have to go?"

"You'll love it," he assured her. "Portland's great. Think of this as your last big hurrah before school."

That seemed to cheer her up. Even when she was reluctant to do something, she usually wouldn't refuse if he asked outright. She was impertinent by Panamanian standards but compliant by Gemman ones. He wondered how long it would take to shake that docility out of her and if he'd be proud or worried when it happened.

As it was, she was looking more and more like a Gemman girl, especially with her love of jeans. She still wore her long hair elaborately braided and wrapped behind her head. It was a little odd and old-fashioned but didn't attract the kind of attention her provincial clothing had.

The ride to Portland took about two hours by high-speed train, but Leo actually lived outside of the city, in the wine country to the west. Limited public transit ran out that way, so hiring a car was required for the rest of the trip. The ride was beautiful, with rolling green hills and sprawling estates tucked in among vineyards. Most of the chaos and degradation of the

Decline had happened in urban centers, and many people had fled to pastoral settings for safety. Some of these houses had been around since those times.

Picturesque or not, Justin had a hard time imagining trendy Leo making a home out in the country. He was—or had been—a city creature if ever there was one. He'd lived in one of the hottest districts in downtown Vancouver, sacrificing space in order to be within arm's reach of the most exclusive clubs and bars. They'd often gone out together, and Justin had spent a few nights passed out on Leo's living room floor.

It was around noon when his entourage finally reached the address. Leo's house wasn't one of the mammoth, century-old estates. It was small, cute, and well kept but could only be described as a cottage at best. The house appeared to be situated on a fair amount of property, with a vineyard stretching out beyond it. It was also the quietest place Justin had been since returning to the RUNA.

"Huh," he said as they walked toward the house.

Mae gave him a sidelong glance. "What's wrong?"

"Just not what I expected." They reached the front of the house, and he was even more surprised to see the cute wooden door rigged with a number of locks and a security panel. Leo had urban sensibilities in a rural setting. "Also didn't expect this place to be sealed up like a federal building."

"I thought there wasn't any crime in the RUNA." He could just barely pick up a hint of mockery in Tessa's voice.

"Oh, we have plenty of crime." He knocked on the door. "We just don't have ordinary people walking the streets with guns."

The door opened, and Leo appeared. Maybe the ravens were right and he hadn't wanted to see Justin, but Leo gave no sign of that as his face broke out into a grin. He gestured them forward, shaking Justin's hand as they stepped inside.

"You're the last person I expected to hear from this week," Leo said. "Or any week."

Leo looked the same as ever, with his slim build and delicate features. His dark hair was slicked back, and he was dressed as though he was about to step out of a Vancouver high-rise.

"I've been busy," Justin responded. "Leo, this is Mae, my aristocratic security, and this is Tessa. She's a friend's daughter who's staying with Cyn and me." It was an unwieldy introduction, but "ward" sounded like he was in some ancient novel. And anything else just conjured up sordid theories in people's minds.

Leo did a double take at Justin as he shook hands. "Wait. You're living with Cynthia?"

"It's a long story. I've kind of been seeing the world."

"I don't think 'seeing the world' ever came up when we were trying to figure out what happened to you," Leo mused. "We had a pool going over in the Internal Security building. The favorite theories were rehab and starting a cult of your own."

"Don't think I haven't thought about it." Justin sat down on a couch in a small living room with rustic pine floors and walls that contrasted with the media screen and sleek black and steel furniture that he remembered from Leo's old apartment. Tessa took the spot beside him, and Mae stood near the fireplace. Her stance was casual, but her eyes were as watchful as ever. "How in the world did you end up here? Can I get in on a pool for that?"

Leo grinned. "I didn't end up anywhere. I chose to come here."

"Why?"

"For the noblest of reasons." Leo nodded toward the living room's doorway. "I got married."

So much for his stunning powers of observation. Justin hadn't even noticed the gold ring on Leo's finger. The man who entered the living room, wearing a matching ring, was pretty much Leo's opposite in every way. Where Leo was tall and slender, this guy was shorter and broad shouldered, with the kind of muscles that came from hard work or expensive fitness devices. He had the common dark hair and eyes, with a close-cut haircut framing his square face, and scarring along his chin suggested he was one of the rare plebeians to have picked up Cain. He was more casually dressed than Leo and clearly much shyer.

Leo caught hold of his arm and steered him in while making introductions. "Dominic, this is the guy I told you about."

Justin jumped up to shake Dominic's hand, wondering what

exactly Leo had told him. "Well, congratulations." Justin put on his sunniest public relations face. "If I'd known, I would've brought you a gift. You look like you could use some nice linens."

Leo laughed, but Dominic said in a very flat voice, "We already have some."

"Justin won't say it, but he's appalled by our living conditions," Leo explained. "He'd never dream of living anyplace so 'primitive.'" Beside him, Justin heard Tessa clear her throat.

"Oh, I'll say it," Justin told them. Dominic situated himself on the opposite side of the room, arms crossed in a standoffish way that oddly mirrored Mae. "Getting married doesn't mean you have to pack up and move to a farm, though. If it does, then I'm even more against it than I already was."

"Dominic's trying to start his own wine business. All the vineyards outside? That's his handiwork." Leo looked up at his husband with unabashed pride and adoration.

"And what do you do?" asked Justin. "Design the labels?" It was impossible to imagine fastidious Leo digging around in the dirt.

Leo shook his head. "Nah, I commute to the city. Well, sometimes. They let me do a lot of telecommuting too. I work for Estocorp's Portland branch now."

"That's a long trip if you do have to go in." "Estocorp" sounded familiar, but it took Justin a few moments to place it. "You're working on contraceptive implants?"

"Pays better than my old job. Maybe even better than yours."

"Not likely," said Justin. "Leo, you could probably hack an identity chip. Why would you waste your time with birth control?"

Leo was still amazingly casual about all of this, but then, he'd had a lot more time to adapt to his change in fortunes. "Hey, it's noble work keeping our population stable. Besides, the Ministry of Health and Social Services is considering switching from their current provider. Do you know what kind of money we'd make with a government contract?"

"*I* can get you a government contract," protested Justin. "I've been back barely a week and already have a case for you to look at."

"Don't you have other people in your department who can look?" asked Dominic. His voice was gravelly and gruff, matching his exterior.

"None of them are as good as Leo." Justin leaned forward, needing to get through to his old friend. "I know you miss Vancouver. Give this up, and come back. You could get your old job again, no problem. You'll get a better deal and more action and adventure than you can handle. My charming companion over there's a prætorian. That's movie-quality stuff."

Justin spoke jokingly, thinking mentioning Mae would appeal to Leo's love of novelty. Instead, it seemed to startle the other two men. Leo even paled. Their alarmed reactions made Mae tense in return.

"Whoa, sorry," said Justin, glancing between Leo and Dominic. "Don't freak out. She's perfectly tame."

Not in bed, said Magnus.

"No one who's pumped full of neurotransmitters on a regular basis is tame," Dominic said, his face growing dark. "And we aren't leaving."

Mae frowned but didn't otherwise acknowledge the slight, aside from a shift in her posture. Justin looked pleadingly to Leo, hoping he'd talk sense.

Instead, Leo said, "This is where Dominic's work is. And I like what I'm doing. Like I told you when you called, it's contract or nothing—and only if it's interesting."

Justin was having trouble maintaining his characteristically amiable attitude. When he'd imagined the reasons Leo might refuse to come back, Justin had never even dreamed that an attachment to some cozy country setting would be the hang-up. If anything, he'd thought Leo might be upset about Justin's disappearing without warning.

Not everything's about you, said Horatio.

But this is absurd, Justin said. *Why would he stay? He once switched apartment buildings because a couple of families moved in and he thought the place was becoming too mainstream.*

He's in love, said Magnus. *That's all the reason he needs. Find another tactic, because if you keep mocking that, you won't get anywhere.*

"Oh, it's interesting," Tessa said unexpectedly. Justin had nearly forgotten she was there. "Justin's working on something that'll blow your mind. No one can figure it out." Justin knew she didn't actually know any of the details of the murders or the shadowy assassin video, but she'd overheard enough of Justin and Mae's offhand comments to figure out something major was going on.

This seemed to amuse Leo more than anything else he'd heard today. "I thought the prætorian was your backup."

Justin realized then that he'd been an idiot. Tessa had jumped onto what he'd missed. He was always so proud of being able to get to the heart of people. He'd tried wooing Leo with money and glamour, but people like Leo didn't become experts in their fields just because of those things. Justin had seen Leo stay up all night trying to solve the unsolvable. He had a passion for what he did, and despite Leo's idyllic claims, even Justin knew contraception was boring work.

Justin suddenly felt back in control. "She's right. No one can figure it out, and we've had every agency looking at it." A gleam of interest showed in Leo's eyes. "You don't even have to leave your love nest, unless you need some Internal Security resources. Then, hey, you guys can have a romantic getaway in the big city."

"I don't like going to the city," interjected Dominic. His eyes narrowed. "Any city."

"Fine," said Justin, trying hard not to show his exasperation. He couldn't imagine what had brought this match about. Dominic's wine probably tasted like shit. "You just come, Leo. We'll close out the Silver Spike like we did in the old days."

Leo didn't answer, but Justin could tell he'd finally gotten through. Leo still had an easy smile on his face, but his interest had been piqued. *No one can figure it out.* Leo couldn't resist that. There was nothing to do now but wait. Justin had played all his cards, and it was time to see if he'd won the jackpot.

"Okay," Leo said at last. Dominic groaned. Or maybe it was a growl. It was hard to say. "I'm in. I'll help you out. When can I see this mind-blowing case?"

Justin stood up and patted the briefcase. "Right now. I've got it all here."

Leo shot Dominic one last hesitant look and then rose as well. "Let's get some lunch first since you've come all this way. Then we'll get down to business. I can't wait for you to try Dom's Pinot Noir."

Happy that he'd gotten his way, Justin gladly put back on his sunny, sociable persona. "I'm sure I've never tasted anything like it."

Afterward, Justin had to admit the wine wasn't *that* bad, but it also wasn't good. It wouldn't win any awards unless Dominic figured out a way to export it to the provinces.

After lunch, Justin and Mae went with Leo to his workshop to go over the video away from Tessa and Dominic. Justin was relieved that Leo actually had a workshop, one filled with all sorts of half-completed projects. It meant the old Leo hadn't entirely disappeared.

He didn't look thrilled to have Mae with them, but he forgot all about her when the video ran. As soon as it ended, he had the same reaction as Justin. "It's fake."

"That's what I said. But they say they can't prove it."

"What else could it be?" asked Leo. If he'd had any doubts about taking this on, they'd vanished. He was hooked.

"That's for your brilliant mind to uncover. Mine's going to work on the rest of this mess."

He left Leo all the other information on the case, as well as a warning to protect the camera and original footage. "It's my ass if something happens to it. You're lucky I trust you, or I'd never leave it with someone unauthorized."

Leo grinned. "That's the nice thing about living in the wilderness. No one's going to come snooping around."

On the train ride back, Tessa surprised Justin by telling him how she and Dominic had apparently become best friends while everyone else was in the lab.

"He's not bad at all once you talk to him," she said. "He's a Gemman citizen but was raised in one of the provinces, so he kind of understood what I'm going through."

Dominic was partially provincial? That explained a lot. "I'm just glad he doesn't seem to ever leave that house," Justin noted.

"He'd probably hunt me down otherwise, and who knows if my gallant protection would come through."

Mae, who'd been gazing out the window, glanced back. "Why wouldn't I?"

"Because you didn't do anything when my sister tried to knock me out."

"You're still alive, aren't you?" She returned to the window.

Tessa had tried a glass of the wine, and it had made her sleepy. She opened her eyes and turned toward Justin. "Dominic wasn't unfriendly when we first got there. He was just shy. Or, well, socially awkward, I guess. He didn't get unfriendly until you told him Mae was a prætorian."

Justin thought back on the afternoon. "No, Dominic had it in for me from the moment I walked in the door. You heard what Leo said—he'd told him all about me."

Tessa shook her head. "You're wrong." Yes, Tessa was definitely getting more defiant.

Because she contradicts you? scoffed Horatio. *Such audacity!*

"Hey, I'm the master here," Justin told her. "You're the apprentice."

"The master was too appalled to be out in the 'wilderness' to notice," Tessa retorted. "I'm telling you, I'm right."

"Next time I'm leaving you home," he said, wondering whether he really was slipping.

CHAPTER 11

LICENSE TO WORSHIP

Although meeting Justin's alleged technical genius had been interesting, Mae was eager to get to the heart of this mission they'd been assigned. She craved action, and even if this wasn't a typical prætorian assignment, there was still justice to be served for the greater good of her country. She didn't entirely know what Justin's methods were, save that they would eventually be investigating suspect and possibly dangerous groups. That sounded promising.

Her disdain for Justin hadn't changed. It was obvious to her he was high each morning, and she had no respect for anyone with that kind of dependence. His dependence on women was equally obvious. Women noticed him, and he noticed women. A few witty words . . . and they were hooked, freely giving away numbers and promises of future dates. It constantly reminded Mae of her own foolishness.

And yet, despite his bad habits, he'd occasionally show those flashes of brilliance that Francis had lauded. Justin latched on to small details, able to make astonishing deductions she never could've fathomed. His dedication to their case was fierce, and when he spoke of it and explained the psychology of religious groups to her, she couldn't help but be fascinated.

The final piece puzzling her was his unfailing devotion to Tessa and his family. Sure, sarcasm ran rampant in that household, but there was no question of his protectiveness toward them. It contradicted Mae's image of his selfishness, and she didn't like contradictions.

Their first few days of investigation took them to the crime scenes on the patrician land grants, something that seemed more like police than servitor work. It mostly involved interviews with the victims' friends and families, giving Mae another opportunity to watch him manipulate people. He didn't approach anyone with a cop's interrogation style. He engaged them in conversation, winning them over and then very carefully studying their words and body language.

"It's not hard," he'd told Mae. "You find what means the most to someone and run with it."

That had come after an interview with a Lakota castal who'd initially been hostile to Justin. Upon noting the man had four children—a rarity among the fertility-challenged castes—Justin had shifted the discussion toward them, playing on the man's obvious pride. The man had been heavily marked by Cain, with asthma and skin lesions, but he'd lucked out with his deceased wife. She'd been extraordinarily beautiful and healthy, with no problems conceiving. By the time Justin was finished with him, they were practically best friends, and Justin knew all about the kids' soccer and dance lessons. The family had no connection to a religion, and Justin also determined that the man was telling the truth about not being involved with his wife's murder. Justin had similar results with other castal interviewees and their claims of innocence.

After three of the crime scenes, he told her they were putting the other two on hold until Leo could come along with them. The people they talked to weren't giving them any leads; they needed to examine the technical side for new evidence. Although Leo had made no progress on the video, Justin was certain his friend could figure out how the victims' surveillance had been disabled. Leo couldn't join them right away, meaning it was time to start checking out suspect religious groups, something Mae had been looking forward to.

They left Vancouver for an overnight trip to the Midwest, to visit a group whose goddess had connections to the moon and silver. Before they went to that church, however, Justin made a side trip to another sect in the same town.

"Favor to Cornelia," he explained when their hired car

dropped them off. "Right around the corner from our church. It's just a standard license renewal—should be a breeze. They're a pretty small and benign group. Still, you'll get to see that this job isn't all glamour and stone-wielding mobs."

They stood outside of a small but pretty building that had all sorts of flourishes. Arched stained glass windows. Gold-painted trim around the windows and doors. Lacy wooden embellishment along the gables. An ornate sign above the door read TEMPLE OF THE LADY OF THE BOOK, MADISON BLUFF, TWENTY-FIRST WARD.

Justin came to a stop on the sidewalk leading up to it and gave the building a once-over. "Well maintained," he said with a frown. "Much better than their last inspection. Good maintenance means money. Money means support."

The door opened as they approached, and a middle-aged plebeian man with thinning hair stepped outside. He looked nervous but gave them a polite smile. "Welcome. I'm Claude Diaz, the priest of Our Lady here. You must be Dr. March?"

"Yes." Justin introduced Mae and then waved his ego over the license beside the door. The square's screen displayed the RUNA's seal in green, along with a date and scrawled signature below it. When the ego passed over the screen, a holographic image of the seal appeared in the air, verifying the temple's license.

Claude urged them inside. "Please come in. I'm so eager for you to see our sacred space and answer any questions you might have."

Mae hadn't been in very many places of worship. She'd been to Church of Humanity services, of course, but those didn't count. Every once in a while, someone in the Nordic caste would try to bring back a Scandinavian religion. Those that didn't fail right away usually only lingered on with scant numbers. Mae's mother had once taken her to a temple when visiting a friend in the Pan-Celt land grant, and Mae remembered it being a terrifying experience for her six-year-old self. The chanting priests had worn hoods and masks, and images of their fearsome goddess had seemed to look at Mae from every part of the room. She didn't remember the cult's name but hoped it had been shut down by now.

Between that memory and what she'd seen of provincial religious practices, Mae was content to stay away from all of it and completely supported the RUNA's stance against religion. People who got caught up in the groupthink of these superstitions were easy to lead into dangerous behaviors, as the Decline had shown. The only thing Mae put her faith in was her country.

This temple bore no resemblance to the one in her nightmares. The space was warm and inviting, smelling of wood, beeswax, and roses. Rows of well-oiled wooden benches faced forward, and shelves of archaic paper books lined the sides of the room. At the front of the room, looking over everything, stood a statue of a woman in flowing robes who held a book in one hand and a lit candle in the other. Incense smoked at her feet.

As Mae studied the sculpture, a weird sense of disorientation swept over her. The statue shifted in her eyes. A sword replaced the candle, and she held flowers where the book had been. An amber necklace hung around the goddess's neck, and on her head, a crown made of tiny sparkling stars bathed her in brilliance. Mae had never seen anything so beautiful, and she didn't even realize it had called her forward until she stood right in front of the statue. The intensity reminded her of that darkness that descended on her in battle, only now she felt a warmth and exhilaration spread through her, making her feel light and radiant.

Justin came to stand beside her. "So what do you—"

He stopped when he saw her face. His expression transformed with wonder, and his breath caught. The world sparked between them. Somehow, he could see that glory burning through her, and he was spellbound. For a moment, she could see herself in his eyes, vibrant with beauty and life. And then, something even more remarkable happened: She could sense a power surrounding him as well. It had a different feel—ancient and wise, rather than sensual and earthy—but its nature was the same as hers. She'd never seen such a thing in any other person.

Suddenly, that icy darkness Mae knew so well slapped her in the face. The radiance burning through her faltered, and she felt the darkness's familiar hands resting heavily on her shoulders, trying to block her from the statue's power. The two forces fought against each other, the statue's warmth calling to Mae as the darkness crushed it. She felt like she was being ripped in two until at last the darkness won. The light and life vanished. Above her, the Lady of the Book stared blankly ahead, a stony scholar once more.

Victorious in its conquest, the darkness lifted, leaving Mae dizzy. She staggered a few steps and started to fall. Justin caught hold of her hand to steady her. She started to lean into him and then suddenly jerked away. "Don't touch me!" she exclaimed.

"Easy," he said. His enthralled look was gone. There was no power there. "Are you okay?"

"I'm fine." She turned in another direction, attempting to avoid eye contact. He moved in front of her.

"Forget that you hate me for a minute. I'm just trying to help."

"You're the last person whose help I need."

"You saw something," he insisted, a sharp look in his eyes.

"Yeah. A lifeless statue."

But his face told her he didn't believe her. He knew what had happened. Or at least he knew more about what had happened than she did.

"Don't you have a job to do?" she asked irritably.

Whatever retort he might have made was interrupted when Claude came to stand beside them and admire the statue. "Her flame illuminates the path to knowledge," he told them.

"It's lovely," said Mae automatically. But that was all it was: a nicely carved piece of stone. There was no life force in it, certainly not one with divine powers.

"It's new," said Justin. He gave Mae one last searching look and then turned toward Claude with his *we're pals* smile. The servitor was back. "It's not on last year's inventory. I'm not an art appraiser, but this doesn't seem to match up with your income—unless you've completely neglected all other operations." Justin glanced meaningfully around. "Which it appears you haven't."

"Oh, no," said Claude. "The temple didn't purchase it. It was a gift. One of the wealthier members of our congregation was kind enough to donate it."

"Ah, I understand. That's lucky." Justin made a note and continued his visual assessment of the facilities. When he finished, he and Claude sat down opposite each other at a desk in the temple's back office. Mae had recovered from her earlier disorientation and took up a spot that was close enough to observe Justin and Claude—and intervene, if the seemingly docile priest surprised her—but otherwise stay out of their way.

"So." Justin settled into the tilting leather desk chair he'd been given. He set his reader aside, projecting the ease and friendliness of someone who'd merely come to chat. "You want to renew your license for worship of a fictitious entity."

Claude, who had almost started to relax in the face of Justin's casualness, flushed. "She's not fictitious, Dr. March."

"I know you think that, but if you can't prove her existence to the government, we have to classify her as fictitious." Justin's tone wasn't unkind, but he spoke in a way that told Mae he'd had to explain this point many, many times. He waved a dismissive hand at his reader. "Now, I've got all the official jargon here, but I'd love to hear about your group in your own words. What you believe. How you operate."

He'd put on that friendly air again, and Claude lit up at the chance to explain his beliefs. "We worship the Goddess of Nine Faces in her scholarly guise. She gives us understanding and insight into the world, allowing us to pursue all sorts of knowledge."

"And wisdom," added Justin.

Claude gave him a gentle smile, and now it was his turn to explain one of his well-worn fields of expertise. "Knowledge is not the same as wisdom, as I'm sure you can understand. A scholar who is always learning and striving to excel in their field possesses knowledge. A ninety-year-old-man who has lived a fulfilling life possesses wisdom. Wisdom is pursued by those who worship our goddess as the Lady of Keys. Despite our different paths, we do have much in common with them, however, and we've been trying to forge connections between our groups. There's a Lady of Keys congregation a hundred kilometers from here that we've begun to be in contact with."

"Ah," said Justin, smiling and nodding along in understanding. "Now I see."

There was no way a servitor wouldn't know every established religion inside and out, especially one as widespread as the Nine-Faced Goddess. Justin most certainly understood the difference between the Lady of the Book and the Lady of Keys. He was still the perfect picture of pleasantness and amiability, but as Mae watched, she could see a cunningness in his dark eyes as Claude spoke. Justin was taking in every intonation, every gesture, and every turn of phrase. Coaxing Claude to talk about the goddess he loved simply allowed Justin to gather more data. It was his technique in action: Find out what means the most to someone and exploit it. Like, for example, the blue mood of a woman visiting Panama.

When prompted, the priest was equally happy to explain how they worshipped. "Many of our meetings simply involve being together and reading whatever we like. Afterward, we share our knowledge and try to learn more from each other through enlightened discussions. Our main weekly service usually focuses on a book the entire group is reading. I write my sermons based on lessons learned from the reading, but of course, all opinions are welcomed, and we urge respectful analysis. Worship of the Lady herself is present too. We sing songs and prayers to her, bedeck her with flowers, and give our blessings to scholars seeking her aid. We read stories and myths of her many guises, as well as those of the other gods. There's enlightenment in learning about the truth of others."

Justin had his reader in hand again and proceeded to go over operating, financial, and tax paperwork with Claude. Mae couldn't see the screen but followed along with it as best she could. It gave her a new appreciation for the many facets of a servitor's job: scholar, psychologist, detective, accountant. She found herself drawn in by the intensity in his already captivating features. It was a single-minded focus she understood.

"I don't even have to study these records to see how well you're doing," said Justin. He paused to look around and admire the room before returning to his reader. "Your congregation's at . . . one hundred and fifty?"

Claude's head bobbed up and down. He was clearly delighted at how well this was going. "Yes, yes. It's quite wonderful. We were only around seventy-five at our last licensing."

The speed at which Justin looked up was Mae's only indication that he was shocked. "You've doubled in a year?" He turned back to the reader and scanned a list. "There it is. You certainly have."

They talked about ten minutes more, and at last, Justin stood up and shook Claude's hand again. "Well, it's been very nice speaking with you."

"Likewise," said Claude. The priest was beaming. "I'm so pleased you were able to see all the wonderful things we do here."

"Me too," said Justin. "And I'm sorry I can't renew your license."

Claude froze mid-handshake. "I . . . I beg your pardon?"

Justin shook his head in sympathy but amazingly still managed to have that upbeat look on his face. "I'm not renewing your license. You'll have to suspend all operations immediately."

Claude's mouth hung open, and he said nothing for almost thirty seconds. "But . . . but we aren't dangerous! We aren't violating any of the country's religious dictates."

"You're violating our tax dictates. That statue may have been a gift, but it's an expensive one and still has to be reported as an asset and filed under your income. As income, it would be subject to taxes—which you haven't paid."

"We were never told of anything like that!"

"It's the law, Mr. Diaz, which you're responsible for knowing. Ignorance is not an excuse."

Justin began moving toward the doorway, and Claude was fast on his heels. Mae moved swiftly after them, just in case the priest surprised her.

"Then give us a chance to rectify the situation! We'll appraise the statue and pay whatever back taxes are necessary—and any penalties." Claude wrung his hands. "Please, Dr. March. Our goddess is the center of my life and the lives of many others. Please don't take this away."

"I don't have a choice," said Justin. "Our government has very strict laws for groups like yours, and I have to follow them, no matter how much I hate to see it happen." The cheery attitude was gone.

"Please," begged Claude. "*Please*. There must be something."

They emerged outside. Justin stopped by the door and took a moment to enter something on his ego. He scanned it over the licensing screen. Immediately, the square turned red, and the date and signature vanished. Justin's signature appeared instead, along with a new date one year from that day.

Justin turned to face Claude and put on a formal expression. "Mr. Diaz, the Republic of United North America is suspending your license to worship. All practices will cease immediately. You have twenty-four hours to remove any belongings from this facility, after which it will be shut down and abandoned. Your organization's financial assets will be seized and held in a federal account. You may not assemble with more than three members of your former congregation in any other place. You may communicate with them via written message, but all correspondence must be copied to the Division of Sect and Cult Investigation. In one year, you may apply for a new license. Failure to comply with any of these edicts will result in your arrest and that of any other accomplices. Do you understand?"

Claude's jaw was on the ground. "Dr. March . . . this can't be possible."

Justin handed over his reader. "Sign here, please."

Mae tensed, wondering whether Claude would comply. This, no doubt, was the point at which zealots reacted badly. But as she studied the sad man further, she knew he wasn't going to break out any stones or torches. Mostly, he looked like he was on the verge of tears. With great resignation, he signed the order.

And with that, the job was done, and Justin and Mae left for the day's real attraction. She would've expected him to be pleased with himself, but as the car ride progressed, it became obvious his mood had plummeted.

"A tax technicality," he muttered. "A goddamned tax technicality."

"It's ingenious," she admitted, hating to praise him out of principle and especially for manipulating someone. "A way to shut them down without making yourself personally responsible."

Justin didn't seem convinced. "He was a nice guy. They're harmless right now."

"Right now," she repeated. "But would they stay that way? Their numbers are growing. They have a reasonable message. You said those were the most dangerous kind."

On their plane ride here, Justin had given her a lesson on what warning signs servitors looked for. Groups who were disorganized and touted nonsensical messages were the ideal candidates for licensing. They made themselves (and religion in general) look bad. The really outlandish and dangerous ones were easy too because they were instant shutdowns. Quiet, friendly ones like Claude's were trickier because they could initially attract followers with reasonable messages, and then eventually blow up in the RUNA's face as dissent among themselves and against authority grew.

He looked over at her with a smile. "And here I thought you weren't paying attention."

"I've got to stay tuned for anything dangerous," she explained.

His smile faded. "Yes. They could be dangerous someday. It's better to stop them now."

"Then why do you sound so unsure?" His behavior made no sense.

"It's just sad, that's all." Justin stared out the window. "His beliefs mean a lot to him."

"Beliefs in a *fictitious* entity," she reminded him, drawing his attention back.

His eyes searched hers. "Do you really believe that?"

"Of course," she said, puzzled that a servitor of all people would ask her about one of their country's founding principles.

And yet, as she spoke, she remembered her vision by the statue. No, not a vision. A hallucination. She really did need to own up and see a psychiatrist. *But am I crazy if he saw it too?* "Don't you?"

"Of course," Justin said, echoing her. His face still looked troubled as he turned away. "We did them a favor."

CHAPTER 12

MIRACLES

"Welcome to the Church of Apollo and Artemis," said Justin when they reached their next stop. The church was a small white building that had been built up to make it resemble a Greek temple. Faux pillars surrounded the doorway, and a Greek inscription was painted in gold about the door. "Know anything about them?"

"No," said Mae. He obviously hadn't expected her to. Religion and myth weren't taught in schools.

"Apollo's the Greek god of light, prophecy, music, and a few other things. Artemis is his twin, goddess of the hunt, the moon, virgins—" Justin came to a stop and frowned as he studied the Greek words. "She's also not mentioned anymore. That's just welcoming us to the Church of Apollo." He took out his ego to pull up a file. "Hmm. I wonder if they dropped her. This place hasn't been inspected in almost eight months. If so, this may be a dead end since she's our moon connection. Shit. The priestess that used to operate here is a piece of work."

"You think she's responsible for the murders? Because she's linked to the moon?"

"No," he said swiftly. "Absolutely not. That's not her style."

Mae frowned. "Then why are we here?"

"Because she's got connections to, uh, resources that might help us. Maybe her old partner can help us find her." Justin looked over something else on his ego, the edges of his lips quirking into a smile.

"What is it?" Mae asked.

"There are reports of this place claiming miracles. That's always a treat." He slipped his ego back into his jacket. The two matched. "Another good reason to have someone like Leo on hand. These groups go to extremes to pull off their scams. Leo's a pro at figuring out what they're doing. Fortunately, I'm not half-bad myself."

Mae rolled her eyes. "Now, now, no need for modesty."

He grinned as the two of them headed inside. "If the same guy's still here, he's not really all that stable either. Actually has the balls to call himself Golden Arrow."

Although Justin had an appointment, no one greeted them at the door, which was unusual. When they stepped inside the church's foyer, they found a full-fledged ceremony going on within.

"Warning sign," Justin murmured to her. He'd once taught university classes and often slipped into lecture mode without even realizing it. "They're feeling cocky if they scheduled a service during a servitor inspection. Worse still that they've got this many people out on a weekday afternoon." He checked his ego. "Looks like a quarter of their regular members are here. And there's the man himself."

Through a doorway, she could see Golden Arrow standing at the front of a large room, wearing a white toga that wasn't even accurate for Roman wear, let alone the Greek culture he was hearkening back to. He wore gold-painted laurel leaves in his dark hair and held his hands upward as he stood over a large smoking bowl sitting on a tripod. Two similarly clad women knelt nearby, one on either side of him. The walls were painted with murals of a blond man in various scenes: shooting a bow, driving a chariot across the sky, etc. Mae squinted at the pictures and then focused back on Golden Arrow.

"There's a little facial resemblance," she noted.

"There certainly is. Bad enough to claim to speak for a god, let alone liken yourself to one. Ah." Justin pointed. "There's Artemis, but significantly dwarfed. They really have dropped her from the act."

The picture he indicated showed Apollo with a dark-haired woman carrying a silver bow. She wore a short gown and a crescent moon on her head. Mae studied the picture for a long time and felt chills down her back. When she dragged her gaze away, she found Justin watching her closely. "Ready to go in?"

"Of course," she said, irritated for reasons she couldn't explain.

He hesitated a few moments longer and then gave her a small nod as he walked toward the main sanctuary, where the ceremony had gone on uninterrupted. Golden Arrow continued chanting in Greek, with his hands and rapt face turned heavenward.

"What's he saying?" she whispered as they started to step through the doorway.

Justin shook his head. "Nonsense, mostly the same stuff repeated over and over. It's all about light and glory."

Golden Arrow's chanting suddenly stopped when he caught sight of Justin and Mae. All of those gathered turned around to stare as well.

"Friends, we have a special guest, Dr. March from the servitors' office. So nice to see you again after all these years. Come, come. Take a seat and join us." He had a good speaking voice, one that resonated. Mae could see how people would be compelled by it.

"Thank you," said Justin cordially. Mae had to give him points for looking perfectly at ease. He sat on a pew in the back and then beckoned her to join him. "Please, carry on," he called.

Even she could see how contrived Golden Arrow's simpering smile was. But after a melodramatic half bow, he returned to his ceremony. The Greek chanting gave way to English, in which Golden Arrow begged Apollo to grace his humble servants with his bliss. He began a refrain that the worshippers echoed as they stomped out a steady beat on the floor. The words grew faster and louder, filling the space with a buzz that set her teeth on edge. Then, through some unseen signal, the noise abruptly stopped. The congregation seemed to hold its breath as it watched Golden Arrow experience what seemed like a cross between a seizure and an orgasm. Maybe, in some cases, the two acts weren't always that different.

Golden Arrow shook violently and fell to his knees, head tilted back and mouth open as he let out a low moan of joy. A rapture even greater than what he'd shown earlier lit his features, and it only seemed to grow more intense when he lay prone on the floor and continued to writhe around. He finally stilled and grew quiet, gasping in a way that made Mae wish she could offer him a cigarette. The two robed women helped Golden Arrow stand and face the congregation.

"Who will the god choose to share his ecstasy today?"

All of the worshippers dropped to their knees and stared upward with eager expressions. Golden Arrow walked among them, peering closely at each face. At last, he stopped in front of a middle-aged woman, murmuring, "Share in the union of our god."

Her face shone, and she followed him back toward the front of the room. There, she fell on her knees, head lowered.

"Here we go," Justin said.

Golden Arrow cupped the woman's face with his hands, saying a quiet prayer Mae couldn't hear. A few moments later, the woman had a startling reaction that mirrored his earlier one. She took on that same orgasmic look, complete with the uncontrollable writhing on the floor. Everyone watched in awe, and when the fit finally passed, Golden Arrow's assistant helped her back to her seat. He then repeated the process with a young man who looked barely out of high school.

Mae was aghast. She whispered, "It's fake, right?"

"That part is." It was a weird word choice. "The question is who's faking it. Him or them."

"One more," the priest intoned. "The god will share his grace with one more. Dr. March, would you like to experience the light of Apollo?"

All eyes turned toward them again. Justin said nothing, and Mae could guess his thoughts. Golden Arrow had timed this ceremony with Justin's visit and was now openly inviting him to participate in a "miracle." There was a dangerous look in the priest's eye that put her on alert. *He expects something to happen. He* knows *it will.* Justin had said miracles were always disproven. It'd be a big coup for a group to demonstrate an act of divinity on the person sent to debunk it—which meant, of course, that Justin couldn't do it. She could see Justin analyzing all of these things, and suddenly, a smile appeared. He turned to her and rested his hand on hers, leaning so close that his lips nearly brushed her cheek.

"Do you trust me?" Before she could answer that disconcerting question, he added, "At least as far as this stuff and our country go?"

Mae glanced up at him and met his penetrating gaze. Did she trust him? Not with women, of course. She thought about everything she'd seen in these last couple of weeks, the way he so keenly observed others in his job, jumping on the tiniest signs of danger. And as for his country? Yes. If nothing else, she believed in his devotion to it. She gave a small nod, and he turned toward Golden Arrow in triumph.

"Thank you for the offer," Justin told him. "But I think I'll pass this time. My lovely friend here, however, would love to commune with your god."

Mae jerked her head toward Justin in alarm, but his attention was all on Golden Arrow. The priest looked disappointed at first but then smiled and shrugged. A servitor's companion was just as good. He gestured for her to follow him.

Trust me, Justin's eyes seemed to tell her. Nodding more to herself than him, she rose and walked toward the church's front. Neurotransmitters surged within her at this threat, and that dark power began to settle upon her, weighing down her steps. For once, Mae didn't entirely fear it. It was almost like armor.

Golden Arrow smiled down at her in glee. "Feel our god's light," he said, resting his hands on her cheeks. Mae tensed, fearful that Justin had led her astray and she'd soon find herself on the ground, writhing for the entertainment of these nuts. But . . . nothing happened. Nothing at all—except a slight flaring of the darkness wreathing her. Golden Arrow's grin faltered, then disappeared altogether. Soon, his face became an almost comical picture of disbelief. She turned as Justin's voice suddenly rang out through the church.

"Mr. Rafferty. You've created a hoax in an attempt to trick others into the worship of a fictitious entity. Your license is revoked, and you will be forced to answer for—"

The young man who'd had the earlier fit sprang toward Justin. Mae saw the attack coming and acted without hesitation. *I can't let anything happen to him.* She was too far away, though, to stop that first punch that knocked Justin back. That was all the guy got in before Mae reached him and tackled him to the ground. Her sharpened senses warned her of others moving in, and once she was certain her target was down, she spun around and blocked the attack of another man who'd come at Justin. The guy was joined by several of his brethren, men and women, all of them worked up over this blasphemy toward their leader. Mae vaguely noted that Golden Arrow himself, along with other more prudent members of the congregation, was uneasily keeping his distance.

She spared them little more time than that, however. Battle mode seized her, driven by both her normal fighter nature and the influence of that dark presence that reveled in violence. That darkness seemed to take especial satisfaction out of battling the servants of a god, and for a moment, Mae had the surreal sense of being involved in something much bigger than what was, ulti-mately, a scuffle with some delusional hotheads. The pews made for awkward fighting, but it was more trouble for them than for her, and as soon as she had a semi-clear space around her and Justin, she took out her gun and fired a shot into the air. Every-one froze.

"Back off," she ordered, moving into a position that gave her a vantage on everyone in the room. "Get over there, against that wall." Power filled her, and she almost hoped someone would try to resist. They didn't and instead scurried to comply. Golden Arrow seemed to realize just how much trouble he was in. The rapture was gone, and he looked like a very ordinary, very frightened man.

"Dr. March, maybe we can clear up this misunderstanding—"

"You can clear it up with them," said Justin, getting to his feet and nodding toward the doorway. Mae could hear voices and footsteps, and within seconds, local police filled the room, notified by a message Justin must have sent off on his ego at the fight's start. Servitors could request instant access from law en-forcement.

Once she and Justin identified themselves, the authorities

took over processing and detaining Apollo's followers. Mae sat near the back of the room with Justin, staying out of the way until they were needed to finalize the official paperwork. The darkness that had aided her in battle was gone, leaving her tired and a little empty.

Justin gingerly touched the spot on his face that had been hit. "Ow," he said. "My stunning good looks are ruined. How will I get by in the world now?"

Mae rubbed her trembling hands together. "You'll manage. There's hardly anything there. Just get some ice when we leave."

He shook his head. "I'd rather have something harder. We're staying in Windsor tonight. You want to go hit some nightlife?"

"Incredible," she said. "You get attacked by a cult, and the only thing you can think of is going clubbing."

"You have a better idea?" He winced. "Goddamn, that hurts."

"Baby. The military infirmary would laugh me out if I came in with that."

"I'm not a supersoldier with a pain-dulling implant."

"It's nothing," she insisted, unable to hide a smile.

"Dr. March." That was Golden Arrow as the police led him past. His earlier fear was gone, and he'd apparently decided to accept his arrest with arrogance. He came to a halt. "You must be very pleased with yourself. No doubt your master thinks he's triumphed over mine."

"SCI's triumphed over worse than you," said Justin cheerfully.

Golden Arrow's eyes gleamed. "That's not the master I'm talking about."

"What happened to your partner in crime?" asked Justin. "I was hoping to see Callista."

"I'm sure you were," said Golden Arrow with a sneer. "She left last year with Nadia."

Justin fell silent as he dredged up the name. "Nadia Menari? That Arianrhod priestess?"

"I'm surprised you remember the lives of those you ruin."

"She was preaching the destruction of men everywhere," said Justin. "She was lucky she wasn't arrested. Why'd she go with Callista?"

"I don't know." Mae understood little of what was being discussed, but from the bitterness in his voice, Golden Arrow had taken these events personally. "To start some überfeminist cult."

"Where?"

Golden Arrow glared. "Hell if I know. They took off with half my money and disappeared."

"If you need to talk more," said one of the authorities, "we can set up an interrogation room at our station."

Justin shook his head. "I'm good." Yet, Mae was pretty sure she heard disappointment in his voice.

"For now," called Golden Arrow as his captors led him away. "Your side hasn't won. Not by a long shot."

"I don't even know what my side is," Justin muttered.

Mae watched Golden Arrow until he left the building, and then she turned back to Justin. "Did what he said make sense? Is Callista the priestess you want?"

"Yeah." Justin definitely looked upset. "The piece of work. It's interesting she went into business with Nadia. She was another priestess. Different religion, but both their goddesses have a real girl-power thing going on—and silver and moon connections. If all our victims were male, I'd say maybe we were onto something." He shrugged and stood up. "Still worth finding them. For now, I'm finding that nightlife, with or without you."

Mae thought he was joking, but after they were settled into their Windsor hotel, Justin came knocking on her door. He'd lost the tie and simply wore a black jacket over a white button-up shirt with the collar open. Even in casual mode, he still looked polished and stylish, and of course, his hair had been repaired after the temple scuffle. After being surrounded by military men whose styling could at best be described as "efficient," she was constantly surprised at the effect his meticulous grooming had on her. He looked her over.

"You're wearing that out?"

"I'm not going out with you," she said, feeling slightly affronted on behalf of her jeans and black blouse. "I told you that before."

"Right, right. Because flawless castal princesses don't lower themselves to the company of common plebeians. Well, rest easy, because this is business. You can't really abandon me to the seedy streets of Windsor, can you? Maybe some vindictive followers of Apollo will come after me. Wouldn't you feel bad about that?"

"Yeah. I'd be heartbroken." Seeing his hopeful look, she sighed. He had a point, after all. "Fine. But I'm not changing."

He looked as though he might protest but shrugged it off. "Something tells me for you, it won't matter. Let's go."

She didn't know how many times he'd been in Windsor, but he managed to find the shadiest, most illicit club he could. It wasn't even an official establishment and was instead housed in what looked like an abandoned warehouse. When they stepped inside, though, she was blown away that a place like this could exist without being known to authorities.

Hundreds of bodies were packed together in relatively little space, and the room reeked of human sweat and smoke from all sorts of substances. It was almost like being in Cristobal's club, except cleaner and more high-tech. The place was kept dark, lit only by pulsing colored lights that seemed to be timed to the loud, pounding, percussion-intensive music filling the air. People talked in clusters around the periphery of the room, while the middle was reserved for dancing, which mostly seemed to consist of a lot of erratic body thrusting and rubbing.

"Wow," said Justin with delight, while Mae felt her body respond to the implant. He made a beeline for the bar, and she fell into step with him.

"How is it possible that someone who bemoaned his fate in Panama for four years chooses the most provincial bar I've ever seen in this country?" she exclaimed.

"Difference is in the clientele," he told her. "These people are civilized."

Glancing around, Mae wasn't so sure. Some did seem to be from Justin's demographic: stylish, affluent people charmed by novel vices. Others looked like the dredges of society and would've fit in well in Panama. The bartender, whose mouth was completely encircled in metal piercings, seemed to be a prime example.

"Black Bay bourbon. Straight," Justin ordered. He glanced

at Mae. "Can't get that in the provinces." He turned back to the bartender. "You got any ash?"

She suppressed a groan, wondering if her position as a soldier of the Republic meant she should be enforcing its laws.

"Oh, yeah, of course," said the man, handing Justin a small glass of amber liquid. "It's good, if you want to get something for your fucking grandmother. You want some serious shit, though, you go for the gates of paradise."

Justin scoffed. "You don't have that here." The bartender reached down and held up a small plastic dropper, earning an exclamation of, "Fuck me. Hook me up."

"The gates of paradise? What is that?" asked Mae as Justin handed over a stack of EA dollars. Their sister country still ran on hard currency, which was fairly easy for Gemmans to exchange. Since it couldn't be traced in the same way electronic funds could, it was frequently used for purchases like this.

Justin accepted the dropper. "The closest those of us without implants can get to being a god." Without hesitation, he held it to his tongue and shook out several clear drops. He closed his eyes, shuddering as an invisible wave swept over his body. "Damn," he breathed. It sounded like a benediction. He opened his eyes again and blinked them several times as though focusing. Even in the erratic light, she could see his pupils dilating. "Heavenly. Would this be wasted on you?"

"Yes," she said sternly. "I don't need drugs to wind down after a hard day."

"Says the woman whose life is dependent on neurotransmitters and endorphins."

She flushed. "That's not the same at all."

"Whatever you say." He knocked back his drink in one gulp and handed the empty glass and vial to the bartender. "Another bourbon." He waved grandly to Mae. "And whatever she wants."

She nearly declined but felt awkward just standing there. "Get me a mojito."

The bartender gave her a flat look. "Does this look like the kind of place that serves mojitos?"

"Surprise me, then."

He made her a martini, explaining, "That's the prissiest I can do."

Mae would've expected Justin to start trolling for women, but instead, he leaned near her against the bar in companionable silence. He watched the room with interest, and she wondered if his brilliant observation skills still worked when he was strung out on illegal substances. At least he was sipping the bourbon this time. He wore his typical amused and confident expression, but when she gave him a more scrutinizing look, she swore she could see a glimmer of the sadness she'd observed in Panama.

"What's wrong?" she asked.

He glanced her way, and she could tell he was on the verge of denying it. Then, studying her, he changed his mind. "Do you know why the land grants are on hold? Why we're looking into cults now?"

"Because one of them is responsible for the murders?"

The ghost of a smile flashed over his face. "Well, yes, but I'd much rather solve all of this through placid forensics work—even though I know that's not your thing." He grew solemn again. "I got a call from the illustrious Cornelia the other day, letting me know how displeased she was at our lack of progress."

Even though she wasn't personally involved with the investigative part, Mae felt offended. "But you're doing everything you can. Your interviews are . . . meticulous. You're getting the data scrutinized again. And we're not done talking to everyone."

"You're a fan after all, huh?" His smile returned, and for a moment, his hand lifted as though he might touch her. Then it dropped. "Meticulous or not, we're stuck, and Cornelia made me very aware of the ticking clock." He stared into the depths of his glass. "And so, we're on to nuts like Apollo's people—but even that didn't pan out. I thought it'd be easy, you know. Just a few strokes of brilliance from me, and it'd be put to bed. Now I may be back in Panama before the month's over."

"Why did you go there in the first place?"

He looked back up, surprising her with a hint of the sadness she'd seen at their first meeting. "You wouldn't believe me if I told you."

Mae didn't want to, but she felt sorry for him. No matter his faults, he'd been put into a bad situation—maybe even an impossible one. Bringing him back had most certainly been an act of desperation on Internal Security's part. "Maybe you can find that woman, Calliope—"

"Callista," he corrected. "And maybe. I don't know. Not many people can disappear, but she could. She's got ties to underground networks of religions, ones that hide from SCI. Those groups stick together and help each other stay under the radar. Most of them wouldn't go anywhere near a servitor like me, but she'd help me. I know she would." He finished the bourbon and gestured the bartender over. "More paradise."

Even the callous bartender looked taken aback. "That first shot should last all night."

Justin put some cash on the bar. "It's been a long day." After a little more hesitation, the bartender swept up the money and handed over another vial. Mae bit her tongue on her own protests and watched as Justin took it down. His depression melted away, or was at least hidden. That dashing charmer returned, and he stepped closer to her. "You want to dance?"

"No. And that's not dancing." She cast a contemptuous look at the dance floor before returning her gaze to him, feeling slightly discomfited by his proximity. "It's just an excuse for people to rub themselves up against each other."

He leaned close. "If memory serves, you didn't mind that once."

"I'm going to ignore that because you're high off your ass right now," she snapped. "And if memory serves, you don't go on second dates."

"I'm not asking you on a date, princess." The intensity of his eyes was all-encompassing, his voice velvety and coaxing. The same voice he used to get what he needed from interviewees.

Her earlier sympathy dried up. "I'm sure you think that over-the-top term of endearment is cute, but it's really not."

"It's not cute. It's true." He looked at her in a way that somehow managed to see both the past and the present. "You know, the first time I saw you—before the alley—my whole world came to a stop. Everything else in that room faded to nothing, and there was only you, with your beautiful neck and your winter-sunlight hair and eyes that commanded the room." He tilted his head in thought. "Do you know stephanotis?"

Mae swallowed, suddenly feeling as though she were back in Panama with a man who knew her inside and out. "Stephan-what?"

"It's a flower. We should find some and go back to the hotel." He reached out and ran a hand over her hair. "We'll make a wreath of them and crown you in majesty, and then the world will ignite between us. . . ."

Mae jerked away, embarrassed to find she was holding her breath. She was a soldier who killed without hesitation, not a woman swayed by pretty words. "Go dance. I'm sure there're plenty of women just as far gone as you who'll be enthralled by your flowers and fumbling advances."

"I've never fumbled in my life."

She turned away, angling her body so that her back was to him. Tense, she waited for more, but it never came. When she finally dared a look back, he was gone. The bartender strolled over.

"Refill?"

She shook her head and left for a wall near a back exit. It gave her a good vantage of the dance floor but kept her away from most of the crowd—not that it stopped her from getting hit on. She should've left. There was no reason for her to be here. She didn't even know why she'd come. Yet, something in her couldn't abandon Justin, especially now that he was in the throes of drugs and alcohol. Not that he seemed to need much help. Each time she caught a glimpse of him, he was talking to a different woman, his face alight and full of that oozing charisma. He seemed to be on top of his game as the night went on, confident and in control, even after a trip to the bar for another drink and vial. It made his earlier proposition that much more insulting. Disgust filled her, and she welcomed it. It was easier to deal with than attraction.

Blinking out of her own troubled thoughts, she focused back

on the dance floor. She couldn't see Justin, but she could make out a few people standing around, looking at something on the floor. One of the gathered people shifted slightly away from whatever they all were watching, and Mae caught a glimpse of the jacket Justin had been wearing earlier. Her adrenaline spiked. She sprinted over to the gathered people, none of whom seemed in any particular hurry to act or move. Her stomach lurched as her worst fears were realized. It was Justin, sprawled on the floor, eyelids barely open as his breathing came fast and shallow. Alive—for now. As she quickly knelt down beside him, she wondered just how much trouble she'd get into if he died.

CHAPTER 13

TWO PERCENT

Justin opened his eyes and promptly closed them again—the light hurt too much. He waited a few moments and then decided to try again, this time using his hand to shade his eyes. Even that small amount of motion was uncomfortable. The muscles in his body felt limp and sore. The view above him revealed nothing, as that was where the light source was, and only made him close his eyes again. With great effort, he tried to shift his body over and look to the side. He was on some kind of hard, uncomfortable bed, and his body complained against it accordingly.

Still keeping his eyes shaded, he blinked rapidly and tried to bring the room into focus around him. The walls gleamed dully in an inoffensive shade of taupe, and a large dark square hung nearby, which he assumed was a window. There was someone standing near it, appearing only as a shadowy figure. That figure approached, and he could start to discern more tangible features: lean body, golden hair. His Valkyrie.

"Hey," he said, surprised when his own voice had difficulty coming out. There was a strange taste in his mouth. "What's new?"

"You're an idiot." His angry Valkyrie.

"That's not really new." She stood in focus now. Her face looked strained, and most of her hair had fallen out of its ponytail. "What happened?" Then, before she could reply: "A bad trip?"

She nodded. "What were you thinking? You could've killed yourself!"

"Hey, it was good stuff. Really good." It had been. In addition to making him feel like he was made of that spun-sugar stuff that kids ate at the Anchorage summer market, it had also distorted his vision so that everything around him was edged in color. Glittering people, ringed in brightly hued auras, left trails of colored light when they moved.

She didn't answer, still keeping her face void of expression, and he somehow felt their relationship had just regressed about two years. At the same time, he had the startling sense that she'd actually been worried about him.

"I had no idea my job would involve protecting you from yourself," she added. "How can someone so smart be so stupid?"

Excellent question, said Magnus.

How could he be so stupid? Well, it was easy because it was hard for him to say no. When it came to the pleasures of life, he had a tendency to think that if one was good, ten were better.

"I don't care how futile the mission seems right now," she continued angrily. "You want to fix things? You want to stay in the country? Then go solve this case! Don't go drown yourself in drugs and self-pity!"

Her words brought back the dismal state of the mission, Cornelia's threats, and Callista's disappearance. That was more than enough to make someone seek blissful oblivion, that and—

"Have you ever not wanted to think?"

Her hard expression turned puzzled. "What?"

He shifted from her and stared up at the ceiling. "I think a lot, Mac. I see a lot. And my brain's always analyzing every detail, over and over and over. This case. Me staying in the RUNA. That church. You." He sighed. "I can't shut my brain off. It's like a hamster wheel. It's why I take stuff to sleep."

"I thought you took stuff to sleep because you loaded up on stimulants in the morning." Her contempt was nearly tangible, but rather than summon his knee-jerk reaction to castal airs, it made him feel . . . unworthy.

Did I do anything I shouldn't have? he asked the ravens.

Overdosing? suggested Horatio.

You know what I mean.

You propositioned her, replied the raven.

Did I? Justin didn't remember that. He remembered very little past dosing with the gates of paradise. From his current state, he must've done it more than once. *How'd it go? I mean, I know the result, seeing as I'm in this bed instead of hers.*

You were very eloquent, said Horatio. *A real poet. I would've gone home with you.*

You offered her the crown, said Magnus much more seriously.

A sinking feeling welled up in Justin's stomach. He was used to doing all sorts of stupid behaviors following a high, but it had never occurred to him that he could've accidentally stumbled into the very thing he wanted to avoid. Now that he was somewhat clearheaded, and in the path of that condescending gaze that stung so much, it was easy to resist her. It was a relief that she was still in full possession of her hatred and plebeian disdain.

"If I ever hit on you again," he said, "you have my permission to punch me."

That, she hadn't expected. "Why on earth would you say that?"

Because if I sleep with you again, I'll be bound into the service of an unknown god.

"Because you've made your Nordic-nine preferences perfectly clear. And I need to respect that."

He hadn't thought much about the last comment and simply wanted to keep her away. He wasn't trying to be noble. Instead, something unexpected flashed over her face.

You just improved two percent in her view, noted Horatio. *That's the first personal comment you've made that doesn't make you come across as an asshole.* The raven sounded pleased, but of course he would. He and his counterpart wanted a reconciliation.

Magnus wasn't so optimistic. *It's going to take more than your fixing that damage to get her again. I told you before, gods follow her. One goddess in particular. You need to help Mae break free, for her own good. You saw how she gets seized in battle.*

The darkness, admitted Justin. He'd seen it, an almost tangi-ble shadow that surrounded her when she fought.

It happens because gods can't communicate with her in the normal way.

What way is that?

Dreams.

Why not? asked Justin.

You tell me, said Magnus.

Justin immediately realized the answer. *Because she doesn't sleep.*

You are *smart,* Horatio said. *Too bad you're so stupid.*

Just be careful, Magnus warned him. *The deity that follows her might start getting suspicious of others. You can deny it, but there's power in you that's detectable by some. She certainly wasn't pleased by that usurpation back in the temple.*

It took Justin a moment to catch on; then he recalled how Mae had shone and become larger than life while standing by the statue of that goddess. She'd been wreathed by a power as intense as the battle-driven one, only it had been warm and se-ductive and full of life, rather than dark and terrible.

What happened? he asked.

Another god tried to seize Mae from the dark one, said Mag-nus.

The Lady of the Book? Justin had a hard time imagining a scholarly goddess going after Mae.

No, just some enterprising deity who tried to take advantage of the situation. Gods sometimes weaken in the territory of other ones.

Mae peered at Justin. "Why are you looking at me like that?"

He realized he'd been staring as he mulled things over. Quickly, he groped for something. "Don't tell Cyn about this."

"Why would I?"

"You guys are chummy. Especially after she made you pan-cakes the other day. You ate twice your weight in them." After a number of shared meals with Mae, he'd discovered prætorians required a lot of food to maintain that superhuman metabolism.

"They were good pancakes," admitted Mae. "And she made a lot. She always makes a lot of everything."

He smiled. "You know why? It's overcompensation."

"For what?"

He hesitated before answering. In trying to avoid a topic Mae didn't want to discuss, he'd strayed into one he hadn't wanted to bring up. There were days he could assess people's life stories with a glance, but he preferred to keep his to himself. And yet, as he met her eyes—a bewitching balance of blue and green today—he felt a strange ache in him that made it hard for him not to talk. Maybe she hated him. Maybe she thought he was weak and manipulative. But suddenly, he wanted her to understand this part of him.

"Do you want to know how a brilliant, murderer-catching servitor got his start? In the dusty stalls of the Anchorage Summer Market. Cyn and I used to earn our keep by doing what you figure I do best: scamming people."

Mae started. "I don't think that."

"Don't you?" He gave her a knowing look, and she averted her eyes, proving his point. "You think every word that comes out of my mouth is an attempt to reel people in. And that's okay, because half the time it's true. The Nordics ever have carnivals or fairs?"

"Of course."

"You know those guessing games they do? Age, weight, stuff like that? That's what we did. Can't you picture it?" He held out his hands, warming to his story. "Two adorable kids—because we were, you know, even then—dazzling tourists with the ability to figure out things no one should be able to know. Cyn was really good at weights. She's got an eye for that kind of thing—it's her genius and totally underutilized mathematical prowess. Me? It was people's stories. The ages. Where they're from. I memorized accents. Pair that with a few seemingly innocent childlike questions, and I could find out practically anything."

"That's not scamming," she said. "That's just being observant."

He shrugged. "It felt like scamming—especially with the way those people reacted. You would've thought it was magic. Brought in a lot of money to the asshole carnie we worked for, of which we saw a fraction. But it was enough to buy food."

"Why would a couple of kids need to buy food?" she asked. She'd probably grown up with cooks and servants.

"Because there wasn't any at home. Our mom didn't work—well, she earned money, but not much of it went toward us."

"What about . . . your dad?"

He shook his head. "Just an anonymous donor somewhere who happened to be a good genetic match for my mom and her stipend."

Mae nodded, looking slightly uncomfortable. "But then you would've gotten federal rations."

"We did," he said simply. "She sold them for anything that could give her a high."

Mae was silent for several moments. "I can't imagine kids going hungry—not in the RUNA, at least. I can't imagine a mother doing that to her kids."

"She had a lot of problems." Boy, was that an understatement. "Cyn says I've got the same addictive personality, you know." He frowned, realizing the irony of bringing it up in this context. "But this is nothing compared to her. And Cyn knows it. She just gets extreme sometimes when she's pissed off. I'm nothing like our mom."

"Because you've worked your problems into a functioning lifestyle."

"Seems like by definition they aren't problems, then," he retorted. "I'm okay. My loved ones are okay. I take care of them." He was a little surprised at the fierceness in his voice. No matter what else happened, looking after Cynthia and Quentin—and Tessa—was always at the forefront of his mind. Maybe he'd deluded himself about inheriting his mother's addictions, but one thing he'd refused to repeat was her abandonment—which was part of what had made exile so agonizing.

"You do," said Mae, no trace of mockery. "You're very good to them. And look at you now. Using all that elite childhood training to get you where you are in the service of our country."

"Not that elite. What I do . . . it's not hard."

"I couldn't do it," she said.

A doctor appeared just then, a stern-faced woman who quickly made it apparent that she didn't find him charming in the least. She lectured him on the dangers of mixing alcohol and drugs, subtly hinting that he was lucky he hadn't actually been in possession of the—illegal—gates of paradise. She gave a set of basic discharge instructions involving rest and water and then scanned his ego so that she could send him "helpful" resources on substance abuse. He accepted all the reprimanding humbly, both because it was deserved and because it got them out of there faster.

Mae said little when they finally left the hospital, but he noticed her giving him the occasional sidelong look. He knew without a doubt she still thought his vices were a sign of weakness, but somehow, between his comment about respecting her and the story of his youth, he'd inadvertently grown a little in her esteem. Worse, he found he liked it. The pride and faith in her eyes had momentarily taken his breath away. Quickly, he reminded himself that she was a supercilious castal who looked down on others, one who'd been far from tactful in her attitudes. He needed to respond in kind, both for his own protection and because he deserved it. He would, as Horatio had observed, be more of an asshole from now on.

I'm sure that won't be difficult, the raven responded.

CHAPTER 14

JUSTIN'S FAVORITE MEGALOMANIAC

"What the hell happened to you?"

Cynthia nearly dropped her frying pan when Justin stumbled into the kitchen. Tessa looked up from the toast she was too nervous to eat and immediately saw what had caught Cynthia's attention. Justin looked pale and haggard, with dark circles under his eyes. He was dressed and groomed to his usual standards but was far from his dazzling self.

"Bad trip," he said.

Cynthia gave him a wary look. "What kind of trip?"

"The one where I battle it out with volatile religious nuts to protect the way you live. Ask Mae. She'll tell you." He started to trudge off down the hall and then noticed Tessa in her maroon school uniform. He patted her shoulder. "Good luck today, sweetie. You'll do great. I can't wait to hear the recap tonight."

She gave him a brave smile and nodded.

Although Tessa could understand Justin's emphasis on getting a formal Gemman education, there was a part of her that thought she could absorb just as much by staying at home with the stream. She spent hours on it every day, amazed at what she learned from both its entertainment and reference options. She had yet to find a topic the stream didn't cover. Some days it was almost overwhelming—but she loved it.

Still, she had to remember that the whole reason she'd been allowed to come to the RUNA was because of a student visa.

Studying at home was a valid option in Panama—the only one, actually, for ladies of her class—but here, the country's standardized education system was the path available to her.

"No private schools?" she'd asked Justin when they'd toured their suburb's high school last week. There were fledgling public schools in Panama, but New Money and the upper middle classes often opted for a slightly more elite choice, if they could afford it.

"None that would let you in. But don't worry—public education's outstanding. It's standardized across the whole country, even for castals and plebeians. Builds the national identity."

That identity was becoming more and more apparent. Even someone like Mae, who'd been raised in a unique cultural environment, still had a strong sense of national pride instilled into her that had existed long before her military service. The RUNA held three things responsible for the Decline: biological manipulation, religion, and cultural separatism. All of the early genetic mixing had gone a long way toward stamping out group solidarity, and the loose Greco-Roman models the country had adopted had provided a new, all-encompassing culture that everyone could be a part of.

Tessa still wasn't sure she agreed with all those principles, but it was hard to overlook the fact that the RUNA had become the most advanced country in the world.

The school had still been on holiday when they'd toured it last week, and Tessa grew nervous as she imagined those vast halls filled with students. She'd gotten better about dealing with the crowds in the city, but sometimes, claustrophobia still kicked in. The principal had made a special appointment with them, coming into the school on her day off. Tessa quickly realized that was because of Justin's profession. People weren't afraid of servitors the way they were prætorians, but there was definitely a lot of respect and awe.

"We've never had a provincial in all the time I've been here," Ms. Carmichael had said, studying Tessa as though she were some new species. Another thing Tessa had learned was that all things non-Gemman were called provincial—and it wasn't a flattering term. They all seemed to use it without thought. "I'm sure it will provide a unique learning experience for the other students . . . though I worry about your ability to, uh, fit into the classes here, dear."

Tessa had picked up on the subtext. Like Justin, Ms. Carmichael believed Tessa's education had involved "insipid reading and remedial math." After some assessment, both Justin and Ms. Carmichael had been surprised to learn her literary and composition knowledge was up to par. But, to Tessa's chagrin, her math skills were indeed remedial.

Now Tessa's first official day had finally arrived. Both Justin and Cynthia had offered to escort her, but Quentin had informed her that would only attract more attention and was most decidedly "uncool." Despite his young age, he hadn't yet led her astray, so she followed his advice.

Ms. Carmichael had assigned her a guide for her first day. Melissa was bright and beautiful and seemed to embody every quality of the perfect Gemman girl. Although she was polite enough, it was obvious that she too regarded Tessa as some kind of freak of nature. She also seemed to think Tessa was five years old and deaf.

"This is a locker," Melissa said, speaking more loudly than necessary, even with the din around them. Her words were also exaggerated and slow. "It holds your stuff. You have to open the door first. Put your hand over the lock, and it'll read your chip. That's the thing that's in your hand."

Tessa had already learned locker operation on her tour. Although there was nothing comparable in Panama, it wasn't exactly a difficult thing to figure out. Still, she smiled at Melissa and said, "Thank you."

"What did you say?" asked Melissa.

"I said, 'Thank you.'" Melissa kept asking Tessa to repeat herself, claiming the accent was hard to follow.

"You're welcome," Melissa practically shouted.

Despite the condescension, Tessa was glad to have Melissa taking her to classes. The halls were as crowded as Tessa had feared, and the uniforms everyone wore made it worse. It all looked the same, making it difficult to pick out points of reference.

"This is your English class," Melissa said when they reached the first room on Tessa's schedule. "This is where you read books. Books have words in them and tell stories or facts."

"Thank you," said Tessa.

"What?"

The classroom was sleek and gleaming, filled with the same white light and metal that permeated most Gemman public spaces. Students sat at desks with built-in touch screens and were ready with readers and egos. No one paid much attention to her as she and Melissa entered, and Tessa hoped she might just slip into a desk in the back where she could quietly take in this new world. Unfortunately, their teacher—who'd been briefed on his new student's background—decided to utilize her arrival as a learning experience.

Mr. Lu made her stand at the front of the room until soft chimes heralded the beginning of class. The students fell silent, and twenty sets of eyes focused on her.

"Everyone, we have a new student joining us. This is Teresa Cruz, who has come all the way from Panama."

All those eyes widened, and suddenly, she could see them judging everything about her. There was something in their faces that made her think they'd expected her to show up in fur and feathers—which, perhaps, wouldn't have been that out of line for someone from Europe. Aside from her hair, Tessa felt confident that the rest of her looked no different from anyone else.

"Teresa, what can you tell us about Panama?" Mr. Lu wasn't quite as bad as Melissa, but he too spoke a bit more slowly to her than he had his other students.

Tessa had no idea what he expected. Some sensational, sordid tale? Or maybe a confession of how much more amazing the RUNA was? Her hesitation only made her that much more conspicuous, so she blurted out the first neutral thing she could think of. "It's in Central America."

Mr. Lu gave her a kind smile. "That's very nice. Why don't you take that desk over there?"

Tessa slinked away, though she knew she was still the center of attention. Some students were at least discreet about their examination. Others stared openly, making no secret of their fascination.

They were in the middle of reading a book by a famous Gemman novelist that Tessa had acquired and read in advance. Rather than letting her listen in merciful anonymity, however, Mr. Lu kept stopping class to ask her if she knew how to use the reader and desk screen. Tessa kept nodding and thanking him for his concern.

The rest of her classes passed in a similar way, with other "helpful" teachers embarrassing her. By the end of the day, she found that word of her arrival had spread, so that her classmates were waiting for her to show up and do something savage.

She felt a little bit of pride at her ability to keep up with English and history. She especially liked the latter since it filled in some of the gaps she had about Gemman culture. Melissa was in the same class and had again felt the need to explain how it worked.

"This is history. It's about the past. We're learning about the RUNA's formation after the Decline and how the castes happened. Do you know what 'caste' means? They're groups that didn't have to follow the mandates because they helped fund the early government. We read books in here."

Tessa simply nodded her thanks for fear of having to repeat herself.

Math proved to be a dismal experience, but her self-esteem was boosted in advanced Spanish. Of course, she wasn't entirely sure why she'd been placed in it. Spanish was her first language, whereas her classmates were still learning and working on translation. Her teacher kept making her say things but would always remind the others, "She has a provincial accent, so make sure you stick to the standardized one." She would then helpfully try to correct Tessa's pronunciation.

By the time she reached her last class of the day, Tessa was exhausted. *One more class,* she kept telling herself. *One more class, and you're free. This is the worst day. It can only get better now.*

After the usual embarrassing introduction from the teacher, she took a seat near the middle of the room. Unlike the other classrooms, biology had no desks. They all sat at long tables with the usual touch screens, as well as another device Tessa didn't recognize. It was round and metal, set with a piece of glass, also round, on top. Tessa could freely admit this was probably beyond her. She clung to the hope that if she studied enough at home, she'd eventually catch up. Cynthia had gruffly offered to help.

Their instructor immediately launched into a discussion of Cain, apparently following up on a lecture that had begun yesterday. Everyone knew about Cain in Panama, and Tessa started to relax, thinking she was in familiar territory. But as the lecture became increasingly technical, discussing how the disease operated at the genetic level, Tessa knew she was once again out of her league. Things grew worse when they received their assignment and Tessa learned what the round device did.

It created a three-dimensional image in the air, showing a model of Cain's proteins and mutations. Manipulating the model proved to be challenging. The image had no substance, of course, but the projector could detect hand movement and "touch," allowing the model to be rotated as needed. The technology was still new in the RUNA, so there was a bit of a trick to it. The other students had practiced before, but Tessa couldn't quite get the hang of it. She didn't seem to touch the image in the right spots to trigger detection, and more often than not, her hand passed right through it. Her classmates had no difficulty jumping right in as they worked through their assigned questions and problems.

After a day of being told how to use technology she'd already learned, Tessa had finally hit a wall. She knew if she went to her instructor, he'd find someone to help her—but that would draw unwanted attention to her and confirm everyone's suspicions about the primitive girl from the provinces. No one had seemed to notice her difficulties—yet. They were all consumed with their own tasks, many of them chatting with friends as they worked. Tessa continued trying doggedly to manipulate the model, succeeding only about a third of the time. When she was able to manage it, she could barely understand the related questions, making the whole exercise kind of futile.

Panic hit her. What was she doing here? Her superficial features might have looked plebeian, but there was always going to be something that made her "other." It didn't matter if she wore the same uniform as everyone else in the school. The maroon pants and white shirt weren't going to disguise what she was. And it wasn't even her hair or accent or lack of technical skills that really made her stand out. It was something more intangible, an attitude and demeanor that screamed to the world that she hadn't been born and raised in this glittering, frenetic society. The students here were just like everyone else she'd seen in the RUNA: confident, purposeful, and so certain of their superiority over the world. Tessa was never going to possess that air.

Clenching her hands, she took a deep breath and tried to seize control. She remembered the way Justin had fought for her with her parents and how proud he'd been when taking her to tour the school. More important, she couldn't shake the way he kept calling her his prodigy. She didn't really know whether she believed that, but the thought of going home and telling him she couldn't do any of this was unbearable. Another breath calmed her, and she resigned herself to asking for help, no matter how humiliating it was.

But when she went to the front of the room, she found her teacher deeply engaged with another student. Standing around made her self-conscious, so she returned to her table to wait her turn. Behind her, Melissa had taken a break in her work—or maybe even finished—and was talking to a cluster of friends.

"I can't understand anything she says," she told them. "And I'm pretty sure she doesn't get half of what we're saying. I don't think they have electricity there."

"Did you see her with the hologram?" asked another student.

Someone else laughed. "She probably thought it was some sort of vision. They've got crazy beliefs in the provinces."

Melissa sneered, marring her pretty features. "Well, I'm just glad I don't have to drag her around tomorrow. If I have to look at that hair one more—"

She froze, her smile slipping as she noticed Tessa watching. Melissa flushed, embarrassed at being caught. Then she became equally conscious of her friends and pushed aside her chagrin.

"Well?" she demanded. Gone was the friendly peppiness from before. "What are you staring at?"

When Tessa said nothing, one of Melissa's friends nudged her. "Forget it, Mel. Look at her. She didn't even understand what you said."

"I can understand bitchiness in any language," Tessa said. A few seconds later, she added, "Do you need me to repeat that more slowly?" She kept her face cold and unrevealing, something she'd picked up after days spent around people who excelled at hiding their thoughts.

Melissa's face said that she had indeed understood. "Who are you calling a bitch?"

"Who do you think?" asked Tessa, growing emboldened. "That's rhetorical, by the way. It means you don't have to answer."

Part of Tessa knew she needed to stop. She was only digging a bigger hole for herself. Melissa didn't seem like the type to defend her honor with fists, not if the way she pranced and kept checking her hair was any indication. But there was a malevolent look in her eyes that made Tessa think Melissa was very likely the type to take revenge in far more subtle and insidious ways. Fists might have been easier.

"That's the part Melissa doesn't understand," a new voice suddenly said. "How not to answer. She can't keep her mouth shut—just ask Silas Moore."

Melissa glared as one of her friends snickered, and then she turned her fury on the girl standing beside Tessa. "Shut the hell up, Poppy! Everyone knows what you did last weekend."

"Funny," said the girl called Poppy. "How come no one ever brags about what they do with you? They always just look kind of sad and disappointed."

"Ladies, why are none of you working?" That was Mr. Rykov, striding toward them. Melissa and her friends immediately began to disperse. Poppy, however, turned toward him and looked him squarely in the eye.

"Just helping Tertia, Mr. Ry," she said brightly. "That's the kind of person I am." She reached toward Tessa's model and deftly flipped the molecule over.

Mr. Rykov looked suspicious. "Well, I suppose that's—you have that abhorrent makeup on again! I told you not to come to class like that. You'll be serving detention with me tomorrow."

"Can't. I've already got another one. But I'm free on Thursday."

"Fine," he grumbled. "Thursday. Now get back to work, and try to accomplish something productive with your last ten minutes."

When he was gone, Poppy turned to Tessa. "You know why he didn't ask me to do detention today? Because everyone knows he goes and fucks Ms. Braeburn on Tuesdays. It's the day her husband works late."

"Oh," said Tessa, not entirely sure how else to respond. "I see. Well, um. My name's not Tertia. It's Teresa. Er, Tessa."

"Got it," said Poppy. "Let's knock the rest of this out."

Without further comment, she took over Tessa's workstation and began entering in answers as she worked through the assignment. Tessa leaned over to watch her, amazed at how much Poppy accomplished in so little time.

The "abhorrent" makeup was heavy black eyeliner and hot-pink lipstick that matched the streaks in Poppy's short, spiked hair. Justin was always going on about how refined Gemmans were, but apparently, he only meant his own demographic.

Chimes signaled the end of the school day, and Poppy stepped back. "Damn. Well, that's most of it. I don't think he'll really care what you turn in anyway. You heard those assholes. No one here even thinks you can read." She suddenly paused. "You can, right?"

Tessa sighed. "Yes. And I'm fluent in English, even though I have an accent."

Poppy shrugged. "The accent's cool."

"I still want to finish this. How do I bring it home?" Tessa gestured to the screen Poppy had entered the answers on. So far, all of Tessa's work had been completed in class, and she'd simply been able to send it from the screens to her teachers.

"Easy." Poppy took Tessa's ego and held it over a small panel. A few taps on the screen, and it went blank. She handed over the ego. "Done. Just upload later. Your model will only be 2D there, though. Unless you've got a projector."

The luxury house had many amenities, but Tessa hadn't seen anything like the projector. Thinking of how little she understood, she said, "I don't think it'll matter."

Poppy gathered up her things. "Where do you live?"

Although Justin refused to call it anything except "the suburbs," Tessa had recently learned the name of her neighborhood. "Cherrywood."

"Hey, me too. We can walk there."

Poppy headed off as though it were a done deal. After a bit of hesitation, Tessa followed. She'd ridden the bus this morning. It was another automated vehicle but one that had a supervisor to keep students in line. True, the distance to school hadn't been very long, but no one like her would walk that far alone in Panama. Poppy had no fear, however, and neither Justin nor Cynthia had seemed to care how Tessa traveled, so long as she made it to and from school.

Poppy lit a cigarette as soon as they were three blocks away. Smoking was a lot less common here, and Justin had held good to his commitment to quit. Those who did smoke were very respectful of laws about where it was allowed, and they always cleaned up after themselves.

Tessa soon discovered Poppy had no sense of personal boundaries. She peppered Tessa with questions about Panama, but it seemed to be out of friendly curiosity and not some sort of perverse condescension. Poppy's reactions ran the gamut of emotions as the many rumors she'd heard were either confirmed or denied. She seemed legitimately disappointed to hear particularly savage stereotypes dismissed—but that was matched by supreme delight at other revelations.

"Really?" she asked. "No gun laws?"

"No. I don't even know how they'd enforce one. You can get guns anywhere."

"Not here." Poppy sounded wistful. "They're hard to smuggle in, and production is pretty closely watched. I wouldn't mind learning to use one."

"Join the military," suggested Tessa.

"Nah. I could never follow all those rules. This is where you live?"

Tessa had come to a stop in front of her house. "Yup."

Poppy gave a nod of approval. "Wow, nice. Your parents must have made out pretty good back in the provinces."

"I live here with friends."

"Cool." Poppy brightened. "Are you like some orphan rescued from the wild streets?"

It was hard keeping up with her sometimes. "Not exactly. My parents are still back there."

"Okay, that's cool too," said Poppy. "You want to get some coffee before school tomorrow?"

Did she? Tessa wasn't sure at first, but then she decided she might as well. Poppy was the only person who'd treated her like a human being today, and besides, she seemed like she might be a good person to have around if Melissa did come after her. Tessa accepted, and Poppy told her she'd be back at six thirty.

As she approached the house, Tessa was greeted by the astonishing sight of a man sitting on the front step. She hadn't noticed him from the street. Seeing her, he flashed her a grin and leapt to his feet. Tessa came to a halt on the walkway, too nervous to proceed. She guessed he was Justin's age and possessed the same powerful presence, albeit in a different sort of way. He was tall and broad chested, wearing a gray T-shirt that showed off his extraordinarily muscled arms. His features were plebeian, tan skin and brown eyes, though his long hair had been dyed blond.

"Finally," he said. He had a rich voice, one that urged her to relax. It only made her more uneasy. "I was about to give up. Is my good friend Dr. March here?"

"Y-you're friends with Justin?"

"Yes, of course. He's my favorite servitor, you know. I've missed seeing him. I'd gotten used to his yearly visits, and then poof! Off he goes without a trace. I was hurt. His replacement was a huge disappointment."

Tessa really had no idea what the correct response to that was. "Who are you?"

He extended a polite hand, one she paused before taking. "You, sweet child, can call me Geraki."

"Oh. I'm Tessa."

"They told me he had a protégée, but I didn't expect someone like you. It's very charming. And intriguing." Behind that amiable face, Tessa caught a glimpse of something shrewd and dangerous.

"He's not here," she said. She pulled her hand back from his strong grip and looked around nervously. One of their neighbors was outside working in her garden, which made Tessa feel a little more secure. She could also see a couple of kids walking home from school, which meant Quentin would be back soon. Cynthia had said she'd be home around the same time. "He probably won't be back for a while. He's out of town."

"Shame. I'd really hoped to catch up with him."

"He's got a prætorian with him." She didn't entirely know what made her blurt that out or why it ended up sounding like a challenge.

Geraki chuckled. "I heard that too. Amazing how he pulled that off."

"He didn't request it." Tessa knew that much at least about Justin and Mae's odd relationship. "I think it just happened to him."

"Things 'just happen' to him a lot, and he doesn't even realize it. Or, if he does, he thinks it's all due to his cleverness." Geraki sighed and shook his head. "I tell you, the ravens are wasted on him, but who am I to dictate to higher powers?"

Tessa was growing increasingly panicked. "Look, Mr. Geraki—"

"Just Geraki, please."

"Geraki, I have to go." She prayed he wouldn't try to stop her. Surely the neighbor would do something if she screamed. "Maybe you can call him."

Geraki's lips twisted into a half smile. "I'm not sure he'd take my calls. Still, I'll leave you to your affairs. Tell him I said hello. And ask him why his employers have gone on a hiring spree." He swept her a gallant bow. "It was lovely meeting you. I'm sure our paths will cross again."

And with that, he stuffed his hands into his jeans pockets and strolled away, whistling as he walked. Tessa watched him for a few moments and then hurried inside, locking the door.

Cynthia and Quentin arrived within the hour, making Tessa feel a lot safer. She hesitated to tell Cynthia about Geraki without first speaking to Justin. Besides, Cynthia wanted to hear all about Tessa's experience at school. When Tessa finished her generously edited report, she found Cynthia had had her own academic experience.

"I had my first class." She didn't seem entirely pleased about that. "I've been trying to make this work for four years, and then my big bad brother waves his hand and gets me in within four days."

Tessa had heard pieces of this story before but never understood the full thing. "At . . . the university?"

"Yup." Cynthia opened up the pantry and began adding up dinner options.

With the way Cynthia oscillated between kind and prickly, Tessa always hesitated to solicit personal information. Curiosity won out this time. "Don't people usually go to college earlier?" She'd nearly said "younger" but thought that would be rude.

Cynthia snorted and dumped a bag of vegetables onto a cutting board. "They do." She glanced briefly toward the living room, where Quentin was watching a show. "And they usually put their kids in national day care while getting an education. But I had an unusual husband who wanted me to stay home until Quentin went to primary school."

Tessa forgot about Geraki. She'd never heard the story of Cynthia's husband, only that he had died when Quentin was very young.

"In retrospect, it wasn't a bad thing." Cynthia's expression softened a little. "I liked being home with him. But it meant I missed my window. Do you know how it works? Higher education is covered up to a certain age. Peter told me it was okay, that when he finished law school and Quentin started primaries, we'd have enough to pay out of pocket for my degree." She paused. "But then Peter died."

"I . . . I'm sorry."

Cynthia's face was very still as she spoke. "It was a car accident. Now, don't freak out—they're pretty rare. But they happen. And when everything was settled, it turned out Peter hadn't actually been saving the money he said. He'd spent a lot of time gambling after his classes. I just can't seem to escape that." She chopped a carrot with particular force. "Anyway, it didn't matter. I didn't want to do anything but mourn, and Justin told me not to worry, you know—in that way of his. He said he'd support us and send me to school when I was ready. Unfortunately, it didn't happen."

That was a surprise. Tessa couldn't imagine him backing out of a promise like that. "Why not?" she asked.

"Because he suddenly dropped off the face of the earth—and all the money dried up. And so, I was left waitressing and petitioning for a special grant." She looked up at Tessa and waved her knife, using it to punctuate her words. "You want my advice? Don't listen to the promises of men, even ones who mean well. Take care of yourself."

Tessa decided then that it was a good time to do homework.

Justin came back late again. Quentin had gone to bed, but Cynthia was still up, watching a movie with Tessa. He had the same worn-out look he had each night and repeated his usual ritual, flouncing back into the armchair with a bottle of beer. Cynthia looked over at him with disapproval.

"Why do you drink that stuff? It's overpriced and doesn't even taste that good. You're such a label whore."

"Nice to see you too," he said. He turned to Tessa. "Let's hear from you. Tell me something that's not going to stress me out. How was your first day?"

Tessa hesitated, not sure how to start. Justin had been regarding her with a lazy smile but suddenly snapped to attention. "What happened?"

"Someone came by today. Someone . . ." She frowned, thinking back to the bizarre encounter outside. "Someone who says he's a friend of yours."

Justin's eyebrows rose. "Yeah? Someone from the university?"

"I don't think so. His name's Geraki."

Justin sat up suddenly. "He was *here*? In our house?"

She cringed a little. That wasn't the reaction she'd expected. "No . . . he talked to me outside. He was waiting there when I got home."

"Were you here?" Justin demanded of Cynthia.

"No," she said. "This is the first I'm hearing about this."

"He said he was glad you're back and that he wanted to see you," Tessa explained. "He also said you were his favorite servitor."

"That's fitting, since he's my favorite megalomaniac," he muttered. His gaze focused back on Tessa. "Did he threaten you? Hurt you?"

Tessa shook her head.

Cynthia regarded her brother warily. "What are you involved in?"

He stayed silent a few moments, but his eyes were troubled. At last, he smiled at Cynthia, but Tessa could still see tension all over him. "Nothing. Just someone I owe money to. Card game gone bad."

"I knew it." Cynthia stood up in disgust. To Tessa, she said, "See? I can't get away from it. I'm going to bed. You should too—it's late."

Tessa hesitated but couldn't fight against Cynthia's logic or stern look. It was only after Tessa was in bed that she remembered that Justin never played cards.

CHAPTER 15

HE'S TALLER

He'd had the video for more than a week, but Leo hadn't been able to crack it in "five minutes," as Justin had assured Cornelia. Leo still swore he'd have the secret of the shadowy figure any day now and finally agreed to go to one of the murder sites to check out the technical and forensic sides of things. Of course, it came with a little complaining about missing his ridiculous day job.

Justin went out the night before the trip and had the good fortune of running into a former student from his days of teaching university religion classes. Aurelia had grown up over the years and was quite taken with the idea of her former professor leading a glamorous servitor's life. She was the first woman he'd slept with since coming home, and the experience was sublime. He supposed, as far as the mechanics went, she was no different from any of the many Panamanian women he'd passed time with in exile, but there was an allure to the idea of finally being in the arms of a Gemman woman again. It had amped up the excitement of it all.

Finally? asked Horatio.

Mae doesn't count, Justin told him.

Justin slinked back to his house the next morning, certain he was there too early for anyone else to be up. He was wrong, of course. Cynthia was in the kitchen, pouring a cup of coffee. Guessing what had happened, she sighed in that angst-ridden way she'd perfected.

"Really? Thank goodness Quentin's still in bed. What am I supposed to tell him when you come home like this?"

Justin kissed her on the cheek. "That I'll have some excellent tips for him in ten years." He reconsidered. The boy was a March, after all. "Eight years."

He headed for his room, unable to keep the spring out of his step.

Mae was there when he got out of the shower. She always claimed she showed up at the house to save them travel time, but he suspected she actually came to get in on Cynthia's ample breakfasts. Today, he was met with the astonishing sight of Mae, Tessa, and Quentin all out in the backyard. Cynthia stood at the glass door, shaking her head in disapproval at what was apparently a tree-climbing lesson. Mae deftly grabbed the lower limb of a large maple tree and effortlessly swung her body up. Quentin and Tessa stared up at her. His face was rapt, hers uncertain. Neither would have had any experience with tree climbing, Justin realized. Tessa's mother would have had a seizure at the thought, and Quentin had grown up in far too urban a setting.

"He'll break his arm," fretted Cynthia. Mae held out her hand to help Quentin up. He took it eagerly. "He can't do the same things she can."

"It's worth the risk for him to actually see a tree." With Quentin successfully up, Mae helped Tessa. "Would you rather have him guessing ages and backstories?"

Cynthia scowled, and they fell silently into their shared memory. With her students safely settled, Mae climbed up into the higher branches of the tree. Joy lit her features, and Justin couldn't take his eyes off her. He'd thought Aurelia might make being around Mae easier, but the girl's face was already fading from his mind the more he watched Mae.

"She's an athlete," Justin observed, more to himself. She effortlessly jumped to the ground from a height that would've broken a bone in anyone else.

His sister gave him a sidelong look. "Really? It took a tree for you to realize that and not the part where she's one of the most lethal soldiers in our country?"

"There's a difference. She's physical for the love of it, not just because she's trained to be." It was a new discovery about her, a puzzle piece in the mystery that was Mae Koskinen. He might adhere to his hands-off stance, but the urge to figure out her inner workings was one of those things he just couldn't ignore.

"You can't sleep with her," Cynthia said abruptly.

He turned to her in surprise. "What?"

"Some women are even out of your league."

If only she knew the hilarious truth, remarked Horatio.

Mae caught sight of her audience and helped Quentin and Tessa down so they could return to the house. Naturally, she hadn't broken a sweat, but there was a very pretty flush to her cheeks and that same delight in her eyes as she stepped inside. "Good morning," she told him, actually sounding sincere. Tree climbing apparently put her in a good enough mood for her to temporarily forget that she hated him. "Hope we didn't take too long."

"No problem," Justin said, more enchanted than he wanted to admit at getting a glimpse of the woman he liked to think of as "Panamanian Mae." "We're right on time. Let's go see what the Nipponese have to share."

He'd scheduled an errand before they had to be at the airport, and he used the trip into the city to tell her about Geraki. She stared at Justin in disbelief when he finished the story.

"Why are we going to the Nipponese grant when there's a religious zealot after you?" she exclaimed. *This* was the kind of danger she yearned for—a threat on his life that he hadn't actually caused. "We should find him!"

"The authorities will. Er, the other authorities. Internal Security's got a warrant out for him. As soon as he trips a checkpoint, they'll bring him in for questioning."

Mae still didn't look convinced. In fact, she looked like she'd have jumped off the train then and there if it was possible. Knowing her, she could probably have done it and survived. "But will they actually be able to hold him?"

"They'll hold him long enough," he said. "Someone like him showing up at a servitor's house is pretty serious . . . but yeah, no one will be able to prove he actually meant any harm."

It was how Geraki worked. He'd been on a watch list for years. Justin knew Geraki was a cult leader, but no one could prove it. It was all instinct and circumstantial evidence, and that just wasn't enough to bust someone as smart as Geraki. Every year, the servitor's office investigated him. And every year, he came up clean. Worse, Justin knew he was one of those people tied to the network of underground religions, just like Callista, the priestess of Artemis. The difference between them was that Geraki wasn't the type to give up useful information.

For his part, Geraki seemed to enjoy the servitor visits—in a smug and condescending sort of way. He was always jovial and cooperative, assuring the servitors they could look into anything they wanted. And all the while, Justin had seen a glint in the other man's eyes that was both knowing and mocking.

Coming to Justin's house was out of character, though. Retribution happened sometimes when religions were shut down, but Geraki had no reason to seek revenge. No one had ever censured him. No one had ever proven he had a following. Nonetheless, Justin didn't want him anywhere near his family.

You should talk to him, said Magnus. *Maybe he has something important to say.*

Justin wasn't convinced. *I know what he has to say. Cryptic nonsense and faked innocence. And all the while, he'll be laughing behind my back.*

Seeing Mae's hardened expression, Justin couldn't help but tease her. "You actually look like you're worried about my safety. And here I didn't think you cared."

"I don't," she said. "I mean—I do, but never mind. I care about religious freaks coming after you."

"Hopefully detaining him'll scare him off, and then we'll get a restraining order to boot." What he didn't mention to Mae was that Geraki was actually the reason they were going on this errand. One thing Tessa had mentioned when quizzed further about her encounter had particularly piqued Justin's interest—Geraki's comment about SCI hiring more servitors. A little poking around had found that was true, but no one could explain the spike in employment.

The car took them to the House of Senators, not far from Hale Square. Despite the early hour, the RUNA's main government facility was already abuzz with activity. Lobbyists and aides hurried up and down the front steps while tourists stopped to take pictures. Guided tours started early, and Justin could hear one guide describing the makeshift building that senators had first used following the Decline. Off to the side, a sign pointed the way to the National Gardens a few blocks away, a vast wonder of horticulture that attracted visitors from all parts of the RUNA and hosted fancy political parties.

And it was here that Mae—who always walked with such confidence and fearlessness—faltered. Justin looked over at her in surprise. The senate overwhelmed a lot of people, but she shouldn't have been one of them. She would've had to see this building countless times, especially since prætorians had a strong presence there.

In fact, three prætorians stood on each side of the building's entrance now, hard faced and watchful as they took in the morning activity. Guns hung openly at their sides, and their black uniforms provided a sharp—almost sinister—contrast against the white marble. People who worked in the building walked past the prætorians easily, but newcomers gave the guards nervous looks and a wide berth.

"Friends of yours?" Justin asked her, still puzzled by her reaction. There was an intensity in her gaze as she stared upward, paired with an emotion he had a little trouble identifying.

Mae recovered herself and gave him a small smile before continuing up the steps. "Just been a while, that's all."

Most of the prætorians gave Justin and Mae the same once-over everyone else received, but a couple looked at her with recognition. She gave them a small nod and kept going through the door, soon slipping back to her cool and collected state.

After they cleared the building's extensive security checkpoint, an aide led them toward Lucian Darling's office. They passed more military scattered throughout, gray uniforms and black uniforms mixed together. Mae took them all in without a word or break in her expression, but when they finally reached the office, two prætorian men stationed nearby shed their stern looks and gave her smiles.

"Koskinen," said one. He had a red pip on his collar. "I guess they let you out after all."

"Look at that neckline," said the other. He turned to his colleague. "I think we should search her. You know, for the sake of national security. Maybe if we're lucky, she'll put up a fight."

The most astonishing thing happened. Mae smiled—a genuine, all-consuming smile. It was Panamanian Mae. That smile shone from her eyes and lit up every part of her. He hadn't thought he'd see that light again, at least not in the face of sexist remarks.

I wonder what you have to do to get a smile like that again, said Magnus wistfully.

Wear a uniform, suggested Horatio. *Or make inappropriate sexual remarks.*

"I heard that's the only way you can get any, Chow," said Mae. "Well, that and ree."

The one called Chow scoffed, but the other prætorian laughed. "Why aren't you here with the rest of us?"

"Forget here," said the other guy. "Come out with us tonight. I hear there's a party."

"There's always a party," said Mae.

The aide cleared her throat. "Um, Dr. March? This is Senator Darling's office." She looked distinctly uncomfortable, probably because she'd never actually heard any of the prætorians here speak—or seen them laugh.

"Right," said Justin, still transfixed by the easy banter between alleged killing machines. "Thank you. We'll take it from here." The aide left, and he hesitated before going into the office. He felt like he'd be depriving Mae of something if he took her away. "You can stay if you want," he said. "You don't even really need to come along. I wouldn't be surprised if there's a wait."

He would've expected dutiful Mae to protest, but instead, she turned that smile on him. "Thank you."

I guess that's what you have to do for the smile, said Horatio. *Be careful or she might start liking you again.*

When he'd told her there'd be a wait, Justin had mostly said it to justify his offer. He hadn't actually expected to be stuck in the reception area for a half hour. Mae stuck her head in three times, anxious about being away, and he waved her off each time. The receptionist responded haughtily when Justin reminded him they had an appointment.

"The senator is very busy. Often his meetings run over."

Justin wondered if that was true or if Lucian had simply fallen asleep in his office. In the old days, that wouldn't have been out of character.

But when the door finally opened, two official-looking women stepped out and shook hands with Lucian, gushing gratitude for his time.

"The senator will see you now," said the receptionist.

"There's a woman with me," Justin told him. "Show her in when she gets back."

"Of course there's a woman with you," said Lucian. "There always is." He shook Justin's hand and beckoned him inside.

Once the door was shut, Lucian sat on the edge of his desk and shook his head. "Unbelievable. When I saw your name on my schedule, I thought it was a joke."

Justin took a few moments to assess his old friend and roommate. He looked just as he had on TV, smiling and charming, with that new tawny hair color that the saleswoman had claimed was "hot."

"That's funny, because I thought the same thing when I saw you running for consul." Justin walked over to a bottle of scotch sitting near the window. At least some things never changed. "May I?"

"Knock yourself out." Justin could feel Lucian's eyes weighing him. "The election's old news, but then, I hear you've been away."

Justin poured a glass. "Yeah? How'd you'd hear that? I mean, aside from me not returning all the calls I know you must've made to me these last four years."

"I did a little investigating when I saw your name come up. Well, my assistant did." Some of Lucian's swagger faded. "What the hell did you do? People don't get exiled. And they certainly don't come back from it."

It was a relief to know that Lucian's access didn't stretch that far, but Justin wasn't surprised. The majority of Internal Security didn't even know his full background.

"It's not really that interesting of a story," Justin said. "Especially compared to how a guy who was once on the committee that regulated pets riding on public transportation became a candidate for consul."

Lucian took the hint and smiled again. "You don't think I care about our country? And its pets?"

"I think you've always been the type to take the easy way out. You always tried to get by under the radar."

"Yeah, well, one day, I made myself a target." Lucian's brown eyes narrowed as he drifted into some memory. "A comment at a lunch about how it was time to get rid of the last of the mandates. It was supposed to be off the record—but wasn't. The next thing I knew, Lucian Darling was the champion of those seeking genetic freedom. My party rode that popularity and convinced me it was an opportunity we couldn't miss." He spread out his hands. "And so here I am, one of the youngest consular candidates in history."

"Having to own your words."

"It's not that bad. I really do believe in what I do, you know." He nodded toward Justin's scotch. "What do you think?"

"Excellent. Of course, I've been in the provinces, so my bar's still pretty low these days."

Lucian laughed. "I heard that too. You know who gave it to me? Religious-freedom lobbyists."

Wow. Lucian really was involved with heavy platforms now. College days and dorm-room parties seemed like centuries ago.

"You're trying to break open everything. Genes and religion. It really is a new age."

"I never said I supported them." Justin noticed Lucian also didn't say he opposed them either. "You worried you'll be out of a job?"

"I'll just run for public office. I hear it's not that hard."

That brought another smile from Lucian, and Justin wondered if it was the one Tessa said they shared. "Don't worry, I have plenty of antireligious ones knocking at my door—and they've got a lot more money. Anyway, to what do I owe the pleasure of your company? You never paid me casual visits before you left."

"I have a favor to ask."

"The last time you asked for a favor, my girlfriend ended up bent over your desk." Lucian poured himself a glass.

Justin sighed. "When are you going to get over that? She was your *ex*-girlfriend, and she really was helping me with my essay."

"Yeah? What exactly was it on?"

Lucian's receptionist suddenly opened the door and stepped aside so that Mae could enter. "Sorry," Mae told Justin. "I didn't realize you'd gone in."

She'd become serious again, back to her professional mode, but he could still see a little of that light in her face. Lucian saw it too. He swiftly set down the scotch and strode over to her, his gallant smile turned all the way up.

"Senator," she said, taking his hand. "It's an honor to meet you."

"You can call me Lucian. We aren't big on formalities around here." Lucian kept holding her hand. "And I can call you . . . ?"

"Mae." She was smiling too, but thankfully, it was with amusement and not that earlier joy.

"*Prætorian* Mae Koskinen," said Justin.

He hoped that would make Lucian back off, but mostly it seemed to intrigue him even more.

"Are you?" Lucian looked her over like he was doing some official assessment of her physical strength, but Justin suspected he was actually checking out the way her chest looked under her clinging georgette blouse. "I can't believe I've never seen you around here."

Keep him away from her, said Magnus, more heatedly than Justin was used to.

I know you've still got high hopes for me and her, said Justin, *but come on. He's not her type.*

Which type would that be? asked Horatio. *The tall, good-looking, powerful, and charming type? He could interfere with your chances.*

I have all of those things going for me, retorted Justin. *Not that I want a chance.*

He's taller, said Horatio.

Surprisingly, Magnus actually sounded frustrated with both Justin and his fellow raven. *It's more than that! The goddess who wants her still hasn't made an official claim. That makes Mae vulnerable to others.*

Magnus had been fairly coherent since their return to the RUNA, so Justin supposed it had only been a matter of time before the raven returned to his old ways. No matter the setting or attire, "vulnerable" was a word Justin had never applied to Mae.

"She's not stationed here," said Justin. He paused dramatically. "She's assigned to me."

This was enough to make Lucian drag his eyes from Mae. He frowned. "What does that mean?"

"Well, you know how dangerous and harrowing my job is, what with the constant assaults on my life and unstable dissidents I face."

Mae gave Justin an incredulous look.

"So, SCI decided to up my protection since I'm so important." Feeling more in control again, Justin poured another glass of scotch. "Mae's my bodyguard. We're off together to the Nipponese grant. She goes with me everywhere. *Everywhere.*"

She picked up on the subtext and fixed him with a chilly look. "That's a bit of an exaggeration."

"He exaggerates about a lot of things to a lot of women," said Lucian. He turned to Justin. "So what's this favor?"

Putting Lucian in his place was an activity Justin never tired of, but the clock was ticking, and he did actually have serious business to discuss. "SCI's been doing a lot of hiring. The number of servitors has shot up in the last six months."

"Probably at the cost of some other worthy government program," said Lucian. "Is this you being worried about your job again? That they might find someone better and cheaper?"

"No, I want to know what the increase is for. We've had things locked down for years. If anything, the numbers should be decreasing."

Lucian decided to let the banter go as well. "You could look in your own backyard for that. Someone at SCI should know."

"I'm sure someone does, but they aren't telling me." The best he'd received was a lot of meaningless "surplus budget" and "extra openings" mumbling—but nothing concrete. Cornelia had blown him off, and he didn't have the access or good graces to badger anyone higher than her. "Someone in Internal Security—or more importantly, a senator with friends there—might be willing to tell a promising young senator who's running for consul. It'd be a great way to curry favor."

"I see." Lucian's lips quirked. "It'd be a weird request, though."

Inspiration struck Justin. "Would it? You've got religious-freedom lobbyists sending you gifts. Inquiring about the servitor's office would be very reasonable."

"You think of everything, don't you?" Lucian didn't make it sound like a compliment. "Did you think of a clever reason for why I should do it for you?"

"Because we're friends. And maybe you'll need a good servitor on your side if those lobbyists turn on you. Or, hell, just do it for old times' sake."

"You mean my girlfriend?"

"Ex," Justin reminded him.

"Fine. For old times' sake." Lucian turned to Mae, who had been watching the exchange with a mix of astonishment and fascination. "But now I have a favor to ask. I have a fund-raising party in a couple of weeks. I don't suppose you'd want to go with me? If you can tear yourself away from Justin, that is."

It apparently was a day of firsts with Mae. It had started with that radiant smile and had now moved on to her becoming flustered. That discomfiture lasted only a few moments, though. She rewarded Lucian with a polite and—Justin was certain—ever-so-slightly superior smile. That was castal upbringing. Debutantes were taught to eat men alive.

"That's very flattering," she said. "But I don't think my commitments will allow it."

Lucian was unfazed. "Well, check on them, and if they change, just let me know. I don't plan on going with anyone else. They'd just be a disappointment now."

Do something about this, snapped Magnus.

"Mae's great at parties," said Justin. He gave Lucian a pointed look. "She's a Nordic patrician, though I'm sure you already noticed that."

Lucian's eyes said he understood what Justin wasn't explicitly saying. No matter how high Lucian's star was right now, no matter how much class tension had eased in recent years . . . any hint of romance with a patrician would be political suicide. Lucian's fellow senators were the ones who cast the votes, and their patrician constituents would raise holy hell at the thought of a plebeian defiling some pure patrician woman—especially if her score came out.

Lucian was too noble to fully backpedal, though his pitch lightened. "Well, just let me know."

Mae didn't speak to Justin again until they were en route to the airport, free of flirting senators and distracting prætorians. "What," she said, "was that all about?"

"It was me tapping inexplicable political connections to get answers that my department won't give me."

She shot him a sidelong glare. "You know what I mean. The presumption back there was off the charts."

"I know," he said, nodding solemnly. "Lucian doesn't know his limits sometimes."

"Not him! You, with all your 'she goes with me everywhere' insinuations."

"It's the truth, isn't it? And how was that worse than his trying to trade my favor for a date with you? I defended your honor, you know. He was objectifying you."

"He was just asking me out." Mae's face turned speculative. "He seems like a nice guy."

"You aren't . . . you aren't seriously thinking about that, are you? And what happened to you not lowering yourself to associate with plebeians? Or do you make an exception for glamorous and powerful men?" The thought of her in Lucian's arms, her face flushed with the afterglow, made Justin feel ill. Over and over, he told himself he couldn't have her, but he didn't want anyone else to either.

She stared out the car's window as it pulled up to the airport's front entrance. "It's my business if I do."

"You don't want anything to do with a guy like that. It's his job to say things to lure people in."

Mae returned her gaze to him. "Tell me exactly how he's any different from you. Aside from the fact that when he says he holds a post in the government, he's actually telling the truth."

Yes, said Horatio. *Please, go ahead and tell us.*

A lot of answers came to Justin's mind, but "I'm more fun at parties" might not have helped his case after the overdose in Windsor. Instead, he simply said, "I had that smile first."

That was apparently the wrong answer, because all Mae said before getting out of the car was, "Point proven."

CHAPTER 16

THE PRINCIPLE AND STUFF

Leo was waiting at their gate. He'd caught an earlier flight up from Portland so that they could all travel together, though he still treated Mae in a standoffish way. Once they were en route in the air, Justin asked him about the video.

"Anything?"

Leo leaned back in his seat and frowned. "No. I've run all the standard tests and a few I made up." His cold attitude vanished as the thrill of his task seized him. "I know some film people I'm going to check with. Don't worry—I'm not going to actually let them see it. Just get some info based on the camera type. This thing'll be cracked. It's just a question of when."

"Maybe you'll have better luck at the house," said Justin. "Figure out how someone got into a room locked from the inside." He grinned. "Aside from turning into smoke and shadows, of course."

Leo nodded. "That shouldn't be a mystery—as long as the place hasn't been altered. The last grant you were at muddled all their data."

"That wasn't my fault," Justin said. "That was their own sloppy police work long before we got there."

Silence fell after that. Justin turned his attention to a reader that held background information on the Nipponese victim. Mae shouldn't have cared, but she felt a need to lighten things between Leo and her. If they were going to be working together, she didn't want him afraid of her.

"I never caught how long you've been married," she told

Leo. She didn't mention Justin's excessive commentary on Leo's rustic living conditions or choice in spouse.

Leo gave her a wary look. "Two years."

She smiled back. Maybe hers wasn't as captivating as Justin's, but she'd been grilled in how to be pleasant and likeable. Good castal girls learned how to excel as hostesses. "Wine making must be an interesting job."

"It's a time-consuming job," said Leo curtly.

He was breaking the rules of small talk and not giving her much to go on. "I was down there once before, closer to the coast than your place. We spent most of our time in a cottage out at the shore but went wine tasting a few times. It's beautiful there."

She didn't know what had made her bring that story up. Just an instinctive need to draw Leo out, she supposed. It wasn't a trip she'd thought of in a while, but in giving voice to it, a jumble of memories suddenly flooded her. The way the ocean had smelled crashing on the shore. The never-ending cacophony of circling seagulls. The taste of Pinot Gris that they'd purchased from a vintner selling bottles out of his garage. The sun on her face. The feel of the sheets on her bare skin as they spent long hours in bed.

Leo again made little response, and Mae gave her last, best effort. "How did you guys meet?"

To her astonishment, Leo launched into an extensive account. "I met him at Li Vale. It's a bar in Vancouver. There's a list to get in, and you almost always see celebrities there. I was supposed to meet a friend there one night, but she was running late. So, I just ordered drinks at the bar. When my third one came, I realized I'd left my ego at home. You can imagine how embarrassing that was at a place like that. All I could do was hope my friend would show up soon and pay my bill. Suddenly, Dom came and sat beside me and told the bartender he'd cover me. I tried to protest and tell him my friend would come, but he wouldn't listen. I thanked him over and over and told him I'd get in touch later and pay him back. He told me he'd rather have me pay him back by buying him dinner the next night. I agreed, and after that . . . we were inseparable."

Mae didn't have to fake her next smile. "That's a great story."

Leo nodded and switched back to stiff mode. He stood up and moved into the aisle. "Be right back." After waiting for a flight attendant to squeeze past him, he turned toward the restroom.

Justin's eyes were still on his reader. "Who was he?"

"Who was who?" Mae didn't know whether he meant Leo or Dominic.

"The love interest you went to the beach with. Some Viking nine?"

"What makes you think he was a love interest?"

"Because friends don't rent romantic cottages on the water together."

"I never said it was romantic."

"Your voice did." He finally looked up. "Everything about you softened. . . ." His eyes lingered on her for a few seconds, and then he went back to his reading. "It's fine. You can keep your sordid tales and ex-lovers to yourself. I mean, well, you can try to. You tell stories without even knowing it."

Mae knew she shouldn't engage him. If she'd learned anything, it was that Justin loved attention. Ignoring him was probably the worst punishment she could dole out. But, as so often happened, he'd managed to reach into her in a way that made it impossible not to respond.

"Why do you think he's an ex? How do you know we're not still together?" she demanded.

"Because you would've said 'my boyfriend and I' when you were talking. You just said 'we.' And although I wouldn't put cheating past plenty of people, you don't strike me as one of them. You wouldn't have sought out a sensational night of sex in Panama if you were involved with someone."

"You have a real cut-and-dried way of analyzing relationships," she said. If he used half as much energy on solving the case as he did on her, then he'd have figured out the murders already. "You probably don't think Leo's story was romantic at all."

He scoffed. "Of course not. It was a piece of bullshit. He made it up."

Mae was floored. "Why would you say that?"

"Because it was too well rehearsed. Couldn't you tell? There was no spontaneity whatsoever. No emotion. He's told that story a hundred times, like he's reading from notecards. Besides, think about Dominic . . . aka Mr. 'I don't like cities.' Can you picture him in Vancouver, let alone Li Vale? That's a place Leo would go, and he's just incorporated it into this fairy tale."

She didn't know what to say to that right away. Leo's story had certainly sounded thorough, but she never would've guessed that it was because he'd made it up. The circumstances he'd described hadn't sounded that contrived either. People certainly met under weirder ones. Her own past was proof enough.

"Why would Leo make something like that up?" she finally asked. Justin was so frustrating, but the inner workings of his clever mind were fascinating.

"That's the question, isn't it?" Justin adopted an overly mysterious voice. "Maybe it's a secret. Or maybe the real story's too boring. It could've just been matchmaking on the stream. Who can say?"

"Are you going to ask him?"

"Nah. I'll find out sooner or later without even trying."

So they were back to the arrogance and self-assuredness. She was starting to think she'd imagined those brief moments of sincerity in the hospital. At least his interest in Leo had distracted Justin from his speculation on her own romantic past. Mae kept it too well guarded in her heart, and there was no way she'd put up with Justin's analyzing that volatile roller coaster of a relationship. Leo's story—true or not—was tame compared to the drama-filled epic of how she and Porfirio had met.

A lot of that night's memories were a blur. Other things stood out in perfect, crystalline clarity. But then, that was how ree worked. As one of the few intoxicating substances the implant couldn't metabolize quickly, its effects surged inconsistently throughout the prætorian body.

Cohorts on city duty sometimes pooled their resources to throw large private parties, since drunken prætorian antics in public didn't always go over so well. The military hadn't gone out of its way to fix the ree loophole, but everyone knew too much abuse might eventually draw the research department's eye. The Maize cohort was responsible for the party in question that night, and it had done its best to make the gathering a showstopper, going so far as to rent out a hall with a live band and bartender. There were about a hundred prætorians there, pretty much anyone who was within a day's travel of Vancouver.

Mae spent most of her night at a round corner table with Val and several other prætorians. Val and an Azure named Albright had just returned from South America and brought back a card game they swore was the Most Fun Ever. Unfortunately, there were a couple of problems. It was a complicated game in and of itself, and neither of them could remember all the rules. Compounded with everyone at the table's being drunk, the whole thing was kind of a mess. Mae didn't really mind, though. She was afloat on a ree buzz and able to roll with just about anything— or so she'd thought.

"That's trump," Albright told Mae as she started to play a card. He'd been particularly solicitous in tutoring her. "Save it for the next round."

Val's brow furrowed in thought. "No, hearts are trump."

"I thought it was spades?" asked some Crimson across the table.

"Hearts," Val insisted.

Albright was an extremely easygoing guy and didn't have a problem with the switch. He leaned toward Mae, putting an arm around the back of her chair as he looked at her hand. "That one, then," he said, pointing.

Mae, who was pretty sure everyone was wrong and that diamonds were trump, played the card without protest. Normally, she would've chafed at some guy attempting to take an instructive role toward her, but Albright did it in such a friendly and laid-back way that she didn't find it threatening or overbearing. She also discovered she was liking him more and more as the night went on. Mild-mannered prætorian men were rare. Usually, they were all brash and outgoing, and she wondered if maybe this particular personality type might be a sound choice to invest in.

"That's bullshit! I know someone who could clean the floor with you!"

Mae and Val both looked up at the same time as a loud, familiar voice carried over to them from several tables away. Even in a noisy, crowded room, the two women were always tuned in to Dag. His back was to them as he stood near a table of what looked like Violets and Indigos. Without uniforms, it was hard to remember. Regardless, Dag was clearly worked up about something as he gestured wildly with a sloshing ree cocktail and spoke to someone Mae couldn't see.

Val shook her head ruefully but didn't look particularly concerned. When you mixed volatile soldiers with intoxication, conflict was inevitable. "I leave him alone for five minutes and look what happens. What are you doing?" That was to Albright.

"You just said hearts were trump," he reminded her patiently. He was the least drunk of all of them, which might have played a role in his also being one of the least obnoxious men in the room right then.

Mae took a sip of her own drink, enjoying the heady rush it brought. She had recently returned from a trip of her own, in the Asian provinces, as backup to the EA. After some of the sights there, she was grateful for this reprieve. "He's right, Val."

Val looked skeptical and gave Mae a knowing look. "Of *course* you'd agree with him."

Dag's voice carried over to them again. "Fifty bucks says she can kick your ass."

This brought cheers and chatter from those seated at the table, and suddenly, half of them were on their feet. More astonishing still, Dag was leading the entourage over to Mae's table. He staggered to a halt and pointed directly at her.

"She's the one. She'll do it."

Mae nearly looked behind her but then remembered she was sitting against a wall. Her whole table came to a standstill. "What are you talking about?"

A man pushed his way through the others and stopped beside Dag. Mae felt her breath catch. He was one of the most beautiful men she'd ever seen, and she wasn't the type who usually looked first and asked questions later. He had a physique outstanding even among prætorians and wore a simple blue T-shirt that did an exquisite job of displaying all those well-sculpted muscles. His face was as perfectly chiseled as the rest of him, with a strong chin and high cheekbones complemented by piercing eyes that were so dark, they nearly looked black. His hair was black too, thick and wavy, pulled back into a ponytail that grazed his shoulder blades. It was the kind of hair women involuntarily ran their hands through; she felt her own twitch.

At first, the tanned skin and dark hair made her think he was plebeian, but then she noted his features were too European. There was a stamp to him that hinted of a Mediterranean caste, which was surprising. She could probably have counted the number of prætorian castals on one hand, and like her, he possessed no obvious signs of Cain. Then again, any castal in the military would have to be in good health.

Those dark eyes looked her over in a way that suddenly made her feel as though he'd just taken off her clothes, and there was an arrogance and smugness there that confirmed his castal background nearly as much as his appearance. She was familiar with that superior attitude, having been bred with it as well. A satisfied smile curled his lips.

"Her? Sure. No problem. It'd be my pleasure."

The cockiness snapped Mae back to attention, and she quickly hid her unwanted attraction with a well-practiced expression of indifference. She glanced at Dag, refusing to give the other guy any more of her attention. "What have you done?" she asked in as bored a voice as she could manage.

"This guy." Dag pointed at his companion dramatically, just to make sure there was no misunderstanding. "He says he was some kind of *canne* prodigy back in his caste. And I was like, 'Whatever, there's only one castal *canne* prodigy around here.' "

Mae's cool mask faltered as she jerked her gaze back to the other guy. "You play *canne*?"

"Other people play it, darling," he told her, still with that damnably self-assured smile. "I live it."

Dag moved in between Val and another Scarlet so that he could lean across the table toward Mae. "Finn, you have to take this asshole out. I've got money riding on you."

"Me too," a couple of people shouted beyond him.

Mae gave Dag an incredulous look. "You signed me up for something without asking me?"

"I didn't think I had to ask," he said. "I thought you'd want to do it. You know, as a matter of principle. And stuff."

A Silver whom Mae knew came up and nudged the black-haired man. "Porfirio, why are you harassing her? Shouldn't you castals stick together? And what the hell is *canne* anyway?"

"A sublime sport for those who are both athletes and artists," declared Porfirio. His gaze fell back on Mae. "A charming ladies' pastime for others."

She could only assume it was the ree that caused what happened next. She shot to her feet. " 'Pastime'? I was nearly professional!"

Porfirio didn't look impressed at all. "Nearly," he repeated. "But you weren't. What went wrong? Not good enough? Baltic boyfriend wouldn't let you?"

Mae was too outraged to correct him. Dag was quicker. "She didn't do it because she joined up with us, dumbass."

"All right, all right," said Porfirio, giving her a lazy, almost predatory smile. "There's only one way to settle this. You and me. On the mat. Then we'll see the difference between a profession and a pastime."

Excitement raced through her body at the prospect, and her implant kicked to life, trying desperately to shake off the ree's intoxication as it sensed endorphins and hormones indicative of some confrontation. "Name the time and place. I'll be there."

Porfirio stepped toward her. "Why wait? We're doing this now."

"Now?" she repeated, but her voice faded among the cheers of the assembled prætorians. Looking up, she realized almost every prætorian in the place had gathered around them now, and they were all riled up for a match, many of them already placing wagers on Mae and her opponent. "There's no room."

"Trying to back out?" Porfirio pitched his voice for her ears alone. "Afraid to go one-on-one with me?" Locking gazes with him, she felt her heart rate pick up. The implant still struggled, unsure whether there was a legitimate threat or not. *That makes two of us,* Mae thought.

"You wish," she hissed. "I just don't want you cheating."

"We have a deposit on the place," muttered a nearby Maize.

"And where are you going to get canes?" demanded Mae.

Porfirio glanced over at an Indigo woman standing near him. "Connie, go see what you can dig up. You're good at this stuff." She nodded and scurried off, which somehow annoyed Mae further. Was that typical of his dealings with women? A quick command and they jumped? Maybe that was why he was so confident in his abilities against her.

Wagers flew fast and furious around them. Porfirio listened with amusement as he carefully retied the ponytail at the base of his neck. When he finished, he smoothed a few wayward hairs into place and then glanced at Mae. "What do you say? Want to put some money on the line? We can keep it low, if you want. I don't want you to have to write home for a loan."

"I don't want your money," she said. She paused for effect. "I want your hair."

A few Indigos nearby fell into awed silence at her words, confirming what she'd suspected. Porfirio was a man in love with his hair. No one grew and touched his hair like that if he wasn't completely obsessed with it. And, if he was like her, he'd probably been raised to flaunt his Cain-free features.

He smiled at her, like this was just some kind of funny joke he hadn't quite caught the punch line on. "My hair?"

"Sure. If I win, I want you to cut it." Mae helpfully mimicked using scissors. "I want to keep it on my dresser."

More people—especially those who knew him—quieted to listen eagerly. Porfirio's smile went away. "I am *not* cutting my hair."

"Of course you aren't. Because you're going to win, right?" Mae felt like she was getting control of this situation now and had taken his measure. She raised her voice, playing to the crowd. "I mean, there's no real risk—unless you're afraid."

This got catcalls and cheers, and then everyone waited in anticipation for his response. After several tense moments, he relaxed, and the old arrogance returned. "Fine. If that's the wager you want, so be it. Like you said—makes no difference to me. But what do I get when I win?"

Mae smiled at the choice of "when" over "if." "Pick," she told him. "You want me to cut my hair?"

He looked her over with as much intensity as he had in his initial assessment of her, a brazen look that had an almost tangible quality. Only this time, not sitting behind the table, she had more to show. Some semi-reasonable voice inside her suggested signing on for a fight in a dress and heels was, perhaps, not the wisest choice.

"That would be a shame," Porfirio said mildly. "Especially since I plan on seeing it fanned across my sheets. When I win, I want *you*. That's my wager. You come home with me."

There was a collective breath. This was high drama. The prætorians loved it.

"Done," said Mae without hesitation. She shook his hand as the others whooped, and she tried not to imagine how those strong hands would feel on her body.

Porfirio's lackey surfaced soon thereafter and had amazingly turned up two sticks, which, although certainly not regulation, weren't that far off from what *canne* players used. A space was cleared on the far side of the room, despite some of the Maize prætorians' unease that their venue was about to get trashed. Mae realized then that they actually had no clue what was about to go down. Porfirio strode boldly toward the makeshift arena's center. Mae followed, and Val fell into step with her.

"You don't have to do this."

Mae scoffed. "Of course I do. Can you imagine their reaction if I bailed? Besides, it's like Dag said. It's the principle of the matter. And stuff."

"Uh-huh." Val's eyes fell on Porfirio's powerful body walking ahead of them. "If I were you, I think I might throw it."

"Never," said Mae fiercely. "I'm going to send him crawling back to his cohort."

Val glanced back and gave her a searching look. "So help me, you're serious. Goddamn it, Finn. Sometimes I don't know what to do with you."

"I do," said Porfirio, catching that last bit. "Let's do this."

Mae kicked off her shoes and took up a position opposite him, both of them striking starting poses. Val subbed in as a ref, beginning the match, and then scurried out of the way as it started. Mae had mostly sobered up by then, and the implant was now fully on board as she engaged in the fight. Its positive feedback system, sensing her body producing neurotransmitters, encouraged it to create even more. Honestly, she didn't even believe she needed the implant to beat him. She'd meant what she said: She'd nearly played professionally. She was good. Very good. And she could tell within the first few minutes that that took him by surprise.

The prætorians also seemed surprised. Most had no clue what *canne de combat* was. All they'd known was that some sort of competition would go down and that floor space was needed, leading most to believe it would involve people and objects being thrown around. In reality, it was far more controlled. *Canne* resembled fencing and involved a lot of the same precision and alertness. Every part of Mae had to be on guard to anticipate what Porfirio would do, both to dodge and to plan her attacks. She became in tune with the way he breathed and the way muscles flexed in that remarkable body. They had agreed on Mae's favorite variant, one that allowed a number of fairly acrobatic maneuvers. Porfirio made a small grunt of approval when she pulled off a particularly graceful backflip that eluded his reach.

"You're flexible—I'll give you that," he said, his eyes watching her with just as much scrutiny. "That'll be to my advantage later, I suppose."

"Yeah?" She tried to get inside his guard, but he was too fast. "Then why haven't you landed a hit on me yet?"

"I don't like to rush things, as you'll soon find out."

Mae made no response as she narrowed her world back into the fight. Exhilaration filled her. She loved this bizarre, antiquated sport with all of her heart, and even though she knew the military had led her to a nobler calling, there was still a part of her that ached with the realization that if not for her mother's strong will, Mae could have very well devoted her life to it. Porfirio had been right that it was an art. She threw herself into this match, and despite his continuing commentary, she loved that she finally had someone to play against who was such an even match. She had him on speed, hands down. That and agility were both skills she'd honed over the years, skills she'd had to develop against male opponents who almost always outweighed her. Porfirio still moved admirably fast, but it was his strength that took its toll on her whenever their canes slammed together. It was magnificent.

The observing prætorians, however, were less enchanted. After the initial cheering and shouts of encouragement, their enthusiasm had dimmed when no real action or hitting occurred. Mae was vaguely aware of shouts of "Get on with it!" and then eventually, no commentary at all. Porfirio noticed as well.

"We didn't set any round limits. We should've had someone timing this," he said. A faint sheen of sweat could be seen on his forehead.

He was right about the time. Matches were usually only a couple of minutes long at most. Neither of them had thought about that when starting. They'd just wanted to get right to it. She had no idea how much time had passed and didn't care.

"What's the matter?" she asked. "Maybe you've got trouble going a long time after all."

"Darling, I can go as long as—shit!"

Mae's stick made contact with his abdomen. Apparently, all it took was one dig about his sexual prowess to throw him off. Typical. She expected some kind of reaction from the crowd but heard nothing. That was when she noticed something that brought her to a stop.

"What's wrong?" he asked, still in his attack stance but not advancing.

"They're gone," she said in disbelief.

He looked at where she nodded, his face mirroring her astonishment. The prætorians, bored, had all gone back to their drinking and bantering on the other side of the room. If he really did share a similar background in *canne*, Mae suspected that he too was used to audiences composed of enthralled fans who could appreciate the subtleties of the sport. Porfirio's lips curled in contempt.

"Children. All of them. Oh, well." And with speed that Mae

didn't anticipate, Porfirio lunged forward and tapped her on the calf—twice. "Match." He tossed his stick onto the floor.

"Hey," she exclaimed. "That's not fair at—ahh!"

He picked her up bodily and literally threw her over his shoulder. "I had more points. Ergo, I win. Let's go home."

She pounded on his back as he effortlessly carried her out of the hall like some sort of war prize. Both knew she was fully capable of freeing herself, or at least doing serious damage—which would've probably restored their audience—but she held back and contented herself with verbal protests and Finnish insults. Once they were outside in the misty night, she finally broke his hold and pushed herself away, settling onto her own two feet.

"You did *not* win," she told him vehemently, fists clenched at her sides. "We didn't establish round lengths or ever discuss—"

Porfirio pulled her to him, his hand sliding up the back of her neck and tangling up in her hair. She felt his lips crush hers in a kiss of victory, making liquid fire ooze through her body. His mouth searched hers, hungry and demanding, and she responded in kind, her body straining toward his, wanting to feel those muscles against hers, those hands on her skin. When he at last pulled back, leaving them both breathless, he asked, "Look, are we going to do this the hard way or the easy way?"

Mae swallowed, still flushed and dizzy from the kiss as adrenaline and endorphins spiked within her. "I guess it depends on what you mean by 'hard.' "

Which was how she ended up in his bed after all—without being forcefully carried there. It was the kind of aggressive, backbreaking sex that prætorians thrived on, and as she stretched out in the tangle of sheets afterward, she experienced a rare moment of exhaustion. It wouldn't last, and if a squad of assassins suddenly burst through the bedroom door, her implant would have helped her muscles and heart get the energy they needed to contend with danger. But even prætorians needed to rest sometimes, and it was a nice feeling to lie there with all of her muscles pleasantly worn-out. It would've been better still to sleep. Post-sex was one of the few times she missed sleep. It seemed like a natural conclusion to the act of passion, being able to drift off in a lover's arms.

There was no sleep for either of them, though Mae stayed in bed while he showered. When he returned, he tossed something on the bed that made her sit up in alarm. For half a second, she thought he'd thrown some animal at her. Then she recognized his ponytail.

"Your hair," she said in amazement, peering up at him. He looked as though he'd simply lopped it off in one cut. The ends of his remaining hair were uneven, but he was still dazzling to behold. "You didn't have to do that. Or you should've at least gotten it done properly."

He waved it off. "A deal's a deal. I didn't win. Well, not in *canne*. You want to keep it as a trophy?"

She wrinkled her nose. "That's actually pretty creepy. I was just joking about keeping it on my dresser."

"Good to know." To her amazement, he unceremoniously threw the hair away and then sat back down beside her in bed. "But now you don't have anything to remember me by."

"Do I need something?" She drew him toward her and felt her pulse start to quicken again. "You aren't going to return my calls?"

He smiled and ran his lips along her neck. "*Were* you going to call?"

"Well . . ." She allowed him to ease her back down on the bed. "I might need another *canne* warm-up. You know, to keep me in practice before a real match."

"Well, then, for that, you can call me anytime."

CHAPTER 17

THE MOST DANGEROUS MAN IN THE REPUBLIC

The Nipponese were pleasantly deferential when Justin and his entourage showed up. Reactions to servitor visits varied widely, and he and Mae had received lukewarm ones at the previous three grants they'd visited. A lot of castals resented federal interference, even if it was for their own good. Servitors especially made them nervous, because if a servitor found a dangerous religious group on the grant, he or she could pretty much call in a military invasion. None of them wanted that. The relationship between the Gemman government and "the patriarchies," as they called themselves, was tenuous enough. The fledgling RUNA, fearing the kind of separatism and resistance to authority that had sparked Mephistopheles's creation, had had to be careful in allowing its wealthy supporters the ethnic solidarity they'd requested. Patricians had been exempted from the mandates, at their own risk of Mephistopheles and Cain, and given their own land—with very strict regulations.

The entrance to the Nipponese land grant resembled that of all the other grants: a gated road with a checkpoint and a sign welcoming others in both English and the caste's native language. The guards were lightly armed, per the agreement with the government. The RUNA's flag was the only ornamentation since no unique castal symbol was allowed either.

Justin's contact inside was an older police officer who went by his Japanese name: Hiroshi. He didn't fall all over himself the way the gate security had, but it was clear he was floored at the idea of hosting a servitor and prætorian in his jurisdiction.

"The victim's wife moved out," he told them when they reached the house in which the murder had occurred. "But nothing has been changed whatsoever in the building. We got extensive pictures and documentation at the time, and I verified this morning that everything is the same." He hesitated. "I hope that's all right."

"That's great," said Justin, earning a relieved smile.

Leo, though pleased at having uncontaminated evidence, was less thrilled at the house's size. "It's huge. This is going to take forever."

To be fair, the house *was* enormous, especially for two people. The architecture was in keeping with common Gemman luxury homes, though the pointed roof and a few other flourishes hearkened back to the caste's Japanese roots. The inside told a similar tale. Painted screens and clean lines paired with trendy lush furniture and media screens. Here was a family in possession of stereotypical castal wealth.

Leo immediately began to take apart the house's main security panel. It monitored every door and window in the house, and like the other sites, initial investigation of the system's memory had shown no sign of entry anywhere. Video surveillance had been disabled, providing the only clue (aside from the dead body) that someone had been inside.

"Remind you of the old Koskinen estate?" Justin asked Mae as they strolled through the house.

"Our koi pond was bigger," she said. She gazed around and walked over to an ornamental tea set. Her features were luminous in the light pouring through the window. He was dying to know more about the ex-boyfriend she'd hinted at on the plane and needed to figure out the best strategy for getting information without receiving bodily harm in the process. The relationships people formed—or didn't form—spoke legions about them, and he was a little surprised that someone who feared others seeing her emotions during sex had managed any kind of long-term relationship.

She didn't say it was long term, said Horatio.

She didn't have to. It was in the way she spoke. When he received no response, Justin couldn't help but add, *I guess I can pick up on some things that you guys can't.*

Of course you can, said Magnus. *Otherwise we wouldn't need you.*

"Dr. March?" Hiroshi appeared with a petite young woman. "This is Mrs. Hata, the victim's wife."

Mrs. Hata looked drawn and nervous, but Justin read it more as a reaction to his presence rather than a sign of any culpability. Police investigations had confirmed her alibi, and she didn't look like she would have had the strength to drive the dagger into her husband's heart anyway. He gave her a friendly smile, hoping to put her at ease.

"It's a pleasure to meet you," he said, shaking hands. "I'm so sorry for your loss."

"I don't understand what's going on," she said. "I've already talked to the police over and over."

"I know. And I'm sorry to keep putting you through this, but we just have a few more questions." He motioned to the dining room. "Can we talk in here? I'll keep it brief."

She sat down opposite him at the table, clasping her hands in front of her. Her features showed the phenotype so prized by her caste: dark hair, high cheekbones, golden skin, and almond-shaped brown eyes. Long, thick lashes crowned her narrow eyelids, giving her an added touch of allure, even if the lashes were false. She wore her hair in a smart haircut that went to her chin, meaning she most likely had a touch of Cain. Genetically pure castal woman tended to show off their undamaged hair by wearing it long, like Mae did. As the light caught Mrs. Hata's hair, he saw an almost lacquerlike sheen, verifying his suspicions. Heavy gloss treatments were a common way to cover the thin and frail hair Cain so often caused. When she brushed that hair aside, she inadvertently revealed a bit of scarring near her ears. There were certain kinds of expensive face-lifts that could smooth out the pockmarked skin of Cain, but they always left slight signs at the periphery. Mrs. Hata displayed most of Cain's detrimental effects and had no children either. He wouldn't have been surprised if she had asthma too.

Justin was ready to reel her in with his charm and pleasantries, but a second glance at her stricken face made him decide not to play any games today. He kept his interview brief, asking the same questions he had before about any questionable religious involvement on the part of the victim. Like his past interviewees, she was quite alarmed at the thought of her family being connected to a cult. In fact, she even adamantly pointed out that her husband had petitioned the grant's government to ban all religions on their land. He'd had a particularly vehement dislike of them. That was an interesting tidbit, and Justin wondered if it was enough to have put Mr. Hata on some group's hit list. The only hiccup in that logic was that a retribution theory implied that a Nipponese religion was involved, which wouldn't likely have interest in other patricians. Still, it was a connection worth noting.

They chatted a bit more, and he finally let her go. She was eager to return to her mother's home. Mae, unable to stay still long, had gone outside, so Justin joined Leo as he examined the site of the murder.

The master bedroom was expansive, the size of three of the bedrooms back at his house put together. A silk coverlet draped the bed, and a small alcove near the fireplace held a table that might be used for reading or tea. Blood stained the carpet. Leo knelt by the fireplace and stood at Justin's approach.

"It's sealed. Only for show." Leo pointed up at a horizontal line of windows near the ceiling. They were the only ones in the room. "Those are too small for anyone to get through."

"And I'm guessing the security system recorded no entry in the door?"

"Nope." Leo walked over to the doorway and ran his hand along the side. "It only recorded his entry before he died and then his wife's a few hours later. If the door's locked from within, only hand chips could open it from the outside—unless you had the demolition equipment to bust it down. Obviously, that didn't happen."

"Then it's the most secure room in the house." Justin examined a picture screen on the dresser that scrolled through various personal shots of the family's life. "Like with the other murders. I'd almost say whoever did this is showing off."

He'd seen a head shot of Mr. Hata in the official case files, but the personal pictures showed a whole different view into the dead man's world. A wedding picture focused in on the happy couple's faces. He couldn't see much of their attire, but she wore a traditional Japanese hood that hid the scarring and short haircut. At a glance, Mr. Hata's face showed no ostensible signs of Cain, but that wasn't uncommon. A family whose child had good genes could arrange an expensive marriage to a family hoping to weed out Cain. He'd observed it in the previous castal investigations as well. It was why Mae's vocation—and the fact that she even had one—was so unusual.

Other pictures showed the Hatas on vacation or with other family members. A pretty portrait showed Mrs. Hata posing in a flower garden, while a more candid shot showed Mr. Hata grinning triumphantly at what looked like the end of a marathon. Still another—

Justin did a double take and scrolled back to the marathon picture. "He was a runner," he told Leo.

Leo was still engrossed in the door. "So?"

"So no asthma." Justin flipped through a few more pictures, scrutinizing Mr. Hata's face. It was as flawless as it had seemed before, emphasizing his wife's very subtle defects. A shot of their extended family showed occasional appearances of Cain, but even among his unmarked relatives, there was something especially bright and attractive about Mr. Hata.

The wheels of Justin's mind began spinning. His instincts told him there was something here. He flipped through all the pictures again, consumed by the dead man's face.

"He's perfect," he said to Leo. "Beautiful and perfect."

"Sad you can't ask him out?"

"I'm just surprised, that's all." Justin could feel it in his chest. He was so, so close. "It's uncommon."

"Is it? Go look at your girl out there. She's sporting a pretty good set of genes."

And that was when it hit him. "So did our last victim. And the others."

Justin took out his ego and pulled up all the data on the case. Mostly, he'd been going by the summary Cornelia had first shown him. Now he delved deeper into Mr. Hata's file, looking for the number he was certain he would find.

"An eight," he said triumphantly. "He was an eight."

Even that gave Leo pause. "Not bad for a castal."

You've got it, said Magnus.

Justin searched through the other victims' files, a thrill running through him at the breakthrough he'd made. "They're all eights and nines. And look at their pictures—beautiful and perfect."

Leo gave up on the door, his own face puzzling out the new development. "Our killer has refined tastes."

Mae stepped into the room and glanced between them. "What is it?"

"A pattern," said Justin. "There's always a pattern."

He scrutinized Mae, for once with little attraction. His view was detached and objective. Another flawless specimen, in the prime of her life. The image of her screen came back to him, providing another shocking revelation.

"You're twenty-eight years old. All the victims were twenty-seven and twenty-eight. All were genetic eights and nines."

"You worried she's next?" asked Leo wryly.

"No," said Justin. "But I think something remarkable happened the year she was born. Were you in vitro?"

Mae looked uneasy at the direction this was going. "Yes. So were my brother and sister."

The answer wasn't a surprise. In an effort to grasp at any genetic hope, most patricians were conceived in petri dishes using their parents' healthiest eggs and sperm. "Were you all made in the same place?"

"I have no idea. It was literally before my time."

Justin barely heard her. He was too excited by the theory developing in his mind. "I would love to know what clever doctor worked on you guys. Leo, they've got full gene analyses of all the victims in the case files. Would you be able to tell if they all had the same sort of manipulation done?"

From his eyes, it was clear Leo had picked up on Justin's train of thought. "Yes. Geneticists who do this sort of thing almost always have their own unique style. It kind of leaves a 'mark.' If their conception was all orchestrated by one person, it should be obvious from a side-by-side comparison."

"You think they were all part of illegal gene experiments?" asked Mae. Her eyes glittered at the thought of this new lead, and then her expression shifted to disbelief. "You think *I* was part of illegal gene work?"

"No," said Justin slowly. "I mean, I don't have proof. But come on, a whole bunch of nine and eight castals born around the same time? It's awfully coincidental."

It would also explain that striking appearance he'd observed from the moment he saw her. No Cain anywhere. Features too perfect for a patrician—maybe even for a plebeian. No way was that natural. It was the work of an artist.

Here's a hot tip, said Horatio. *Do not expound on that. Look at her face. She doesn't like it.*

The raven was right, as usual. Mae was horrified. "Eights and nines can occur naturally all the time, even in castes. And if you knew my parents, you'd know my dad would've never agreed to anything like that. Don't drag me into this with your convoluted theories."

Justin made sure to note her words, that her *dad* wouldn't have agreed to it. No mention of her mother. Data for later.

He tapped his ego. "Aren't you at least curious? Even if no shadowy creature's coming after you, there's an awfully big coincidence here."

"I didn't have an illegal conception," she said. There was fire in her eyes, which now favored green in the bedroom's lighting.

"Then let's prove it. Give Leo some blood, and he'll run an analysis for you."

"Leave *me* out of this," said Leo.

"If you're so sure of yourself," Justin continued to Mae, "then what's the harm?"

"Don't try that ploy with me," she warned him. "I've been watching your games for almost two weeks. You're not going to lure me in with a dare."

"It's not a dare." Okay, it kind of was. "I'm just trying to do my job *for my country*. I thought that was your goal too, loyal soldier. On the very, very, very remote chance I'm right, think what you could do for the mission! And if you're not a match, then you'll have bragging rights for proving me wrong."

"Wow," she said. "That'll really impress my friends."

For the first time in their acquaintance, Leo looked as though he might actually like Mae.

Justin scowled. "Fine. Let's make it an outright wager."

An odd expression crossed her face. "I don't really like wagers."

"Everyone likes wagers. What do you want if I'm wrong?"

"Nothing," she said. "Because I'm not doing this."

"So. You do suspect something."

Mae's frustrated expression rivaled one of Cynthia's. "Fine. You can buy me some ree when you find out you're wrong."

That momentarily derailed Justin's satisfaction at getting his way. "What's ree?"

"Prætorian poison," said Leo, chuckling. Mae smiled hesitantly back at him, and Justin kind of wished they'd go back to their awkward relationship. He didn't want them ganging up on him. "Expensive prætorian poison. The only thing that can get them drunk."

"It's an obscure children's cough syrup," she explained. "The implant doesn't recognize it as a toxin. Take it in large enough amounts, and you get a pretty nice buzz."

"Buzz?" Leo's amusement turned to disapproval. "I've seen prætorians on ree. It's a little more extreme than a buzz. And while I respect you guys' having a loophole, intoxicated supersoldiers make me a little nervous."

Justin found it fascinating but had to focus back on the real revelation. "We've got a deal," he told her. "So you'll give him the blood?"

"Thanks for signing me up without asking. Do you know what a pain it is transporting blood?" Leo turned to Mae. "The military would've done an analysis when you enlisted, and you have open access. Save me the hassle and just send that file. Do it soon so that we can all enjoy the satisfaction of him being wrong."

"I'll make it a top priority," Mae assured him. "In the meantime, what are you going to do with the actual connection between the other victims?"

"I'm going to use it to make a profile of the killer. I don't think this is religious at all. It's some pissed-off geneticist going after his or her—most likely his, from the dagger's force—creations. Maybe because of guilt. Maybe because the families didn't pay. Whatever it is, it makes a hell of a lot more sense than a murderous cult," said Justin.

"But why use such a weird weapon?" she asked.

"And what's up with the video?" asked Leo.

"I'm working on that." Justin brushed past it, not wanting to admit he had no clue about those connections yet. Sticking his head out the door, he called for Hiroshi.

The Nipponese cop appeared almost instantly, eager to help. "Yes?"

"Is your ego wired into all local law enforcement records? And citizens' records?"

Hiroshi looked surprised. "Of course. What do you need to know?"

"Citizen records first. I need a summary of genetic scores for all Nipponese births twenty-seven and twenty-eight years ago. No, wait." Justin reconsidered and changed his request to cover thirty to fifteen years ago. Hiroshi put in the request without question and then had the ego organize the resulting data into a chart. Justin peered at it in triumph.

"There we go. Two eights and a nine in those target years—higher than would be natural for a caste. Then it just drops off into typical numbers."

It was true. After those years, the scores abruptly returned to average levels. There was one six and no sevens at all. The rest ranged from two to five. No eights or nines.

If Hiroshi was shocked at hearing the word "caste," he didn't show it. "What else can I help you with?"

Justin thought about it carefully. "Crime stats from the same date range. Especially pertaining to any illegal bio-research."

"What are you getting at?" asked Leo as Hiroshi put in the request.

"I think if some shady lab abruptly stopped making their perfect babies twenty-seven years ago, then they probably got busted and shut down," Justin explained.

"No biogenetic indiscretions in fifty years," Hiroshi said a minute later, scanning the screen. "And the one on record back then was pretty sloppy." Most were. Genetic manipulation at conception was a sketchy science that actually rarely yielded good results, which made numbers like this pretty astonishing.

"The lab could've operated in any of the other grants or even a plebeian city," Justin murmured to himself. He stared blankly at Hiroshi's ego, desperate for some lightning bolt of inspiration. He went back to the original theory. "Any records of suspicious religious activities over the years?"

"I figured you'd already know that," said the man. "No offense, Dr. March."

"None taken. Just humor me."

Hiroshi shrugged and performed the search, finding nothing there either. Justin was on the verge of wrapping things up when an idea occurred to him. "Were there unusual criminal activities of *any* kind in that time span? Anything at all out of the ordinary that made the police's radar?"

"That's a broad request," Hiroshi said.

"Humor me again."

This took more time as Hiroshi made the request and then manually skimmed the data to draw his own conclusions. "Nothing." Then he hesitated. "Nothing here."

A chill went through Justin. "What do you mean?"

Hiroshi grew pensive. "I remember it. There was a lot of weird stuff outside the grant. Huron, Sioux Falls, some of the other neighboring cities. Some missing-persons cases and a higher-than-usual number of deaths. Most accidental, but a few homicides too. None of it was in our borders, but we had a lot of federal and local investigators coming through."

Justin had the scent. He could barely contain himself. "How many?"

Hiroshi turned back to his ego. "Twenty-five, spread out over a two-year period—but they're one off from the two you're focusing on. Twenty-nine and twenty-eight years ago." When no response came, he tentatively asked, "Is there something else?"

"No," said Justin, slowly shaking his head. "You've been more than helpful. Thank you."

When Leo finished up his assessment of the house—finding no definitive answers—he, Justin, and Mae decided to catch dinner in the grant before their flight. That was one perk of visiting land grants. Sure, outsiders often received cold treatment, but if you could suffer through that, the cuisine was outstanding. The three of them found a sushi place that served plebeians, though Justin barely noticed the excellent food. His mind was still trying to find the pattern, to beat sense out of the jumble of data he'd been given.

"So what did you learn today?" Leo asked. "Because I can tell there's something going on in your head. Our cute waitress smiled at you, and you didn't even notice."

"I noticed," said Justin. "And I learned all sorts of things. One is that a bunch of castal eights and nines were born twenty-seven and twenty-eight years ago and that our victims are among them. Twenty-nine and twenty-eight years ago, a bunch of plebeians died near castal borders."

"And?" asked Mae. "What's your brilliant deduction?"

Glancing at her, he momentarily lost his train of thought. How did she fit into this? Despite her claims, it seemed too incredible that she couldn't have some connection to the other victims. Of course, he was missing an awful lot of connections right now and had to admit as much.

"I don't know. The only thing I'm pretty confident of is that we're dealing with some pissed-off geneticist. I'm working on the rest."

He wouldn't give them any more than that, and after a while, his silence turned them to other topics. In fact, by the end of the meal, Mae and Leo seemed to be on pretty good terms with each other, which was a nice change. Justin's ego rang just after he paid the bill, and he excused himself from the table when he saw the call was coming from Internal Security. He returned a few minutes later and found Mae and Leo looking remarkably serious as they talked. Both fell silent in that sort of uncomfortable way that indicated they didn't want him to know what they'd been discussing.

"Everything okay?" Mae asked after several moments.

"Yeah, actually. They brought in Geraki. You want to go meet the most dangerous man in the Republic?"

The predatory look in her eyes was answer enough. Justin didn't share nearly the same excitement. He didn't want to talk to Geraki at all. But he had to find out what had prompted the house visit with Tessa, and SCI had said in their call that they probably couldn't hold Geraki too long. If Justin wanted a shot at talking to that madman, he'd have to do it when they got back to Vancouver. Fortunately, Internal Security's detainment center had open visiting hours, and he and Mae went straight there after their flight landed, leaving Leo to connect to Portland.

They went down to the building's lowest floor and waited in an interrogation room while a soldier fetched Geraki. When he was brought in, Mae sized him up with a glance and waved off the soldier's offer to stay or at least restrain the man. Although Justin and Mae remained standing, Geraki took a chair and leaned back, putting his feet up on the small table. He looked about the same as he had four years ago, except maybe even smugger.

"Dr. March, at last," he said. "I've been looking forward to welcoming you home."

"By intimidating my—family?" Justin supposed Tessa might as well have been.

Geraki made a dismissive gesture. "Bah, I did nothing of the sort. I just had a chat with that girl, who's adorable by the way. You should adopt more provincial orphans."

"She's not an orphan."

Geraki had already moved on, his gaze settling on Mae. "And you . . . you really *are* magnificent."

Justin was used to Mae's admirers. It happened a lot in their travels. But as Geraki's dark eyes swept her, Justin somehow knew it wasn't her beauty Geraki was complimenting. He was assessing something else in her, something more intangible. *He can see it, those powers that come and go, even if they aren't possessing her right now.*

They leave a mark, Magnus confirmed.

Why have you guys been so quiet? Justin asked them. *I thought you wanted me to talk to him.*

We do. We just don't like being around the wolves, said Magnus, enigmatic as usual.

Mae was at full alert, her body crackling with tension and power as she looked Geraki squarely in the eye. Justin was suddenly reminded of their first encounter in Panama, when she'd stood by him in the alley, wearing the plum-colored dress and bracing herself for action. She was like that now, coiled and ready to spring if Geraki did anything remotely dangerous. Recalling the exhilaration in her eyes each time she fought, Justin wouldn't have been surprised if she actually wanted Geraki to attack.

"You're a lucky man, Dr. March." Geraki's awed expression finally shifted to admiration—no, not quite. More like wistfulness. "I have twice as much devotion and not half as many blessings. But I suppose eventually your job will be greater than mine."

"Tell me more about your devotion," said Justin amiably. "I'm sure it's fascinating." Even as he spoke, he had no delusions that Geraki would actually admit his religious involvement in a room with a surveillance camera.

Geraki chuckled. "Oh, it's not that different from yours. You and I are both devoted to our causes and ambitions . . . always confident, always questioning, and guided by the voices in our heads."

Justin kept his condescending smile in place, refusing to flinch at the last comment. "I don't hear voices, but again, I'd love for you to tell me about yours."

"I was referring to my conscience, Dr. March," Geraki said smoothly. "What else did you think I meant? You shouldn't take things so literally."

"My mistake," said Justin. "Now, can we hurry up and get to why you're so eager to talk to me? Prætorian Koskinen and I have had a long day."

"Of course. I wouldn't want to inconvenience you. Unofficially, I was just curious if you'd learned anything in your time away." There was a meaningful pause. "Obviously not."

"Does that mean I'm not your favorite servitor anymore?" Justin gave Mae a brief glance, but nothing had changed since the last time he'd looked at her. She was still tense and ready, her face cool as she stared unblinkingly at Geraki.

"No, no." Geraki laughed. "You'll always be my favorite. Anyway. Officially, I have two messages for you."

"From who?"

"Who do you think?"

Justin shook his head. "I honestly have no idea."

From our master, said Magnus.

I don't suppose you'll tell me his name yet? asked Justin. Naturally, they didn't. They never did.

"No matter," said Geraki. He sat up in the chair, putting his feet on the floor. "The first message: You awarded the golden apple but haven't upheld your share of the bargain."

He's right, said Horatio.

We've been over this, Justin retorted, his eyes darting briefly to Mae. *I don't have to fulfill any bargain. I haven't technically accepted the compensation.*

"Nor have you submitted to training," added Geraki. "You crave knowledge. Once you embrace your role as a student, many of your questions will be answered."

Justin crossed his arms and leaned against the wall, forcing Mae to shift slightly so that she still kept her body angled between him and Geraki. Justin kept his face as blank as he could, refusing to show that the words meant anything. "You know what? I did learn something in Panama. I've learned just how much I missed your incomprehensible rambling."

Geraki held up two fingers. "My other message is to yield your stars and flowers and accept the clever compromise."

No, said Magnus swiftly.

You don't even know what the clever compromise is yet, said Horatio. It was another of those unusual arguments between them.

It doesn't matter. We know what the stars and flowers are. Yielding her is out of the question.

Not if it's an order from the boss, said Horatio.

If we lose her, then the bargain is void, argued Magnus.

Geraki was still speaking about the clever compromise. "You may not like it at first, but the consequences will be worthwhile. It may also knock some sense into you."

If that's true, said Horatio, *then we certainly shouldn't discount it. We must trust in our master.*

"Anything else?" asked Justin, faking a yawn. "Because I'm ready to call it a night. And I'm sure you're ready to return to your cell."

"It's actually a very nice cell. And we both know I won't be staying there for long. You're lucky I think so well of you, or else I might have filed for unlawful harassment."

"*You'll* be charged with unlawful harassment if you come near me, my family, or my home again." It was one of the things he'd worked in his call with Internal Security: a restraining order.

Geraki shook his head, turning absolutely serious—or, well, most likely pretending to be serious. He was one of the more difficult people for Justin to read.

"Dr. March, if you believe nothing else, then believe me when I say I hold your loved ones as dear as my own. You're practically a brother to me, and I want to help you. If I can ever do you a favor, you need only ask."

Justin held back from an eye roll. "I've done fine without a brother, thanks." As he spoke, a strange thought occurred to him. "Unless you know what happened to Callista Xie or Nadia Menari."

Geraki's face was guileless. "Why would I know anything about them? Aren't they illicit practitioners?"

Justin felt his pulse quicken. Although he still favored the idea of a vengeful geneticist over an unholy cult, he was in no position to rule out the latter, especially with time ticking down. He'd mourned losing Callista as a link to the underground religions, but here was another link, right before his eyes—one claiming to be cooperative.

"You know about any illicit practitioners murdering patricians?"

Geraki said nothing. He was very good at keeping his expression neutral, but there was the faintest glimmer of surprise in his eyes. He hadn't expected that question. Well. Justin supposed he should be relieved that Geraki's madness didn't extend to gruesome murders. At least not these gruesome murders. Still, it would've been handy if his new "brother" could've delivered an easy answer to all of this.

Justin straightened up and said to Mae, "Let's go."

"Wait," said Geraki. He studied Justin for several more heavy seconds. "I don't know where Callista and Nadia are. They cut themselves off from everyone. I do know, however, that they talked a lot about enlightening those who still believed. Nadia especially talked about returning to the devout. She seemed to have some place in mind."

"That you don't know," said Justin, again scrutinizing Geraki for the truth. Yet, one word had stood out: "returning."

Geraki smiled. "I don't really know any of this. It's all speculation, seeing as I have nothing to do with such groups."

"Of course." Justin turned to Mae again. "*Now* we're going."

She wouldn't move from her position until Justin was out of the room. A few moments later, she joined him out in the hall, and as the door closed, Justin saw Geraki still smiling. "Don't forget what I said, Dr. March."

Mae didn't relax until they were on the subway, and although she tried to hide it, her hands shook. She'd perceived Geraki as enough of a threat to wind up into fight-or-flight mode.

"You weren't kidding about him," she said. "You think he'll break the restraining order?"

Justin thought about it for several seconds. "No, actually. I don't know why I think that. Just a gut instinct."

"Does your gut have any insight about the rest of what he said? Does he know something about the murders?"

"No. That caught him off guard, and it showed. He was telling us all he knew about where Callista and Nadia went." Justin leaned his head against the subway's window. "Someplace where people still believe. Where would that be?"

"Nowhere in the RUNA," said Mae.

Justin was in the middle of yawning as she spoke, and her

words jolted him awake. He took out his ego and told it, "Bring up Nadia Menari's bio." When it appeared, it took him only a second to find what he needed. Exhaling, he put the ego away and settled back into the seat.

"What is it?" asked Mae.

"I think my 'brother' may have come through for us after all."

CHAPTER 18

A CHURCH WITHOUT A GOD

As Tessa's first week of school went on, she surprised herself with how quickly she adapted to the schedule and technology, even though she still had trouble with some of the content. When she'd told Cynthia about the Spanish class, Cynthia had been furious and marched into the principal's office for an unannounced meeting. Tessa wasn't entirely sure what was said, but afterward, she'd been offered a choice between several artistic electives. She'd ended up choosing one on video and film. The constant media on the stream and the almost exhibitionist style of this society continued to fascinate her, especially after living in such a cloistered way.

The impact of Poppy's friendship soon became apparent. Her endorsement of Tessa provided access to a larger social circle of people who stood up for her against those who were far less accepting. Even if she was still learning the intricacies of Gemman school life, Tessa immediately picked up on the fact that Poppy's friends weren't exactly model companions. Half of them seemed to be in detention at any given time. Still, they never asked Tessa to do anything she was uncomfortable with, and underneath their rebellious exteriors, they were genuinely nice people.

One day, Poppy even provided help with a matter she'd clearly never expected to deal with.

"Have you ever been to a Church of Humanity service?" Tessa asked. They were in their last-period science class, and despite her flippant attitude, Poppy excelled at the subject. She always finished early, which meant Tessa also finished early.

Poppy glanced up from her reader, where she'd been looking at pictures of an actor she adored. "Sure. My parents make me go on holidays."

"I want to see a service."

Poppy snorted. "Why? It's boring as hell. And you can watch one on the stream."

Tessa already had but still wanted to experience it in person. Watching wasn't the same as *feeling*, and she needed to understand the concept of a church without a god. She missed the church services her family had regularly attended, and even though she knew there were Christian variants in the RUNA, she also knew that someone in a servitor's household participating in anything other than the state's sanctioned "religion" would draw attention.

"I just want to," said Tessa. "Would you go with me?"

"Hell no. No offense. You'd know I'd do just about anything for you, Tess, but I've got to draw the line at lectures on morality."

"Okay." Tessa tried to hide her disappointment but must have failed, because Poppy sighed heavily.

"Damn it, don't look like that. It breaks my heart." Poppy peered around and focused on a boy with curly dark hair, who was leaning over his assignment. "Yo, Dennis," she called. "Come here."

He looked surprised but walked over to their table. "Hey," he said.

Poppy nodded toward Tessa. "Will you take her to church one of these days?" To Tessa, she explained, "Dennis comes from a nice, well-behaved family. Well, aside from Rhea."

Rhea was another friend of Poppy's, one who'd been suspended after being caught in a compromising position with a teacher.

Dennis gave Tessa a nervous smile. "Sure. I'm going after school today if you want to come."

Tessa froze, but Poppy answered for her. "Of course she does. And tell Rhea she still owes me money."

Dennis went back to his seat, and Tessa turned on Poppy in

horror. "I can't go with him! Not *alone*. We need . . . I don't know. A chaperone or something."

"Are you serious?" Poppy looked her over. "Wow, you are. Look, this isn't a date. It's church. It's broad daylight. Even your provincial hang-ups can't have a problem with that. It's not like you're going to go make out in an abandoned building. And besides, this is Rhea's brother. He's cool."

Poppy always talked about Tessa's provincial habits as though they were cute, not primitive. Usually, Tessa conceded to her friend's advice, but this involved a line Tessa didn't think she could cross. It didn't matter if it was daylight or public. Going out alone with a boy was completely unheard of in Panama. Even if Tessa knew it was fine by Gemman standards and not really that dangerous, old teachings were hard to shake.

She made herself feel better by calling Cynthia after school and asking permission.

"You want to go to church?" Cynthia was out somewhere and answered with voice only, but Tessa could imagine her incredulous expression.

"Is it okay?" Tessa hesitated before delivering the big blow. "It's with a guy. Alone."

"Is he thirty or something?"

"No. He's in my grade."

"Then go with my blessing. Learn something wholesome."

Cynthia wasn't exactly the authority figure Tessa'd originally believed she was. Justin had recently called his sister out on that, asking if she was doing a good job in parenting Tessa. Cynthia had been indignant. "What's there to parent? She does her homework right after school and helps with dishes. You give me more trouble than she does. The most rebellious thing she does is walk to school with that delinquent."

And so, Tessa soon found herself riding into downtown with Dennis. Maybe he was Rhea's brother, but he didn't have much in common with her—much to Tessa's relief. Dennis seemed as shy as Tessa felt and did his part to help along their awkward small talk. He at least seemed genuinely interested in Tessa's background and, much like Poppy, didn't find it anything to be ashamed of.

"My parents like us to go twice a week," he explained to Tessa, switching back to the topic of church. "They think it develops character."

"Rhea goes too?"

"No, she just says she does, and I cover for her." He laughed to himself. "They're able to make her go while she's suspended. It's probably the worst part of the punishment for her."

Although the Church of Humanity had worship centers everywhere, its main cathedral was in downtown Vancouver. The videos Tessa had watched of services had been in places that typified Gemman public areas: simple, clean, bright. She'd expected the same of the cathedral, just on a larger scale. So, it was a surprise to walk into the building and find that it resembled some of the churches back in Panama.

The most notable part, to Tessa, was the abundance of wood and marble, providing an aged look so different from the modernity of everything else in the RUNA. The vaulted ceiling was arched, and large windows allowed afternoon sunlight to pour into the nave and onto its ornate wooden pews. Pillars lined the sides of the room, coming together in more pointed arches. Tessa almost felt as though she'd been transported to some other country until she saw the media screens scattered throughout the space. That was more in line with what she expected. She and Dennis sat down about halfway back in the pews, allowing her to notice one more notable feature: There were no symbols or pictures of any kind, aside from the Gemman flag.

"Only about half-full today," Dennis told her. "More people come on the weekends."

"It's beautiful," she said. It might have been the most beautiful thing she'd seen since coming to the RUNA. "All of this, for no god. It's so strange."

"Why?" he asked, looking legitimately puzzled.

"It's just how I was raised, that's all."

"You worshipped a god?"

It sounded weird when he put it that way. "My family did."

"Which god?"

"Er, God, I guess."

The officiant began the service. He actually wore the kind of elaborate robes she'd seen on other priests, though these were done in the Gemman national colors. Dennis leaned close to whisper in her ear, "Sometimes on the weekends, Angela herself officiates here."

Tessa didn't know who Angela was and mostly felt startled at Dennis's proximity. It didn't send any thrills of attraction through her. It was just something she had absolutely no experience with.

Everyone stood and sang the national anthem, and then the officiant urged them to take their seats again. He welcomed the congregation and launched into his talk. And that was what it was: a talk. Or maybe "lecture" was a better term. It certainly wasn't a sermon. In fact, as the screens lit up, showing a bulleted list, Tessa felt as though she were back in school.

Today's topic was contraception and how it was necessary for an effective society. Hearing sex discussed so openly in a church made Tessa blush—especially while sitting next to Dennis.

The officiant's powerful voice rang throughout the cathedral, as powerful as that of any priest Tessa had heard. "A society that creates planned and purposeful children is a superior society. We aren't like the provinces, with packs of children running underfoot in families that can't afford to feed and clothe them."

Tessa would've almost taken offense, but she'd already grown used to the astonished looks she received when revealing she had four sisters. Gemman women were usually sterilized when they reached their standard allotment: two children, unless they definitively proved that their social and financial means could support more. Even then, four was the maximum. No exceptions. Justin had explained to her how the castes constantly challenged this law and lobbied for the removal of those limits. "They think their non-Cain members should be allowed to breed like dogs," he'd told her.

"The law ensures we keep ourselves strong and orderly, though occasionally girls slip through the cracks," the officiant said, raising his hands for drama. "If you know of anyone who has dodged the fourteen law, do your civic duty and report it immediately."

Tessa knew the law. Girls were required to get contraceptive implants when they turned fourteen, unless they hit puberty earlier. No legal doctor would remove the implant until the woman turned twenty, at which point she had the freedom to get pregnant. With a jolt, Tessa suddenly realized she had no implant. She wasn't trying to dodge any law; it had just never come up. Maybe no one cared about non-Gemman citizens "breeding like dogs." Regardless, it was a moot point. Tessa had no intention of having sex anytime soon.

Contraception laws were so ingrained into Gemman society that the officiant was able to keep his advocacy brief. The congregation already believed. He was simply reaffirming what they were doing—how good it was, how smart, how superior. He also mentioned the government and national identity a lot. He reminded everyone how lucky they were and how wise their country's leaders were. Looking around her, Tessa could see it on everyone's faces: rapture and adoration for the jewel of the world.

The service closed with the anthem again, and Tessa left with Dennis. "I was wrong," she murmured. "There is a god. The RUNA itself. All that beauty and splendor to inspire wonder in its citizens."

Dennis frowned. "What are you talking about?"

She shook her head. "It doesn't matter. Thank you for bringing me." She knew he wouldn't understand. He'd been born into that propaganda and couldn't even imagine any other way of life. And it wasn't a bad way of life, she admitted to herself. She'd seen firsthand what the officiant warned about: unplanned pregnancies and excess children, some of whom were abandoned. The message was fine. It was the way it was delivered that amazed her.

Dennis gave her a tentative smile as they walked to the subway station. He seemed to have forgotten about her potentially being a member of a dangerous cult. "Did Poppy tell you about the concert we're going to next week? It's Vital Lucidity."

Tessa couldn't even begin to parse what he'd said. "Vital Lucidity?"

"They're a band. An awesome one. They're playing outdoors at Westfield Plaza. A bunch of us are going, and I could pick you up and bring you."

"Is this a date?" she asked. She felt blunt and stupid asking outright but figured this was a matter that required complete clarification.

He shuffled his feet and looked away. "I guess so. If you don't want to—"

"I do," she said. "That is, I just have to ask permission." A concert like he described would have been out of the question in Panama, and she was curious to go, even if she didn't entirely understand what Vital Lucidity was. It couldn't be too dangerous, especially if Poppy was going, but once more, her instincts wouldn't let her go unchaperoned without permission. "I'll let you know soon."

That satisfied Dennis, and he gave her another smile. "Cool."

They parted ways later, and Tessa walked back to the house with her mind full of questions. She hoped Justin wouldn't be too late tonight, because she wanted to dissect what she'd seen at the church. He was as hip-deep in Gemman rhetoric as anyone else around here, but he was probably the only person who might be able to understand her observations.

He actually came home early for a change, shortly after dinner. "No travel," he explained. "Just some local licenses. Only two more big trips left, and then hell if I know what's going to happen." That last part was more to himself, and Tessa was afraid to ask him to elaborate. She knew he was working on something a lot bigger than standard servitor work, something that he and Mae often spoke about in hushed tones. Whatever it was, it kept him away a lot, and although Tessa understood that was his job, she missed talking the way they used to.

He wandered off toward the study he'd claimed as his office, and she deliberated over whether to bother him about her church day or not. Finally, deciding he couldn't complain about her exploring the society he'd brought her to, she followed. She heard voices when she reached his door and started to turn back, realizing he was on a call. Her curiosity was piqued when she recognized one of the voices as Dominic's, and, going against all her good breeding, she hovered just behind the ajar door and peered in.

Sure enough, Dominic's face was displayed on Justin's wall screen, looking irritated. "Leo's in his workroom. I've got to take my portobello casserole out of the oven first, and then I'll get him. It dries out if it's left in there for more than seventeen minutes."

Justin groaned once Dominic disappeared and muttered to himself, "Man, he sucks."

Leo appeared soon thereafter. "Here for your results?"

"You got the reports?"

"Yup." Leo's face broke out into a grin. "Looks like you owe Mae a drink. The victims all match. They were done by the same person, but she wasn't. She doesn't have the same signature."

It was a rare moment of astonishment for Justin. "What does that mean? It's not possible. She's a nine from the right time period."

"It means you were wrong. I know it must be a new experience for you. If it makes you feel better, I think there was a little gene manipulation going on with her."

"How so?" Justin still looked dumbfounded.

"Her genes are outstanding," Leo told her. "Too nice to be natural, in my opinion. They're just not as nice as the victims'. Those are like . . . art."

"So she has no connection to the case," said Justin flatly.

"Not from what I can tell. Don't sound so sad. She's still a badass prætorian and all that."

"I know." Justin smiled fleetingly. "Did I ever tell you about this Apollo temple we were at? You would've loved it. This guy had subcutaneous microfilaments delivering ecstatic drugs. You should have seen his face when I sent Mae as a volunteer. She didn't even twitch."

Even Leo was amused at that. "She must've twitched a little."

"No, the implant protected her."

"Yeah, but it'd take a moment for it to identify and metabolize the drug."

Justin was obstinate. "Well, I know what I saw."

"And *I* know prætorians."

"Well, do you know anything yet about mysteriously altered videos?" Justin shot back, not liking the contradiction.

Leo's good mood dimmed. "No. But I got a good lead on an experiment for the video. I'll keep you posted." He disconnected.

Justin stared at the screen in silence for several moments before saying, "You can come in."

Feeling foolish, Tessa entered the office. "Sorry. I was coming to talk to you."

He waved it off as he sat in his chair and put his feet up on the desk. "Tell me this, prodigy. Six patricians born within a year of each other, all with high scores, all showing signs of genetic manipulation done by the same person—except one. Why would that be?"

Tessa leaned against the wall. "Because the sixth one wasn't done by the same person."

Justin didn't look appreciative. "Thanks for that. So it's a coincidence?"

"I don't know enough about it," she said with a shrug. "Do numbers lie?"

"Not when Leo runs them."

"Then it *is* a coincidence."

He nodded, though his face still showed skepticism. "How about this. A bunch of plebeians die the same year some perfect patricians are conceived. Is that a coincidence?"

She shook her head. "I don't know any of the context here either. Is this your case?"

"Yes. And don't tell anyone we're having this conversation."

It didn't sound like it had much to do with religion. "I guess you have to ask why that would happen. Why would plebeians die when patricians were conceived? If there's a reason, then it's not a coincidence. Sorry," she added, realizing it wasn't much of an answer. "Guess I'm not much of a prodigy tonight."

"You're good enough." He straightened up in his chair. "So. What did you want to talk about?"

"I went to a church service today. Church of Humanity," she clarified. "I thought it would be like a guide for moral living and human principles. But mostly it seemed like a way to enforce loyalty to the country's policies."

"They're the same. That's what religions do—a higher power tells people how to live. Only, this message comes from a reasonable set of humans, not a capricious made-up entity."

"Religions give you a sense of purpose. They connect you with something bigger in the universe and help you understand why you're here," she argued.

He gave her a teasing smile. "Isn't that what I just said?"

"No. I don't think so." She frowned. "If I find a church—a real one, like the one I went to back home—will you arrest me? Or will it get you in trouble?"

"Only if you attempt treason. There are two here in the city that are pretty good matches. Licensed and harmless. You can go if you want."

She didn't say anything, but she wondered just how much the RUNA's idea of "licensed and harmless" would truly match the faith she'd been raised in. Instead, she told him, "Oh. I kind of have a date."

That snapped him to attention. "What? With who?"

"The guy I went to church with." Tessa shifted uncomfortably. "Cynthia said it was okay when I asked earlier."

"That's because she was never a teenage boy," he said. "Two weeks here, and you're already giving me gray hairs. Give me his name so I can run a check and then make sure he comes by to meet me."

Tessa couldn't help but be a little surprised. Thus far, Justin hadn't really seemed all that interested in her activities.

"I'm just going to a concert," Tessa said, trying to reassure him. "I'm hoping it'll give me some footage for my class."

"Footage?"

"I'm in a media class now. Part of our project is to do a documentary, and I'm doing mine on Gemman culture from an outsider's perspective." Tessa was excited about the prospect, and not just because it freed her from inane Spanish lessons.

"Huh," he said. "Budding reporter. I never saw that coming. Don't record anything around here without asking me."

"I know."

He stared off thoughtfully. "There's a lot of power with cameras and editing, you know. It lets you define the truth."

"Isn't that what you do?" she asked. "*Servitor veritatis.* 'Servant of the truth.' Don't you define the truth too?"

That got her another laugh and a rueful head-shake. "Go to bed, prodigy. You're too smart for your own good. And mine."

CHAPTER 19

GRATEFUL TO BE IN THE FOLDS OF CIVILIZATION

Mae wasn't thrilled that she and Justin were down to their last land-grant investigation: the Nordics. She had no desire to visit her homeland and secretly hoped he'd cancel the trip altogether since he was now caught up in the idea of a vengeful geneticist being behind the murders. He had inquiries out to the various castes, requesting records of any other "genetic indiscretions," as they were officially called. Although he believed in the geneticist theory, she knew he wasn't optimistic about getting results. Most patricians were conceived in vitro, meaning there was a wealth of fertility clinics out there that were always coming and going.

He'd also requested information from the various families about the victims' conceptions but had received muddled answers. Some swore they hadn't used in vitro. Others provided the names of doctors who didn't seem to exist. Confusing things further was that many castals resented the RUNA's prohibitions against genetic research, some of whom worked at high levels of castal government and could help cover up illegal clinics.

In the meantime, Justin still doggedly pursued his religious leads, though Mae suspected it was out of desperation. He kept up his overconfident persona, but she knew he was getting anxious about time. They were more than halfway through the month now, and each day that passed meant they were closer to another murder and his potential return to exile. He claimed he'd gotten a lead from Geraki's tirade, which surprised her since little of that madman's ramblings had made sense. She was even more surprised when Justin said they'd be going to the RUNA's borderlands.

The RUNA had spent a number of decades establishing itself and building its power. Once it felt secure, it had begun to slowly expand its territory on the continent. Some regions—such as the lands southwest of the RUNA—had transitioned more easily. They had formed a loose configuration of city-states after the Decline and eventually welcomed being annexed by their powerful neighbor.

Other regions weren't so thrilled. The RUNA's other neighbor, Arcadia, had formed when the southeastern region of the former United States had chosen not to band with the rest of the country and Canada because they opposed the harsh mandates. Mae was familiar enough with Arcadian culture to know that "chosen" wasn't the word they used in their history. Arcadia claimed it had been abandoned because the early RUNA couldn't maintain that much territory. The truth lay in the middle of those theories, and despite ravages by Mephistopheles and Cain, Arcadia had managed to pull itself up into a relatively stable country, due largely to an iron-fisted and religion-driven government.

Relations between the countries had been tense, especially because the RUNA had its eye on some of its neighbor's resource-rich land. Gemman energy favored renewable resources, but oil and natural gas were still in demand. As a result, Arcadia's western border was constantly in dispute as each country tried to stake its claim. The RUNA possessed superior technology and weapons, but the Arcadian military was vast and had been building up weapons that, while less sophisticated, were still problematic.

Justin's destination wasn't in an Arcadian borderland but was instead in a region that had been annexed only within the last five years. Although the Gemman government worked very quickly to bring its new territories into the uniform cultural fold of the rest of the nation, these new territories still had a reputation for recklessness and dissent—nuisances combatted by a very strong military presence.

Mae got the call from Leo about her test results on the way to Justin's house. She wasn't surprised to hear she wasn't a match to the victims. She'd expected that, no matter how much Justin advocated his conspiracy theory.

It was the *other* results Mae was interested in, the ones she hadn't told Justin about. When Justin had left to answer a call during their Nipponese lunch, she'd taken a leap of faith and asked Leo for a favor. Their relationship had warmed up enough that it was worth the gamble. She'd handed over the lock of hair that Emil had given her, feeling both terrified and excited over what Leo might uncover. He'd promised discretion and hadn't asked many questions.

"It's a hit," he told her when he called. "Definitely a relative of yours."

Mae sat on the train, her ego pressed to her ear in voice-only mode. "How close?"

"Twenty-five percent match to you. That's a grandparent, half sibling, niece or nephew, aunt or uncle." He paused. "Double first cousins too."

"I see." She took a deep breath. "Can you tell which?"

"No, all I can go by is the number of genes that match. Send me some of your immediate family's stats, and I could get a closer hit."

Good luck with that. Mae entertained a brief fantasy of stealthily cutting off a lock of her sister's hair. "I don't think that'll be possible."

"Does it help you at all?"

Did it? Mae didn't know. The only thing it proved for sure was that Emil had obtained some relative's hair. Of course, there was still that picture, but that wasn't hard evidence, no matter the family resemblance. Someone like him could've combed through archives of children's pictures to find a Koskinen likeness.

"It helps," she told Leo. If nothing else, it showed her the extent to which the Brödern was willing to go for a prætorian asset. "Thank you. I appreciate it."

She could sense his discomfort. Their relationship still wasn't entirely firmed up. "Glad to help."

"And thanks for not telling Justin. . . . You didn't, right?"

That brought on a snort of laughter. "If I had, he probably would've been at your door this morning demanding answers. This is the kind of mystery he lives for."

Mae had to concur as they disconnected. She might have been just a conquest, but that didn't mean he didn't still try to wheedle information out of her—or anyone else he encountered. Maybe he couldn't help it, as he'd claimed, but she wasn't going to take any chances.

Unsurprisingly, the borderlands didn't have many direct flights, and it took them the better part of the day to reach their destination. When they stepped off their plane, Mae caught her breath. Spring had come to Vancouver, but it was nothing compared to the evening warmth of Mazatlán. The ocean had glowed in the setting sun as their flight had descended, and now, with darkness falling, the twinkling lights of buildings could be seen in the distance, where the bulk of the city sat on a hill.

"This could be a vacation," Justin mused.

"I'm surprised it doesn't bring back traumatic flashbacks of Panama."

"Not as humid. That, and it's safer."

"You sure about that?" she asked. She'd been in enough borderlands to know that unsavory elements lurked beneath the surface, those who weren't quite on board with their new government's policies.

"There are dissidents," Justin said in agreement. "In fact, we may run into a few when we go out tomorrow, but it won't be anything major. Once they have more time to adjust, they'll be grateful to be in the folds of civilization."

Near the airport, state-funded light-rail tracks were under construction, promising the efficiency the rest of the country enjoyed. Driverless cars had spread to this region, however, and it was easy enough to catch one into the city. There, she found Justin's vacation comparison might have been more accurate than she'd realized, seeing as they were staying in a beachside resort.

"SCI's paying for this?" she asked in disbelief. Mazatlán's buildings were a mix of new and pre-Decline, and this one was one of the new ones, beautiful and filled with modern luxuries. Yet, as they approached the entrance, she couldn't help but notice the large number of police and regular military patrolling the streets. That certainly wasn't something you'd see in a posh resort elsewhere in the RUNA.

"Our tax dollars at work," Justin told her. "Enjoy it, because tomorrow we're going to see the dredges of this town."

They spent the night outside in one of the resort's many restaurants, enjoying dinner and drinks as a local band strummed guitars. Beyond them stretched an expansive beach that gave way to the darkness of the ocean. Mae could just barely make out the sound of the surf.

Justin, naturally, drank heavily the whole time, but at least he didn't take anything else, hopefully reducing his odds of an overdose. She didn't want to find out firsthand if Mazatlán's medical resources were up to normal Gemman standards. He'd said very little about Windsor, but she'd noticed that aside from his morning stimulant, he hadn't strayed to anything harder than alcohol.

All this time spent together . . . the hotels, the meals. Sometimes it felt like a parody of dating. Except no date would constantly be checking out other women. His gaze in particular kept going back to a young, red-haired bartender.

"Go tell her you're an EA diplomat," Mae said. "I bet that'll go over well."

He snapped his attention back to her. "For someone who claims that's in the past, you sure can't seem to let it go. You never let me explain."

"Is there more to it than you using it to get me into bed?"

"Was that what did it?" he retorted.

"No," she admitted. It had been his wit, his sexiness. The sense that he was interested in what was within her, rather than just the natural-blond exterior that dazzled so many men. It had even been a little of that bravado, something she apparently couldn't stay away from. Most of all, it had been a sense of connection. She would never give him the satisfaction of telling him, but sometimes, in the rare moments when they weren't sparring, she still felt it.

"The jacket was my friend's," said Justin. "He'd lent it to me, and when you thought I was him . . . I just went with it. Less depressing to be a diplomat than an exile. I didn't expect things to pan out like they did." He laughed softly to himself. "I wonder where Huan is now. He wouldn't believe this change of fortunes. Aside from Tessa's dad, he was my only real friend there."

"Not Cristobal and all those admirers of Gemmans?"

"No. Definitely not." His eyes were piercing as he studied her. "Nordic Nine, you must have been a diamond among ashes growing up. I don't know how or why you got out, but I know you must've been paraded around and put on display. Your family could do nothing less."

Mae didn't want to give him the satisfaction of letting him know he was right, but it wasn't exactly that difficult a conclusion to reach. "Yes."

"Did you like it?"

"Sometimes," she answered honestly.

"Did it get tiring? Always having to smile and say polite things? Knowing people were watching and speculating? Knowing they were flocking to what you were and not who you were?"

His ability to so perfectly capture something like that was both amazing and disturbing. But again, she answered with truth. "Yes."

He spread his hands out. "Then there you go. Welcome to being a Gemman in Panama."

His words drew her up short. She had never once thought they might have any sort of shared experience like *that*. With a jolt, she realized that his difficulties in Panama might have extended beyond just being surrounded by provincial primitiveness. There was a social aspect she'd never considered. And with that conclusion, she suddenly drew an even more startling one. The sadness and loneliness she'd sensed from him might not have been faked. That didn't mean he still hadn't had ulterior motives—especially if his "second date" speech was any indication. Nonetheless, it cast him in a new light. She couldn't fully articulate her thoughts and simply stayed silent. She didn't know what expression she wore, but after several moments of studying her, Justin looked away and downed his drink.

"Well," he said, getting to his feet. "The night's not getting any younger, and her shift'll probably be over soon. I can take it from here, noble defender. Charge anything else to my room." He gave her a mock salute and sauntered over toward the bartender, wearing an expression very similar to the one he'd used on Mae in their first meeting. The young woman looked interested, but then, who wouldn't be in the face of those good looks and charm? Angry about her moment of sentimentality, Mae left as well—for her room, alone.

He was in good spirits the next morning but said nothing about what had happened. She certainly wasn't going to ask. They took another car, this time òut to the edges of the city, which became significantly less affluent the farther they went. The military presence also diminished. There were a few new construction projects, but many buildings were pre-Decline or had been hastily thrown up immediately after in an attempt at safety when chaos roamed the streets. The people they saw here were obviously working-class, and even if they now had the same health and education access, it was clear these new citizens were a long ways from their more fashionable counterparts. Signs in Spanish showed many hadn't yet learned their new national language.

Mae expected they'd go to another church, but instead, the car dropped them off at a tattooist's shop. "Are you going to immortalize this trip?" she asked.

"Maybe later. Right now we're visiting the family of Nadia Menari."

"The woman you asked about back in Apollo's church."

He nodded. "Geraki said she was returning to someplace where people still believed. These annexed borderlands are hotbeds of religion. Even after SCI sweeps them, plenty slip through the cracks. Nadia grew up here, and even though I couldn't find anything on her, some of her family moved back after I shut her down. If I were going to set up a low-profile cult, I'd come here."

"And Nadia can help us?"

"Maybe. I'm more interested in finding her associate—Callista. She's the one that'll help us."

Mae had a hard time imagining groups that had been busted by servitors wanting to help him. "Are you sure?"

"Very sure."

They stepped inside, out of the heat, finding no air-conditioning in the empty shop. A dirty glass case displayed potential designs. Mae had had a childhood fantasy of getting a tattoo but was pretty sure she wanted no part of this place's unhygienic practices.

"Can I help you?" A tall, lanky plebeian man stepped through the door leading to the back of the shop. Justin stepped forward.

"Yes, I'm—"

"Justin March." The man gave him a slow, long look. "I remember. I was there when you visited."

Justin forced a smile. "Ah, well . . . nice to see you again. I'm, uh, here for the same reason as before. I'm trying to find Nadia."

"Nadia? My cousin? You already disbanded her church."

"That's not why I'm here. Do you know if she's in Mazatlán? I just need to speak to her."

Mae approached, her wariness triggering the implant's response. She didn't like the man's body language. He was nervous.

"Yes . . . yes, of course. I just need to get ahold of her." The man managed a smile. "You know how she is."

Justin nodded, still smiling but also confused.

The man moved back toward the door he had just come through. "Let me call my brother and see what he knows. It'll just be a moment. Can I . . . get you anything while you wait? A chair? Something to drink?"

"We're fine."

The man disappeared through the door, which he left ajar,

and Mae heard his one-sided conversation in Spanish. The only words she picked out were "Nadia" and "Justin March."

"Something's weird," she said. "He's too uneasy."

"Yes," Justin agreed. "But he knows what I am. These people are more afraid of federal visits than castals are."

The tattooist returned, his smile bigger and more natural this time. "My brother knows where she is. He's going to bring her over."

"Excellent," said Justin. "Thank you."

Justin and Mae milled around the storefront, which saw no customers, for about ten minutes. Then they heard a door open in the back and a low conversation. Their host appeared and beckoned them forward. "Right this way."

The back room looked like any messy workshop type of area. Assorted tools and outdated readers littered the tables and benches, and a large, wicked-looking metallic contraption hovered over a long pallet where the tattooing most likely took place. A bed suggested the tattooist lived here.

Mae knew immediately there was something wrong, because instead of a woman, she found three men waiting for them—three armed men. She promptly knocked Justin down, so strongly that he cried out in surprise. Her gun was out before he hit the floor, and she unflinchingly shot one of the attackers in the arm. One of his colleagues had the wisdom to drop to the ground also, and another joined him after Mae disarmed him and belted him across the face with the gun. She was on to the one who'd tried to elude her when she heard a voice behind her say, "Easy there. Drop your gun, or Dr. March's career ends."

Mae slowly turned toward the speaker. It was the tattooist, and he too was armed—holding a gun to Justin's head. These damned annexed regions were still able to smuggle guns in. This would never have happened in civilization. She knew she was faster than the tattooist and could save herself, but that didn't mean Justin would walk out alive. And as she met his eyes, her heart clenched. She felt a terrible, gripping fear—not for the mission, but for the loss of *him.* A scuffle at the back door told her others were joining them, and gritting her teeth, Mae set her gun down.

*　　*　　*

The motley Mazatlán cronies were poor excuses for captors, and their detainment was made more embarrassing when Mae thought about the lethal combatants she'd fought over the years. But she'd been stuck with that gun to Justin's head, leaving her in this predicament. The two of them were kept tied up in the back room until darkness fell outside. That was when their captors decided they were safe to transport.

She studied the men all day and found only one who acted as though he might have had militia training from the region's pre-RUNA days. He wasn't adept enough to identify her guns as military issue, nor did he think to check her boot. She couldn't use the knife while bound anyway, but she felt more secure knowing it was there.

The group led Justin and Mae to a large, worn-down building that might have been an office space in better days. They entered through a side door, and she blinked as bright light shone down from an old incandescent fixture. The room they stood in was small and cramped, and it looked as though it had once been an administrative office of sorts. A door opposite the one she had entered stood firmly closed, but unless she was mistaken, she thought she could hear the sound of people on the other side. A lot of people.

Two plebeian men waited in the office, and they tensed when Mae's entourage entered. One was older, with graying hair, but the two men shared such a strong resemblance, she assumed they must be father and son. The son looked to be a little younger than she was, but he was built like a tank, with well-defined muscles all over his body.

"Is this him?" demanded the elder, walking over to stand in front of Justin.

"Yes," said the tattooist.

The older man struck Justin hard across the face, and Mae flinched inside, seething with anger as he staggered backward from the blow. She tried to surge forward, despite her bindings, but two sets of hands jerked her back harshly. The older man's eyes flickered to her. "Who's the castal?"

"I don't know," the tattooist said. "She was armed to the teeth, though."

You don't know the half of it, she thought bitterly. She looked forward to beating these people up once she was free and Justin secure.

The older man eyed her with disinterest and turned back to Justin. "You bastard." The man's voice rang icily. "You fucking bastard. Because of you, I lost my daughter!"

Justin made a quick assumption and blanched. "Nadia's dead?"

"She might as well be! After you shut her down, she came here to start a new life but decided she needed guidance from her goddess. Nadia left to commune with her in the jungle . . . and crossed the border! She wasn't allowed back in."

"She's a citizen," said Justin. "They should've let her back when they scanned her chip."

"She removed it for the journey," said the man mournfully. "She wanted to purify herself and be free of all man-made devices. Now border security won't let her back, and there's no way to put it back in out there. We've been trying to petition, but in the meantime, she's stuck. And it's all your fault for shutting her down!"

It was, quite possibly, one of the stupidest stories Mae had ever heard and furthered all she believed about religion. Everything from the idea of communing with divinity to removing the chip—a major crime—had been foolish.

"Hey, I saved her from a prison sentence," snapped Justin. "I shut her down for a paperwork error, rather than the fact that she was preaching sedition!"

The man hit Justin again, and this time Mae—prepared for the hands restraining her—skillfully slipped underneath them and managed to place a hard kick in the older man's stomach. His eyes widened in pain as he fell while many hands now restrained her, shoving her forcefully up against the back wall. Her head hit hard against the surface, and the implant quickly compensated for the pain.

The solidly built younger man lunged at her. "You bitch—"

"Whoa, whoa, hey, wait there, Eugene. Save your strength for the fight," soothed one of Mae's captors, moving in front of her.

"Fight?" asked Justin. Half of his face showed an angry red mark from the blows, though he hid any pain he might have felt.

"Yes," wheezed the older man, allowing one of the others to help him up. "The *danza*."

The tattooist, seeing their blank looks, explained, "The *danza* is a fight used among Clans to settle matters of honor."

"What kind of fight?" Mae asked.

"What kind of matters?" Justin asked.

"A knife fight," declared the young man, Eugene.

A knife fight of honor? Clans? Mae was amazed. This place really did have a long way to go.

"Tradition requires it, as does our goddess," explained Nadia's father. "We must avenge what you did to her."

"What are the rules?" Mae looked expectantly between her captors and the grieving father. "You can't expect him to fight in it without knowing the rules."

The tattooist shrugged. "The rules are simple. The combatants must stay within the marked boundaries. Each combatant gets two knives that they are allowed to use in any way on the opponent. The winner is the one still standing at the end. The loser is the one who bleeds to death."

Playing to the death seemed right on par with the rest of this melodrama. It was straight out of a movie: an honor-avenging duel. Crude or not, Justin wouldn't stand a chance, especially against Eugene. The man could probably win by mass alone.

"How are the combatants chosen?" she asked, trying to puzzle a way out.

The older man made an impatient gesture, clearly annoyed by her questions. "We have no time for this. The crowd is waiting."

She shifted uneasily and glanced at the door, where she could still hear a low roar. "We have the time." She forced as much bravado as she could. "If this is really as honorable as you claim. Why him? Why is he fighting and not him?" She gestured to Eugene and the tattooist respectively. "Aren't you all family? Isn't the whole family's honor at stake?"

"Yes," said the tattooist in agreement. "Anyone could have

done it. Eugene was simply the one chosen to represent our side."

Ah. That was what Mae had been waiting for. Justin might live another day after all, much to the relief of gullible women everywhere. "So the combatants are representatives for the various sides?" she repeated. The men nodded. "Then I want to represent Justin. I'll fight."

"What? No." The older man was livid now. "You're wasting our time." A dangerous gleam flared in his eyes. "I want to see March bleed."

One of Mae's captors, the scarred man who had originally held the gun to Justin, swallowed uncomfortably. "Uncle Raoul, she has the right. The rules of the *danza* say—"

"I'm not going to fight *her*," said Eugene, his dark eyes running over her with disgust. "I could break her in half. It wouldn't be right."

The tattooist and a few of the others who had fought her at the tattoo parlor didn't look so convinced. She idly wondered what had happened to the guy she shot. "She has the right," the tattooist insisted. "You have to let her, if March says it's okay."

All heads swiveled to Justin. "By all means, go for it," he said immediately. "Although . . . if she loses—er, dies, or whatever, what happens to me?"

"Then your side has been proven guilty, and we get to kill you."

"Great."

"And if I live," prompted Mae, "then Justin lives too?"

The tattooist looked at Eugene, who nodded reluctantly.

"Fine," snapped Raoul. "Let's just get this over with. If they're both intent upon dying, so be it. At least this way, I can actually pull the trigger on March myself."

Justin's gaze flickered to Mae, and she tried to give him a reassuring look as the whole group began moving toward the door. It opened, revealing a large, vaulted room. It was hard to say, but it might once have been the kind of work space that held cubicles and desks. They'd long since been cleared out, and the dull hum she'd heard earlier strengthened to a roar. At least a hundred people were gathered along the room's sides.

An audience, how perfect. It would be just like a *canne* tournament.

Passing near her, the scarred captor gave her a curious and almost sympathetic look. "I hope you're good with a knife."

She smiled.

A TICKING TIME BOMB

Justin stared around the "arena" in amazement. He supposed he should have felt flattered that this many people had turned out on short notice to witness his so-called punishment. Rickety makeshift bleachers ringed the room's periphery, and nasty barbed wire lined a large, rectangular space that formed the match's ring. Unless he was mistaken, dark blotches on the floor looked suspiciously like bloodstains.

It actually wasn't the first time he'd seen something like this. In Panama, grisly duels to the death popped up a lot among rival gangs as a more "civilized" way to deal with disputes. It was, however, the first time Justin had been at the center of one, and he certainly hadn't expected it to be happening within Gemman borders.

Mae stood only a few feet away from him, and judging from the cool, predatory look on her face, she was busy studying her surroundings, sizing up the layout. He hoped she had a plan. He'd seen her in action enough to know she was good, but that Eugene guy was huge. And solid. Beside him, her slim body seemed hopelessly outmatched.

You've seen her take out guys just as big, said Horatio.

I know. But it was never to defend my honor. That, and from the looks of this rabble, I'm not convinced we'll make it out alive even if she does win. For a moment, he forgot she was a trained warrior. She became that breathtaking lover, the one who'd lounged in his bed and given him a smile that undid him.

He suddenly didn't want her to fight. He wanted to rush forward and protect *her*.

Give her something to help, said Magnus.

An automatic weapon? suggested Justin.

No! Magnus sounded irritated. *A blessing. Protection. It's within your limited powers.*

No, it's not, argued Horatio. *He hasn't learned any of the runes.*

We could show him, insisted Magnus.

Horatio was still obstinate. *Showing isn't the same as teaching. It takes years to learn them, to sear their meanings into the mind. That's what he should've been doing in Panama, instead of chasing other men's wives. Besides, he'd need to touch her to do a proper casting. Their hands are tied.*

He could kiss her. Magnus sounded hopeful.

The crowd had cheered when they entered, and now they quieted as Nadia Menari's father began speaking. He said nothing that hadn't been said earlier—mostly how Justin had wronged his daughter by disbanding her church in Chicago, forcing her to flee here and go into her eventual self-imposed exile. If his life hadn't been on the line, the whole thing would've been comical. Justin had seen Mae's face when Raoul Menari told them the story of how Nadia's vision quest had panned out. It was easy to understand why Mae held religions in such contempt, when foolish gods made people do foolish things like that.

Nadia's goddess isn't the one to worry about, said Magnus. *Another's moved in here. Can't you feel it?*

Justin started to say he couldn't, but when he focused and made himself aware of his surroundings, he could detect a faint tingling along his skin and something inexplicable that danced along the edges of his mind.

It's going to get even more crowded, added Horatio. *Mae's goddess won't let her fight alone.*

Raoul finished his rant. Two men came forward and pushed Mae toward the ring. Justin felt himself tense up, but she showed no fear as she strode forward. She kept her head held high, walking purposefully and determinedly. Someone undid her bindings and handed her two knives. She studied them carefully, tested their weight, and flipped them in the air, catching each one deftly. Satisfied with what she had found, she stripped off her overshirt, leaving herself in only a tank top. A few men in the audience whistled. She then struck a stance in her corner and watched as Eugene moved to the opposite one.

Raoul came to stand beside Justin, pure malice gleaming in the older man's eyes. "Your castal whore is going to die for you, you know. I suppose this way, you'll at least have company when you burn in the underworld."

"Arianrhod big on that kind of thing?" asked Justin carefully, recalling Magnus's comment about another goddess's presence.

Raoul shook his head. "We no longer worship Arianrhod. We've since learned that she's only an aspect of the true great goddess. That's why Nadia went into the wilderness, to seek greater understanding."

Justin wanted to ask more, but things were happening in the ring. A man stood in the center, holding a flag up. He glanced between Mae and Eugene, shouted something indecipherable, and thrust the flag downward. He promptly scurried away as the combatants approached each other.

Justin wasn't entirely sure what a to-the-death knife fight of honor should be like, but he found it a lot less action packed than expected—initially at least. Oh, the tension in the room was through the roof, no doubt about that. He could see it written all over the fighters' bodies, and the surrounding crowd was screaming for Mae's—and his—blood. Neither combatant lunged or wrestled the other, however; things were surprisingly calm. Mae and Eugene stalked around the ring together, almost in a parody of a dance, sizing each other up.

She still had that calm, dangerous look on her face, and she seemed almost—exultant. *She's enjoying this.* He was reminded of when she'd fought in Apollo's church. Her expression had been the same then—not exactly showing pleasure, but still a sort of fierce triumph. It was impossible to take his eyes off of her. She was fierce and beautiful, her presence too big for this small room.

Told you, said Horatio.

It took a moment for Justin to understand. He blinked a

few times, tuning in to those powers that danced beyond normal senses, and caught faint glimpses of what could only be described as black sparkles trailing Mae. They were hard to focus on, though, and if he hadn't seen the same thing when she fought Golden Arrow's worshippers, he would've thought he was imagining it now or had something in his eye.

Divine glamour, said Horatio, being surprisingly helpful. *It happens when a god seizes someone who doesn't have the control to handle it.*

Can everyone else see that? asked Justin.

No. Only adepts. Horatio's tone said he didn't like giving Justin that kind of credit. *Look. Her opponent isn't alone either.* Justin squinted at Eugene and could just barely make out a faint shimmer around him too.

The dancing stalemate ended as Eugene surged toward Mae, his knife aiming for her upper torso. She flowed away from him like water, her movements so fast that it seemed she must have started moving before he did. Clearly surprised, he tried again with similar failure—only this time, after evading his attack, she snaked forward with one of her own and dragged a blade across his arm. A hiss of disapproval ran through the audience, and deep red showed against Eugene's tanned skin.

His face darkened with anger, and he returned to feinting, as though buying time to reassess her. Mae wouldn't give him that luxury, however, and came forward to strike twice more. One of her attacks drew blood again, but the second one missed. He had finally anticipated her—though just barely. He followed through with a full-body attack, apparently deciding to push the advantage of his greater mass since he certainly wasn't making any grounds with speed.

Mae dodged his lunge, but he still caught part of her leg and knocked her down. Her back brushed briefly against the barbed-wire ring as she fell, and Justin winced when he saw the bloody tears in her shirt. Falling to the floor, she and Eugene rolled around a moment, away from the wire, each one vying to pin the other. Justin flinched again as one of Eugene's knives sliced at her shoulder. The crowd roared with delight, even though he couldn't actually manage to keep Mae down.

If the injuries fazed her at all, she didn't show it, and in an eyeblink, she jumped back on her feet again. Eugene tried to follow suit, but she was faster, and she came at him not with a knife but with a kick of staggering proportions. She executed it gracefully, packing a force that no one her size should have been able to deliver, not even a prætorian. Eugene staggered to his knees, and then she was on him once more. He dodged her attack clumsily, avoiding her knife somewhat, though not enough to miss being swiped across the cheek. Justin could see that she'd originally been targeting the man's neck.

Raoul Menari, standing near Justin, drew in his breath as Eugene quickly wiped at the large, bloody gash on his face, inadvertently smearing more dark blood across his skin. He sweated and breathed heavily now, clearly in the throes of physical exertion. Mae showed less distress, but it was obvious from her expression and posture that every ounce of her being was wrapped up in this fight. That glittering dark aura continued to intensify, and as it did, he saw the change in her. Her expression grew harder, her moves faster, her strikes stronger.

They paced around the ring again, with Mae now feinting, drawing him out so that he would lock up into defensive maneuvers that never followed through. His effort to keep up grew while hers stayed the same. Justin tried to gauge Eugene's glamour but couldn't see it anymore.

Because his goddess left, said Magnus. *She recognizes a losing match, and she isn't that well established yet.*

Who? demanded Justin. The ravens didn't answer, keeping to their policy of caution with gods' names.

Finally, growing frustrated, Eugene rushed forward, again attempting a full-body assault. Mae met him. She avoided his attack and inflicted far more devastating damage on him. Her two knives slashed across his chest, cutting deeply through both skin and fabric. Justin heard the other man cry out, and with another swift kick, she knocked the knife from Eugene's right hand. It flew off to the far side of the ring behind him, too far out of reach for him to easily retrieve it without exposing himself further to her.

Tired and bleeding, he switched his remaining knife to his

right hand, just as Mae came at him in full force. Maybe no one else could see that dark fire, but judging by some of the faces around Justin, it was obvious that the power with which she moved wasn't natural. Kicking and hitting, she knocked Eugene to the ground and this time, he couldn't overcome her. Fear was written all over Eugene's face as he looked up into Mae's. Her expression was terrifying, filled with bloodlust and exultation. It was Mae's face and yet not Mae's face.

In a movie, perhaps, Mae would have spared Eugene in this moment of triumph. She would have looked up at Raoul, blade poised above his son, and made some dramatic speech about how she wasn't going to stoop to their level, how killing wasn't the way. Justin knew that ending wasn't going to happen today. She was going to kill Eugene. She *wanted* to. Justin could see the desire in her eyes. She wrested Eugene's other knife away from him and brought her own knife down to his throat, apparently in preparation to slit it. She froze at the last possible moment as a shrill, piercing sound suddenly tore through the crowded warehouse.

The crowd's screaming and chanting faltered, and all turned to the sound of the noise. Mae remained paused in her killing stroke, but when Eugene attempted to use the opportunity to move, she slammed his head back against the ring's floor and pinned her blade to the exposed vein on his throat. He didn't move again, and she peered around, a snarl on her face, as she sought out the interruption.

Following everyone else's gaze, Justin looked toward an aisle between the bleachers that led from the front door right to where Justin stood with Raoul Menari. The noise had apparently come from an ego gripped by a bland-faced plebeian man Justin had never seen before. Raoul, trembling with fury, took two steps forward down the aisle.

"What is the meaning—"

A woman suddenly stepped out beside the man. Raoul paled as he saw her, and several others in the crowd gasped. Justin, meanwhile, wasn't sure whether he should welcome or fear this new development. She was older than Justin—early forties, if he remembered correctly—but still possessed a hard-edged beauty that struck him deeply. The high, square cheekbones of her Korean grandmother distinguished her plebeian features, and she wore her dark hair in a chin-length, asymmetrical cut. She strode forward, as others parted, and finally came to a stop in front of Justin, resting her hands on her narrow hips.

"It really is you," she said in a low, throaty voice. "I thought it was a joke."

"Hello, Callista." He did his best to put on his game face and act like he wasn't in a bloody makeshift arena. "I wish this was a joke, believe me."

Her lips quirked into a smile, and she gave him a long, languid once-over. "Untie him before Internal Security finds out you idiots abducted one of their employees," she snapped. Raoul pushed forward.

"No! We demand vengeance for Nadia!"

Callista fixed him with a hard look. "Raoul, I'm very sorry for your loss, but what happened to Nadia was Amarantha's will. Rest assured, there's a purpose for her absence. Surely you aren't questioning the goddess?"

Amarantha. Justin hadn't heard that name in a while. She was a post-Decline one, a merging of other goddesses, though her followers had been scanty last he knew.

Raoul acquiesced to Callista after a few more grumblings and then ordered two of his lackeys to go help Eugene out of the ring. Everyone seemed to have forgotten about him and Mae in the wake of Callista's entrance, and Justin was surprised to see the two were in exactly the same position: Eugene pinned down, a knife against his throat. Mae stayed where she was until one of the guys tried to pull her away. In one fluid motion, she leapt up and spun toward him, shoving his body into the barbed-wire perimeter. The guy wailed, but no one really noticed because in the space of a heartbeat, Mae had punched the other guy and followed through with a rib-cracking kick. Justin heard the click of guns and Raoul shouting for reinforcements.

"Stop!" yelled Callista, her sharp eyes quickly assessing the tinderbox they were in. "Stay where you all are. You." She leveled a glare at Justin. "You've got a lot of nerve bringing someone like her here."

"*I* didn't bring her here," he exclaimed.

Callista pointed. "Go get her out of there."

Mae had returned to a crouching position near Eugene, knife still in hand as she scanned around for anyone else who might dare to intrude. The glamour was still on her, as was that expression of dark power and need for destruction. Justin hesitated only a moment before making his way forward and slipping through the opening in the barbed wire that the others had used. Mae's eyes tracked him as he approached, but she didn't move.

Don't touch her, Horatio warned him. *The fight's done. She'll get herself back soon.*

Justin knelt beside her, grateful to see that Eugene was still alive. "Mae. Time to go," Justin told her. "You won, and we've got a ticket out."

Mae didn't even blink, and he wondered whether she'd heard him. Her chest rose and fell rapidly, and there was savagery in her gaze.

"Mae," he said more loudly. "Come on. We have to get out of here." He rested his hand on her shoulder, and like that, she was in front of him, the knife at *his* throat. Whatever words he might have said next died on his lips.

Told you, said Horatio.

She won't hurt me. Justin wasn't so sure he believed that, though.

Her goddess would. She's starting not to like you.

Swallowing, Justin looked Mae squarely in the eyes. "Put the knife down, and let's go. I need you to protect me."

It took several more seconds, but those were the words that penetrated the divine haze. A part of him hoped it was feelings for him that drove her, perhaps some leftover sentiment from Panama, but most likely, it was her sense of duty that triumphed. Whatever it was, she focused on him and nodded. As he squinted, the glittering around her faded, and her face once again became that of the woman he knew. When the ravens okayed it, he held out a hand and led her away. Her legs trembled, though Justin had no idea whether it was from simple exertion, unmetabolized chemicals, or recovery from divine possession. Maybe a combination of all of them.

He kept his arm around her as they headed out of the ring and found the fabric of her shirt's back wet and sticky with blood. He knew she'd recover from it and that it couldn't be too severe, but he still felt a sickening sense of guilt knowing she'd been wounded on his behalf.

If you had cast a blessing, she wouldn't have been injured as much, Magnus told him. *Your continuing denial and refusal to learn is already having consequences. Just because you can't fight like she does, it doesn't mean you can't take part in battle.*

I don't want any part of that, said Justin. *I tolerate you guys. That's the extent of my divine involvement.*

Then why are you here? asked Magnus.

By the time they reached Callista, Justin could tell Mae had fully returned to herself—which meant she was still lethal and watchful, especially as she looked Callista over. Nonetheless, Mae handed over the knives and struck a protective stance near Justin.

"Now, then," began Callista. "If you've got a moment, we should—"

"Bastard!"

A cry behind Justin interrupted her. He turned to see what it was, but Mae was faster, of course. She spun around, reaching for her boot, and Justin was just in time to see her throw her own knife at a charging, gun-wielding Raoul. The man gasped as the knife plunged into his chest, near his collarbone, sparing him from a killing blow. He yelped and staggered back, dropping the gun. At a nod from Callista, one of her cronies dragged him away. She narrowed her eyes at Justin.

"We need to talk."

"I would love that," he said.

As a sign of goodwill, Callista made sure their egos and Mae's guns were returned. She invited them back to her home, but not without first asking, "Can I expect a military raid?"

He smiled sweetly. "Depends if I make my flight tomorrow."

"Understood." Callista was smart. As soon as he'd received his ego back, he'd activated its GPS signal and sent a message to local authorities to track him if he didn't check in by a certain time tomorrow.

Callista's house was in that old, run-down region, but it in no way resembled its neighbors. It was new and expansive, with grounds extending in all directions. Guards stood outside its fence, though they didn't display any guns. Borderlands might have been able to sneak weapons behind closed doors, but security guards in the open could hardly flaunt guns when regular Gemman patrols continually passed by.

Mae remained silent for the journey and said nothing until they were escorted into a luxurious sitting room decorated in an Old World Spanish style. Left alone, Justin reached for a pitcher of water and a cup sitting out on an ornate wooden table.

"You think that's safe to drink?" asked Mae.

"We're fine. I've got Internal Security tracking us now." He poured the water.

"You should've done that the instant we stepped off the plane."

"Yeah, well, I didn't think we'd traveled back in time to some barbarian civilization. This place has been Gemman for five years."

"It takes a long time for people to give up on their old ways. I still see it in the Nordics, and it's been almost a century."

The door opened, and Mae jumped up, readying herself for a threat. What actually came through, however, was a young girl, probably only a year or so shy of hitting puberty. Extremely pretty, she possessed Callista's exquisite features and carried a tray containing bandages and a dark glass bottle.

"My mother wanted you to have this," the girl said shyly, setting the tray on a small table. "She's finishing up some business but will be ready to talk soon."

Justin vaguely remembered a name. "Persia?"

She flushed with pleasure. "Yes." To Mae, Persia said, "Do you need help?"

Mae glanced at the tray, face cold. "No. I'll do it myself."

Persia gave a small nod of compliance and moved toward the door. "Thank you," said Justin, not entirely sure how to interact with this serious-eyed woman-child. She nodded again and disappeared.

Mae picked up the bottle Persia had left, uncapped it, and

sniffed. Seeming satisfied with what she found, she began cleaning and wrapping the cuts on her arms with military efficiency. When she finished the ones she could reach, she turned around and peeled off her tank top, glancing at Justin over her shoulder. "Will you help me?"

Not even he could find that sexy, though he was charmed at her modesty, considering everything she'd done. His efforts were clumsier than hers, and he cringed when he applied the antiseptic to the cuts caused by the barbed wire. For her part, she didn't even flinch.

"Are you going to finally tell me about Callista?" Mae asked.

"She's the one who used to work with Golden Arrow." He paused to tape down some gauze. "She's apparently traded employers, though. Or, well . . . just morphed her goddess a little. Amarantha's kind of a combined goddess, drawing mostly from Artemis and Hecate, the last I knew. It's not that out there, since the goddesses have some overlap. In the ancient world, they got blurred together a lot, and some viewed them as faces of a triple goddess: virgin, mother, crone. I guess the virgin thing—Artemis—wasn't working for her." That must have been what Raoul meant about Nadia's changing allegiances. She'd left her Celtic moon goddess for this Greek one and pooled resources with Callista.

He finished his first-aid handiwork. Mae donned her tank top and overshirt again before turning to face him. "How can a goddess be all those things? Or a merging of multiple ones?"

"It's a common thing in religions. Deities are all-encompassing."

He didn't quite know how else to articulate it, and she obviously didn't follow. Gemmans who didn't make careers of religious history had very two-dimensional views of gods and goddesses.

"You seemed surprised by all of this," said Mae.

"The knife fight? Yeah, that was definitely a surprise." Bringing it up made him think of the elephant in the room, the topic Mae was pointedly avoiding: the part where she'd gone on a superhuman rampage. Ignoring it for now was fine with him, because he didn't really know what to say either.

She shook her head. "I mean the religious developments. Even I know this group isn't licensed, and there's no way they fall under the law for acceptable religious practices. Even the secular practices don't. You're going to report this, right?"

He shifted uncomfortably. "We'll see."

Her eyes widened in disbelief, but her protests were interrupted as the door opened again. Persia returned with two armed guards. "My mother will see you now—just Dr. March."

Mae strode across the room in seconds. "No. No way is he going without me."

Persia turned nervous, but a stone-faced guard took over. "Callista's orders. He goes alone." He tightened his grip on his gun, and Justin could tell from Mae's face that she was already planning how to disarm him or pull her own gun.

"Let me go," Justin told her. He'd seen too many guns today and didn't want a shoot-out. "Everything's okay."

"Going off with unlicensed zealots with illegal guns?" she asked incredulously. "Nothing about that is okay."

The guards' faces darkened. Persia stepped forward. "I swear, nothing will happen to him. My mother just wants to talk."

"Please," said Justin, meeting Mae's eyes. "Trust me on this. Remember—we're tracked. And you've got your ego too if I don't come back."

Mae said nothing for several tense moments. Finally: "Fine. If he's not back in an hour, I tear this place down around you."

The guards looked skeptical, but they stayed outside the door when Persia led him away. She took him to the far side of the house, to double doors that opened into a bedroom. Callista sat at a vanity, clad in a long silk robe, brushing her hair in the mirror. She glanced up at their approach. "Thank you, dear. You can go." Persia retreated, closing the doors behind her.

Justin stood there waiting as Callista finished her hair and then rose gracefully to her feet, managing to do it in a way that let the robe make the most of her body. "Always drama with you," he said as she walked over to him. "But I guess that's part of the job."

She brushed her lips against his cheek. "Lovely to see you again. Shall we talk?"

"Here?" he asked.

"I didn't think you'd mind, but if you've gone chaste on me, we can go outside." She glided over to a set of glass doors and stepped out into the warm night. Justin followed, finding a table already set with candles and wine on a garden terrace. More drama.

Callista poured him a glass without asking and then leaned back in her chair, crossing her legs so that the robe slipped off of one of them. She gazed up at the starry night and then looked back at him with a smile. "Are you here to arrest me? How did you even find me?"

"Luck, more than anything else." He took a drink of the wine, some kind of deep red that Dominic could've learned a lot from. "I got a tip after paying your former associate a visit. I actually came here for Nadia, though you were the one I ultimately wanted."

"So flattering. How is Mr. Arrow these days?"

"Awaiting trial. He tried to drug servants of the government."

Callista's lips curled in disdain. "He was always so stupid. Using tricks instead of the discipline needed to get real power. It's half the reason I left."

"That, and it's easier to gather followers in unregulated borderlands?"

"It's becoming more and more regulated every day," she said. "Bit by bit, the RUNA's blanket of uniformity is enveloping this place."

Justin wasn't fooled. "Don't act like that's a bad thing. You grew up in civilization. You know it's better than having a bunch of armed nutjobs running around, no matter how gullible they are."

"Speaking of armed nutjobs . . ." Callista's expression of easy charm transformed, making her the hard-edged leader who had ordered around Menari's people. "What the hell were you thinking bringing her here?"

"Why do you keep saying that? I didn't bring her to you. We were captured."

Callista traced the edge of her wineglass, gazing into its depths by the candlelight. "I never thought I'd see the day someone like you was traveling with someone like her. Of course, from what I can tell, a lot's changed with you."

"Traveling with a prætorian's not that weird," he countered. "Especially in light of today's events."

Callista jerked her head up. "She's a prætorian?"

"Isn't that what you're talking about? How else do you think she did what she did?"

"You know how she did what she did! She's an undisciplined and uninitiated elect," she snarled. No more flirtation now. "Chosen by someone powerful from the looks of it. It was a wonder the rest of them couldn't see the glamour—and don't act like you couldn't. You've got a lot more control since the last time I saw you. I didn't actually think you'd embrace your calling."

"I haven't," he said firmly.

Callista's face said she didn't believe that. "What god follows her?"

He hesitated. "I don't know. It's not my concern."

"It should be! A prætorian elected by something that strong? That kind of combination is a ticking time bomb waiting to go off."

Justin decided it probably wasn't a good time to bring up Mae's nigh-perfect genes.

"She needs to deal with whatever's following her," continued Callista. "She needs to either embrace it and get some control or else get rid of it."

"I don't even think she knows it's there," he said.

"Well, she should. You should enlighten her." She seemed to calm down a little and poured more wine for both of them. "It's fitting that you've found this path, you know. There's no better advocate than someone who used to persecute believers. Do you know the Christian story of Paul?"

"Of course I do. And don't use the past tense. I still 'persecute' believers."

"You let me off," she said softly. "And that was before I slept with you."

He said nothing right away. Neither of those past actions had been smart. "You were the first person I ever saw who . . ."

Even now, he couldn't give voice to it. It was something he'd kept buried inside all these long years, the secret he'd told no one. The secret that could have worse consequences than what he'd already faced.

"Who showed proof of the supernatural?" Callista said.

"I'd lose my job for that," he said. "Or worse."

"Your secret's safe with me. I could tell then you had the signs of an elect. The potential for power wreathed you. But you had no god then. Who do you serve?"

"I don't serve anyone, Internal Security aside."

"But you've got something with you," she insisted. "It isn't blatantly out of control like hers, but I can sense it."

"It's unwanted," he said.

That hurts, said Horatio.

"And I don't know who," Justin added. "As I'm often told, gods don't like to give up their names."

Callista reached across the table and put her hand over his. "I'd be happy to help you explore . . . a number of things."

He smiled but didn't take back his hand. "Thanks, but—"

"Callista!" A man came frantically tearing out of her bedroom door. "Juan and Eduardo are unconscious, and the castal woman's gone!"

"What?" Callista jumped to her feet. "Get the others and find out where—"

"Relax," came a smooth voice from the darkness. "I'm right here."

Mae strolled out of the shadows of the nearby trees, a gun in her hand and displaying a casualness that made Justin despondently think she'd been at ease there for a while. And, judging from the look on her face, she'd also overheard a number of things she shouldn't have.

Well, said Horatio optimistically. *It had to happen sooner or later.*

CHAPTER 21

CONFLICT OF INTEREST

"My job's to protect him," Mae told Callista in a voice that chilled the warm night. "Admittedly, I didn't really realize what kind of danger he was in."

Justin had the grace to look embarrassed, but Mae wasn't sure exactly what part of the madness she'd just heard was responsible for it. It could've been anything from the part where he had slept with a cult leader to him admitting he was a believer in the supernatural. For now, she couldn't spare the mental energy to process it all, not when Callista's guard held a gun and others were coming.

"I thought we were here to track down a ritual murderer," added Mae.

That actually seemed to startle Callista. She turned to Justin. "What?"

He sighed and apparently decided to just make the best of the mess he was in. "Call off your dogs and let Mae join us. Secrecy's blown, and she already knows what I've come to talk to you about."

Callista gave Mae a long, considering look. "If she puts away the gun."

Mae glanced at the guard. "Him first."

Callista gave a small nod, and he lowered his weapon. Several moments later, Mae followed suit. Callista dismissed her reluctant guard and beckoned Mae over to sit.

"I can get you a glass." Despite the offer, Callista didn't

sound nearly as hospitable as she had for Justin. Had Justin really slept with her? Had he liked it? Mae refused to speculate.

"No, thanks."

Callista shrugged. "Suit yourself. Now, what's this about murders?"

Justin looked like he wanted to sink into the ground—as well he should have—but recovered himself enough to begin explaining the story. He told Callista everything. *Everything.* Even the part about the video they weren't supposed to talk about. Whatever regard Mae had developed for Justin began to crumble away as he spilled secrets to this zealot-turned-lover.

When he finished, Callista took her time to process his words. "So. You've come to me because you think I might know something about a moon deity whose followers wield silver daggers." She gave him a sidelong look. "Or maybe you think I serve one."

"Probably not," he said. Mae wondered whether he'd used his brilliant deductive skills to come to that conclusion or was simply too blinded by her.

Callista chuckled, though there was no amusement in her eyes. "Thanks for the vote of confidence. And no, I don't know about this. I have no reason to kill patricians." Her eyes rested meaningfully on Mae as she said that. "I don't know of any other group who'd do something like this either . . . but I'd be very interested in finding out more. There's power in blood. You could be dealing with a very, very strong deity."

"So you favor a cult over a vengeful geneticist?" he asked.

"Why are they mutually exclusive? I wouldn't mind a few genetically perfect followers. The gods are choosing their elect. You think they choose randomly? There's a reason you were chosen. Both of you," Callista added reluctantly.

Mae couldn't take it anymore. "Are you seriously saying these make-believe entities of yours are part of this case? That they're interfering in our lives? It's insanity!" She could perhaps understand it from Callista, but Justin? That was still the mind blower, and Mae secretly hoped to find out everything he'd said was just part of a clever ploy to reel the other woman in.

"You of all people should take this seriously," said Callista. Her condescending tone irritated Mae further. "And if you don't want anything to do with this 'insanity,' you need to break out fast. Find out who's trying to control you and sever their power."

"How?" asked Justin, as though that were actually a real thing.

"Gods consolidate their power in places and people. Breaking belief is the biggest way to hurt one. You do that by disbanding their followers. Gods need people to believe in them. Could be as simple as someone like you revoking a license." Callista considered. "Or it may take more drastic means. Destroy their place of worship. Take out some of their leaders. Once the followers start to stray, the god weakens. It's why they're all scrambling right now to build their power—and followers."

"Enough of this," said Mae, unwilling to hear more. If Justin wasn't going to do his job, then she would do it for him. "Can you or can't you give us any leads on this killer?"

Callista shot her a glare. "I told you: I don't know who would do this. No matter what you believe about the faithful, most of us don't embrace bloodshed. Those who do wouldn't share that fun fact with others. I don't think it's that far-fetched that a god would want genetically superior servants. I do think it's weird that he or she would then kill them off."

"You said blood is power," Justin reminded her.

"Yes, but the choice of victim is a waste. A god could take a sacrifice from any number of other sources."

Justin caught his breath. "Like a bunch of plebeians."

He met Mae's eyes, and for a moment, she forgot about all the reasons she had to be upset with him right now. If Callista was right, if crazy groups sacrificed for imaginary power, then Justin might very well have one piece of the puzzle.

"Do you know any groups, any at all, that could be worth checking out?" Justin asked, his voice urgent. "Ones I wouldn't know about."

The unlicensed ones, Mae realized. The ones that operated in the shadows. Like this one.

Callista met his gaze levelly. "Justin, there are a lot of groups you don't know about. There's been a surge in them over the last few years. I could give you at least two dozen groups with ties to the moon and some obsession with blood and silver. You think you can check them all out in the next week and a half?"

"You could if you turned the list over to SCI," said Mae pointedly. "They could send out other servitors."

"And pick me up along the way, no doubt," said Callista.

Justin shook his head. "We won't do it that way. Send me what you can, and I'll see if I can make any connections between that and the other evidence. If I get any hits, can you help me find where they're hiding?"

"Some of them."

"Okay. We should go." He stood up and glanced at Mae, who immediately rose as well. "I think we have a lot to talk about. Thank you for your help—and, uh, timely intervention."

Callista joined them and caught hold of Justin's hand. "Be careful. There are dark forces at work, and I'd hate to lose my favorite servitor."

"You know, Geraki calls me that too. I'm glad I have such a great reputation."

"Geraki . . ." Callista arched an eyebrow. "I haven't heard from him in a while. He might have some answers for you."

Justin grimaced. "Mostly all he's got are riddles, though he was the one who gave me the clue about Nadia. It *is* too bad about her. Shitty luck."

Callista smiled in a way that made Mae tense for danger. "Luck had little to do with it. I was the one who suggested she go on her vision quest."

"What? I thought she was your friend."

"She was. She is. But we were starting to disagree on how to run things. So, when I encouraged her little journey . . . I mentioned that Amarantha would prefer she do it unchipped. Don't look at me like that," she told Justin. "I've made inquiries. She's fine. And with the way the RUNA's spreading, the territory she's in will be annexed soon anyway. Besides, things are a lot smoother now that it's just me running the faith."

"Aside from when her family—who blames me for what she did—decided to take some sideline revenge," he reminded her.

"I saved you," said Callista. "And I'll keep them in line. They're all still unruly and half-provincial, but they fear Amarantha."

Justin seemed to accept this, which just increased the absurdity of this night. That kind of behavior—dissension in groups that made them turn against one another—was exactly the reason religions weren't supposed to grow.

Callista caught Mae's sleeve as she started to walk past. The flirty, irreverent nature was gone. "You need to deal with your problems," she hissed. "Until you do, you're a danger to yourself. And to others. And to him."

Mae jerked her arm away. "Fiction offers no danger. Only its followers."

One of Callista's lackeys delivered Justin and Mae back to their hotel. It was a long, awkward car ride in which neither said anything. When they made it back, Justin told her good night and headed for his room. Mae, aghast, grabbed him in the hall and pulled him to her with more force than she intended. He stumbled and put a hand on her shoulder to steady himself, triggering a jumble of emotions in her as she tried to figure out who he was. Romantic confidante? Schmoozing womanizer? Secret zealot?

"You are not going to bed! We have to talk about what happened!"

"It's the middle of the night." He looked both physically and mentally weary. "And you won't believe anything I say anyway."

"I believe that you'll be back in Panama if SCI finds out you pick and choose which people you turn a blind eye to. *And* that you believe in your own deity or power or whatever. That's a conflict of interest. As is sleeping with people you're supposed to license!"

He sighed. "Are you jealous? If it makes you feel better, I had a better time with you—well, during sex, at least. After is a whole other story."

Mae rarely lost her temper. She'd had too much discipline drilled into her to let her emotions get the better of her, which was why the lapse with Kavi had been so shocking. Mae nearly lost it again now and just barely stopped herself from slapping him, which probably would have knocked him into the wall. She took a deep breath.

"We're going to talk now."

For a moment, she thought he'd protest. Then a remarkable transformation came over him. A hard expression she'd never seen filled his face, containing both impatience and exasperation. He too was nearing a breaking point. "Do you want to know why I'm back? Why they went to all that trouble? Do you want to know why I left?"

She blinked in surprise. Those weren't exactly the answers she wanted tonight, but they'd certainly been on her mind. Something about the intensity in his face cowed her. "Okay."

They returned to his room, where Justin promptly poured himself a shot of tequila from a bottle that looked like it had been tapped last night. He downed it and then, after a moment's thought, simply picked up the whole bottle. He sat down cross-legged on the bed and patted the spot in front of him. "Have a seat." Mae hesitated, but there was nothing even remotely sexy going on. She joined him.

"Do you remember when I was first with Cornelia, talking about a group that tried to set me on fire? It wasn't a joke. That was my last assignment before exile. Those nuts never should've reached that point. Whoever did their last evaluation had fucked up pretty badly for them to have progressed that far." Mae bit back a suggestion that maybe the group's last servitor had slept with one of their members and turned a blind eye. "I actually had to get some military out there to break up their compound." He shook his head at the memory. "Until now, that was probably the craziest thing I've ever investigated."

He took a drink from the bottle. "Anyway, they shut things down and rounded up most of the group. They were in a pretty remote place, and I had to stay at this little country inn. Not the most glamorous accommodations, but it did the job. My security guy went out for a good time, and I went to bed satisfied with a job well done."

"A good time out in the middle of nowhere?" she asked,

though that wasn't nearly as surprising as the idea of his body-guard taking off.

"The nearest real town was about ten miles away, and they had a licensed brothel. So, he took the car out there." Then, maybe because the tequila was already in effect, Justin randomly added, "I've never paid for sex, you know. No matter what else you think of me, I've never done it."

"Noted."

"Anyway, I went to bed and had this dream. That's where things get messed up."

"More so than being set on fire?"

"In a different way." His gaze turned inward, and the expression on his face grew troubled. No, more than that. Pained. "I had this dream that felt really real. I mean, a lot of dreams do, but you've got to believe me when I say it about this. *Really* real. I was out in the woods at night, but there was a brilliant full moon that lit everything up. I sat on the ground, and three people sat in front of me. I was holding a golden apple." Justin gave her an expectant look. "Does that mean anything to you?"

"No. Should it?"

"A golden apple initiated the Trojan War." Her face said she didn't understand that reference either. "The short version is that a mythological war began when a Greek goddess of chaos gave a golden apple to this guy named Paris. He was supposed to give it to the most beautiful goddess, and three of them tried to get it by bribing him. The details don't matter, but the results of who he chose caused a war."

"Okay."

"Anyway, I had this golden apple, and these three people wanted it."

"They wanted you to pick the most beautiful?"

"No." He frowned and seemed to be grasping for words. "It's hard to explain. The apple wasn't about beauty here. It was more than that. The choice was about—I don't know—power. Power and allegiance."

"Allegiance to what?" she asked.

"To one of these three. Giving the apple was a commitment, I guess." The more he spoke, the more obvious it was that this dream had deeply affected him. "They told me I had power with the apple, but that if I gave it to one of them, they'd give me something in return. And just like in the story, they tried to bribe me.

"One of them was a man wrapped in smoke and darkness. I couldn't really see him, but he spoke in this deep voice that made the ground shake. He told me if I followed him, he'd give me power and authority. He said I'd have wealth and influence and people scrambling to serve me. That they'd fear me. It was kind of intense, and he made some cryptic comment about how he knew my adversaries and could help me fight them. The woman—there was only one—was a little gentler. But still dangerous. And alluring. I could see more of her. Her skin was pure white, and she had gray eyes and silver hair. Not like graying silver. Like, real silver. Brilliant and beautiful . . . It nearly hurt to look at her. . . ." He trailed off for a moment. "She told me she liked clever men and that if I gave her the apple, she'd give me wisdom that could unlock all the secrets of the world. I told her I already had wisdom."

"Of course you did," said Mae. Even in some life-changing dream, his self-confidence would still be going strong.

"She said I was wrong, that I had knowledge and cleverness—but not wisdom."

"Like the Lady of the Book versus the Lady of Keys."

The reference seemed to surprise Justin, but he nodded slowly. "I suppose so. The third guy was older, and I could only see half of his face. The rest was in shadows. He said no one could *give* wisdom, that it had to be earned. He said he'd teach me and that his thought and his memory would guide me. He also said he'd show me how to outwit my enemies and that I could have love that would make others stop and stare. That kind of pissed off the woman. She said, 'So love can be given, but not wisdom?' And he said that he never said he'd give it to me . . . just that I *could* have it, like, if I worked for it. She called him a cunning bastard."

"I'm surprised you didn't give him the apple just for that. He sounds like a kindred spirit."

"I didn't get a chance to mull it over," said Justin, though he had the first genuine smile she'd seen since they got back. "Because then the smoky guy scoffed and said that he could do that and more, that he'd give me more women than I'd know what to do with."

"I assume you told him the impossibility of that," Mae interjected.

"You're on a roll here, aren't you? Never thought I'd have a heckler while I was pouring out my heart and soul."

"Okay, sorry." She had to remind herself of all that was at stake.

"The old guy said I'd only need one woman, and that the one he'd send me would mirror me in light and shadow, that I'd know her by a crown of stars and—" Justin faltered for a moment and then cleared his throat. "He said she'd be carved of fire and ice, that she'd scorch me in my bed and live and die for me outside of it."

Mae would have accused him of embellishing the story, but with his memory, he was probably reciting the flowery words verbatim.

Justin took a deep breath. "I ended up giving him the apple."

"Because you're a romantic at heart?"

"Because of what he said next. He told me he could also save my life. And even though I was in the dream, I suddenly realized the room I was sleeping in was on fire. He took the apple and said, 'Follow the ravens.' I woke up in a burning room."

Now they were back to the arson story. "And you escaped."

He met her gaze. "You ever been in a room that's on fire? Been surrounded by flames? It was so hot. Probably hotter than the woman who was going to scorch me in bed. The heat smothered me, and I was choking on smoke. I couldn't see anything but sheets of fire. Pieces of the roof were starting to collapse . . . and that's when I saw them. The ravens."

"The ravens?"

"Yup. Two big black birds, hovering in the air. They flew over to a corner of the room, and I followed them. I don't know. Maybe I just didn't have any other choice. And there, I saw that part of the wall had collapsed and that there was a small opening to the outside. Mae, you have to believe me. I couldn't see that spot from the bed. There was no way I could've known about it without those birds." His eyes suddenly became wide and desperate.

"I believe you," she said, not sure if she did.

That seemed to satisfy him, but he still looked anxious and frantic as he dove into the old memories. "I managed to get out of it, though my shirt caught on fire. I had to kind of flounder around to put it out on the ground, but I managed. Got a few burns in the process. I saw a specialist later who was able to fix most of them up without scarring—except this one."

Justin unbuttoned his shirt and opened it to show her the side of his torso. Mae moved over beside him to look at a spot he pointed to just below his rib cage. There was a scar there, but it was barely visible, just a small mark of raised skin nearly the same color as the rest of him. She wasn't even sure she would've seen it if she wasn't looking for it. It was only a few centimeters long. Without thinking, she touched it with her fingertip and traced its odd shape. They weren't perfectly straight, but she could make out a vertical line that had two shorter lines extending from its top at a downward diagonal. It reminded her of a slanting F. He tensed at her touch, and without thinking, she splayed her fingers and rested her palm on his skin. It was warm and smooth, and a jolt of memories went through her. She jerked back.

"Sorry."

"No problem." He buttoned the shirt back up.

There was a weird moment of awkwardness between them, and she tried to remember the narrative. "So you made it out of the fire?"

"Not exactly." He fell back into the stride of his story. "It was just as bad outside. We were by some woods, and it was almost impossible to make anything out. It was the middle of the night, and there was no moon, like in the dream. The smoke didn't help. There was more light near the front of the inn, but that's where most of those zealots were. Apparently they'd had more followers than we realized in the initial arrest. I started moving blindly into the woods, but one of them saw me and yelled for his colleagues. I ran but couldn't see where I was going and could hear them approaching. That's when I started following the ravens."

"The ones who showed you the opening in the wall."

"Yes. It was weird too—and not just because I was following two birds that had appeared out of nowhere. I mean, it was dark out, and they were black, but somehow I knew where they were going. They took me through this crazy convoluted path in the woods, finding openings in the trees I never could have seen on my own. I lost the pursuit, and after what seemed like forever, I emerged out near this road . . . just as some police and fire trucks were coming by. And the ravens vanished."

Mae didn't know what to make of the raven part, but the rest was certainly amazing. "You got lucky."

He nodded. "Very. They got me back to civilization and caught the remaining members. Bruno—my security guy—got fired. I went back to the office and wrote up the report on what had happened. I didn't say anything about the dream . . . but I did mention the ravens."

Mae couldn't respond. Bad enough for a servitor to harbor beliefs in the supernatural. But to write them up in an official report?

"I described how they'd led me places I couldn't have known about and how they appeared and disappeared out of thin air. I didn't even try to find a reason for it. I just wrote, 'Perhaps there are supernatural forces in the world we can't rule out.' Cornelia wrote those same words on her note in Panama."

Mae made the connection. "The letter I delivered."

"Yup. It was Cornelia's sign that the offer to come back was authentic. She wasn't very happy about it at the time of the report, though. You wouldn't believe all the shit I got from others. A servitor acknowledging something supernatural in an official report. My whole job is to show that stuff is make-believe and that those who subscribe to it are deluded. They berated me to redact it. They threw all sorts of theories at me, about how I'd mistaken things in the dark or that the ravens were just products of my subconscious showing me things I already knew. It would've been easy to delete it too. One line, Mae. One line, and it would've all gone away. But I just couldn't do it."

"Because you couldn't explain what you saw."

"Well, that, and because the ravens never left me."

She waited for more, but it didn't come. "You said they vanished."

"They did—in physical form. But they went in here." He tapped his head. "They live here in my mind. I don't see them, not exactly, but I feel them there. They're with me all the time. They *talk* to me. They want me to swear fealty to their god, but I dodged it with a, uh, technicality."

"Justin . . ." Mae was floored. She had no ability to deal with something like this, except to suggest he completely stop all drugs and alcohol. Her earlier outrage was gone. Now she felt sorry for him. "You can't . . . You must be mistaken. You went through a lot. If you thought you saw them that night, then maybe you . . . I don't know. Maybe you convinced yourself they were real and just developed some kind of . . ." She hated to use the word, but there was no other. "Delusion."

He collapsed back against the bed and laughed without much humor. "Oh, believe me. You have no idea how many times I told myself that. How many times I still tell myself that. I didn't mention that in the report, though. I wasn't that crazy. That one line got me into enough trouble, enough to get me exiled. Imprisoning me was too dangerous. What if I told someone else about what I'd seen—or thought I saw? They just had to get rid of me, get me away from honest Gemmans altogether. Three days after I filed that report, I got a military escort to the airport and was told to pick a place to go. 'Anywhere but here,' they said."

There was an earnestness in his face and more of that desperation from earlier. Whatever was going on here, Justin believed it was true. Mae didn't. She couldn't because she didn't believe the world had things without explanation.

"Justin, I don't know what to say."

"You think I'm crazy. I've thought about it myself."

"No . . . I think you're dedicated and astute and actually kind of brilliant. But you went through a lot."

"The ravens are real," he said adamantly. "I don't understand the how or the why, but they're real. I denied it for a long time, but they've been with me for four years. They know things that I couldn't possibly know."

Just because something had been with you for four years didn't mean it was real. If anything, Mae just thought it was proof of a serious problem. Unwilling to say so, she switched subjects as a realization hit her. "SCI already knows about your beliefs."

"Well, not all of them."

"But the report is why Cornelia wanted you back?"

"It's why Francis did," Justin said. "They don't understand the video, and he must've read the report. He's a believer in something—I can spot that stuff—and figured maybe the only servitor who has gone on record contradicting his job's premise might be able to do something on a case that defies the RUNA's founding principles. That, and I've seen other things. . . ."

"Like what?"

"Things I can't explain. Feats of power. People like Callista."

Mae didn't really find Callista to be proof of a higher power. "What's so special about her?"

He studied her. "You don't see it? It's hard for me sometimes, I guess. Some can hide it. But there are people out there who sometimes shine with power. Every once in a while, if I look just right, I can make it out."

The words sent chills down her spine. "What kind of power?"

"I don't know. Callista was the first person I ever saw who manifested that—and it freaked me out. I didn't know what to do. It was why I didn't write her up."

"Was that why you slept with her?" Mae asked archly.

"I slept with her because she was hot and wanted me. Maybe we're dealing with the supernatural, but *I'm* still human. I never told Cornelia about Callista, but I occasionally hinted at some of the other things I saw—off the record. Cornelia told me to forget about them and didn't seem to think they were a big deal, at least until I put one of them in writing."

Mae mulled over the subtext. "Are you saying the head of SCI believes there are higher powers at work in the world?"

"I don't know if she believes in them, but she knows the reports are out there. And even if she doesn't like it—or me—I'm here because they're grasping at straws."

Numbed, Mae lay down beside him and stared at the ceiling. Such an amazing mind . . . bogged down by delusion. It was a pity. But then, after what he'd gone through, how could he not be scarred? Which now left her with a problem. What did she do with everything she'd learned? Because she'd learned *a lot*. There was an unlicensed cult stockpiling weapons in Mazatlán, as well as a priestess with information about other unlicensed groups. There was a servitor who believed he had supernatural creatures living in his mind and who had all but admitted to a belief in gods interfering in mortal lives. Of course, if what he'd said was true, SCI might already know where his beliefs were . . . but did they realize the extent? Would they care? They would probably care that he wasn't reporting dangerous factions.

"What are you going to do?" asked Justin quietly, guessing her thoughts.

"I don't know."

"Horatio tells me you have a lot of control right now."

"Who?"

"One of the ravens."

"That's his name?" she asked. "Horatio?"

"I didn't give it to him. The other's Magnus. But he's right. You can make or break me, Mae."

She pondered it for several more moments. "I want you to break this case. And right now, no matter how, um, confused you are, I still think you're the only one who can do it."

He turned to her and smiled. "You've got a lot of faith in me."

"Faith in your powers of observation and deduction. I don't know about the rest." Some of Callista's words came back to her. "What did Callista mean when she was asking who'd chosen you? Did she mean the ravens?"

"No." His smile faded. "According to them, they're just the messengers—of the god I gave the apple to. I'm supposed to follow him."

She caught the wording. "Are you saying you don't?"

"I'm saying I've found a few loopholes in the agreement that night that have spared me from officially signing on with this god who's claimed me."

"You really believe there's one?"

"I believe there's something interfering in my life." He paused. "And in yours."

Mae jerked upright. "No. Do not bring that up."

He sat up as well. "Mae, maybe you can doubt me, but you can't ignore what happened tonight. Didn't you feel it? During the fight? I could see it! There was something with you, something spurring you on. You're one of the elect."

"Elect?"

"Someone a god has staked out and chosen. You've got one following you, and Callista's right. It's a hell of a lot more dangerous than my ravens."

"Nothing's following me or choosing me or whatever you insane people want to believe," she exclaimed. No way would she tell him how terrifying that knife fight had been—terrifying and exhilarating to have that tremendous, dark power filling her and driving her, making her invincible. "You saw the implant in action, that's all. It has that effect in battle sometimes. All the chemicals get churning and—"

"That wasn't the implant. And I'm pretty sure the implant didn't protect you from Golden Arrow's drug either. I think that was your unwelcome patron. Leo said you shouldn't have been that impervious."

"Leo can't figure out that faked video," she retorted. "He's not the genius you think."

Justin was surprisingly calm. "Mae, I know you can feel it. I've seen the fear in you afterward—and I've seen *it*. This thing that wants you to serve it. And when we were in the Lady of the

Book's temple, the ravens say another god made a play for you. They say you're the kind of person that gods want to—"

"No more." Mae scooted off the bed and stood up. She'd hoped he'd forgotten about the statue, but she should've known better. Crazy or not, he didn't forget anything. "Justin, I'm not going to report you. And I'll accept without protest that you believe what you've seen is real. But don't drag me into your philosophies. There's nothing you can say that's going to convince me of magic powers in the world. There might be . . . there might be something wrong with me, something biological. But that's for me and a psychiatrist to work out—not a god. I don't believe in them. I can't. I've seen too many horrors in this world to think any deity could willingly allow such things. Please don't bring this up again."

His dark eyes held her in deep thought, but she couldn't read him. At last, he sank back into the bed. "Okay."

"Thank you. And thank you for talking to me." She glanced at the time and winced in sympathy. Not everyone could forgo sleep. "Get some rest. We've got a long trip tomorrow At least you can sleep on the plane."

He nodded, looking as though he might fall asleep before she cleared the room. His eyelids started to droop and then blinked open. "Oh, hey. Can you do me a favor? One that has nothing whatsoever to do with . . . any of this?"

"What is it?" she asked warily.

"You think when we get back home, you could go get your uniform and come over to my place?"

Mae made no effort to hide her surprise at the bizarre topic change. "Why would I do that?"

"Tessa's got a date today. Er, tomorrow. Whatever. You hang out with me in black while I meet him, scare the hell out of him, and we won't have anything to worry about."

A sickening feeling welled up in Mae. "No. Absolutely not."

"After everything else that's happened, is it that big a deal?"

"It's wasteful," she said, mustering as much scorn as she could to hide her sadness over her ban from wearing the uniform. "I'm not putting on the uniform of the RUNA's greatest military branch for your own amusement. You should be ashamed for asking."

He sighed. "You should be ashamed for putting Tessa's virtue at stake."

"She's a good kid. Nothing's going to happen."

"I'm not worried about *her*. Come on, be a team player. Can't you give me something to work with here?"

Mae considered for several long moments and finally nodded with resignation. "I think I know what I can do."

CHAPTER 22

THE MISCREANT TERRORIST GIRLS' REFORM CAMP

Tessa didn't understand why Mae was around when Dennis came over. Tessa also didn't understand why Mae chose that particular time to clean her guns.

"So," Justin said. "Tell me where you guys are going tonight."

He'd received them in his office, sitting behind the wide oak desk he'd recently acquired. His hands were clasped in front of him, and Dennis stood before him in the way a supplicant might when pleading before a judge. One screen on the desk faced Justin, but a larger one in the wall behind him was viewable to everyone else in the room. It displayed the locked menu for Justin's work, showing the RUNA's seal and: *Warning: Authorized Personnel Only, Ministry of Internal Security.* Maybe other people would've found that intimidating, but not Dennis.

That was because he couldn't take his eyes off Mae. She sat near Justin's desk, at a round table that had two guns and a knife lying on it. Her legs were folded under her on the chair, and she looked casual in jeans and a pullover. Everything about her was easy and relaxed, except for the fact that she was systematically disassembling each gun, cleaning the parts, and putting them back together. Then she'd repeat the process. Although it was weird, Tessa didn't find it that alarming, but she reminded herself she was more used to guns than the average Gemman. What she found more disturbing was a bruise and small cut on the side of Mae's face that were visible whenever she brushed her long hair away.

Mae finished putting together her larger gun for the third time, checking it in such a way that it pointed directly at Dennis. He flinched and backed up, nearly running into Tessa. It took him several moments to realize he'd been addressed and finally turned his wide eyes toward Justin. He gulped.

"Westfield Plaza, sir."

"Outside or inside?"

"Outside."

"General seating?"

"Yes."

"You bringing blankets?"

Mae loaded a cartridge into the other gun with a bit more force than she probably needed. Dennis jumped again.

"Y-yes, sir."

Justin said nothing right away and simply stared at Dennis in a way that seemed to terrify him more than the guns. Tessa could see lines of fatigue on Justin's face and was surprised he could be so intimidating. He and Mae had only just gotten back from their recent trip an hour ago, and from the tension between them, things hadn't gone well.

"How many other people are going?" asked Justin.

"Six."

"Poppy's one of them," said Tessa, feeling a need to help Dennis.

Justin scoffed. "That's not reassuring. You're the kid who goes to church, right?"

"Yes, sir."

"Are they still preaching that cr—stuff about virtue and pure bodies?"

Dennis nodded eagerly. "Yes, yes. They just had a lecture last week."

Justin subjected him to more dramatic scrutiny. "Okay. You can go . . . but I did a background check on you. I know where you live. She's back by eleven, understand?"

Mae finished putting together a handgun and practiced aiming this one as well.

"Absolutely, sir. Thank you, sir."

Tessa and Dennis hurried away.

"Wow," he said once they were en route. "It must be pretty brutal living here."

He sat almost a foot away from her on the train downtown, and Tessa had a feeling she didn't have to worry about him attempting moves on her virtue tonight. Or ever.

They met Poppy and the others at a busy fast food place near the concert venue, which was a far cry from the fine dining establishments Justin frequented. Watching the way the servers churned out food didn't inspire confidence, but it did give Tessa material for her film class. She'd taken to bringing her camera everywhere lately so that she could film snippets of Gemman life for her project. Her instructor was the only one who seemed to think Tessa's background could actually offer something useful in observing the RUNA. Part of this included candid interviews, something her friends were more than happy to do.

"I was worried you wouldn't come," Poppy told her later. "Thought those provincial hang-ups would get the best of you." As usual, though, she spoke of those "hang-ups" fondly.

Poppy was dressed like a girl Tessa had once seen on a corner while traveling by car with her family. "That girl didn't listen to her parents," Tessa's mother had said ominously.

"This is going to blow your mind," Poppy added. As the others chatted excitedly, she leaned toward Tessa and lowered her voice. "What do you think of Dennis?"

Tessa glanced across the table to where he was chatting with his sister, fresh off her suspension. "He's okay," whispered Tessa. "But I don't think he's the one for me."

"Who needs the one?" Poppy grinned. "Nothing wrong with having fun with a guy."

Tessa didn't think she would ever be into the kind of "fun" that Poppy was referring to, at least not in a casual way. Maybe there was nothing more to attraction and Tessa was just deluding herself. Just like Dennis, no guy at school had really wowed her. No girl had either. She would've blamed it on a cultural contrast, but she'd never met anyone of interest in Panama.

Poppy seemed to love a different guy every week, and Tessa feared there might just be something wrong with her.

The fact that the concert was outdoors helped with Tessa's crowd claustrophobia. It was the music itself she had trouble with. She'd meant to preview Vital Lucidity on the stream but hadn't gotten around to it. They caught her totally off guard and were like no band she'd ever heard before. The lyrics were indecipherable, and the background music sounded jarring and discordant. Worst of all, everything was just *loud*. All conversation had to be shouted, and Tessa half expected hearing loss later. Sitting outside in the spring evening was pleasant at least, and recording her friends' enraptured faces provided more material. Rhea was a particular fan and kept going on about how much she knew about the band, all the paraphernalia she'd collected, and all the stats on their next album. It was another of those moments when Tessa was struck by how an antireligious country managed to find gods without even realizing it.

"You want some?" Poppy offered her a flask at intermission.

Tessa hesitated. One glass of wine at Leo and Dominic's had nearly knocked her out. "I don't know if I should."

"There's another one in my purse. I stole it all from my dad's liquor cabinet—not that he'll even notice. I swear, he drinks more than anyone else in the world."

After living with Justin, Tessa wasn't so sure about that.

Dennis overheard and moved to their side of the blanket, panic all over his face. "*No.* Absolutely not. If she goes home drunk, they'll kill me."

"He didn't say anything about alcohol," said Tessa. It surprised her that she'd suddenly feel irritated at the thought of Dennis dictating her actions. And Justin had started off the night doing it as well. *I've been here too long,* she thought. *Already resisting authority. I never would've questioned any order back home.*

"Whatever," said Poppy, still wielding the flask. "A couple drinks won't get her drunk."

But by the end of the concert, Tessa was drunk.

It was a new experience, and she was surprised at how much she liked it. Maybe Justin was onto something. Her head felt pleasantly fuzzy and light, and everything was extra funny. She didn't feel as shy as usual around the group and enjoyed putting herself into the conversation for a change.

As they walked down the street afterward, Tessa noticed that Dennis was the only sober person in their group. He kept casting nervous looks at both Tessa and the time on his ego. Justin and Mae's presentation had apparently hit home.

They ended up in an area of the city Tessa had never seen. A large pillared building loomed up before them, with cleverly aimed spotlights adding to its powerful presence. "What is that?" she asked.

"The House of Senators," said Rhea's latest boyfriend. "How can you not know that?"

Embarrassed, Tessa groped for something to say that would redeem her. "The guy I'm living with knows a senator. They're practically best friends." Her foggy brain tried to remember the name she kept seeing in the news. "Lucian Darling."

"Really?" asked Rhea. They all looked impressed, and Tessa swelled up with pride. "He's gonna be consul."

"And he's hot," added Poppy. "The senator, I mean. Well, and the guy you live with too. I don't have a problem with older guys, you know."

"Everyone knows that," said Rhea's boyfriend, eliciting snickers.

They walked a few more minutes and came up on a large stone wall surrounding several city blocks. "What about this?" Tessa asked.

"The National Gardens," Dennis told her. He looked down at his ego. "You should start heading home."

"You need to come here in the day, when they're open," said a girl named Sibyl. "Awesome place to make out."

Rhea had come to a halt and was staring at a tree farther down the wall's side. "I heard you can get in if you climb that tree."

The others turned on her incredulously. "That's crazy," said Poppy. Tessa was pretty sure it was the first time she'd ever heard her friend describe anything that way.

"No, no. My friend's cousin told me." Rhea pointed. "Look,

it almost touches the wall. You climb it and jump over, and then you're down. It's easy."

"That drop isn't easy," said Dennis. He tugged Tessa's arm. "Come on."

"There's a bench on the other side," Rhea insisted. "You just aim and land on that."

Even Poppy wasn't on board. "I don't think you could get over from the tree."

Tessa blinked the world into focus and studied the tree in question. "No, no . . . you can. Look. You have to swing onto that branch off to the side, and that'll get you up to the limb by the wall."

Despite Cynthia's constantly saying a prætorian wasn't a realistic instructor, Quentin and Tessa had kept up with tree-climbing practice. Even if they'd never developed Mae's easy skill, they'd both managed to finally get up the tree on their own.

Emboldened by that success (and the alcohol), Tessa thought Rhea's proposal was perfectly reasonable—aside from one small flaw. "How do you get back out?"

"The inner wall is textured," Rhea said promptly. "Get back on the bench, get a handhold, and you're back on top to the tree." She caught hold of Tessa's arm. "Want to do it?"

Dennis displayed the same panic he had with Mae's gun pointing at him. "No! You can't. Do you seriously think it's that easy? The whole place is rigged and monitored! You can see the guards right there."

It was true. Scattered along the wall were gray-and-maroon-clad military, keeping watch on their surroundings. Rhea was unconcerned.

"You guys distract them. Make a big scene. We'll go over."

Poppy clearly was wavering between her normal impulsive instincts and a logical voice that had apparently decided to show up tonight. The former won out. "Okay. We'll help."

Rhea grinned at Tessa. "You in?"

"I'm in."

"You guys!" exclaimed Dennis.

But everyone else was already in motion. Poppy led the others over to a soldier while Tessa and Rhea slinked off in the other direction. The group laughed uproariously and stumbled more than they had earlier. Tessa heard Poppy say, "Hey, mister soldier guy. Do you know where we can get some tapas around here?"

"I don't want any fucking tapas," said Rhea's boyfriend. "You said we could get pie."

"You always want pie," said Sibyl, earning more laughter.

The soldier said something Tessa couldn't hear, probably about how they all needed to go home. Another soldier strolled over to see what the commotion was, and Rhea shoved Tessa. "Let's go."

The tree didn't have nearly as many branches as the one at home. Tessa scraped her hands trying to get ahold of the lowest one, which wasn't as sturdy as she'd thought. Her disorientation didn't help matters, and she nearly lost her balance twice. Still, she was pleased that she did a better job than Rhea and actually jumped to the wall first—though not without nearly falling again. She managed to hold on to the top of it as she crouched and willed the world to stop spinning. Once her rapid breathing calmed down, she moved over, and Rhea joined her.

"Fucking awesome," said Rhea.

Tessa had to agree. The gardens spread out before them, so beautifully designed that they didn't seem real. Hedges were trimmed to perfection, lining stone paths that wound around everything. Trees Tessa had never seen before swayed gently in the evening breeze, with beds of flowers surrounding them. She couldn't quite make out the colors in the poor lighting. The gardens had the same kind of spotlights as the front of the senate, but they were pointed up at statues of important historical figures scattered along the path.

And just below them was Rhea's bench.

"It's really there," said Tessa, not realizing until that moment that she hadn't been sure. It didn't look quite as high as Rhea had led her to believe.

"Yup."

Without further warning, Rhea jumped. She actually managed to land on the bench but couldn't get her footing. She swore as she fell to the ground but soon stood up and gave Tessa a thumbs-up. "No broken bones."

A reasonable part of Tessa was beginning to sober up and tell her this was a terrible idea. But Rhea had already invested in the venture, and peer pressure ran strong. Tessa jumped with similar results, hitting the bench and falling. Unlike Rhea, Tessa felt pain shoot through her ankle as she landed ungracefully. Rhea helped her up and had that big grin on her face again.

"What should we do first?"

Shouts told them they wouldn't be doing anything. Tessa spun around, wincing as her ankle yelled at her. Still, she was about to jump on the bench and climb out when she noticed something important.

There were no handholds on the wall. It was perfectly smooth. Her jaw dropped, and she turned to Rhea.

"You said—ahh!"

Something big slammed into her body, forcing her to the ground and knocking the wind out of her. A nearby cry suggested Rhea had met the same fate. Strong hands jerked Tessa upright. A dark figure peered down at her and sighed.

"It's just a fucking kid," he said.

"Mine too," came a female voice. "So much for the world's best security."

"It's not like they got into the senate itself," said Tessa's captor in a surprisingly light tone. He steered her forward. "Come on."

She tried to walk but stumbled. "M-my ankle."

"Serves you right."

He slung his arm around her and half dragged, half carried her toward the main building. Tessa thought her heart would explode. Until then, she hadn't believed anything could be more terrifying than that first day in the Gemman airport. Blood pounded in her ears, and she really couldn't make any sense of her surroundings except the rapidly approaching building.

The man scanned his hand at a door and unlocked it. Light spilled out when the door opened, making Tessa squint at the dramatic change. She and Rhea were led down an empty, sterile hallway toward a large door that read SECURITY. Another hand scan gave them access, and they entered a room filled with monitors and gray uniforms. One of the soldiers looked up in surprise.

"What's this?"

"Our perimeter was breached by highly trained assassins," said the man holding Tessa. He gently pushed her into an empty chair, and a moment later, Rhea sat beside her, looking as though she might pass out.

Now that her eyes had adjusted to the light, Tessa managed to get a good look at their escort. When she did, she thought she might be sick.

Prætorians.

All the larger-than-life horror stories she'd grown up with returned. These two weren't like Mae, who joked and smiled and wore pretty clothes. Both were clad in black uniforms that made them seem like death incarnate. The man who'd held her was huge, his muscled physique apparent even under the black jacket. The woman who'd held Rhea was shorter and slimmer, but her strength was obvious. Both wore guns at their sides and possessed hard, deadly expressions.

The regular soldier who'd greeted them brought over a scanner and checked Rhea's chip. "I'm sure your parents are going to love meeting with military police tonight. You're lucky you're a minor." When he scanned Tessa, his snide look vanished. "Huh."

" 'Huh' what?" asked the female prætorian.

"She's a Panamanian national." The soldier stepped back, floored. "This is an attack on Gemman soil. She's technically a terrorist."

The male prætorian snorted. "She's a kid. And she's drunk."

The woman moved to look at the scanner. "Is there a guardian or some contact information?" She looked over the screen, and her eyebrows rose. "Justin March."

She and the big prætorian exchanged looks.

"Let us take her," said the female prætorian. "We'll deal with her."

The soldier gaped. "You can't! Do you know how serious this is? I have to make calls and—"

"Hector," said the woman, her voice like ice. "Let us have her. We'll make sure she's dealt with."

"How? I'll get in trouble if I release her."

The big prætorian pointed at Rhea. "You've got one. There'll be enough drama over her, and then it'll blow over."

The man in gray obviously didn't agree. "It's trespassing on federal property."

The three of them went back and forth, and all the while, Tessa tried not to hyperventilate. In the end, the prætorians won. They started with logic and eventually resorted to intimidation. The soldier was trembling by the time they finished and gave the prætorians a nervous salute as they led Tessa out. She shot Rhea one last desperate look, but her friend was too shocked to even notice.

The big prætorian helped her walk again but didn't restrain her with handcuffs or anything. Considering how quickly he'd subdued her in the garden, she probably wasn't a big security risk. They took her to other rooms, going about some other business she couldn't follow. When two other equally terrifying prætorians showed up, they all saluted one another, and her escort received permission to leave.

She expected to board a military plane straight back to Panama, but instead, they rode the subway—which actually might have been worse. The stares she'd received on her first day in the RUNA were nothing compared to what she got now. The prætorians sat on each side of her, stiff and formidable, and Tessa hunched over, wishing she could melt into the seat. Despite the gawking, the other passengers kept their distance, and Tessa didn't blame them. She and her companions rode in silence, which was broken only once, when the man said, "You are in *so* much trouble."

One sentence, but it was enough to make every awful scenario play through Tessa's mind. What would happen? Deportation? Losing her visa was probably the best thing she could hope for. Even imprisonment wouldn't be as bad as other fates they might have in store. After all, the man at the security office had said she was a terrorist. Couldn't something like that result in execution?

By the time they reached the March house, she no longer had to worry about hyperventilating, because she practically couldn't breathe at all.

The prætorians still flanked her as they marched up to the front door. Lights shone through the window, and some hysterical part of her wondered whether she'd made curfew.

Justin opened the door and took in the sight before him with remarkable calm. "Oh. Wow."

"Are you Justin March?" demanded the woman. When he nodded, she said, "We have a situation."

"Yes," he said slowly. "I can see that we do."

"This girl invaded the National Gardens," explained the male prætorian. "That's practically an act of terrorism."

Justin could only stare.

The woman continued on, her voice low and cool. "Because she's a minor, we might be able to lighten her punishment."

"Don't get me wrong," said the man. "Prison's still the most likely option. But if she's lucky, she might just serve a few years in the Miscreant Terrorist Girls' Reform Camp."

Justin's eyes had been kind of dazed, but with those words, that razor-sharp focus Tessa knew so well reappeared and fixed on the prætorian. "The Miscreant Terrorist Girls' Reform Camp?"

"Yes," said the woman. "I'm sure you know its reputation."

"Some girls never make it back," said the other prætorian ominously.

Justin seemed slightly more relaxed, maybe because execution hadn't been mentioned yet. "Well. Sacrifices have to be made for the sake of our country."

The female prætorian nodded. "Normally, we'd detain her right away, but since you work for Internal Security, our superiors decided she'd be safe to leave in your custody."

"Especially since you have a prætorian working with you," added the man. "I, uh, don't suppose she's here right now?"

"No, she went home."

"Ah." The prætorian sounded disappointed. Maybe he wanted the extra level of security for Tessa. "Well, then, it's on you to make sure she doesn't escape."

Justin gave Tessa a sharp look. "Oh, I assure you, she's not going anywhere."

"We'll decide her fate tomorrow." The woman made a grand gesture toward the house. "You may go now."

Tessa hesitated and looked to Justin.

"Go," he said.

"And get some ice for your ankle," added the guy. For half a second, she thought she saw his lips start to twitch into a smile, but then his face was all hard lines again.

Tessa gave hasty nods and then scurried inside, afraid that they'd change their minds if she looked back.

CHAPTER 23

THE BALLAD OF
MAE AND PORFIRIO

Justin listened as Tessa went into the kitchen, opened the refrigerator, and then headed off to her room. When he heard her bedroom door close, he finally spoke to the stone-faced prætorians.

"So," he said. "You must be friends with Mae."

And then the most extraordinary thing happened. The terrifying prætorians started cracking up. The man actually burst into outright laughter and nearly had tears in his eyes. The woman buried her face in him and shook as she tried to keep her own laughter quiet.

"Oh," he told her, "that was so mean. And hilarious."

The woman was still trying not to giggle. "Really? The Miscreant Terrorist Girls' Reform Camp?"

"It was all I could think of on the spot," he said. "And it worked, didn't it? Did you see her face? Poor kid."

Justin looked between them, not entirely sure how to handle this situation. He'd accepted that his life was becoming increasingly surreal these days, but it apparently still held new and exciting ways to surprise him. "Would . . . you like to come in for a drink?" He remembered belatedly that alcohol was useless on prætorians, but it seemed like appropriate compensation. He wasn't sure what had just happened, but instinct told him the prætorians might have just done Tessa a huge favor.

"Sure," said the woman. She held out her hand without hesitation. "Valeria Jardin. My friends call me Val, and you can definitely be one of my friends." Justin often likened Mae to a lioness when she was ready to fight. There was something feline about Val too, but of an entirely different nature. She was sleek and sensuous—but most certainly had claws of her own.

"Back off," the man warned Val. "You heard what she said."

"Mae?" asked Justin. "What did she say?"

"She said you were cute," said Val.

The prætorian man rolled his eyes. "She did not. She just told you to stay away."

"That's practically an admission of lust from her."

"It is not. She just doesn't want you complicating things, Val."

Val looked up at Justin through long lashes, a demure look in her dark eyes. "I never complicate anything," she purred. "Not too much, at least."

"I need that drink," the guy prætorian said, stepping around her. "Hope you're well stocked."

"Extremely," said Justin. He was still a little mystified. "I didn't catch your name . . . ?"

"Dag," called the man, not elaborating on whether that was his first or last name. He was already striding toward the kitchen, with the self-assurance of one who knew he could go anywhere.

Justin showed them the liquor cabinet, which met with their approval. They grabbed two bottles each and looked at him expectantly. "Out to the patio," he said. He took a bottle of bourbon for himself and three glasses, not that the prætorians seemed to need any vessels. "Everyone else is asleep."

The expansive backyard patio was far away from the bedrooms, which were clustered together. Like everything else around here, it was opulent and lovely. It had a slate floor set with patina-covered furniture and a trellised cover wrapped with vines that offered protection on hot days. A fire pit sat off to the side, ready with warmth on cooler days. The whole area was ripe and ready for entertaining, but backyard parties hadn't exactly been on Justin's agenda recently. He never would have guessed he'd be breaking it in with two prætorians.

Both of Dag's bottles were whiskey. He set one on the table and then immediately began drinking the other, no glass required.

"Isn't that"—Justin groped for the right words—"kind of a waste? With the implant and everything?"

"He's slamming the implant," explained Val. She opened a bottle of tequila. "If he can down that bottle in a couple minutes, he'll get a buzz. A short one, but hey, you take what you can get." From the way she then dove into her own bottle, she was apparently "slamming" her implant as well.

This was news to Justin. "Seems like you'd mostly get alcohol poisoning."

"Nah." Dag paused in his drinking. He was about halfway through the bottle. "The implant will catch up. I'm just getting a head start."

"I see." Justin watched them continue their binge drinking and felt a little lame for sipping his own drink. He had no delusions about trying to keep up, though. He'd probably have been dead already.

They both finished and looked supremely pleased with themselves. Dag gave Val a high five. "There it is."

She sighed happily and settled back into her chair. "Fun end to a fun night."

"What happened tonight?" Justin asked. "Why is Tessa a terrorist?"

That brought the grins back. "She scaled the wall into the National Gardens," said Dag. "Happens every once in a while. I mean, there's so much surveillance there that they're always spotted before they even get to the wall, but they should really cut that fucking tree down."

Justin didn't even hear the part about the tree. "Tessa broke into the gardens? Why would she do that?"

"Because kids do that with other kids," said Val. "And she was drunk."

Justin nearly dropped his glass. "No. Not her. No way."

Dag actually looked sympathetic. "I know it's hard to accept, but no matter how innocent you think they are, teenage girls are always going to do things you don't want to believe."

"Oh, I have no delusions about teen girls, believe me. But not her. If you knew her, you'd understand. Hell, she put on her first pair of jeans two weeks ago and still gets freaked-out about how cars have no drivers."

Val laughed. "Well, she was lucky this time, so keep her out of trouble. Next time federal security drags her in, she may not have two gallant heroes to rescue her."

"Something tells me there won't be a repeat." Justin toyed with his glass and used the opportunity to mull over their story. "How'd you know who she was?"

"Finn—er, Mae—told us everything, and there aren't that many Panamanian girls wandering Vancouver." Dag was already eyeing the second bottle. "Then we just tracked you down."

Justin thought back on recent events. "Mae did too good a job at teaching her to climb trees."

That made Dag laugh. "She's good at everything. You should see her in combat."

Val nodded along with Dag's words. "I mean, we're all good, but she's *really* good. Even before she had the implant, she was kicking ass. She got a lot of crap for being castal when she joined the guard. I think she beat up three people that first day, and no one ever messed with her again. Well, not in our cohort, of course."

Justin knew enough about prætorians to understand the color-coded system. Their pip color was visible in the dim light. "Red cohort?"

"Scarlet," they said in unison.

"Why do you call her Finn? She already fits into your monosyllabic club."

They found that hilarious. "Dag couldn't remember her name back then," said Val. "But we could all remember she was Nordic. Hard not to. And 'Finn' is a cuter nickname than 'Swede.'"

Silence fell as the prætorians cracked into their second bottles. Justin still couldn't get over the weirdness of this situation. Before that miscreant-camp nonsense, even he'd been taken aback when they'd shown up at his door. The faces . . . the posture . . . those uniforms. His own heart had nearly stopped. He'd also seen Mae in action enough to appreciate just how lethal prætorians could be.

Which made it completely ludicrous that he now had two of them before him, trying desperately to get drunk as they made wisecracks and congratulated themselves over a prank played on a teenage girl. The government took nearly 40 percent of his paycheck, and he felt kind of affronted that this was what his taxes paid for.

"And so you guys are guarding the gardens?"

Dag nodded. "Yup. Pretty sweet deal. Easy work and lots of time off."

"I'm free tomorrow night," said Val meaningfully.

"I kind of miss the field." Dag stared wistfully at his bottle. "I'm ready for action."

Val touched his arm. "Soon enough. Maybe we'll go together. Maybe Finn too. They can't stick her with this job forever." She glanced up at Justin. "No offense."

That instinct rose up in Justin, the one that said something was about to happen. "Why would I be offended?" He examined her words. "And what do you mean she's stuck?"

"You don't know?" Val looked legitimately puzzled. "You're punishment."

"That's harsh. I mean, someone had to be with him, right? It's not like they just designed this job to teach her a lesson." Dag turned thoughtful. "But I don't think she would've gotten it if she hadn't done what she did. She'd be with us in the gardens."

The big man sounded sad, but there was an almost accusatory note in his voice. Justin didn't know whether it was directed toward him, Mae, or some other mysterious factor. All he knew was that he was being left behind in this conversation, and he needed to catch up. The idea of his being someone's punishment didn't make any sense.

Horatio laughed, inasmuch as a raven could. *Right. Because how could your company be anything but a delight?*

"What did she do? Why is she being taught a lesson?"

Val and Dag exchanged looks. Their happy-go-lucky natures

had vanished. "I don't know if we should tell," said Dag slowly. "I mean, if she hasn't told him, maybe she doesn't want him to know."

"Well, it's not exactly a big secret," Val pointed out, a bit of her swagger returning. "Hell, practically every prætorian knows the Ballad of Mae and Porfirio." She laughed at her own word choice, and Dag soon joined in.

But Justin wasn't amused. He was too caught up in the glimmer of insight he was starting to feel. "Porfirio . . . that's him, isn't it? The beach guy."

Val turned from Dag. "She *did* tell you."

"No . . . not exactly." How could he explain all the telltale signs he'd gathered? The way she wouldn't meet his eyes when any whisper of this came up, the way her whole body went still. "I just kind of guessed something was going on."

"Oh, believe me, I don't think you could guess all of this. It's one of those stranger-than-fiction things." She looked back at Dag. "Do you want to tell it?"

"You start," he said. "I'll correct you when you're wrong."

She elbowed him with a force that would've knocked an ordinary person out of his chair. "I know the story. I was there when it happened."

"So stop wasting time, and tell it," Dag ordered.

"Fine, fine." Val took a deep breath. "So, about two years ago, we were at this party. Since it was an election year, they had a bunch of us in town—it'll happen later this year too. Too many important people around who need protection. Guarding politicians is a lot like guarding the gardens. Lots of ceremony, lots of time off—and lots of ree parties. One night, this guy— Maize, I think—rented out a whole hall. I swear, half the guard was there."

"Wasn't it his engagement party?" interjected Dag.

"Maybe. I don't remember."

"See? I knew you wouldn't."

"I know the important parts," she snapped.

"The party," said Justin, trying to get them back on track. "Ree. Half the guard."

"Right," said Val. "Okay, so yeah. Lots of us there, lots of us trashed. Dag's walking to the bar and overhears this group of Indigos. One of them's bragging how he used to do *canne de combat*. Do you know that sport?"

"I must've missed that somewhere," Justin told her.

"It's nuts," said Dag. "Imagine fencing with wooden poles. And a lot of acrobatics."

Justin could not imagine that. "It's a real sport?"

"Yup. Finn's awesome at it." Dag looked as proud as he would have been of a star pupil. "Castals really dig it, but you find plebeian leagues too."

Val was ready to move on with the story. "So, this Indigo guy, Porfirio, is—was—an ex-castal. Iberian." Outside Mae's caste, Justin realized. "And so, he's there bragging about how great he used to be, and *someone* feels the need to call him out." She paused and shot a glare at Dag.

"Hey," he said, throwing his hands up indignantly. "You should have heard him. He was an arrogant prick. He *always* was, right up to the end. He needed to be put in his place."

Val pointed accusingly. "If you'd kept your mouth shut, none of this would've happened."

Dag fell silent, contemplating her words.

"So," she continued. "Dag tells this guy—Porfirio—how his cohort sister could totally kick his ass. This gets the Indigos all riled up, and everyone starts making bets. The next thing I know, Porfirio's swaggering up to the table I'm at with Finn, ready for a fight she doesn't even know about."

"Arrogant. Prick," muttered Dag.

"That one Azure guy was hitting on her, you know." Val's brow furrowed in thought. "Albright, that's it. He's a nice guy. If you'd left well enough alone, she might have gone home with him. It would've saved us a lot of trouble."

"Stop getting on me for stuff that's already happened!" Now Dag pointed reproachfully at her. "And you know it never would've worked with Albright. She's all stiffly proper in every part of her life, except relationships. Then she somehow ends up with the most messed-up guys out there. Cocky. Full of themselves. Makes me want to punch all of them."

Justin shifted uncomfortably in the chair.

Somehow, despite constantly distracting each other, the two of them managed to relate the most bizarre story about Mae wagering sex in a fight involving sticks. In his mind's eye, he could perfectly picture Mae—fast, deadly, graceful—engaging in this duel. He leaned forward, riveted by the drama of the story.

"It was all foreplay," said Val as she neared the ending. "You could cut the sexual tension with a knife."

"What happened?" asked Justin. "Who won?"

Both Val and Dag hesitated. "I'm not really sure," she said.

"*What?* I thought you guys were there."

"Oh, we were," she said adamantly. "But it just went on forever. We got bored, and then this fight broke out in the Violets because one of them was cheating or something . . . so, we all just went over there."

Justin was stunned. How could Val and Dag have been leading up to this big, climactic moment, only to drop the story now? Even more incredible was how blasé they were about it.

It doesn't inspire much faith in the country's defenses, does it? asked Horatio.

Justin agreed. *Let's just hope they're more competent on the battlefield.*

"I think she won," said Dag. "Porfirio cut his hair the next day."

"No," said Val. "I think he won. I saw her. You know that look she gets after sex. She's less tense for, like, five minutes."

"Maybe they both won," he said.

"Or lost," suggested Val.

Justin wanted to beat his head on the table. Instead, he poured another glass of bourbon. "Is there more to this? What about the part where I'm punishment?"

Val gave up on analyzing the fight's outcome. "I'm getting to that."

Maybe by tomorrow, said Magnus.

"Whatever happened, they were together after that. And they were glorious. Her all fair and gold, him like some dark Mediterranean god."

"He wasn't that good-looking," grumbled Dag.

"Yes, he was," she retorted. "They didn't serve together much. Word gets around, even to the higher-ups, and they keep couples apart so there's no conflict of interest. But whenever they had time off together, they'd hole up and stay in bed for days." Val's gaze shifted inward. "I *think* she was happy."

"Apparently not," said Dag ominously.

"Maybe." Val focused on Justin again. "About six months ago, he proposed. I don't know how he did it. He was always over-the-top, so I'm sure it was something gorgeous and dramatic. Didn't matter, though. She said no."

"Why?" Justin was getting hooked again and was barely aware of how much bourbon he was taking down.

Val shrugged. "I don't know. That's her business. But he certainly had all sorts of theories. He blew up and went off on her about everything. It was all behind closed doors, but I heard enough of it from her. He accused her of not being able to commit. He said she was too proud to leave her caste. He even told her she must have been cheating on him. I think he was pretty desperate to rationalize why she wouldn't run off into the sunset with him. Whatever it was, it got pretty ugly, and if I *had* been there to see it, I would've made sure he never fucked anything again."

Dag nodded in agreement, and Justin once again looked into the faces of the prætorians who'd been at his doorstep. No more levity. No more antics. They were hard and deadly, and if Porfirio had been there right now, Justin was pretty sure they would've ripped him apart.

They love her, said Magnus.

Justin agreed. *Yes, they do.*

Unhinged, wacky, lethal . . . these prætorians were many things, but they were also devoted to Mae with an intensity he rarely saw in the world. And although she hadn't mentioned them yet, he would have wagered all he had that she felt the same way about them.

How does devotion like that happen? he asked. *Is it because they have all that national loyalty drilled into them, and it just gets transferred to those they serve with?*

There doesn't have to be anything complex behind love, said

Magnus. *People just care about each other . . . because they do.*
Friends are like that. Lovers are like that. You should try it
sometime.

I love Cyn and Quentin. Are you going to demean that?

No, that's real, conceded Magnus.

Who are they more loyal to? Each other or the RUNA?

The ravens didn't answer.

"Porfirio didn't take it very well," said Val, finally gaining
enough control to continue on with the story. "He kind of got
out of control. He wanted to prove himself. And he wanted to
get away from her. He requested an assignment over in
Europe—you know what a mess that is."

"I do," said Justin. Europe had never been a consideration
for his exile. "What happened to him?"

"He died," said Val simply. Her and Dag's faces were grave.
"Killed in combat from some explosion. I don't know the details. I don't want to know. When word got back, a lot of
people—especially his cohort—said what happened was her
fault."

"It wasn't," said Dag fiercely. "That was that bastard's own
mistake."

Val obviously agreed. "But plenty didn't think so—still
don't. His funeral was three weeks ago, and one of the Indigos
picked a fight over it."

Dag lit up a little. "Finn cleaned the floor with that bitch. It
was amazing. Kind of scary too. I mean, like we said, she's
good . . . but wow. It was unreal."

"It was real enough to our superiors," said Val dryly.
"Drunken fights at parties are one thing. Disorderly conduct at
a military funeral is completely different. She spent some time
in confinement and then got officially reprimanded. They
stripped her of her uniform and—"

"Wait," Justin interrupted. "What's that mean?"

"It means she can't wear a prætorian's uniform until the ban
is lifted. If she has to go in military wear, it's got to be gray and
maroon." Val's eyes were troubled, filled with sympathy for her
friend. "It's a pretty big deal."

A uniform didn't sound like a big deal, but every cue from

Val and Dag said it was. After a little consideration, Justin could understand it. The prætorians were very, very self-satisfied, confident in their power and position. The uniforms were a symbol of that. They were part of the public's image of them: deadly, black-clad warriors. The greatest in the Republic. Being denied that had to be like losing a part of oneself, and with a pang, he suddenly realized why Mae had been so hostile when he'd suggested she dress up to meet Dennis.

"She also got cut from both active duty and ceremonial duty." Val allowed a dramatic pause as the story finally neared its end. "She got assigned to you."

"And that's why I'm a punishment," he concluded. They nodded, and Justin made no attempt to conceal his feelings.

"Don't take it personally," said Dag, almost kindly. "Your life's kind of exciting."

"But it could be a lot better," said Justin.

A long pause followed, and then Dag repeated, "Don't take it personally."

Justin managed to summon his customary smile—though it was harder than usual tonight—and act as though he was taking this all in stride and had enjoyed their lively story. He tried to think of a topic that wasn't his being a punishment.

"I'm kind of surprised she was openly involved with some-one who wasn't Nordic," he said. An outside castal was consid-ered the same as a plebeian. "I figured she would've been put in some well-arranged marriage."

"Her?" Val's earlier levity returned. "Hell, I don't think she's ever dated a Nordic guy. At least not as long as I've known her."

"But she's still got Nordic citizenship. Seems like she'd want to stay on good terms."

"Apparently not as much as she wants to sleep with dark-haired guys," said Dag. "And as long as she's not married or knocked up, she can flaunt a guy she really likes as much as she wants."

A couple of things about that bothered Justin. One was that Mae had lied about her inability to be with someone like him. The other was the subtle assumption that she hadn't "flaunted" him because he wasn't a guy she really liked. She was still off-limits, but that old sting to his pride remained.

He finished his current glass and offered them more, but a check of the time made the prætorians realize they were missing another party.

"Thanks for the hospitality," Val said, standing up. She touched his cheek. "I'll have to repay you sometime."

"Val," warned Dag.

She merely laughed and gave Justin a wink as she sauntered out. Dag started to follow and then turned back. "Leave your girl hanging for most of tomorrow. Then finally tell her you got a call from the authorities, and they're letting her off—this time. It'll stop it from happening again."

"Thanks for the parenting tip."

Dag grinned and left with Val.

Justin stayed at the table and poured another glass. There was a storm of emotions raging within him, something he hadn't experienced in a very long time. He was hurt. Hurt, sad, and angry. He gulped down half the bourbon and slammed it on the table.

He felt like an idiot.

It hadn't seemed possible that his tangled relationship with Mae could get any weirder. Apparently, he was wrong. Looking back on everything now, he felt sick thinking about some of his behaviors.

You're sick because you've been drinking too much, like usual, said Horatio.

I'm sick because she's been keeping this tragic love story locked inside her. How long does it take to get over something like that? I knew she was sad in Panama. I could see it, but I went for it anyway. I shouldn't have.

You didn't know. And you were drunk then as well, said the raven.

Magnus was kinder. *You didn't act alone. She went for it too, and she was sober.*

Why? asked Justin.

Because women find you attractive. Magnus's tone sug-

296 • *Richelle Mead*

gested he didn't entirely understand that. *And you were sad too. Like calls to like.*

My life has improved since then, Justin reflected. *Well, kind of. But hers got worse. I knew she wasn't thrilled about an irregular assignment, but I didn't know I was a punishment! And here I've been the whole time, arrogant and presumptuous, giving her a hard time over what happened between us, just because I was offended she wasn't drooling over me. I'm as shallow as she claims.*

When the ravens didn't deny it, Justin stood up on unsteady legs. "I'm going to see her."

That's a bad idea, said Horatio as Justin went inside.

It wouldn't be my first, Justin replied.

A check in the mirror showed he was presentable. His clothes were neat and unwrinkled. Every hair was in place. He didn't even look that drunk.

He could feel the ravens' incredulity at that last thought.

He double-checked Mae's address and then caught the purple line downtown. A transfer took him out to her neighborhood, an older but upscale district with well-established trees and pretty brick buildings. Mae lived in a town house with cherry trees out front, and he paused to admire it as he stood outside. It wasn't quite as sleek as his last apartment had been, but it was still the kind of place he should've ended up in, rather than his sister's house. He really needed to fix that and move to the city.

He braced himself as he went up the stairs, trying to stay cool in the flood of anxiety and eagerness filling him. He still didn't know what he was going to say, but if he talked to her, they could fix things. He needed to make sense of all of this, to understand why—

"Hello?"

A strange man opened the door. He wore only jeans, showing off a bodybuilder's chest. He had sandy-colored hair that looked damp from recent washing. After a few initial moments of shock, Justin decided that he must have the wrong place.

"I—I'm sorry. I made a mistake."

The man gave him an easy smile, and Justin realized he

wasn't a stranger after all. He was one of the prætorians from the senate. "You looking for Kosk—er, Mae?"

Justin could only give a mute nod.

"Come in, and I'll get her." The guy stepped aside. "She just got out of the shower."

CHAPTER 24

THERAPY

Mae hadn't expected to get as much amusement as she had out of Justin's treatment of Tessa's poor date. Maybe after everything that had happened in Mazatlán, that little bit of comic relief was what she needed. It didn't change Mae's overall mood, of course. She was still reeling from everything that had happened, still trying to find a way to process the unimaginable: that a man she'd come to respect—despite how infuriating he was at times—was being driven by delusions of the very thing he was supposed to be fighting against.

As she started to climb the steps to her town house, she remembered a message that had come to her ego about a package that had arrived for her. She changed course and walked to the building next door, where her landlord lived. His lobby held all the tenant mailboxes on that block, as well as larger compartments for packages. Kneeling down, Mae located the one indicated and scanned her ego over the digital lock. The door clicked open, and she found a bouquet of long-stemmed white roses, their petals delicately edged in pink. She picked them up in surprise, searched for a card that wasn't there, and headed back to her home.

She couldn't remember the last time anyone had sent her flowers. Maybe some love-struck former soldier from back before she'd joined the prætorians? Porfirio hadn't been much for gestures like these. Sure, he went for the dramatic sometimes, but it would be things like a candlelit bedroom, the kind of act that usually resulted immediately in sex. For half a second, she wondered if they were from Justin as a sort of *Sorry for completely deceiving you about my involvement in illicit religions* apology. But no. The flowers had arrived while they were traveling to Mazatlán.

She put them in a vase and received an answer far more quickly than expected when her ego rang with a call. The display showed a shocking name, and she switched the call over to her living room screen. Lucian Darling's smiling face appeared, as handsome and polished as anything she'd find at a press conference.

"Senator," she said in greeting. "I figured you'd forgotten about me."

His grin widened. "Impossible. Just been caught up in the whirlwind of campaigning. Not that that's an excuse."

"I don't know about that. It's actually kind of a good one, what with you preparing to lead the country and all that."

"Does that mean you'll urge your representative to vote for me?"

She laughed and settled onto the couch. "Sure."

"Then I'm one step closer. Was it the roses that won you over?"

"No, but thank you." Despite all the ease and charm he radiated, she felt a little flustered by the gesture. It kicked his flirting from their first meeting up a notch, something she wasn't sure she wanted. "You didn't have to."

"Of course I did. I needed to secure your vote. That, and I was hoping I could get you out for a late dinner."

The unexpected just kept coming. "Tonight?"

"Sorry about the short notice." Something in his manner made her think he wasn't *that* sorry, that he still figured she'd jump at the chance. He and Justin weren't that different after all. "An event just got canceled, so I'm homebound in Vancouver for the night and thought you might like to come over. Don't read that as presumption," he added. "It's more for convenience. I'd gladly take you out somewhere, but I don't think you'd like the attention."

"Probably not," she said in agreement. Remembering Justin's observations about the political fallout of a plebeian senator dating a castal, Mae knew Lucian wouldn't like the attention either.

"Fortunately for you, I can cook the kind of steak most people only dream of. You'll be a believer." That smile was in overdrive now as he waited for her response.

"That's sweet. And flattering," she said honestly. "But I literally just walked in after a long trip and don't think I'm up to getting out." *Or navigating the treacherous waters of this sort of liaison.* "I'm sorry. But thank you."

His face fell only a little. Undaunted, he asked, "I'm out of town tomorrow but back the next day. How's Monday night work for you?"

She shook her head. "I'm out of town. Justin and I are going to be out at the Nordic land grant."

He arched an eyebrow. "Taking him home to meet the parents?"

"Business," she said, shuddering at the thought of unleashing him on her family.

"Well, that reminds me . . . I also called because I've got an answer—sort of—to Justin's question about servitor hiring."

She'd nearly forgotten about that. "Why not call him?"

"I'd rather talk to you. Besides, he'd give me grief about not having much that's conclusive."

"What'd you find out?"

He shrugged. "Mostly that the number of servitors has increased because the demand has increased."

"Are you sure?" Mae tried to recall what Justin had said. "I think he checked the number of cases SCI's got. There's no significant difference from last year."

Lucian's eyes sparkled, probably at one-upping Justin. "He checked the *national* cases. But not ones in the protectorates and provinces."

She was startled. "I didn't think we sent many servitors there. Especially the provinces." Protectorates weren't that surprising. They were usually on track to being annexed, so it made sense that the RUNA would start cleaning house in advance.

"We do now," said Lucian.

"Why?"

"No one gave me an answer on that. But I also found out some of the national cases are getting multiple servitors investigating them." He tilted his head to study her. "Is that helpful?"

"I don't know," she admitted. "Justin will have to make the call on that. I'll pass it on. Thank you."

The grin was back. "Happy to help. Especially if I get to talk to you again. Don't worry—we'll make something work out one of these days."

"Thanks," said Mae, who hadn't been worried.

There was something appealing about him, but again, it was a mess she didn't need. After a little more flirtation, Lucian disconnected and Mae stood up, stretching her muscles. The activity in Mazatlán hadn't wearied her. If anything, it had made her crave more physical action. The odds of finding a *canne* partner this time of night were pretty low, though.

In a heartbeat, she made her decision—an ironic one, considering she'd just rejected Lucian. But she needed a simpler man now, one who didn't travel with reporters in tow and could help her with this physical restlessness in as simple a way as possible.

"Call Giles Whitetree," she told the screen.

He answered quickly, looking pleasantly surprised to see her face. "Koskinen."

Whitetree had been on her mind since she'd seen him at the senate. He was a Scarlet too, one of the nicest guys in her cohort. Little stressed him out, and he didn't kiss and tell. His liaisons sometimes did, and what they told was always favorable.

"What are you doing tonight?" she asked.

"About to head over to some Celadon's place across town. Rumor has it he got some ree."

"You want to come over here instead?"

Whitetree paused and gave her a considering look, perfectly understanding the subtext. "Have you moved?"

"Nope."

"I'll be there in fifteen."

They disconnected, and Mae wondered if she should make it easy on him by changing into a robe. Her implant would encourage her body to increase the chemicals of lust, just as it did those of battle. That surge in sex hormones sent women to heart-racing levels of arousal—men into blind frenzies. Normal male sex drives had a tendency to be stronger in general. Paired with an implant, those sex drives could grow out of control. However he was traveling here, Whitetree had fifteen minutes to think about sex, which was an eternity for the implant's effects to keep building and building. Prætorians took nonprætorian lovers often, but it could sometimes be difficult for civilian women who weren't prepared for that roughness. Although it was rare, prætorian men occasionally found themselves accused of rape.

"Look at you, courted by politicians and warriors alike."

Mae immediately turned toward the voice that had come from the dark hall leading to her bedroom. Her guns were on the kitchen counter, and she couldn't risk exposing herself to retrieve them. She picked up the first weapon she could find: a heavy stone bowl she'd brought back from a mission in Asia.

Emil, the man from the Brödern, materialized from the darkness. At least he wasn't armed again, but that didn't rule out a threat, especially seeing as he'd broken into her home. "How the hell did you get in here?" she demanded.

"I get where I need to go," he said mildly. There was such an irritating casualness about him that Mae half expected him to go help himself to something in the refrigerator. "And it's hard to find you in one place these days."

She kept her grip on the bowl. "Really? And here I thought your group's influence reached everywhere."

"No, though it goes far. Did you get the hair examined?" Now that he was in better lighting, she couldn't detect a trace of Cain on him.

"Yes," she said reluctantly.

"And?"

"And it could still be a ploy. You could've gotten it from my aunt, and it'd have the same match."

"That's a lot of effort for one ploy."

"Ploys generally work that way, especially if you really do want some enterprising prætorian to join up with you. You want to convince me? Give me an address and location. Or doesn't your reach go there either?" While she spoke, Mae's mind was racing, figuring out the best way to subdue this guy. If she'd had her ego within reach, she *might* have managed a covert call to the authorities. As it was, he couldn't be that hard for her to take out herself, so long as he didn't have a gun concealed somewhere. Even organized criminal groups had difficulty obtaining guns in the RUNA, but they were more likely to have them than average civilians.

"It's hard for anyone to reach into Arcadia," he said. "We lost track of her shortly after the picture was taken, but we can help you get to her—if you help us and take your rightful place."

Mae didn't hear anything past one key word. *Arcadia.* "You're lying. They wouldn't have sent her there."

"Wouldn't they?" Emil asked, meeting her eyes levelly.

Yes, she thought bleakly, *they might very well have done that.* "What do you want from me?"

"What we've always wanted: you to take your rightful place in the group you were born into and step up now that we need you."

"Step up how?" She didn't want to negotiate with these people, but it had suddenly become impossible to shake the image of that small girl in the desolate reaches of the RUNA's tyrannical neighbor.

"By doing what you do best. We need you to kill someone."

"Oh, is that all?"

He frowned, momentarily caught up in his own thoughts. "You kept company with the servant of another goddess this weekend, one our mistress doesn't like. You need to eliminate her."

"I don't 'need' to do anything," snapped Mae, trying to hide her shock at the reference to Callista. How did they even know about her? "And I'm not an assassin for hire."

He shot her a wry look. "Really? Then why do you collect a government paycheck? Don't be stupid about this. It's your last chance to embrace your destiny. . . . Otherwise, you'll face the consequences."

Her body tensed. "Threats now if I don't do your killing?

Why would you even care about some zealot in the border-lands?"

"Because she and her goddess present a risk."

"A risk to the Br—" Mae suddenly cut herself off as a terri-ble, sinking feeling emerged within her. It seemed as though Justin wasn't going to be her last wacky mistaken-identity mis-hap. "You aren't with the Brödern."

Emil was briefly thrown off. "The Swedish mafia? Those underlings?" Slowly, almost comically, realization dawned on him as well. "You don't know, do you? You have no idea who I am."

"I know you're a guy who broke into my house and dangled promises of my niece in order to get me to commit murder. Seems like that's plenty."

His eyes were full of wonder. "Unbelievable. They broke the rules and never taught you her ways. I just figured you were one of the many who stray, but you were never even set on the path. It's a shame," he murmured. "You're too dangerous to change now."

"You don't know the half of it."

She threw the bowl, clipping Emil in the head. It made him stagger, and then with astonishing speed, he melted back into the shadows. She sprinted to the hall in a few easy steps and found no sign of him. It was impossible. He couldn't be faster than her. Without stopping, she headed toward the bedroom and flipped on the light. He wasn't there either. Swearing, she spun around and headed to the bathroom, wondering if he'd side-stepped into it. It too was empty. Her heart racing, she hurried back to the living room. Emil must have slipped into the bath-room while she was in the bedroom and then doubled back out. It was the only explanation . . . but it was improbable. This whole chase had lasted only a matter of seconds. She'd heard no door or window, and neither was open. The bolt to the stor-age area on the second floor was still in place.

She searched the apartment again, looking in every possible place: closets, under the bed, etc. No sign. He was gone, van-ished without a trace. How had he done it? She paced around, more out of agitation than anything else. What did she do now?

Calling the police over a break-in wasn't unreasonable, but what was she supposed to say?

"Damn it." She sat on the couch again, trying to calm down and figure out what to do. Except, there was nothing to do. *It's your last chance to embrace your destiny.* Ominous words. She wanted desperately to tell someone about this, but who was there?

And more important, who was Emil? With his blond looks and information about her niece, it'd been easy to assume he was one of the mobsters she'd long beseeched for help. Clearly, that wasn't the case. Weirder still, he seemed to think she should've known who he was, furthering the mix-up. She wished she had Justin's talent for memorization so that she could analyze all the tiny details of the conversation. Surely there was a clue in Emil's words. The most she could draw on was his mysterious use of feminine pronouns and his reference to some "mistress."

The chiming of her doorbell made Mae jump. She'd nearly forgotten about Whitetree. Sex was suddenly the furthest thing from her mind, but he was on her before she could shut the door. There was an animal look in his eyes as he pulled her to him and crushed her mouth with a kiss. The kiss was unexpected and was what convinced her to shove Emil from her mind. The encounter with him had amped her physical responses up, and she suddenly wanted an outlet for them. Usually prætorian men didn't waste time with kissing. In fact, in a remarkable show of restraint, he actually managed to carry her off to her dark bedroom rather than taking her on the couch, against the wall, on the floor. . . .

But after that, the primitive urge took over, and their clothes were off in seconds. There was too much testosterone churning through him, and any rational thought he might have had was swallowed by his body's out-of-control need to mate. She'd only just managed to lie on the bed when he threw himself onto her body, and like that, he was in her. No preamble, no foreplay. Mae made no attempts at resistance as he took out that animal fury on her. It was hard and it was rough, but her own desire had spiraled up enough to welcome it.

It was also brief. Prætorian sex almost always followed a

similar pattern. That initial burst of lust was mindless and raging, and his body needed the relief as soon as it could manage it. He collapsed onto her, his breathing ragged and his skin already slick with sweat. This pure, basic need was a welcome change to all of the muddled goings-on of the last few days. Nothing esoteric here. Just nature.

With that initial blind lust sated, Whitetree's desire—though still strong—eased a little. He rolled over, his breathing relaxing. It wouldn't take long for him to recover if they wanted to do it again, and although it'd still be fast and furious, the second time usually managed to last a little longer and *sometimes* even allowed for foreplay.

But for now, Mae was content. Fast or not, her body had still found release, its bliss momentarily trumping her troubled mind. With their needs temporarily satisfied, the implant wound down, no longer needing to increase the hormonal output. Their hands trembled as the excess chemicals were metabolized.

"Lucky me," said Whitetree at last.

"I've been kind of stressed."

He laughed and brushed back her hair. "Well, if you need therapy again, I'll be around. I've got another month here."

"Doubly lucky," she said, surprised at the bitterness in her voice.

"Hey, you'll be back in the game soon," he said, trying to reassure her.

Mae put her hands behind her head and sighed. "I should've just skipped the funeral."

He shifted to his side to look her in the eyes. "She asked for it, Koskinen. She provoked it. You've got a hundred witnesses."

"People keep saying that, but it doesn't matter. I should've done the noble thing and walked away." Thinking about Kavi was killing some of the afterglow happiness. So much for a reprieve. "The only upshot is that I didn't cause anything worse than a quick hospital stay and physical therapy."

"Not that quick," he said. "She's still hospitalized."

Mae sat up abruptly. "What? It's been three weeks! It takes a fraction of that time to set and bind a broken bone. She should be home recovering on her own."

"I'm no doctor. That's just what I heard. Addison was over there the other day after getting in a fight—defending your honor, by the way."

Mae barely heard him. She was still reeling from the news. Why in the world would they still have Kavi at the base's hospital? True, she'd been pretty messed up afterward, but there was no way she'd still need intensive treatment . . . would she?

"Just let it go. It's over and out of your hands." Whitetree gently drew her back down. "One more time?"

Mae nodded, if only to have an excuse not to think about Kavi. When they finished, he offered to stick around for more, but she declined. He asked if he could use the shower, and she directed him to it and the towels. Pushing Kavi out of her head, Mae just tried to lie in bed and revel in her body's satisfaction. It didn't work, because her mind wandered to Panama and the tantalizing way sex had been drawn out there. Plebeian men might not have been able to keep up with prætorian frequency, but they more than compensated with the ability to make sex last and build up the anticipation with long lingering touches. . . .

Mae suddenly grew angry at her traitorous thoughts, especially in the wake of her current mess with Justin. She almost considered asking Whitetree for a third time, if only to blot out her memories, but was no longer up to it. When he finished in the shower, he encouraged her to come out to the Maize party with him, but she declined. In a particularly gallant gesture, he told her he'd wait around until she showered. It would have been perfectly normal in the world of prætorian sex for him to take off.

She was halfway through blow-drying her hair when she heard him knock at the bathroom door and call her name. She turned the dryer off. "What is it?"

"That guy's here. The one you were with at the senate."

Mae was certain she'd misheard. She put her robe on and stepped outside. In the living room, she found that Justin was very much there and also very, very drunk. He held out a bottle of ree to her.

"I come bearing gifts. But I guess next time, I should call first." Mae could only stare in disbelief. She wasn't ready for this. She still needed to process the revelations in Mazatlán. And Emil.

Whitetree pulled on his shirt and kissed her cheek. "My cue to go. Call if you change your mind."

As he left, Mae thought that a glass of ree might not be such a bad idea after all.

"Get some water," she told Justin. "I'll be right back."

Whatever was about to happen, she wasn't going to do it half-naked. She put on a T-shirt and flannel pajama pants. Her damp hair wasn't particularly elegant, but as she returned and looked at Justin, she doubted he'd even remember tomorrow.

He'd ignored the water order and sprawled out on her couch, with his arm tossed over his head. She sat down in an armchair opposite him and waited expectantly.

"So was that his one time?" Justin asked. "No second date for plebeians, right?"

"Why are you here?" she demanded. She reminded herself that she'd promised to be patient with Justin, in light of his mental state, but it was kind of hard under the circumstances. "It can't be just to interrogate me about my personal life."

"No," he said in agreement. "That was just a bonus. You wouldn't believe all that's happened since I saw you earlier." Considering she'd been asked out by a senator and ordered to perform an assassination, Mae was pretty sure she could believe any number of things had happened. "Did you know Tessa's a terrorist? She invaded the senate. Er, the gardens."

Okay, that wasn't one Mae had expected. "How much have you drunk tonight?"

"I'm serious," he said, studying her face. "She and some of those stupid kids climbed the garden walls. Bad enough for any of them, let alone a Panamanian citizen."

He was actually serious, she realized. "Is . . . is she in jail?"

"No. She had the astonishing and improbable good luck of being caught and brought home by two prætorians. Two prætorians who are big fans of yours."

Mae closed her eyes for a moment. "You can't be serious. Not Val and Dag."

"They drank half my liquor cabinet, you know." He paused.

"Okay, that's an exaggeration. There's plenty where that came from."

For some reason, it bothered her that Justin had met her friends. There was nothing illicit about it, but it was just something she'd never shared with him. "That's why you're here? Do you want me to reimburse you for what they drank?"

That brought a flicker of a smile to his lips. "No. It was worth it to meet our country's noble defenders." He glanced away for a few moments, and when he looked back up, all traces of humor were gone. His dark eyes bored into her. "Why didn't you tell me? Why didn't you tell me about Porfirio and that funeral?"

Mae froze, unable to respond for several seconds. "How do you know about that?" she asked in a low, low voice. But it was a stupid question. Val and Dag had spilled everything because they had no control switch.

"You should have told me." There was a surprising desperation in him. "You should've told me that you were only with me as a punishment. And that you were in mourning after some ill-fated romance. Fuck, Mae. If I'd known that, I never would have . . . I don't know. I would've done things a lot differently."

The world spun for a moment and then abruptly snapped back into focus. Something exploded in Mae's chest, and she shot to her feet. "No!" she exclaimed. "You can't know that. It's *mine*. Everything else you've clawed out of me. That was the one thing I still had. The part of me you hadn't figured out with your goddamned 'amazing' sleuthing skills. You can't know everything about me. You have no right!"

She was surprised to find she was clenching her fists. Even the implant had spun up a little with her agitation. It wasn't the content that bothered her so much. The story of Porfirio and the funeral was widely known. But in seizing that last piece of her life, it was like Justin had unraveled everything about her. She was open and exposed. There was no escaping, and she suddenly hated him for it.

Perhaps the only satisfying thing here was his complete and total shock. She didn't know what he'd expected from her, but this outrage obviously wasn't it. Finally. Something he hadn't figured out.

"Mae . . ." He faltered. There it was, another rarity: him without a clever response.

"You think you're so smart," she continued. "You think it's a game—that it's some right you have—to pry and crack open other people. But you can't! You can't do that to people."

His face was perfectly still as he processed her words. "I told you before that I can't help it," he said finally. "I can't help seeing the things I do."

Mae crossed her arms and stalked away to the kitchen. She opened the bottle of ree he'd left there and, without any formalities, took a long drink before speaking again. "You don't have to flaunt it."

She didn't want to look at him. She didn't want him to see something else in her. Seeing the outside of her body was nothing compared to seeing the inside. Even now, he was probably analyzing her outburst, and she already felt too raw and exposed. If she kept her back to him, maybe she could hide the hole in her that she felt he'd ripped open. The silence that stretched between them was agonizing. When he spoke again, his voice was very, very quiet.

"I'm sorry."

Somehow, she knew he didn't apologize very often. If ever. That didn't mean all was right with the world, but she felt the need to acknowledge his words. Slowly, against her better judgment, she turned around and felt the first flush of the ree hitting her, bringing a slight tingling to her limbs.

"That doesn't change things," she said.

"No," he agreed. "I can't take back what I said. Or what I know. I'm sorry."

There it was again. She swallowed and forced that calm indifference onto her face. "Nothing to be done. But thanks for the apology."

"But it's not accepted."

She threw up her hands. "What do you expect me to say?"

"I don't know." He slumped back. "I meant what I said back in Panama: You're hard to read. And I don't know how to deal with that. You're still that devastatingly beautiful Nordic nine who looks so sad sometimes and is terrified of losing control. I want to understand that. I mean, I guess I kind of do now, but still. I know you think I have no respect for women, but I really wouldn't have taken advantage of you back then. And when I gave you that asshole line about no second dates, I really wish that—well." He shook his head. "Forget it."

"You didn't take advantage of me." Mae took another long drink of ree. "And I'm not in mourning. I mean, I didn't want him to die. I'm sad for that—I am. But everyone seems to forget I ended things with him. I refused him."

"Why did you? From what Dag and Val said, you guys were—" Justin abruptly stopped and looked sheepish. "Sorry. Horatio's just tactfully reminded me I'm doing it again—pushing you. It's none of my business."

Horatio. The raven that lived inside Justin's head. She'd almost forgotten about that in the midst of this new drama.

"What else do they say?" she asked. As the ree continued to work, talking about imaginary ravens didn't seem that strange.

"They tell me you've already forgotten about the guy who was here."

Mae supposed that was true. It also was a conclusion Justin himself might have subconsciously drawn. She sighed.

"Do you want to know why I have control issues?" she asked. "It's because people have been trying to control me since birth. Only my dad didn't, and he's been gone for years." Mae wasn't sure where her next words came from. "I know what else you want to know," she said. She wanted to believe this admission was ree-driven, but some part of her also needed to let out what was inside. He'd shown discretion with everything else he knew about her, and besides, she kind of had leverage over him. "You want to know how a Nordic nine ended up in the military."

His eyes said yes, he very much wanted to know that. "It's not my business."

"It is now. Get comfortable."

CHAPTER 25

HOW MAE GOT HER PURPOSE

Mae didn't think of herself as much of a storyteller, but as she stretched back into a chair and began to speak, she found herself forgetting where she was or that Justin was there. The past took over, and memories she tried to keep locked away suddenly burst forth.

After her father's death when she was sixteen, she had meekly gone along with her mother's shift in parenting style. Part of it had just been grief. The rest had been an inability to fight her mother. Mae had dropped *canne*, as well as her dream to study something sports related in her tertiaries. There was a limited number of subjects a girl of her class could study, and Mae had chosen music, the lesser of the evils. She'd clung to the idea that it might get her a job and some glimmer of independence, but she'd been naïve to think Astrid Koskinen would allow her daughter that kind of life.

Her mother had planned for Mae's debut party to take place two days after her tertiary graduation. Mae had been no fool about that part. She understood the point, that her mother wanted to show her off in the hopes of landing her a husband as soon as possible. After all, that was what girls of her class did. Plenty of young men had already trolled around before then, and despite her mother's opinions on certain ones, Mae had been able to rebuff them all. That, at least, had been a small measure of control, and even if she resented the formalities of her debut, she knew marriage wasn't something they could force her into.

There'd been no avoiding the pale pink dress. That was the

tradition for all debutantes. Mae's confidence grew when she got to choose the style: matte satin with a short-sleeved off-the-shoulder neckline and long, slim skirt. She remembered the dress perfectly, just as she did everything else from that night.

Mae's mother had been intent on making the debut *the* social event of the year. She'd bought new furniture and decorations and even hired extra servants to staff the party. She'd also invited every influential Nordic person she could think of and even a few visiting plebeians of importance—like General Gan.

Mae had played her role to perfection. Putting on a good face, no matter what she felt on the inside, was bred into her: dancing, flitting around, smiling at the congratulations of all her guests. She'd felt like a show horse, or even a mannequin on display, beautifully groomed and meant to be stared at. It had been grating but was all part of the act. And always, always there were men around her. It was as if all the suitors who'd come calling when she was younger had suddenly ganged up together. They asked little about her and mostly spent their time telling her about all that they could offer in material goods.

When Gan had spoken to her, she'd felt a little intimidated at meeting a plebeian military leader, but her sense of etiquette wouldn't allow her to show it. He'd given her the usual congratulations and then said something wholly unexpected, triggering a conversation forever etched in her memory.

"I saw footage of some of your *canne de combat* matches," he told her. "You were remarkable. I'm surprised you didn't compete professionally."

No matter her opinions on the matter, Mae wasn't about to confide her woes to a stranger. "It was a childhood game, sir. I had to grow up and move on to more important things."

"I don't think there's anything particularly childish about embracing your natural talents. I'm guessing you're quite the athlete and do well in other pursuits."

"When I have the time." He was the only person who'd spoken to her about such things, and as much as she longed to delve into a discussion about sports, she knew better.

"What will you do with your time now?" he asked with a small smile. "Get married?"

"Maybe," she said automatically. "My tertiary was in music. Maybe I can do something with that."

He nodded. "So I heard. A pretty vocation shared by half the girls here, I'm sure. Hardly what I'd expect of such an athletically talented young woman." The tone of his voice left no doubt about his thoughts on that "pretty vocation," and Mae suddenly felt humiliated. Still, she kept smiling.

"I can't compete professionally anymore, sir. Even if I wanted to." Which she did. "I'm past my prime to start down that path."

"You mentioned earlier that you were moving on to more important things." There'd been an intensity in his eyes that Mae would see through the rest of their acquaintance over the years. "Maybe you're past your prime for *canne*, but you are right in it for the military."

For a moment, she thought he was joking, but his face said otherwise. "The military? I . . . I don't know. It's not something I've ever thought about. It's not something someone like me could do." And by "someone" she meant a patrician woman. Even a male patrician would hesitate to enlist, not if he could live off of family money and drink cocktails on the veranda.

"It's exactly what someone like you could do," he said gravely. "You were made for greatness. It's written all over you, and there's no greater thing than serving this country. Have you ever been outside the RUNA, Miss Koskinen? No, of course not. You've probably hardly ever left this grant. But I'll tell you what you're missing: savagery. If you could see the rest of the world, you'd understand what you have here—and you would want to lay down your life for its glory. We are the last bastion of light left on this planet. You could go far, achieve rank and responsibility far more worthwhile than anything you'd accomplish as a landowner's wife."

His words had left her breathless. Or maybe it had been the light on his face. Whether his motivations were honorable or not, he believed wholeheartedly in what he was saying.

"Begging your pardon, sir," she said quietly. "The military is all about following orders. How is that any different from around here?"

Gan smiled. "Because you *choose* to follow them. And because they give you purpose. Do you have a purpose, Miss Koskinen?"

The question sent chills down her spine, but she tried to put on a mask of indifference. "Of course," she said politely. "But I appreciate your advice. You've certainly given me a lot to think about."

His expression told her she wasn't fooling anyone. "I'll be sticking around here for another hour or so if you'd like to talk more, but then I have to head back to the Gustav. Early flight—otherwise I'd stay longer."

"I understand."

Someone called her away then, and she murmured a polite farewell. Her heart was racing, but she wasn't entirely sure why. Maybe it was the glory he'd described. Maybe it was the thought of simply not doing what she'd been raised to do here. Or maybe it was just someone speaking to her candidly for a change. She never bothered to find him, though.

The night wore on. More smiles, more compliments, more dancing, and more champagne. She felt a headache coming on and slipped away from the party to find a painkiller in the kitchen. Before she could reach it, however, someone caught hold of her arm. She flinched.

"Mae, come here."

Kris Eriksson stood in the doorway to her father's office, a conspiratorial grin on his face. "What are you doing here?" She was more surprised at someone intruding in the sanctuary of her father's office than Kris's soliciting her attention. The Eriksson family were longtime friends of the Koskinens, and Kris was one of her more persistent admirers. She liked him well enough but had never given him anything more than friendly thoughts.

Glancing around to make sure no one would see her sneaking off with a guy, she followed him into the office and shut the door behind her. "What's going on?"

His blue eyes were alight with excitement. "It's all settled," he said. "I didn't think it would happen this quickly. I thought we'd have to wait weeks after tonight. Maybe even months. I knew you'd be getting lots of other offers and didn't think your mother would take ours so soon."

Mae felt as though she were trying to understand a conversation in another language. "What's all settled?"

"You and me." Kris moved close and clasped her hands in his. "Getting married. Our families worked out the details. Your mom's going to get a partner's share in our stock, and we can get married within the year." He put on a mischievous grin that didn't quite manage to reach his cheeks. The Erikssons were heavily affected by Cain, and Kris had had a number of skin treatments. "I'd rather have it sooner, but I suppose we'll have to take the time to do a wedding right."

A cold lump settled in her stomach. "No one asked me. It can't be settled. And I wouldn't—" She hesitated, unable to say that he was no one she'd choose. Not that it really mattered who they'd "settled" on.

Kris didn't seem deterred. "I can ask you now."

And then, to her complete and total horror, he got down on one knee *in her father's office* and produced a ring box from his coat pocket. He opened it up with a flourish, giving her a glimpse of some glittering mess.

"Maj Erja," he said, still grinning like they were in on a joke together, "will you do me the honor of becoming my wife?"

Mae stood there for several agonizing seconds, her mouth agape. Finally, she simply blurted out, "No. I can't. This isn't right. Something's not right."

Not waiting for his response, she nearly ripped open the door and tore down the hall to the kitchen. There, her mother was engaged in some kind of altercation with Claudia, Mae's sister, while their brother Cyrus leaned against the wall and looked on with amusement.

"Mother," exclaimed Mae. "What in the world is—"

Her mother held up a hand for silence. "Be quiet. Something important is going on."

"More important than you selling me off?"

The angry expression reserved for Claudia shifted to confusion and then understanding. "Ah, that."

Mae felt her eyes widen. "Yes, that! How can this be some

kind of afterthought? We're not in some kind of Regency novel where you trade me for a dowry!"

"So dramatic." Her mother tsked. "You know these kinds of business transactions are made all the time."

It was true. Although antiquated by plebeian standards, marital arrangements involving exchanges of goods weren't uncommon among the castes, especially the upper classes.

"Yes, but usually the parties involved get asked!"

"Why? Is there someone else you wanted?"

"I didn't want anyone!" Mae told her. "Not yet."

"Maj." Her mother put on what was apparently supposed to be a kindly look, but it came across as condescending to Mae. "You can't really have thought you were going to flit your days away doing nothing of use, did you? Look at you. You are our last, best hope to turn this family around. You need to redeem us, save us from the ruin others would see us plummet to."

She directed a glare in Claudia's direction, and that was when Mae got her first solid look at her sister's face. "Something important" might have been an understatement. Claudia was pale and looked as though she'd been crying. Mae glanced between them uneasily.

"What . . . what's happening?" she asked.

"What's happening," their mother said, "is that your sister is a slut."

Claudia's white face turned red. "That's not true! It's not my fault!"

"Really? Someone else was whoring herself out?"

"It wouldn't have happened if you'd let me keep my implant!" Claudia cried.

Their mother's expression could have frozen the room. "Well-bred ladies don't need contraceptive implants once they're of age. It's an insult to keep them . . . which reminds me, Maj. You can get yours removed now too. You'll want to once you're married anyway."

"Really?" demanded Claudia. Her eyes shot daggers at Mae. "Even now, you manage to make this about her?"

Mae was still a few beats behind. "Are you . . . are you pregnant?"

"You win the prize," said Cyrus with a chuckle. "You're going to be an aunt. She beat Philippa and me to it."

"But that's good news," said Mae slowly. "I mean, there'll be talk since you and Marius aren't married yet, but still . . . a baby so soon. . . ." Claudia was late getting engaged since she hadn't had all that many boyfriends after her debut, but pregnancy at the beginning of a marriage was a dream come true for most Nordics.

"It's not Marius's," said her mother flatly. "It's not even Nordic."

"Oh." Mae didn't need to hear any more to understand now why things were so grim. A plebeian had gotten Claudia pregnant. It was pretty much the most scandalous thing that could happen to a young patrician woman. They'd all had the importance of virtue driven into them from youth, with plebeians especially being regarded as the dirtiest of the dirty. Why would anyone risk sullying their genes? "What are you going to do?"

"Well, we can't terminate it. It's impossible to find a safe doctor to perform that off the grid. If we go to a qualified doctor, there'll be a record of it. Even if it's confidential, we can't risk word of this getting out." Her mother sighed and shook her head. "No, there's only one choice. We'll have to send her away and find some reason to delay the wedding. There are places that specialize in this. It doesn't require much skill to have a baby—or to make one, apparently—and then after that, we'll have it sent out of the country."

Mae hadn't really thought anything could shock her more than Kris's proclamation. "Just like that?"

"It's easy," said Cyrus. "I mean, not as easy as Claudia is, but it can be done. It happens more than you think, and I know some people who can help." Mae didn't acknowledge that. She'd heard rumors that her brother was getting involved with the Brödern, but it wasn't a topic she wanted to pursue right now.

"How can you just send away another person?" Mae turned to Claudia. "How can you send away your own child?"

Even irreverent Cyrus seemed surprised. "What else do you expect her to do? She'd lose Nordic citizenship."

"That baby's a plebeian." Their mother practically spat the word out. "Generations of pure genes mixed with who knows what kind of background. What kind of child would that be? Certainly not one we can keep around here. I'm sure it'll have a nice home wherever it ends up. Now stop looking so appalled. It's not like this happened to you, thankfully. Go back to your party. And you, go to your room. I don't want you ruining Maj's day." That was to Claudia, who skulked away after leveling glares at everyone in the room.

"Hold on," Mae told her mother. "We have to talk about the Erikssons."

"Now isn't the time or place."

"It's the perfect time and place."

"Maj." There it was, the patronizing voice again. "You have two hundred guests to entertain. Go back out there, and we'll discuss this in the morning. Avoid Kris if it makes you happy, but after you sleep on it, I'm sure you'll see what an ideal match this is. Like I said, you're our last, best hope. I know you won't disappoint us."

Refusing to hear anything else, her mother glided out of the room. Cyrus followed, after first slapping Mae on the back. "Congratulations, little sister."

Mae remembered very little of the party after that. She resumed her role but didn't even know what she said half the time. Her thoughts kept flipping between her forced engagement and Claudia's pregnancy. After a while, Mae began to feel her own identity merged into the baby's: both of them tossed heedlessly around by people too entrenched in a shallow and antiquated culture. She'd gone through her upbringing with little questioning, not even when her mother had denied Mae the future she wanted. Now it was as though Mae was able to step back and see all the pettiness and empty tradition that had shackled her for her entire life. There was no reason for it that she could see.

There was no purpose.

Mae left the gallery without another word and went back to the kitchen, where servants had returned now that the family drama was over. None of them paid much attention to her as she cut through the room, straight to the back door that led out to the house's side. All was quiet and dark here. Guests who had wandered to the expansive patio had done so at the other end of the house. Packing or changing didn't even cross her mind. She had what was left of her dignity, as well as a clutch purse containing her ego. Those were all she needed.

She walked off into the night, which was heavy with summer's humidity and abuzz with the songs of insects. She found the dirt road that wound away from the estate and followed it to where it joined up with the main highway leading into New Stockholm. Two hours into the trip, she took off her high-heeled shoes and continued barefoot. Three hours into the trip, a storm rolled in and unleashed a torrential downpour. Six hours into the trip, she reached the edge of downtown.

Everyone knew where the Gustav was. It was one of the largest buildings on the west side and was the only hotel plebeians were allowed to stay at in the land grant. Through some serendipitous twist of fate, Mae walked up to it just as General Gan emerged and turned toward a waiting car. When he saw her, he came to a total standstill. Mae had the impression that the general had seen many, many things, but a bedraggled girl with bleeding feet and a soaked debutante's dress probably wasn't a sight he'd run into before.

"Hello, General," she told him. "I've decided I'd like to have a purpose after all."

When Mae finished her story, she thought Justin, who was stretched out on the couch, had fallen asleep. Silence fell, and he opened his eyes.

"If it makes you feel better, you win the dubious honor of completely surprising me. I never would have guessed any of that. My prevailing theory was that you ran off after some infatuation with a soldier."

She smiled at that, pleasantly astonished at how good it really had felt to get this off her chest. She'd never told it to anyone. "Infatuation with my country, I guess."

"Spoken like a true soldier." He stifled a yawn. "That's why you turned Porfirio down—too many scars from the thought of engagement."

She supposed he was close to the mark, though Mae should've been used to that by now. "That, and he was pretty heavy-handed about it. I think he thought asking was kind of a formality. He couldn't imagine I'd say no." Startlingly close to the way Kris had behaved, she realized. "And I think being his wife . . . I don't know. He didn't have a lot of the sexist views patricians have, but there was still an overconfidence about him. He would've assumed I'd always go along with him. Kind of like the proposal—he couldn't imagine I'd refuse." She swallowed as she recalled their last meeting.

"You were afraid he would've tried to control you," Justin said, summing it up. "Like the others."

"It's what people do—they're always trying to get power over each other. The fact that it all went down when Claudia was pregnant just made it worse. More callous control of other lives."

"What ever happened to the baby?" asked Justin.

"I don't know. Sent away." He was too tired to pick up the lie in her voice, or she was just that good. She'd given him a lot, but Emil's mysterious leads and her own obsessive inquiries over the years about Claudia's daughter were staying inside Mae's heart. "I was long gone by then."

Justin's eyelids were drooping again, and she got to her feet. The ree had long since worn off and rarely left a hangover. "Get some sleep. We can do psychoanalysis of my dysfunctional life another time."

"Everyone's dysfunctional. There's no such thing as normal." When she returned with the blanket, his eyes were closed again, but he asked, "Is it boring, not sleeping? Do you mind it?"

"No, it's actually useful."

"Because you can fight at a moment's notice?"

"Well, yes . . . but I've been a bad sleeper my whole life." The next admission wasn't one she made often. "I used to have nightmares. But not anymore."

"No nightmares. No dreams," he murmured. His breathing grew regular, and she knew he was asleep. She studied him for long moments, admiring not just the lines of his face but also this rare moment of peace, when the churning of his mind wasn't tormenting him.

She passed the night in her bedroom, spending equal parts of it ruminating over the last few days, reading, and watching documentaries. Occasionally her eyes would lift to the window as she pondered what had happened to Emil. Who was he? And what was she supposed to do about him?

When morning came, she'd reached a decision. She showered and dressed and was in the middle of making breakfast when Justin finally woke up. He seemed startled that she was cooking.

"Why would you assume I can't?" she asked, feeling mildly offended. It was only scrambled eggs, but still.

"I figured you grew up with cooks and then just ate from a mess hall." He winced at the light. "Got any aspirin?"

"No. I don't use it."

"Caffeine it is, then."

He declined the food and contented himself with a giant mug of coffee. She was also pretty sure he must have slipped in some Exerzol, because he was bright-eyed and upbeat within the hour.

"How are you spending your Sunday?" he asked.

"I'm going to see Kavi."

He arched an eyebrow. "Is that a good idea? I mean, I wasn't there, but by all reports, she might not take a visit well."

"I know," said Mae glumly. "But Whitetree told me she's still in the hospital. I can't believe I did that. This is something I have to understand." The pillow talk had hit her hard. Maybe it was all this rumination on life and death, but Mae had to see for herself what she'd done to Kavi, even if it would end in ranting and hostility.

"Understood. I'll leave you to it." Justin downed the last of his coffee and set the empty mug next to her vase of roses. "Nice flowers. Did your gentleman caller bring them?"

"No . . . Lucian sent them." She braced herself for snark, but none came. "Nothing to say?"

"You can do what you want." But he still hesitated. "Will he get a second date?"

"He hasn't gotten a first one."

That satisfied Justin. He left shortly thereafter, and Mae

headed to the base, which she hadn't been out to since the funeral. The hospital wing's receptionist directed her to Kavi's room, which was in a secure hallway guarded by regular military. It increased Mae's unease, but she reminded herself that a prætorian was no ordinary patient. Of course she'd be in a special section. The room was the farthest one in the hall, again adding to its importance. The door was open, and a monitor outside it read KAVI, DRUSILLA—PRT. Mae readied herself and entered the room. No going back now.

Kavi sat up in a standard hospital bed, the broken leg wrapped in a bandaged cast. A picked-over food tray showed she'd just had breakfast, and her eyes were on a screen running a story about Lucian Darling, of all people. She turned as Mae took a few more steps forward, and then, the most astonishing thing happened.

Kavi smiled.

Mae couldn't remember the last time she'd seen that happen. Kavi was always prickly, and even when Mae and Porfirio had dated, Kavi had never seemed impressed with her cohort brother's girlfriend. But there was no mistaking it now. Kavi was smiling, and there was nothing forced or polite about it.

"Mae," she said, her face filling with delight. "What a nice surprise."

The use of her first name startled Mae almost as much as the smile. "Kavi—er, Drusilla. It's nice to see you too. You look good."

Kavi chuckled and ran a hand through her hair. "Thank you for being so nice. I need a haircut. Or at least a decent blow dryer."

Mae tried to smile back, but the completely unexpected nature of this encounter had left her off balance. "How are you feeling?"

"Good. Everyone here is so nice. I wish I could go home, but they say I need more time. Doctors know best."

"I suppose they do." Mae still couldn't understand the extended stay. What had she done? How could one broken leg be so debilitating? "Are you in much pain?"

"No pain at all." She nodded toward a table by the wall.

"Look at those lilies Newton brought me. The Indigos are always coming by with flowers. Isn't that nice?"

The dreamy quality of Kavi's voice, the distracted look in her eyes, and her fourth use of "nice" finally tipped Mae off. Kavi must have been drugged. Nothing sedative, obviously. It was just enough to make her . . . well, nice. Why was that necessary for a leg injury? Maybe Kavi had annoyed the doctors so much that they'd decided to make their lives a little easier when dealing with her.

"They're beautiful," Mae told her. "I should've brought you some too." She could've used Lucian's roses.

"It's okay. I know how busy you are."

Mae took a deep breath and plunged forward with her whole reason for visiting. "Look . . . Drusilla . . . I just wanted to apologize for what I did at the funeral. It was wrong, and I'm so sorry."

Kavi's smile never dimmed. "You don't have to apologize. We were all a little worked up."

Mae wasn't sure "worked up" was exactly adequate. Kavi had called Mae a fucking castal bitch, and Mae had beaten her face into a bloody pulp.

"I still shouldn't have done it," she said lamely.

"We all miss him." At last, Kavi lost a little of her happy haze as she stared off into space. "I used to talk to him. Porfirio. Or, well, I thought I did. The doctors said it was part of being sick. They gave me more medicine, and now I don't see him." She turned back to Mae. "Do you ever see him?"

"I—no, of course not. He's dead. The dead don't come back."

"I suppose not." Kavi brightened again. "If he did, I know he'd forgive you. He loved you very much."

Mae bit her tongue. Porfirio would forgive *her*? She'd kept the memories of their last time together tucked far, far away in the back of her mind, but Kavi's words suddenly brought them out. Until that last day, he'd been content to vent his feelings in calls and messages. He'd at least upgraded Mae from a "castal bitch" to a "Nordic bitch," and as the harassment continued, Mae had found it easier to endure. She had just shut down more and more, refusing to feel anything. After a while, he must've realized that, so he'd finally decided an in-person visit might actually have an impact.

She'd let him inside, hoping the gesture might allow a civilized conversation, though she should've known better. His accusations always varied, and that day he'd decided she must have refused his proposal because she was cheating on him.

"Who are you fucking?" he'd yelled. "Who are you fucking?"

No protest of hers could've gotten through to him, and her silence infuriated him. In fact, his reaction had been similar to Kavi's at the funeral. Once again, she became a Nordic bitch, a heartless one who was incapable of any real feelings.

Porfirio, however, had had no shortage of emotions as his rant continued. "What does it take? *What does it take for you to feel anything?*"

And that was when the familiar refrain had ended. Mae's reflexes and instincts had failed because she'd never dreamed that Porfirio, even in the throes of his grief and rage, would attack. He'd thrown her to the floor, pinning her wrists and holding her down with his greater weight. The screaming stopped, and the sudden lowering of his voice was actually more menacing. "You *will* feel something," he'd told her. "You're still mine, and I will make you feel."

Mae had felt something. Fear. She'd never given rape a second thought in her life until that moment. Her status had kept her too sheltered on the Nordic grant, and a few fights after joining the military had caused both men and women to tread lightly around her. She'd lived confidently with her own skills and strength. But there on the floor, Porfirio's were superior. Maybe in a *canne* match, her speed would've compensated. Her implant provided extra strength, but his did the same for him. Ultimately, his natural edge in strength had dominated.

Prætorians joked about ripping one another's clothes off, but Mae had never had it literally happen. It had occurred to her that there'd probably be no repercussions either. The fast and furious nature of prætorian sex danced on such a dangerous line that it'd be hard to differentiate between that and rape. It was entirely possible that she'd be accused of using makeup sex as some sort of revenge. As he struggled to get his own pants off while still restraining her, she saw none of the amped-up desire that usually characterized prætorian men. Sure, there was lust, but it wasn't born of affection or even friendly attraction. There was rage in it, a need to punish and possess.

She'd used every weapon she had to fight what he wanted to do—kicking, clawing, screaming. It shouldn't have worked. It *shouldn't* have. Even now she believed that. But somehow, she'd managed a burst of strength that threw him off enough for her to crawl toward her coffee table. He'd caught hold of her leg, but not before she grabbed her gun.

Even while churning with chemicals, Porfirio wasn't so far gone that he would foolishly challenge that. He'd scrambled back as she stood up and screamed at him to leave. He'd tried to stammer out something that sounded more like an excuse than an apology as he fumbled with his pants. Mae wouldn't listen to any of it and had advanced on him with enough confidence that he'd finally taken off. She'd never seen him again.

She'd never told anyone what happened, though Val and Dag had noticed the bruises on her wrists. They probably hadn't believed the story she'd given them, but they had no way to argue against it. If they'd had proof of what he'd tried to do, Porfirio wouldn't have lived long enough to die in an explosion.

As she stood there in Kavi's room, holding on to that strained smile, Mae had a startling revelation. She'd never focused too much on what she'd been thinking during the attack, mostly because there hadn't been a lot of coherent thought. She'd been all instinct and reaction, her only goal being escape. But now, she realized there had been more than just fear and the need to fight back.

With brilliant clarity, she now remembered another set of feelings that she'd buried with everything else. Outrage. Indignation. Even a sense of sacrilege. Who was he to think he could force her into submission? She was no man's possession. Her body was a gift she bestowed on those who earned her desire. It could not be taken.

Maybe those weren't such weird sentiments. Not wanting to

be possessed was certainly a valid response. But there had been something more to her haughty reaction, a sense that she was glorious and sacred, making his attempted violation that much more shocking. At the time, she hadn't recognized it as anything more than out-of-control emotions. She'd always assumed that burst of strength came from her implant's response to fear being greater than his implant's response to rage.

But no. She knew now that she'd thrown him off her because of that dark *otherness* that kept seizing her. That same powerful presence had fueled her thoughts of holiness and profanity. And thinking back to his terrified face as he'd backed away, she wasn't sure if he'd been afraid of the gun or the divine power that had surrounded her. Had he seen what Justin claimed was with her in moments of action and violence? A deity trying to possess her? It was absurd.

To Kavi, Mae simply said, "I should go."

Kavi nodded, still with that dreamy smile. "Of course. I hope you'll visit again. I'd like for us to be friends. I'm sure Porfirio would've wanted that."

"Yes," murmured Mae, turning toward the door. "I'm sure he would have."

CHAPTER 26

EVERYONE'S SO BLOND

Exerzol and caffeine had let Justin put on a good face for Mae, but by the time he arrived home, his skull felt like it was going to explode out of his head. At least no one was around. He wasn't ready for Cynthia's chastisement or noise of any kind. Hoping they'd all stay gone for a very long time, he staggered to his bedroom and dug out a bottle of potent painkillers. At first, he automatically emptied out as many pills as he could take without putting himself into a coma. Several seconds later, he reconsidered and kept only the number of pills actually needed to dull the hangover's legacy. The memory of Windsor still weighed heavily upon him.

Great restraint, said Horatio. *Of course, with as much tolerance as you've built up, they probably won't do anything.*

Quiet, Justin told him. *Voices inside my head are just as grating as ones outside.*

His clothes were already a lost cause, so he just left them on and collapsed into the bed. It felt like he'd closed his eyes for only a few seconds, but when his ego woke him with a call, he saw he'd been out for two straight hours. Cornelia's name was on the display, and he almost considered ignoring her until a hopeful part of him said maybe she was calling to tell him they'd found the murderer and the case was closed. He answered in voice only.

"Do you realize," she said coldly, "that you are down to a week until the next full moon?"

"I'm very aware of that," he told her.

"Then why do I have nothing more to show from your work than massive receipts? Your food bills alone are ridiculous. There's no way you and Prætorian Koskinen eat that much, so I'm guessing SCI is paying for an extended cocktail hour."

"Prætorians need a lot of food," he countered.

"Well, I don't need an extra servitor, so you should think a bit more seriously about earning your keep." Mae had told him about Lucian's findings in servitor hiring, and Justin nearly considered pointing out that Cornelia apparently needed lots of extra servitors. "You're only here by Director Kyle's good graces, and if your incompetence lets another murder slip by, you'd better hope your Panamanian friends will take you back. Now. Tell me you have something."

Justin hesitated. Although he had gathered a fair amount of information, he hated to share it now because a lot of it didn't make sense. He hadn't found the pattern yet, and it was hard to admit to others that he didn't know something.

But if she was talking about Panama, it might be worth sharing his good-faith efforts. So, he told her as much as he could, starting with all the theories about a geneticist going after his creations and then expanding to how the many plebeian deaths might also have been part of some larger sacrifice. He made sure not to mention Callista but hinted at "connections" that might help him to track down the guilty group if they could only make a positive ID.

Cornelia sounded more impressed than she wanted to be but still couldn't deny the obvious: "You have no idea how this all ties together."

"No," he said in agreement.

"And your tech friend hasn't found any tampering with the video."

"No."

She gave a melodramatic sigh. "Which brings us back to your having one week left and no results."

"We're visiting the last land grant tomorrow. The Nordics. It may very well hold the key, especially if Mae's connections can get us in deeper." That last part was complete bullshit, but he hoped it sounded convincing.

"Let's hope so," said Cornelia. "Stay in touch." She disconnected.

Justin stared at the ego in dismay and then dragged himself
out of bed to become human again. The others had come home
from whatever outing they'd been on, and he ended up spending the rest of the day in with them. It earned him a lot of points
with Cynthia, though not so many with Tessa when he told her
she was the butt of a prætorian joke. She'd apparently spent the
day skulking in terror that the authorities were coming for her
at any moment, and rather than provide relief, this new information only seemed to enrage her.

Still, the day passed in a relatively ordinary way, and he welcomed this eye in the recent hurricane of his life. When he got up
the next morning, however, another phone call made it clear the
universe was done cutting him breaks. As soon as the call ended,
he headed into the kitchen, where the normal breakfast routine was
going on. Mae had just shown up and was accepting Cynthia's offer of food. She gave Justin a cordial greeting and in no way acted
as though she thought he was a deranged religious freak.

"Take the uniform off," he told Tessa. "You aren't going to
school today."

She looked up from her eggs. "Why not?"

"Because young budding terrorists apparently get suspended
for crimes against the country."

Her mouth opened, but nothing came out at first. "You said it
was a joke! That I wasn't in any trouble!"

"You aren't," he said. "But your principal doesn't feel it's
right to have a girl who's been carted off by prætorians back in
school right away. Sets a bad example, violates the school's
code of conduct . . . something like that. You're off for a week."

Once she accepted she wasn't being deported, Tessa was
okay with it. Cynthia was the outraged one. "What? That's absurd! They can't suspend her for personal activities. They're a
public institution, obligated to provide her education."

"Well, technically, she attacked the public. I'm joking," he
added quickly, seeing Cynthia's face darken.

"You should've sent her to a private school. Surely you've
got enough money for them to overlook where she's from."

"I've tried." Tessa never complained, but he knew that there was still a little friction in her adjustment to the school. She would've done better elsewhere, but the places he wanted her in had strict admissions policies. If he'd foreseen that problem, he would've worked it into his initial employment agreement. "Look, if you want to go in and fight to get her back sooner, be my guest. I would, but I've got to go see the Nordics today."

Cynthia glowered. "I'll try. My day's not much better. The least you can do is take her with you."

Justin, Mae, and Tessa all turned to her in surprise. "I'm going to work, Cyn," he said. "It's not a vacation I can just bring her along on."

"What are you doing? Renewing some licenses? It's all formality and paperwork," said Cynthia, who apparently had little regard for his job. "I'm sure you'll have downtime."

"I'm fine here," said Tessa.

Cynthia was obstinate. "Glued to the living room screen? No. That's not what Justin brought you here for. You need to live. Go experience how the other half lives. Think of the photo ops for your class."

Tessa brightened at that, and Justin deliberated. Tessa really had no business going along on SCI's most important case, but Cynthia was right about how Tessa would spend her day if left behind. He looked at Mae for help.

"The downtown area's safe," she said after a moment's thought. "She'd be fine exploring on her own while we're out."

That was good enough for Justin, largely because they were running out of time before they needed to go. He managed to book Tessa a ticket on the way to the airport, and they decided she could just share Mae's hotel room, lest another expense get back to Cornelia.

To the girl's credit, Tessa handled this trip much better than her first flight. Sure, she still kept a white-knuckled grip on the seat, but she didn't look like she was on the verge of passing out. She entertained herself with a reader and made occasional conversation. All in all, she handled it like a pro, even when Justin had to send her off on her own. They'd checked in at a hotel on one side of downtown New Stockholm and then traveled to a police station on the opposite side. Tessa went with them to the station and then prepared to strike out.

Mae pointed out a trolley running up and down the street. "This whole stretch and the adjacent streets are shopping and touristy stuff. Plenty to see and do. You can just work your way back to the hotel."

Tessa nodded, eyes wide. "Everyone's so . . . blond."

"Yes, they are," Justin said, glancing at the sea of golden hair. It made everyone look alike, and he could understand how that might actually make her fear of crowds worse. But, just like with everything else on the trip, Tessa mustered her courage and gave a resolved nod. "Here," he said. "Let me see your ego." He made a few adjustments on his and then scanned it over hers when she offered it up. "There you go. Walking-around money. Don't spend it all in one place."

She grinned and surprised him with a hug, promising she'd call if there was a problem. He watched her disappear into the crowd, hoping an area this tourist-friendly wouldn't go too hard on a provincial girl.

Their contact among the Nordic police was a woman named Dahlia Johansson, a veteran detective who obviously didn't like federal involvement but disliked having an open case even more. She escorted them to her office and then leaned against the wall with crossed arms.

"Clara Arnarsson." Johansson pointed at a screen on her desk, displaying a head shot of a young woman with strawberry blond hair. "Twenty-seven, killed with a silver dagger."

Justin was following along with the victim's profile on his ego. "And she was an eight, of course. Looks like she's the only one who wasn't killed at home, but . . . I'm guessing there were still no witnesses and a mostly inaccessible room?"

"Correct. She was killed in her office." Johansson glanced at Mae. "Do you know the Sturluson Building? She was on the tenth floor, in a secure hall only accessible to those with the correct key cards."

"Was there a window in her office?" asked Justin.

"I can't imagine that being used as an entrance," said Mae, eyes narrowed in thought. "That building wouldn't be easy to climb, and it's on a pretty visible corner. Was it during business hours?"

Johansson nodded. "Yes, which makes it even more unbelievable."

"Let's head over and take a look, then," said Justin. He didn't exactly feel defeated yet, but he had a suspicion the same pattern was coming: no clues at the scene, no obvious religious involvement, and security info sent to Leo that would reveal no obvious alteration.

That wasn't far from the truth. The office was just as difficult to penetrate as Johansson had implied. The police had at least documented an extensive amount of information on the place, meaning Leo would have solid evidence to sift through later. In a surprisingly helpful gesture, Johansson's team cleared out most of the staff on that floor of the building, so that Justin and Mae could have an easier walk-through. Johansson even saved them a trip by bringing the victim's husband in for questioning. Justin went through the usual interrogation and couldn't help but feel bad for Mr. Arnarsson. He was clearly grief-stricken and wore the look of someone who couldn't yet accept his reality. And just like all the others Justin had interviewed, Mr. Arnarsson firmly denied any religious involvement on his wife's part.

When Justin finished, he sought out Johansson to wrap things up but found her engrossed in a heated discussion with a few of her officers. "Come on," Mae told him as they waited a respectful distance away. "Let's wander. I saw a vending machine by the elevators. They might have this drink I used to love."

The section by the elevators had actually remained unsecured, and a few curious coworkers lingered near the edge of the police lines, whispering and speculative as they waited for the authorities to leave. There was a counter along the wall that contained assorted beverage machines, and Mae bought some sort of carbonated fruit beverage that she assured him he'd adore.

"Needs vodka," he told her.

While they lingered, a nervous Nordic woman in her forties approached. She gave them tentative smiles and then glanced around for any onlookers. Satisfied, she moved closer and said, "You're with SCI, right? I heard they think there's a cult involved in this."

Mae looked understandably annoyed at the security leak. "I'm sorry, we can't discuss the investigation."

"Of course, of course." The woman's eyes darted around again, first to her colleagues, then to the police, and then back to Justin and Mae. "Have any of you looked into . . . the man?" Despite her unease, the woman seemed to enjoy the drama of the moment, and Justin's senses went on high alert. Interpersonal gossip could crack something like this wide open.

"The man?" Justin asked, giving the woman one of his best smiles. Whether she went for plebeians or not, she seemed to like the attention and flushed with pleasure.

"Clara's boyfriend. She tried to keep it quiet, but I saw them at restaurants a couple of times. They always seemed to be having really intense conversations. I don't know if I can blame her. The guy was gorgeous—a little different from Siegfried, if you catch what I'm saying."

Yes, Justin certainly did. The victim had been beautiful, as would be expected from an eight, but her husband showed heavy damage from Cain. It was the same pattern they'd observed in the other murders.

The woman had overcome her anxiety now and was loving her captive audience. "If you want my opinion, you shouldn't be checking out cults. Look to her husband or her boyfriend. One of them might not have liked the, uh, arrangement anymore."

"That's good insight," Justin told her, which pleased her more. "And astute of you to notice all that at the time. You're in the wrong line of work. You should be a cop with those instincts. Do you know his name or anything else that could be helpful?"

Her face fell a little. "No . . . but I could tell you what he looked like. And I can tell you the restaurants they were at."

Mae called over an officer and asked him to take a thorough description of the alleged boyfriend and the couple's outings. Meanwhile, Justin sought out Johansson.

"Is her husband still here?" he asked her. "We might want to ask him if he knew about any affairs."

As Johansson went to retrieve him, Justin wondered if this new lead could actually be useful. Naturally, he'd take any piece of knowledge they could get. On the other hand, something as mundane as an act of passion didn't fit into the neat raging-geneticist theory or even the murderous-cult theory. Nonetheless, he interrogated Mr. Arnarsson and was met with even greater incredulity than the religious questions had received.

"He seems sincere," Justin told Mae afterward. "But if he did do it, he may have had a while to prepare himself. There's also the small question of how he or the other guy would've gotten into this inaccessible office. Who knows? Maybe the boyfriend's a contortionist or something. That might add to his appeal, along with his good genes."

Mae frowned at that and looked like she was about to speak when Johansson returned and said they had a call for her in their makeshift command station. Mae straightened up as though her general were right in front of her and hurried off.

Meanwhile, the sketch was complete. The image compiled by their witness and the police certainly gave credence to the idea of a desirable lover. The guy was close to the victim's age, with blond hair and flawless skin that the victim's coworker was obsessed with. "It was perfect, I tell you. Not a mark," the witness told Justin. "Just like that woman you were with."

Identifying the man was in the hands of the police now. Justin glanced at the time and saw it was later than he'd expected. They'd have to find Tessa soon and get dinner. Seeing as she hadn't called, he could only hope she hadn't committed any other acts against national security.

One of the officers directed Justin to the office they'd set up their equipment in. There, he found Mae engaged in conversation with someone on a screen—but not the stern general he'd expected from her stories.

"Because I'm here on business!" Mae exclaimed.

"And that doesn't warrant a call?" The speaker was one of those older women who were described as "handsome." Her dark blond hair was wound up into a high bun that showed a face with taut, smoothed skin that suggested a recent face-lift. She had a heavier brow than Mae and lacked the high cheekbones, but the woman's eyes were the same shade of greenish blue that he'd come to admire.

"I'm just busy, that's all. This isn't a good time."

"It's never a good time, Maj." The name sounded like "my" to Justin's ears. "It hasn't been for three years, apparently."

"Mother, please. Now isn't the time." Justin knew Mae well enough now to recognize the signs of when she was fighting to keep control.

"Are you working all night?" her mother asked insistently. "Surely you have to eat. Come over tonight, and I'll gather your brother and sister. Bring your associates." The woman's eyes suddenly flicked to Justin, and he flinched. He thought he'd been standing out of the camera's range. "Is that one of them?"

Mae spun around in surprise, exasperation crossing her features. "Yes. Mother, this is Dr. Justin March. Justin, this is Astrid Koskinen."

With nowhere to escape, Justin stepped forward and went into action. "Mrs. Koskinen, it's a pleasure to meet you. I can see where Mae gets her stunning looks."

Astrid didn't even blink. "Dr. March, do you and my daughter have dinner plans?"

He faltered. "Well, I . . ." A glance at Mae told him what the correct answer to give was, but he was too slow.

"That's what I thought," said Astrid triumphantly. "Both of you come over at seven."

"He's a plebeian," Mae said bluntly.

"Yes, I can see that, Maj."

"And we have someone else with us." Mae paused for what had to be dramatic impact. "A provincial."

Her mother wouldn't be dissuaded. "Bring whoever you want, if that's what it takes to get you here. Besides, you know how open-minded we are."

"No, I didn't know that, actually."

"See you soon." Astrid's face disappeared, and Mae kicked the desk.

"Goddamn it," she growled.

"I'm sorry," said Justin. "I didn't think fast enough to—"

"No, no." Mae waved off his protests. "It's not you. It's all her. And whatever friend she has around here who recognized me and tattled that I was in town. My ego's set to automatically send her calls to voice mail, but she tricked me by going through the police."

"I'm sorry," he repeated. He actually meant it. Sure, there was some perverse part of him that wanted to see where she'd grown up, but after hearing her stories on Saturday, he didn't want to subject Mae to a return to that place. "Maybe we can get out of it. Say something came up."

She sighed. "No. That'll make things worse. I'm just going to have to suck this up." She walked out of the office with a forlorn look on her face, though she paused to give Justin a humorless smile. "On the bright side, if there's anything about me you don't know yet, it'll probably come out tonight."

He gave her a small smile in return, little knowing how true her words would be.

CHAPTER 27

KOSKINEN DECORUM

They had to hire a car. Her mother lived outside of the city, and no public transportation ran out to it. Mae looked like she was going to her own funeral as they sped by the wheat and corn fields, which were green and growing now that spring had moved in. The castes had been founded by families who already had personal fortunes that could help the fledgling republic, fortunes they used to buy themselves out of the mandates. Over time, those families had ended up turning to enterprises that were suited to their land, such as the expansive growing of crops that fed the RUNA. Dark clouds gathering above the fields threatened a storm, which Mae remarked was fitting.

At first glance, the Koskinen house seemed as though it had ridden the success of Nordic farming. The estate—because there was no other word for it—was like something out of a movie. A huge pillared porch with etched-glass double doors welcomed guests with grandeur and intimidation. Identical wings extended from each side of the entrance, beautiful in their symmetry. The house had two floors, and the second one had balconies extending from many of its rooms. There were even a couple of turrets. It was set on sprawling grounds, some of which were obviously just for show and not practical use. Looking beyond the house, Justin could see vast fields dedicated to farming. There the symmetry ended. Half the land showed that green haze of new growth. The other half was bare and neglected.

Walking toward the house told more tales. The tan paint was

worn and chipped. Bushes and hedges were messy and over-grown, while weeds poked through the flower beds. It was all subtle. The house wasn't in ruins, but it definitely showed signs of disrepair.

A plebeian woman wearing a black uniform let them in, murmuring a deferential, "Miss Mae."

Mae smiled and gave her a small hug as they entered, something that seemed to embarrass the other woman. "Hello, Phyllis."

The central part of the house was the tallest, and the foyer took full advantage of that. A huge chandelier hung from the vaulted ceiling, and Justin counted seven tiers of crystals. He also noticed that some of the lights had burned out. Dusty art displaying Norse knot work adorned the walls. To the side of the room, a spiral staircase with a wrought-iron railing stretched up to the second floor. Within moments of their entry, Astrid Koskinen descended the stairs with a showy, measured stride that made him think she'd been hovering at the top, waiting to make this grand entrance.

"Maj," she said, pausing to kiss Mae on each cheek. "How lovely to see you."

There was no warmth in the greeting or in Mae's answering one. "Mother, this is Dr. Justin March and Tessa Cruz."

At a glance, Justin knew this was no time for, "Mother? Really? I would've guessed sister." He opted for pleasant—but not too pleasant—formality. "Mrs. Koskinen, thank you for your hospitality."

"Yes, thank you," said Tessa, a bit cowed by this introduction to the castal aristocracy.

Astrid frowned. "Could you repeat that?"

"I said 'thank you,'" repeated Tessa more loudly.

"Ah. Well, I could hardly turn down the opportunity to host Maj."

"You shouldn't have gone to any trouble," said Mae.

"Come," said Astrid, ignoring her. "Everyone's seated for dinner. Normally we eat at seven." There was an accusatory note in her voice. An old-fashioned grandfather clock proclaimed that it was 7:10. "Thank you for dressing up, Dr. March, Miss Cruz."

She was absolutely serious, the unspoken message being that Mae had not dressed up. He'd worn a navy suit and silk tie, typical for official visits, and Tessa had impulsively put on a dress purchased on her outing today. Meanwhile, Mae was in black slacks and a green tank top. It was elegant and refined, like everything else she wore, but he supposed it might have been considered casual next to Astrid's calf-length taffeta dress. Though he scoffed at Cynthia's "label whore" accusations, Justin *had* made a quick study of the fashion trends he'd missed in exile. It was a leftover habit from when he was younger and had tried to hide his lower-class background. Mae was at the height of style, as always, even when casual. Her mother's dress was from last year. A small detail, but notable among castals.

He wasn't entirely sure who "everyone" was. Astrid led them to a dining room with heavy wainscoting and wallpaper adorned with a swirling blue design. Two women and two men sat at a long table, along with a boy a little older than Quentin. All had the blond hair and blue or green eyes typical of their caste. Erratic signs of Cain marked the group, and Mae stood out from them like some star in a cloudy sky. If not for scattered shared features, Justin wouldn't have guessed they were related.

Introductions named the other guests as Mae's siblings and their spouses. The boy, Mae's nephew, went by his Nordic name, Niklis. Aside from Mae's mother, everyone else used a Latin or Greek name from the National Registry, which was telling. It suggested they were more progressive. Maybe they were, but one thing soon became clear: They hated Mae.

Maybe "hated" was too strong. "Resented" might have been more accurate.

It wasn't so obvious at first. Everyone was so, so polite. A written transcript would have shown nothing untoward, but listening to it in person was a different matter. Every comment contained a barb for Mae and occasionally Justin and Tessa as well.

"Well, Mae," said her sister, Claudia. "It was nice of you to come by. I know Mom appreciates it. I know she especially appreciates you bringing your friends." She peered over at Tessa as the housekeeper set down chipped bowls of yellow pea soup. "Do you guys use silverware in the provinces?"

"Of course they do," said Mae, the outrageous question breaking even her composure. "For goodness' sake, Claudia. She's from Central America."

Claudia sniffed at the rebuke. "Well, it's not like I have that much time to study the provinces." She fixed her attention on Justin and gave what he suspected was meant to be a seductive smile. "So, Dr. March. What do you and my little sister do together exactly?"

Cyrus and Claudia's husband snorted in amusement. Astrid blanched. "Claudia!"

"What?" asked Claudia innocently. "I want to know about their work." She fluttered her eyes at Justin. "A servitor's life must be fascinating."

She's so bitter and jealous of Mae that she can barely sit there, Justin observed.

Can't you see why? asked Horatio.

Justin could. Claudia was short and dumpy, with none of the beauty and grace of her younger sister. Cain had dulled Claudia's hair, and judging from the family's finances, she wasn't able to afford any treatments. That, and she had the drained look of someone who'd never left her hometown and had little to occupy her time. From the sharp looks she also gave her nephew, Mae wasn't the only sibling Claudia envied.

She's jealous of you too, said Horatio. *You're unsuitable by their standards, but you represent another thing Mae has that she doesn't: dashing, exotic, good-looking.*

Are you trying to take me home? Justin asked.

You know what I mean. And look who she's with.

Justin couldn't fault that logic either. Claudia's husband was a lump of a man, with a thick jaw and soup running down his chin. He mostly communicated through grunts. A lowly plebeian might have been preferable to that. In fact, recalling Mae's story, Claudia *did* have a thing for plebeians. With her airs, it wasn't that hard to imagine her giving away a baby to save face. It especially wasn't hard to imagine Astrid encouraging it.

"My job's not that interesting," said Justin, fully in public relations mode. "Mae just comes along to make sure no zealots get out of line. She keeps me safe. You never know what they'll do."

Mae's eyes rested on him briefly, and Justin realized she was mentally assigning him to the zealot category.

Niklis brightened at Justin's words. "Aunt Maj, do you have a gun?"

"Of course she doesn't," answered Astrid. "Maj would never bring a gun into this house."

"I have two," Mae told her nephew.

Astrid gasped. "Why would you do such a thing?"

"Because I'm on duty, Mother." Mae had simply been stirring her soup and now pushed it away. Her face had on that emotionless mask she excelled at maintaining.

"More exciting than being Kris Eriksson's wife, I suppose," said Cyrus. He wasn't exactly antagonistic toward Mae, but he definitely had a mocking attitude. It was one he dealt out to his entire family, so at least he was fair. He topped everyone's wine off without asking. "Mae ever tell you about all the proposals she turned down? She could've made this family's fortune."

"Mae's always done what she wanted," grumbled Claudia. "Gone where she wanted. Run around with who she wanted." She gave Justin and Tessa supercilious looks as she spoke.

That, more than anything else, cracked Mae's tough exterior. She snapped some sharp Finnish retort to her sister, earning snickers from Cyrus and his wife, who seemed to think this was dinner theater. Claudia responded with something that must've been equally venomous, judging from Astrid's scandalized expression.

"Show some manners!" she scolded. "Our guests are more civil than you are." The subtext, of course, was that it was a huge embarrassment to be shown up by a plebeian and a provincial. "Remember that our family is built on principle and decorum."

Awkward silence fell. Mae's face became blank once more. Claudia glowered, and Cyrus kept pouring more wine than even Justin could drink. Glancing over at Tessa, he saw that the girl looked like she wanted to be anywhere but here. He couldn't

blame her. Surprisingly, it was Claudia's dull husband who resumed some sort of civil discourse.

"So," he said. "Did you hear that the Comets made it to the
play-offs?"

Justin didn't care much for sports, but he'd learned long ago
that other people did, making it an excellent topic to build rapport with. So, he kept up with all the latest headlines, something
that came in handy now as he engaged the men in conversation.
They warmed up to the subject and seemed to forget they were
talking to a plebeian. The Koskinen women, however, remained
quiet and sullen.

When dinner mercifully ended an hour and a half later, Mae
offered to show Justin and Tessa around the house.

"Remember that this house isn't a museum," her mother
warned her.

"Yes, yes," said Mae. "We'll stay out of your bedrooms."

Maybe the house wasn't a museum, but it was certainly
dusty enough to be an artifact. Justin had always hired cleaners
to do his housework but was on the verge of asking for a broom
to lend a hand now. He found out that the family had once employed a large staff to maintain the house, though their numbers
had dwindled as the Koskinen finances did.

"What happened to your family's money?" asked Justin as
Mae paused in front of the doorway to what looked like a cluttered
office. A moment later, she kept going and showed them into a
conservatory that could've been straight out of an old movie. He'd
asked her a personal question, but Mae seemed too preoccupied
with her own thoughts to reprimand him for it. That, or maybe
she'd just accepted there were few secrets between them now.

"I don't know. I think my mother just mismanaged it after
my dad died."

Mae ran her hand along the top of a piano, her fingertips
leaving trails in the dust. Justin had a sudden and startling
memory of that night in Panama when Mae, wet and bedraggled but still dazzling, had sat down and played Saint-Saëns. It
certainly wasn't an erotic image, but it triggered a reminder of
that initial, burning attraction, when he'd looked at her and
thought she was the most amazing woman in the world.

She still is, said Magnus loyally. *You could have her, and your world would change.*

Justin felt a pain in his heart and made no response.

Tessa joined Mae at the piano. "This is pretty. Nicer than ours." Tessa played a few lines of something Justin didn't know, reminding him that she too had taken lessons. He supposed it was something upper-class young ladies did.

"Where did you learn to play?" asked Claudia incredulously, standing in the doorway.

Tessa took her hands back. "At my house."

Claudia's face said she couldn't have been more surprised if a cat had learned to play. "Mae, Marius and I are leaving."

Something in Mae's face sharpened. "I'll walk you out. And I'll show you guys my room." She led Justin and Tessa down the hall and pointed to a doorway at the top of the stairs. "Right there. Probably hasn't changed since I left. I'll be there as soon as I talk to Claudia."

Justin was astute enough to pick up that there was more than a good-bye involved, but he left Mae to her own affairs. Besides, he quickly became consumed by her old bedroom. It was another piece of her to collect. Like every other room, dust reigned. The décor was a mix of the two worlds that had always pulled on Mae. All the furniture was ornate and expensive, the kind of stuff a mother would pick out, not a child or teen. The partially ajar closet was filled with old evening gowns that made Tessa ooh and ahh. Juxtaposed with that glamour were old poster screens that, when turned on, displayed images of various athletes and teams. He even found what must have been a *canne* stick leaning against a corner. He really needed to look that crazy sport up.

Tessa found an open jewelry box on the dresser and couldn't resist the curiosity of looking through it. "Wow." She lifted a bracelet encrusted in sapphires that still glittered. "Mae left so much behind."

"You see any engagement rings in there?" he asked. He smiled at Tessa's startled look. "Never mind."

"They're awfully mean to her, though. I guess I'd abandon a lot to get out of here too." She swapped the bracelet for a pearl choker. "Did she leave in a hurry?"

"How would I know?" he asked lightly.

Tessa glanced away from her treasures, giving him a wry look. "How could you not know? You used to watch her with this look. . . . It was hungry. Like you were going to die if you didn't get inside her head."

"Used to?" he asked.

She shrugged and returned to the jewelry box. "You're still alive. I figured you must know everything now."

Justin laughed in spite of himself. "You know, if I'd realized back in Panama that you'd—" He stopped speaking when he saw her next find. "What is that?"

Tessa lifted a silver necklace with a large pendant hanging on it. The pendant consisted of elaborate silver knot work shaped into a bird. "It's pretty," she said. "Looks like a raven."

It's a crow! exclaimed Horatio indignantly. *Can't she tell the difference? Some prodigy.*

Crows are stupid, said Magnus. *I hate crows.*

"It's a crow," Justin told Tessa, stepping closer.

"Same knot work they've got all over the house."

"No . . . it's a very slightly different style." He frowned. "I've seen this before. Where have I seen this before?"

Tessa obviously didn't know. She started to put it back, but he took it from her, trying to dredge up an image from the files of his mind. Suddenly, his breath caught. He took out his ego and pulled up the video that still continued to baffle the RUNA's best technical minds. The display was smaller than a true screen, so it was more difficult to make out the details as he watched the red-haired Erinian woman take off her jewelry for the night. But there it was—he was certain of it. The necklace she removed was the right size and shape, and he knew if he looked at a larger screen, he'd see a replica of the one Tessa had found.

"It's Celtic knot work, not Norse," he murmured.

"Why would Mae have Celtic jewelry?"

"Why would Mae have this at all?" he asked. His mind was reeling, and for all his cleverness, he couldn't find a way to make this work into any of his theories. It tore them open.

Mae entered just then, her angry expression suggesting her

parting conversation with Claudia hadn't gone well. "Are you guys ready to go?"

Justin held up the necklace, still stunned. "Where did you get this?"

"I don't know. Half that jewelry's been around forever. Heirlooms and stuff." She did a double take, picking up on his state of shock. "Why?"

"The Erinian woman in the video had one just like this."

"What? I don't remember that."

"Well, I do, and I just replayed it to check. Why would you both have this?"

Mae shook her head, nowhere near as blown away as he was. "I don't know. Because it was mass-produced by some designer that castals like? Coincidences like that happen all the time."

"But it's Celtic! Why would you have Celtic jewelry?"

"Because sometimes we visit other castes. My mother has Celtic friends. It's probably from one of them." She was starting to get irate. "What are you getting at here? Because obviously, there's something."

"'Something' is that you're part of this!" He set the necklace down and began to pace as he organized his frantic thoughts. "We were wrong. Somehow we were wrong. You're tied to them, Mae. The other eights and nines. I *knew* it was too big of a coincidence."

She looked aghast. "We already went over this, and Leo told you I wasn't a match. I wasn't worked on."

"You were," he said slowly, fully realizing his next words might cause considerable damage. "He . . . he said you showed signs of genetic manipulation. It wasn't the same kind as the victims', but it definitely wasn't natural."

Wide-eyed, she opened her mouth to speak, but nothing came out right away. "He never told me that. *You* never told me that." It was a small detail, but Justin noticed she had a greater expectation that he would tell her the truth than that the person who'd actually run the test would. "There's a mistake. I wasn't part of any illegal genetics."

"Were you not there at dinner?" he asked. "Do you seriously

think you came out of that bunch *without* some sort of serious intervention from science?"

"I'm not a match," she said through gritted teeth. "Leo said so." He could see the panic rising in her, a panic that wasn't so much just about illicit practices. It was the fear of being part of something she'd had no say in, a future that others had chosen for her. If he wanted to keep any of her regard for him, Justin knew he should back off . . . but he couldn't. Not when he knew he was right.

"Maybe you were a trial or something. I don't know. But look at the facts! You have the right score, the right age. You had some kind of work done. And now there's this 'coincidental' necklace, which I'll bet anything you want has some sort of re- ligious meaning—and which I also bet we'll find with some of the other victims."

"Which is it?" she demanded. "A vindictive geneticist or a crazy cult?"

"I think it's what Callista said: both."

"Right," said Mae, scoffing. "Because she's an authority. Don't drag me into your fanatical theories of—"

She stopped abruptly when she saw her mother standing in the door. Judging from her shocked expression and Tessa's paleness, he and Mae had gotten pretty loud. He'd been too caught up to notice.

"Is everything okay?" Astrid asked.

"Everything's fine," said Mae. "I apologize for the distur- bance." She was the ice princess again, but there was fire in her eyes.

"Everything is not okay!" Justin said. "You guys are so caught up in your polished images and passive-aggressive com- ments that no one ever comes right out and says anything. Well, I'm going to." He stared Astrid straight in the eye, uncaring if she thought he was a plebeian savage. "Mrs. Koskinen, was there or was there not genetic manipulation used when Mae was conceived?"

Mae gasped, probably as much from someone actually speaking openly in this house as from the topic itself. He kept his gaze on Astrid, looking for any telltale signs of lying in that impassive face. She was clearly someone who'd perfected controlling what she revealed to the world years ago. Her whole life was built on appearances, and while Mae was good, she was a novice compared to her mother. As it turned out, though, Justin didn't have to read through any lies.

"Yes," said Astrid. "Yes, there was."

CHAPTER 28

HER DRUG

For a moment, Mae couldn't breathe. She stared at her mother, waiting for something else, some explanation or—preferably— the revelation that this was all a joke. But Mae should've known better. Her mother wasn't the joking type.

"You . . . you can't be serious."

"Oh, I'm perfectly serious." Her mother strolled with complete ease into the room, settling down on the plush, satin-covered bed as though she were at tea. "Dr. March's observations were very astute. Did you really think you were the result of some freak chance? After your siblings?"

"They aren't that bad. They're your own kids!" Mae frantically tried to remember how much of the case she and Justin had inadvertently discussed just now. Tessa had been hearing pieces of it for weeks, but it wasn't her discretion Mae was worried about.

"Yes, Maj. They are. And I love them, just as I love you. I loved you enough to give you your best fighting chance in the world."

Mae swallowed, still unable to believe this conversation was taking place. "What you're saying . . . You broke the law. It's illegal. It's unethical."

Her mother shrugged. "Is it unethical to want healthy children? The government's too paranoid. What harm was done? You're here; you're healthy. Mephistopheles wasn't unleashed on the world again."

"I can't believe Dad would've agreed to it."

"He didn't need to. You were all in vitro. It was as simple as giving the lab what they needed and letting them do their business. It was what we did at other places for your brother and sister. Your father had no reason to think any more than normal fertilization was going on. I got pregnant, and we got you." She made it sound so nauseatingly easy.

Justin crossed his arms and leaned against a wall, thoughts churning behind his dark eyes. "He must've suspected something later when he saw this perfect face and athletic skills that'd be mind-blowing in a plebeian, let alone a cas—patrician."

Her mother didn't deny it. "What was he going to do? Return her?"

Mae felt dizzy and rested a hand on the dresser, steadying herself. That her father had had no part in this was the only piece of sanity in this increasingly unbelievable tale.

"You know the name of whoever did the work?" asked Justin.

"I don't remember." Mae's mother waved a dismissive hand. "I'm sure I could find it in our records somewhere, though they're not in business anymore."

"I'm sure they aren't," said Justin. "And I'm sure whatever name you've got will be untraceable anyway."

"You should've told me this," said Mae. It was all she could manage.

Her mother actually seemed to find that funny, though there was venom in her voice. "Why? Would that have changed anything? Would you have stayed behind and done your duty? Married respectfully and helped us recoup our losses instead of sleeping around with plebeians?"

There was a lot of Astrid's response that was out of line, but one word caught Mae's attention. "Recoup . . . that's not why you ran out of money, is it?"

"I took out a number of loans to pay for you," her mother said, confirming it. "Loans that came due around the time of your disastrous debut. It cost a lot to make that 'perfect face.'"

"Did you pay in blood too?" asked Justin.

Mae's mother seemed to have momentarily forgotten he was here. Her defensiveness and contempt faltered at his words, and astonishment crossed her harsh features. "What on earth are you talking about?"

"I'm talking about the cult you signed on with to create Mae, the one that requires human sacrifice." Justin watched her so, so carefully, on guard for any twitch. Mae's mother, however, looked floored. It wasn't something Mae saw very often.

"That is . . ." Her voice trailed off as though she needed to replay Justin's words in her mind and make sure she had them right. "That is absurd." A few moments later, her bafflement turned to outrage. "Is that supposed to be some kind of sick joke?"

"Where did you get"—Justin walked over to the jewelry box and held up the necklace—"this?"

Her mother squinted as the pendant caught the light. "How should I know? It's Maj's. Ask her."

Mae didn't want to play into Justin's madness but couldn't help elaborating. "It's nothing I ever picked out. It's just been around."

"Then it was probably part of your grandmother's collection." Frowning, her mother glanced back and forth between their faces. "What's this about?"

"Nothing," said Justin, snapping a picture of the necklace with his ego.

Mae had no doubt it'd be sent off to the other land grants' law enforcement offices in an attempt to find a match among the various victims' possessions. They wouldn't find one, though. Mae was certain of it. *I have no connection to the rest. Leo said so.* Of course, maybe she shouldn't have put that much stock in Leo, seeing as he had yet to explain the shadowy figure in the video. Justin wasn't coming out and saying it, but she knew he no longer believed the video had been manipulated.

"It's late. We need to go," said Mae. Justin's head swiveled toward her.

"But we—"

"You're not going to find out anything else useful," she told him. "Because this—as ludicrous as it all is—has nothing to do with our work."

He opened his mouth to protest again, and she shot him a hard look that finally made him back down. Tessa looked all too relieved, and Mae's mother had recovered herself enough to act as though it were all no big deal. Mae hesitated by her before walking out the front door after Justin and Tessa.

"Why tell me all this now?" Mae asked.

"Because your 'friend' caught me off guard. That, and it's all in the past. Nothing to be done for it now, and there's no hard proof of my guilt if you were going to turn me in." She crooked Mae a smile that held no warmth. "And I don't believe even you would sell your own family out."

It was ironic she'd mention that, since Mae, before going up to her old bedroom, had had a heated argument with Claudia about the baby they'd smuggled away. Mae had demanded to know if Claudia knew her child had ended up with the savages in Arcadia. Claudia had been aghast—but not because of the girl's fate.

"What are you thinking looking into this? Do you think you're actually going to find her and bring her back?" Claudia had exclaimed.

"I don't know," Mae had admitted. "I'm just looking."

"You'll ruin my marriage if this gets out! Not to mention get me arrested. Are you really cold enough to do that, Mae?"

Mae hadn't had an answer. The little girl seemed too far away, too impossible to ever find. With no proof of her existence, there was no proof of a crime.

The car ride back to the hotel was full of tension. Justin was too smart to say anything more in front of Tessa. And Tessa was too smart to push on something she knew she probably shouldn't have heard in the first place. She was also tactful enough to ask if she could go for a walk when they got back to their hotel. No doubt she assumed Mae needed some quiet time.

"Stay around this block," Justin told her. "It's getting late." It was still well lit and full of people out for the evening's entertainments, especially since the rain had held off. Across the street from their hotel, a band was having an outdoor concert in a small park. Tessa assured him she'd stay safe, and once she was gone, Justin beckoned Mae upstairs. "Let's talk."

Mae trudged along beside him. "I don't want to talk."

"Yes, you do."

She followed him up to his room. He immediately turned toward the minibar, then caught himself and took a seat on the bed instead. He patted the spot beside him.

"Haven't we done this before?" she asked morosely, sitting on the bed's edge. "Except last time you were confessing to believing in the supernatural."

"Well, now it's your time to shine. How do you feel? What do you feel?"

"Nothing. I feel empty."

"That's impossible after what you just heard. You have to feel something."

She stared bleakly ahead. "Mostly I feel that I should've figured all this out on my own. Maybe I was naïve to think I could really be a natural nine and a professional castal athlete."

She spoke as calmly as she could, even though she felt sick on the inside. Knowing she'd been conceived in a petri dish had never bothered her. Knowing someone had altered her DNA was an entirely different matter. Everything about her own body took on a sinister edge. Looking at her hands, she had a surreal sense that they were not truly part of her, as though they were foreign objects.

"Everything about me is a lie," she told him.

"That's not true." He put an arm around her. "The beginning doesn't matter. Where you are now is what counts."

She leaned into him. "You do self-help now? In addition to prying into others' secrets?"

"They're one and the same." She didn't know if she agreed with that, but at least when someone knew *almost* everything about you, they could understand where you were coming from. It still didn't change the awful truth.

"I was a commodity. Born for her own gain."

"Not much different from being a stipend baby," he pointed out.

"Oh." She felt stupid for her misstep. "Sorry."

"Don't be." He looked her in the eye with that intensity that seemed to peer right into her very essence. She fell into it.

There was no scam here, no schmoozing. "Look, I meant what I said. It's where we end up. My mom had me to get some extra cash for her drug habit, and I became an academic turned government agent. You were intended to be some pretty, compliant little creature who could be sold off to breed the highest bidder's children. Instead, you answered your country's highest calling."

"Guarding you?"

"That's the second highest. I meant the part where you fearlessly walk into danger to further the RUNA's glory. You turned it around, Mae." He gently touched the side of her face. "You're the one who took control of your life."

His words wrapped around her, reaching a part of her that few ever acknowledged. The pain of what she'd learned still remained, but there, sitting with him, it lessened slightly. And like that, one of those boxes she kept her emotions locked in burst open. It was where she'd swept away all that desire from Panama, all the longing and infatuation for a magnetic man who'd made love to her with an assurance that wasn't so much dominance as it was the claiming of something both of them sought.

Before she could change her mind, Mae leaned forward and kissed him. She'd intended it to be a sweet and simple gesture, but it hit her with the same intensity as their first kiss, sending fire through her from head to toe. It also lasted a lot longer than she'd expected. A *lot* longer.

"What was that for?" he asked when they broke away.

"Really? There's something you can't figure out?" She stayed close, close enough that she could see the individual lashes that framed his eyes and smell his cologne, which was probably the latest and greatest creation of some trendy designer.

He pondered for a few moments, unable to resist the challenge. "Is it because after a lifetime of having men fawn over you and promise devotion, I'm one of the few who actually doesn't try to control you and even acknowledges that your own self-control is actually a positive thing?"

Mae shoved him away. "Damn it! Why do you have to ruin everything?"

He laughed and caught her hand, pulling them back together. "Does that mean I'm right?"

"Of course you're right. You're always right. Although, admittedly, I wasn't really thinking of it in such clinical terms."

His smile grew as he leaned toward her, and despite the anger and hurt she still carried from the aftermath of their last liaison, the feelings that had burst open within her remained. Suddenly, Justin faltered and let go of her hand. He averted his eyes and shifted away. "Well," he said, voice neutral. "Glad to know my skills are still razor-sharp."

Mae was at a loss. He wanted her; she knew it. Then, a smarting truth hit her, and she felt like an idiot. "Justin . . . I need to apologize for what I said a long time ago. The whole thing about 'someone like me' and 'someone like you.' Obviously, you know now about my nonexistent Nordic dating habits. I just lashed out at you then because I felt hurt and humiliated over what I thought was some scheme of yours. I don't believe that anymore. I know you weren't using me."

A flash of pain crossed his features, gone as quickly as it appeared, and he gave her a small smile. "Yeah, but I'd be using you now. You just had your whole world rocked—badly—barely an hour ago. That's not going to go away if you get your world rocked in a different way. Passion born from emotional upheaval never ends well."

She slinked over to him again, resting her hand on his leg and curling her fingers into him. "Maybe I'd be using you. You of all people understand the need to stop thinking for a while."

"Yeah, and that philosophy landed me in the hospital," he said. Despite the flippant tone, there was a tension in his body and a catch in his breath that told her he wasn't unaffected here.

Mae was undaunted, absolutely confident of how this would end. She moved up on her knees and cupped his face in her hands. "Be my drug," she said in a low voice. "Help me forget."

His hands wrapped around her waist, then slowly slid down to her hips. Such a small, subtle touch, but it was exactly the kind of thing prætorians lacked. For Mae, in that moment, it was almost more powerful than if he'd simply thrown her down on the bed.

Indecision burned in Justin's eyes. It was a rare moment in someone usually so overconfident. "Mae . . . this is a bad idea. . . ."

She lowered her lips to his ear. "We can leave the lights on."

That undid him, and seconds later, they were both trying to pry each other's clothes off. And as Mae had hoped, she *did* forget. He became her drug, making her drunk with a desire she hadn't felt in a very long time. She wanted him so badly, it hurt.

The fallout from today's disastrous revelations vanished, and all that mattered was the warmth of his skin and the way he felt against her. She met his mouth with another kiss, nearly dizzy with the heat and desire coursing through her. She'd forgotten how gorgeous his body was, how deceptively strong it was underneath the expensive suits. Her body demanded his, and her mind demanded release of a different sort, a freeing from everything that had been weighing on her.

When their clothes were nothing more than haphazard piles on the floor, she moved on top of him, straddling his hips as she had once before. He was hard beneath her hands, and her blood burned with the need to possess him. She held back—not easy to do with the implant's influence—but she wanted to savor this for as long as she could. There'd be plenty of opportunity for animal passion soon enough. She slid her hands up his chest, leaning forward so that her face was near his. Beneath her palms, his heart raced.

"You are so beautiful," he breathed. "Still devastatingly beautiful. Doing this in the dark was a crime." He tried to push some of her hair away from her face, but it fell right back.

"It's unruly." She hoped he wouldn't notice that his reference to the dark had stirred up her old insecurities about lovers seeing the depth of her emotions. It had taken her ages to leave the lights on with Porfirio. . . . Surely Justin hadn't progressed to that privilege already, had he? It didn't seem possible, but as she allowed herself to accept this vulnerability, she discovered there was a rightness in granting him this. It still scared her . . . but it thrilled her too.

"It's glorious," he told her. He tucked the hair back again, gave up when it escaped, and instead trailed his fingers along her neck, down to her shoulder, and then along the curve of her breast. It was another small touch, another one with monumental effects.

"Even without flowers?" she teased.

His hand froze.

"What?"

She laughed softly and brushed a kiss against his lips. "You don't remember? Your eloquent proposition in Windsor?"

Not waiting for a response, Mae kissed him again, harder this time. Her whole body ignited, and the time to savor was over. She shifted her legs so that she could take him within her and relive those earth-shattering moments from Panama. There was an urgency driving her actions now, one that needed the feel of him inside her again, to revel in the union of—

Justin gripped her shoulders and gently moved her, just enough to break the kiss. "What did I say?" he asked.

"What?"

"The proposition in Windsor. The flowers."

Mae, adrift in a sea of lust, couldn't even process the demand right away. She was operating on primal instincts now. "We can talk later. Right now, the only thing I want to do is—"

"What did I say?"

The harshness in his voice cast a brief chill over the heat of her desire. She frowned. "I don't remember it all. You were just going on about getting some kind of flower—something shaped like a star—and you were going to put it in my hair and—"

Something completely unexpected happened then. Justin pushed her away and moved out from underneath her. It was agonizing, having been so close to that fulfillment, only to have it abruptly ripped away. But even that wasn't as bad as the look on his face as he sat up. Gone was the humor, the rapture and adoration. Even the arousal was rapidly dissipating.

Mae's was still going strong, and she couldn't figure out what had brought about this change. "What's the matter?"

He raked a hand through his hair. "This is a mistake. We can't do this."

She reached out to touch his arm, but he pulled it away. "The hell we can't. We should've been doing this a long time ago."

His eyes met hers, and she caught a fleeting glimpse of that earlier pain—and longing. It transformed into a steely resolve. "No. We can't. I can't. Look . . . you're gorgeous, no question. And men have every reason to line up around the block for the chance to be in bed with you. The thing is, I already have been."

"What . . . you think someone else needs a chance?" she asked.

He shook his head. "No, no. I'm just saying, for me . . . well, the thrill is gone."

She looked him over. "You seem thrilled to me."

"Not in here." He tapped his head. "You weren't a conquest, not exactly, but some of what I said back in the ministry was true. I usually don't see women more than once, not because of some sinister motive, but because I can't help it. Once I've been with a woman, there's no mystery. No novelty. There's no reason to go back once I know what it's like. And . . ." He held out his hands helplessly. "I know what it's like with you."

Any residual lust within her had dried up and blown away. "You're lying."

"The lie would be going through with this, and I respect you too much to play these kinds of games. I like you. I like the time we spend together and don't want to ruin our working relationship—which is why you need to know the truth. And right now that truth is . . . I'm just not interested in having sex with you."

Mae didn't want to believe it. She couldn't believe it. After all, she'd seen the enthralled way he'd looked at her only moments ago. Of course, she could also see the way he looked at her now, and there was no tenderness or rapture here. His unflinching gaze and level words made her doubt herself, and with that doubt came anger and humiliation that he'd led her to this situation. She seized the former and let it empower her, wrapping it around her like armor so that he couldn't see the terrible hurt he'd just inflicted. She fixed him with the iciest look she had.

"Get out."

CHAPTER 29

TECHNICALITIES

"It's my room," he reminded her.

Mae had that ice princess mask on, though it had come too late to hide her earlier look, the one that said he'd just punched her in the heart. He tried to focus on the hatred in those sea-colored eyes, because if he looked too hard at anything else, he was going to crack. She was too full of distractions—the breasts, the lips, the neck. Even the tousled hair was a turn-on, as he thought back to how his hands had just been in it. If she touched him again, he'd take her with no more protests or lies, selling himself into the servitude of an unknown god in order to have one more night with her.

But she didn't touch him. She stood up and began furiously searching for her clothes. Wordlessly, he tried not to watch as she dressed, but it was kind of impossible not to. And so help him, it was far more provocative than it had any right to be.

Why does her underwear have to be black? he thought despondently. *This would be a lot easier if she'd worn beige.*

This would be a lot easier if you were making love to her and taking your rightful place in the service of our master, chastised Magnus.

"I'm going back to my room," Mae said once she was dressed. "I'll meet you in the lobby tomorrow to go to the airport." She strode toward the door.

"Mae—"

She paused and looked back at him over her shoulder. For the slimmest of moments, he knew he could still save this. He could find some clever, endearing way to take back the god-awful spiel he'd just made up. Or, unbelievably, he could even tell her the truth. But he didn't say any of those things, and she walked out the door.

Justin sank back onto the bed, still naked, trying to make sense of what was completely nonsensical. Lying there only made him think of her again, especially since the scent of her perfume lingered on the sheets. Frustrated, he stood up and put the rest of his clothes back on. The brief tumble hadn't wrinkled them, which was a small blessing. After a little touch-up to his hair, it was almost like the debacle had never happened—aside from the hurt lingering inside him.

I didn't want this. I didn't want any of this! Why couldn't your god have left me alone? he demanded of the ravens. *I wouldn't have been exiled. I wouldn't be in this mess with SCI. I wouldn't have had to say those things to her.*

You're one of the elect, said Horatio simply. *So is she. When gods choose you, you have to face the consequences.*

Justin had done a good job alienating her. He'd seen it as every word that came out of his mouth hit her like a physical blow. It was especially effective because there'd been some truth to what he said. There were, shameful as it was, plenty of women who lost their appeal after that first time. Mae wasn't one of them, but she didn't know that, not after his magnificent, bastardly performance. There'd be no recovery from this.

He supposed it was his own fault for letting things get so far. He'd been caught up in a need to comfort her after all she'd been through today. Then . . . he'd recognized the warning signs and tried to pull back, with little success. The more she'd touched him, the sultrier her voice had grown, the more luminous those desire-filled eyes had become . . . well, the easier it had been to forget sketchy dream promises. Even when she'd been on him, with the light shining all around her, every bit the woman among women he'd been promised in his dream . . . even then he could almost forget. But she'd brought him back to reality with her words—his words, actually. Those stupid flowers.

It was time to go. There was a small casino next to the hotel, and he suddenly craved his old vice. He craved a number of vices, actually. He needed to drown his melancholy in as many distractions as he could find, because he was going to go crazy if he stayed here and pined.

Maybe I'll have more success with the dice, he told the ravens.

Horatio's helpful response was: *I don't see how you couldn't.*

But he couldn't easily forget Mae as he walked downstairs. Once more, he toyed with the idea of telling her the truth, and once more, he dismissed it. He knew she was only just barely tolerating what she saw as his irrational belief in the supernatural. How would she handle it if he described the rest of the golden apple dream to her? The part where she'd been offered to him by a god?

He'd given Mae a very good recounting of the dream, but he'd edited crucial details of the conversation that had sealed his fate, ones that his sharp memory couldn't let go of.

"Give me the apple," the half-shadowed god had said in the woods, "and I will show you the path to wisdom. My thought and memory will guide you, and we will give you the tools to outwit your enemies."

"I offered him the same thing," the silver goddess had said in protest. "And I'd make it far more enjoyable."

"My wisdom is greater and older than yours." The half-shadowed god had turned back to Justin. "You're too ambitious to let your cleverness go to waste. When you're sworn to me, I'll share my knowledge and teach you spells and charms, the likes of which the world hasn't seen for ages."

"I don't believe in spells and charms," Justin had said, even as a chill of anticipation ran through him.

The god had snorted. "You will. And I know you believe in the charms of women. I'll send you one. A woman carved of fire and ice, who will scorch you in bed and live and die for you outside of it."

"Wisdom can't be given, but love can?" protested the goddess.

"He didn't promise love," Justin had found himself saying. "He insinuated it." That had brought a chortle from the half-shadowed man, whom the goddess had then called a cunning bastard. The smoky god, however, had been indignant.

"You want women? With the power I'll give you, you can have more women than you ever dreamed of."

"He only needs one," the half-shadowed man had insisted. Even without seeing his eyes, Justin had felt that dark gaze boring into him. "A woman among women. You'll see. You'll know her by a crown of stars and flowers, and then when you take her to your bed and claim her, you will swear your loyalty to me." Suddenly, almost comically, the god had jerked his head up in surprise. "Damn. You're no use to me dead."

A surreal feeling had swept Justin, of being simultaneously in the dream and back in his bed at the inn. And back in his bed, the world was burning around him. He'd managed to blink the dream back into focus and plead with the half-shadowed man. "Save me, and I'll give you the apple."

"And agree to the rest of my terms? All the words that have passed between us are binding. When you swear in a dream, you swear with your soul."

"Yes, yes. Just get me out of here." Justin had tossed him the apple and woken up to ravens.

Aside from the fact that he had two possibly imaginary birds living with him, Justin hadn't thought much about the dream in exile. There'd been no glorious woman, no spells or charms, no godly apparitions. Mae had therefore caught him off guard, and he'd just barely been able to twist the god's words around and dodge the deal. *You'll know her by a crown of stars and flowers, and then when you take her to your bed and claim her, you will swear your loyalty to me.*

Justin had argued that according to the words of the deal, he didn't have to swear loyalty until *after* he'd claimed her as the one crowned in flowers and stars. Since he hadn't known who she was the first time, he therefore hadn't technically claimed the crowned one. It was tenuous footing, but that technicality kept him safe, so long as he didn't screw up again. He'd used a similar technicality to save him from the training in charms and spells the god had offered—and that was the key. Offered. Justin hadn't actually promised to do any of it. The god had just assumed Justin would jump at the chance.

Our master isn't going to assume anything with you anymore, Magnus said ominously.

When Justin arrived at the casino, the crowd was split pretty evenly between plebeians and patricians who had all sorts of relationships with each other. Most plebeians who came to grants were there on business. They were easy to spot, some in groups of their own while others mingled with Nordic associates. Other plebeian and Nordic pairings looked friendlier and of a more personal nature. Romantic pairings between groups were nowhere to be seen. That didn't mean they didn't happen, of course. In fact, he could already see groups of Nordic mixers—the slang term for patricians who went slumming—on the prowl, hoping for a discreet hookup.

He scanned his ego at the table to buy his chips, fully aware he wouldn't have been setting out such a big amount if his emotions weren't in such turmoil. It didn't matter, though. He had plenty of money to burn, and as Horatio had pointed out, it didn't seem like his luck could get any worse.

And it didn't. That wasn't to say it improved significantly either, but at least he more or less kept even, allowing him to lose himself in the thrill of random chance. Servers brought him drinks, dulling his memories of Mae. Other players moved in and out, and at one point, a young Nordic woman came and stood beside him. She placed no bet and simply watched the game unfold.

"Do you play?" Justin asked her.

She gave him a shy smile and shook her head. "No. I can't follow the bets."

"It's not that hard," he said. He generously gave her some of his chips and proceeded to explain some of the rules. She couldn't grasp all of the strategy, but she caught enough to make some simple bets. A few paid off, and she clapped her hands in delight each time she won. It was cute.

They played for another half hour, and then the girl—who'd introduced herself as Katrin—took a step nearer him and murmured, "I actually didn't come over here to learn to play. I came here for you. But I wouldn't mind teaching you a few things."

Don't, groaned Magnus.

Justin looked down at her, and her early demureness was gone. There was a forward look in her eyes that brought back all the unfulfilled desires he'd been forced to shove away earlier. She wasn't a tall, gorgeous ice princess, but she had pouty lips and a dress that managed to display a knockout body while modestly showing little skin. *And* she was blond. He'd found a mixer after all and hadn't even had to put forth much effort.

"I'm always happy to learn new things," he told her, just as quietly. He kept his eyes back on the table, trying not to be obvious to others.

"Some men find the things I teach . . . intimidating."

"I don't scare easily."

You are so stupid, said Horatio.

A hot Nordic woman wants to do "intimidating" things with me, Justin retorted. *What would be stupid is not taking advantage of this opportunity.*

Justin nearly asked her back to his room, but memories of Mae suddenly popped back into his mind. He didn't want to take Katrin into that bed.

"Do you have any place we could go?"

She didn't answer right away, which only made things that much more tantalizing. He gripped his bourbon glass tightly, waiting for a response that seemed to take forever.

"You said you don't scare easily," she finally said. "Are you afraid of the women's bathroom?"

Whoa. He hadn't expected that. He'd figured she'd give him an address that they'd slip off to separately. Not that he had a problem with bathroom sex. In his younger days, when privacy hadn't always been so easy to come by, it had been a necessary option sometimes.

"It takes more than that to scare me," he assured her. And actually, the more he thought about spreading her legs on a bathroom counter, the more on board he was with the idea. There was just one problem. "But it might not be the most, uh, secure place—which could be an issue here."

"Not the ones on this floor," she said in agreement. "But there's one in the basement for employees that doesn't get used much. Do you see the stairs over there? There's a service door that'll take you down."

She seems to know that bathroom pretty well, observed Horatio. *I wonder how many men she's held "class" for down there.*

"I'll go now," Katrin continued. "Meet me in five minutes."

She cashed out and, without another glance, sauntered away. Justin played a few more rounds, watching every second on the clock, and then left for the rendezvous. He had to seize a moment when no one was near the stairwell before slipping into it. They might very well have had cameras in it, but he was pretty sure that bathroom sex, while frowned upon, wasn't actually a crime, even among castals.

The lower level was a daylight basement, and the long corridor he entered ran down to a glass door that opened out to the casino's back property. Otherwise, there was little activity. A few servers scurried back and forth between stockrooms, but no one was down at the end that contained the restrooms. With a deep breath, he strode toward the door marked WOMEN and knocked softly when he reached it. For half a second, he had a panicked thought that Katrin might have played him and some dour Nordic matron would open the door.

But it was Katrin who answered, with a sly smile on her lips and fervor in her eyes. She beckoned him in and locked the door. For a moment, he was a little thrown off by the bathroom. First of all, it was a lot bigger than he'd expected. Everything in it was aqua blue, from the paint to the satin-covered chair near the entrance to the two faux-marble stalls. Soft violin music was piped in from unseen speakers, and everything smelled like freesias. Justin wasn't sure whether this was a castal thing or some secret of women's restrooms he'd never known about. It kind of took away from the kinky element of everything, but that was a concern easily forgotten.

Katrin wasted no time in pushing him against a wall and kissing him with an almost ferocious intensity. Her mouth tasted like rum and strawberries, and her teeth nipped at his lips. He moved his hands down her hips and pulled one of her legs up, bending it so that he could slide his hand up the back of her thigh. Her skin was sleek and soft, and the fabric of her dress yielded easily as he pushed it up. Yearning flooded him as she ground her body against his, giving him one of those rare moments where the continuous spinning of his mind stilled and gave in to instinct and emotion.

He still held high hopes of getting her onto the counter and wasn't really picky about which way she faced. But when he tried to move her in that direction, she pushed back, her hands resting on his chest to keep him pinned against the wall. Maybe this was part of what "intimidating" meant. It reminded him a little uneasily of Mae's dominance, and he hoped this would have a happier outcome.

It didn't.

He had Katrin's underwear partway off when he felt the wire against his neck.

The kissing also abruptly stopped, and when he opened his eyes, he saw that the ferociously passionate look on her face had simply become ferocious. He tried to speak, but the words were choked off as the wire bit into his flesh. With a strength born out of sheer terror, he pushed back against her and managed to momentarily escape the wire. Katrin surged toward him again with remarkable strength, but he dodged in a way that kept his neck from strangulation. He managed to wriggle away and grabbed the first weapon he could find: a ceramic vase filled with freesias. With no thoughts of chivalry, he swung it toward her and managed to clip the side of her head. It slowed her for a moment, and then, improbably, she came at him again and hardly seemed fazed at all.

Ironically, he found he was the one backed up against the counter. He swung the vase again, managing to keep a small distance between him and that wire while he frantically tried to figure out what to do. Offense wasn't really his style, but staying on the defense didn't seem like it would get him anywhere. He advanced forward as he wielded the vase, allowing him a little progress until she knocked it out of his hands. It fell to the ground and smashed into pieces. He kicked out at her and managed to hit her leg, but much like the vase, it only seemed to annoy her.

Those small delays allowed him a little movement, however, and he was able to reach the door. Unlocking it took long enough that she was able to grab his arm and jerk him backward. His other hand held on to the doorknob firmly, and for a moment, he felt like he'd be ripped in half. He pulled away and managed to open the door, shoving it into her as he did so. It threw her off, so that she missed when she tried to grab his shoulder. Shouting for help, he made it into the hall and had another split-second decision to make.

To his right was the way he'd come, and at the far end of the hall, he knew there had to be employees working. To his left, not very far at all, was a glass door leading outside. He didn't know where it went, but surely it would go somewhere with people and safety. That was the way he chose.

But when he reached it, he found that it was locked. He couldn't find any obvious way to open it, and the delay cost him. Katrin caught him by the shoulder this time and jerked him away from the door. Unexpected pain shot through him at her touch, like several blades scratching his flesh. Snarling, she lunged toward him with the wire, but it wasn't an ideal weapon for a moving target. When he dodged again, she dropped the wire and pulled out a shiny black knife from somewhere in that tight dress.

"Shit."

The long hall beyond her offered freedom, but he couldn't figure out how to get past her. The best he could do was awkward hitting and dodging that slowed her a little but in no way seemed capable of stopping or even tiring her. She appeared to be evenly matched in strength with him, which was equally frustrating. At one point, they got tangled in each other and fell to the ground, rolling around in a way that was not at all like what he'd originally imagined when coming downstairs. Her hand raked down his back, causing more of that pain. If her nails were that bad, he couldn't imagine what the dagger would do.

He finally kicked her off enough that he could crawl into a nearby storage closet. He shoved the door in her face and held it shut with his entire body while he groped for a light. When he found it, he could barely believe how the world had fucked him

368 · *Richelle Mead*

over today. The glass door he'd wanted to open had had a lock, and this one, which he needed to stay closed, had none. There was nothing he could do but try to hold it closed with his own weight. On the other side, Katrin turned the knob and pushed hard against the door, making it open a few centimeters before Justin was able to throw himself back against it. With one hand, he fumbled for his ego but couldn't really get out a message while trying to hold the door.

Well, now what? asked Horatio.

Justin was about to say he was open to suggestions when he realized Horatio was talking to Magnus. In all the time he'd carried them in his head, the ravens had never conversed with just each other. It added to what was already a maddeningly surreal situation.

We have to do something, said Magnus.

What—claw her eyes out? Horatio sounded incredulous. *We can't directly intervene. We aren't even technically supposed to be here until he's sworn.*

Well, it'll never happen if he's dead, will it? And we only need to assist, not intervene.

Katrin launched herself at the door and must have had a running start. It pushed open more than it had during her previous efforts, and it took Justin several seconds to fight against her and slam it shut again.

Okay, said Horatio reluctantly. *What do you have in mind?*

You stay here, was Magnus's bizarre response.

And then, suddenly, Justin felt a searing pain and the sensation of having something ripped out of his skull.

CHAPTER 30

THE RAMBLINGS OF A MADMAN

Tessa might not have understood the big picture of what Justin and Mae were involved in, but she knew enough about genetics and the RUNA to realize the implications of what Mae's mother had revealed. That kind of research was unheard of in Panama, and Tessa was honestly surprised that Mae had handled it as well as she had. But maybe that had been for the benefit of her mother, whom Tessa found even more terrifying than her own.

Regardless, Tessa had decided it was best for her to clear out in case Mae needed time to herself. Tessa didn't mind going back out anyway. Once she'd adapted to the weirdness of being in a city where everyone looked alike, her natural curiosity took over. She was fascinated by a group of people who'd clung to their identity so fiercely, they'd been willing to risk the consequences of Mephistopheles and Cain. Even now, after years of progress, they still maintained their separation from the rest of the country while simultaneously being fiercely loyal.

Most people mistook her for an ordinary Gemman plebeian. There were a handful of others like her on the streets—seeing as their hotel was the only plebeian-friendly one—and most Nordics took them in stride. Mae had explained that farther outside the city, they'd find more prejudice. Here, no one paid much attention to Tessa as she wandered into shops that were still open. She even stopped in a café and bought a pastry stuffed with lingonberries. She'd never heard of lingonberries, but Nordics seemed to love them. Munching on it, she eventually made her way back to the park across from the hotel to listen to the band. A group of people chatting nearby described the music as "Norwegian fusion folk synth." Tessa had no idea what that was but decided the whole scene would be worth filming for her class's documentary—presuming she was ever allowed back to school.

She was so engrossed in her camera that she was taken completely by surprise when a hand clamped onto her arm. Gasping, she turned and found a young Nordic man standing next to her. He appeared to be only a little older than her, with bright blond hair and a wild look in his eyes. Tessa was too shocked to act right away and wondered if she'd found some plebeian-hating patrician.

"You're with SCI," he said.

That was unexpected. "I—what? No."

"I saw you outside the police station," he insisted. "I know you guys were here today to look at the Arnarsson crime scene."

"Er, no. Those were my, um, friends. I'm only sixteen. I'm still in school." She calmed down a little, telling herself she was out in public. He couldn't do anything to her. Although, as she began processing what he said, it occurred to her that he may have been stalking them all day.

"You have to come with me," he said, still holding on to her. "I've been trying forever to get SCI to come here! They never answer my requests. But you can't put it off anymore."

She gulped. "I told you, I'm not with SCI!"

He leaned close. "I know things. I know things that'll help solve the Arnarsson case. She wasn't the only murder."

That got Tessa's attention, though she wasn't entirely sure what to do with it. Murder investigations were out of her league. In fact, she got the impression they were out of Justin's league, but for whatever reason, that was what he'd gotten involved with.

"I can't help you," she said. "But I can get you the actual servitor that's here. You can talk to him."

The guy hesitated and then gave a slow nod. He released her, and she took out her ego to call Justin. He didn't answer, and things were further complicated when Mae didn't answer either. So much for "Call if you need anything."

"I can have them get back to you," Tessa said apologetically. "But right now—"

"No!" he exclaimed. "They'll never get back to me. I know how bureaucracy is. And they don't even think it's a real murder."

She shifted uncomfortably, suddenly worried she wasn't dealing with someone who was completely sane. "Um, what is 'it' exactly?"

"My brother. They killed him. The same people who killed Clara Arnarsson. I can help SCI get to them."

"Why don't they think it's a real murder?"

"Because there was no body. They just think he's missing," he explained. "But I'm telling you it was them! He was murdered by the servants of an evil goddess of death and war. Come talk to my dad—he'll tell you."

Tessa didn't know what to do. His story seemed absurd—especially the evil goddess part—but if there was a chance he knew something about Justin's case, it would be invaluable. Justin hadn't directly said it, but she'd begun to pick up on signs of unease that made her think his continued stay in the RUNA might very well hinge on this case. She tried again to get the Nordic guy to wait, but he was obstinate.

"No. Now. Look, I'm not taking you into a dark alley or anything. My dad's in a convalescent home not far from here. Totally public."

"Why is he in a convalescent home?" she asked.

"Because they think he's crazy."

This wasn't really reassuring her. But as she studied him, she began to feel sorry for him. His face was so earnest, his eyes so pleading. . . . Whatever was going on was real to him. He was cute too, and while that shouldn't have affected anything, it *did* make her feel more kindly toward him.

"We'll stay out in the open to get there?"

He held up his hand. "I promise. It's a fifteen-minute walk from here, all busy streets."

She hesitated only a few moments more before finally agreeing. The guy—who introduced himself as Darius—lit up and actually grabbed her hand to lead her from the park. He was true to his word. The walk was safe, the convalescent home nearby. Along the way, Darius apparently decided Tessa was his new best friend and launched into the story of his brother.

"Ilias was older than me," he began. "Almost ten years. Our parents weren't very fertile, and it took them a long time to have me. We didn't grow up playing together with the age difference, but he always looked out for me and helped teach me things. He was great. Outgoing, good-looking. Everyone loved him." Darius's face fell for a moment, and then he rushed forward. "Last year, this guy kept showing up to see Ilias and our parents. I don't know who he was or what he said, but everyone had a different reaction. Ilias always treated him like a joke. He was like that. Thought everything was funny. He talked about the guy like he was crazy. But our parents . . . they were different. They were upset every time he visited. Not upset—scared. After a while, they were just always on edge. You could see it all over them. And one day . . . my mom just cracked. She committed suicide. Cut her wrist in the bathtub."

Tessa flinched. "Oh, my God. I'm so sorry." Conversation faded after that.

The facility that Darius's father lived at tried very hard to pretend to be something else. Its façade was nearly as grand as the Koskinen house, though better maintained, and even its name sounded more like what you'd find with a country manor: Rose Grove. A clock in the lobby said it was nearly eleven, making Tessa worry about whether his father was still up.

"He doesn't sleep much," Darius explained. He led her upstairs to a room on the third floor. A sign outside read OLAF SANDBERG.

Olaf had the look of someone who'd aged before his time. He sat at a table in his room, talking to himself as he slid around puzzle pieces on a screen. "Red line matches red. . . . Start with the corner, then find the others. . . . Can't match blue with yellow . . ."

Darius took a chair on the opposite side of the table. "Dad," he said gently. "I have someone who wants to talk to you."

"That's nice. Very nice." Olaf's eyes never left the screen.

"She wants to talk about Mom and Ilias."

Olaf's hands faltered on the screen, and pain crossed his face. "Over and done, over and done."

On impulse, Tessa set up her camera on a nearby table. It wasn't ideal, but she thought this might be worth recording for Justin. She then sat in an empty chair between the two men, more than a little unnerved by Olaf's disposition. She was no interrogator, nor did she even really know why she was here. She let Darius take the lead and witnessed a remarkable change in him. The frantic desperation was gone, replaced by a calmness and heartbreaking affection for his father.

"Dad, she wants to know about the goddess you're always telling me about. The one you made the deal with."

"Over and done," repeated Olaf, his voice shaking.

"Did she kill Mom?"

"No." The old man's head shot up, and he doled out glares to each of them. "No one took her. She gave herself up. Do you understand? No one took her. She was strong."

Tessa wasn't sure about that if she'd killed herself. Darius's resigned expression said he'd heard all of this many times and was simply trying to draw out his dad's story for Tessa's benefit.

"She gave herself up for Ilias," said Darius, seeking confirmation.

"She wanted a life. It should've been enough."

Tessa hadn't wanted to get involved, but again, her mind was trying to understand. "Your wife wanted a life?"

"No! Of course not." Olaf paused to slide some more puzzle pieces around. "*She* did. The dark one."

"The goddess?" asked Tessa.

"She wanted a life. That man said it had to be Ilias's, that that was her payment. But why should it matter?" He looked back up again, desperation in his eyes. "Why should it matter? Isn't any life enough? We repaid her."

Tessa felt as though she too were sliding pieces of a puzzle around, trying to make sense of this scattered information. "What did you repay her for?"

"For Ilias."

"Because she gave him to you," said Darius, prompting him.

Olaf dropped his hand and spread it flat on the screen. "But he was never ours. They got a fortune. They got that poor plebeian boy's life to make Ilias. But it wasn't enough. They wanted Ilias to serve, but he wouldn't, so they took him back." He took a deep breath. "I should've joined Siiri. Maybe we owed another life. One for the plebeian boy, one for Ilias. If we'd both given ourselves to her, she might have let Ilias go free."

There was more here than Tessa could understand. Suddenly, a memory tickled her brain: Justin, brainstorming with her in his study. *A bunch of plebeians die the same year some perfect patricians are conceived. Is that a coincidence?*

"What was Ilias's score?" she asked.

"He was a nine," said Darius.

"Cost a fortune," lamented Olaf. "And it was so much more than money. Much more. They wanted him to serve her."

Tessa tried to think like a servitor. "You mean to join her cult?"

"Ilias laughed that man away. Should he have? I don't know." Olaf stared off into space. "Maybe he took the high road. She didn't deserve him. She's evil and twisted. We said we'd let them teach him, but we didn't. We shouldn't have promised him to her, but we didn't know what would happen. We didn't realize what would happen to that boy."

The nouns were hard to follow. "The plebeian boy?" Tessa asked, trying to clarify.

"He was innocent, but we didn't care. What was a plebeian to us? But now I see the blood on my hands." He turned his hands over and studied them. "We both did. But Siiri set herself free. It just wasn't enough to save Ilias."

Tessa began stringing together his narrative, patching it with all the things she'd heard Justin and Mae tossing around. "So . . . this goddess and her people . . . You made a deal to conceive Ilias through illicit genetic manipulation—"

"No. Magical manipulation," said Olaf. "She needs no lab."

"Um, okay. So, then they took money for it and a plebeian sacrifice. . . ." Tessa paused at that, overcome by how awful it was. "And they also wanted you to raise him in her service. But you didn't, so they came back and . . . took him."

Tessa felt sympathetic enough toward the old man and his son that she couldn't say the word "kill." She also decided not to say anything more about Siiri Sandberg. Somehow, Siiri had known this cult was after Ilias and had killed herself in the hopes that she could pay the price for her son. Apparently, this goddess's followers had required premium genes.

"What was her name?" asked Tessa. "This goddess?"

"Death and darkness and war," murmured Olaf.

Darius shook his head. "I've never heard him say a name in all the times he's told the story. He either doesn't know or won't say."

"What about the man who kept visiting?" asked Tessa. "Was he the one saying they'd take Ilias back?"

Olaf's eyes grew moist. "He warned us. He tried to persuade Ilias to join them when he was older, but he wouldn't. He was a good boy."

"Did the guy who threatened Ilias have a name? Do you know anything about him?"

Darius answered when his father wouldn't. "No name, but he was one of us. Blond. Not much Cain." He frowned. "No, there wasn't any Cain. He was like Ilias."

When it became obvious Olaf would say no more, Darius made motions to leave. He gently helped his father get into bed, and the old man fell asleep almost instantly.

"Can you help us?" Darius asked once he and Tessa were outside again. "Can you find these people?"

"I told you . . . I'm not part of this." She put her camera back in its bag. "But I'll tell the people I'm with that—"

Her ego rang with a call, and she saw Mae's name appear. Tessa answered.

"Is everything okay?" asked Mae immediately, her voice hard and tense.

"Um, yeah," said Tessa. "They're just weird. Where are you guys?"

"I'm at the rooftop bar in our hotel." There was a long pause. "I don't know where Justin is."

"Okay. I'll meet you there. We have to . . . talk."

Tessa disconnected and turned to Darius. "I'm going to see one of my friends right now, but it's my other one who'll really be able to do something." If there was anything to be done. For all Tessa knew, she'd just listened to the ramblings of a madman.

Darius nodded eagerly and surprised her by clasping her hands between his. "Will you call me when you find out? Please? I have to get justice for Ilias."

"Sure," she said. They synced their egos to trade contact information, and she wondered whether she could expect hourly calls.

After an outpouring of thanks, Darius went his own way, and Tessa returned to the hotel. It was after midnight, and she was exhausted, but she still found her way up to the rooftop bar. The place was busy with late-night socializing, and the terrace had a nice view of the park. From the way people were starting to disperse over there, the band must have been wrapping up. She found Mae sitting alone, gazing off into the distance. There was a rare expression on her face, troubled and forlorn, though it immediately vanished when she noticed Tessa.

"Hey." Tessa sat down opposite her.

"Hey." Mae had an untouched mojito in front of her. "What's going on that's weird?"

"It may be nothing . . . but I just got accosted by a guy who thinks he has information about that murder you guys are here for."

Mae straightened up. "Accosted?"

"I'm okay," said Tessa swiftly. "And it was more of a request, I guess. A very emphatic one. But I had my camera and—ahh!"

She screamed as an enormous black bird suddenly swooped low over the deck—and landed right on their table. Tessa sprang up in panic, backing into a chair behind her. Mae remained where she was, but her eyes were wide. The bird paced around on the table a little and then stopped, staring directly at Mae.

Weirder still, Mae seemed totally transfixed. She met the bird's gaze unblinkingly and seemed to be holding her breath. Then, without warning, the bird gave a croak and lifted up on strong wings. It flew across the deck again, frightening more patrons, and then paused on the railing of an emergency staircase. It glanced briefly back at Mae and then flew down.

Mae stared after it for a few seconds, and then, without a word, she tore off after it down the stairs.

CHAPTER 31

AVENGING VALKYRIE

Mae was fully aware of how crazy it was. And as she sprinted down the stairs three at a time, she wondered if she was soon going to feel like an idiot. But in that moment, when the bird—no, raven, she somehow knew—had been staring at her, she'd felt suspended in time. The world had stopped, and there'd been nothing in it but those beady black eyes. Then, most improbable of all, she'd sworn she heard a voice in her head when the bird croaked: *Come*. An overwhelming sense of urgency had swept her, and without further hesitation, she'd followed the raven.

It was waiting for her at the bottom of the stairs. Once she hit the ground, it flew off toward a small building next to the hotel, hovered a few moments, and then soared off into the dark sky. Mae looked at where it had paused. Several steps led down to a lit-up glass door in the building's lowest level. Mae could hear thumps and see some sort of movement within. She jumped down to the base of the stairs and was met with the unexpected sight of a Nordic woman in a copper-colored dress throwing herself at a wooden door. Puzzled, Mae tried to open the outer glass door and found it locked. The woman glanced over at Mae, her face filling with shock.

That was all Mae needed. Fight-or-flight mode seized her, banishing all thoughts of her mysterious winged guide. With little difficulty, she picked up a heavy stone planter sitting nearby and swung it at the door. The glass shattered, and without hesitation, Mae slipped through the jagged opening she'd created, heedless of cuts on her arms. The woman backed up and threw some kind of black knife at Mae. Mae dodged it, but in those seconds as it flew, she saw improbable black flame ringing the blade. It landed on the ground, smoking.

It didn't even slow Mae down, which came as a surprise to the woman. She looked legitimately scared, and that was when the truly unbelievable part happened.

She transformed into a jaguar.

At least Mae thought that was what it was. She was no expert in large felines or wildlife in general, but when you didn't sleep at night, you ended up watching a lot of weird TV, including nature shows. She had no time to ponder how she had stumbled into this insanity because her reflexes were kicking into action as the jaguar sprang toward her. Mae was strong but couldn't fight against that kind of weight and impact. The cat knocked her to the ground, slamming her head against the floor. Mae was able to shake the pain off. Unfortunately, she couldn't shake the jaguar off as those heavy clawed paws pinned her down and dug into her skin. It snarled, revealing a mouthful of sharp teeth as it readied for her death.

Suddenly, that icy darkness that was normally so unwelcome surged through Mae. Strength and power flooded her, and she jumped up and pushed the jaguar off of her. It started to charge her, then hesitated. Mae also wavered. The battle lust radiating from her seemed to be hitting a wall that she couldn't move past. The jaguar also seemed immobile. A few seconds later, Mae won out. The world started again, and the jaguar took off down the hall, with Mae in pursuit. As she went after it, she caught sight of Justin peering out of the mysterious door, a hand on his head and his face full of shock.

Not even a prætorian could keep up with a jaguar, but as it neared the hall's end, it transformed back into the woman. Mae took out her gun and fired but missed as her target rounded a corner toward some stairs. Mae wasn't concerned. She had absolutely no doubts about being able to close the distance, now that she was no longer pursuing a beast of the jungle. It was just a matter of time.

They reached the casino floor and the woman dashed through, oblivious to the people around her. Some were pushed out of

the way. Some she actually knocked over. Mae anticipated another opening and fired. The bullet grazed the woman's shoulder, causing her to stumble a few seconds before continuing her
frantic race. Gunfire in such a crowded room didn't go over
very well, and screams and panic filled the space as bystanders
dropped to the ground or trampled one another. Mae ignored it
all. Her whole world was focused solely on the woman, who'd
made it to the outside door.

When Mae emerged, she saw the woman shove her way
through pedestrians in a crosswalk. The crowd in the park had
thinned considerably, but there were still enough meandering
people for the woman to disappear into.

"*Jumalauta,*" Mae swore, knowing she'd need a new tactic.
Adrenaline filled her with a power she never realized she missed
in ordinary days until she was back in the throes of it. It also
sharpened her mind, allowing her to quickly and clearly make a
plan.

She reached the edge of the park and leapt up onto a table,
ignoring both the food on it and the cries of the startled occu-
pants. From that height, it was easy to spot her prey. The
woman was weaving through the crowd as Mae had, creating a
conspicuous path. Mae jumped down and raced off in the direction she'd seen the woman run, continuing to leap on and off
tables as she continued the chase. The crowd slowed both of
them down, but Mae was faster and gaining steadily. At one
point, using another table, she saw her quarry start to turn
toward the makeshift stage. Mae was on the ground in a flash,
tearing toward the center of the stage, her heart pounding and
muscles responding without delay.

The woman made it up on the stage first, much to the astonishment of the band, who faltered and then stopped altogether.
She grabbed the lead singer and held him in front of her, with
another shiny black dagger at his throat. Mae came to an abrupt
halt, breathing rapidly as she assessed this new development.
The dark force urging her forward disappeared, giving her complete and total control of her thoughts and actions. The crowd
gasped and screamed at the scene onstage, but few moved. This
was prime entertainment.

"Back off!" yelled the woman, slowly retreating with her hostage. He covered up most of her body, creating an effective shield. "I'll slash his throat open."

Shooting an erratically moving target had been difficult. A slow-moving one, even with a small space to hit, wasn't difficult at all for someone like Mae. In the space of a heartbeat, she raised the gun and shot the woman in the head.

That caused a reaction, similar to the one in the casino. Guns on Gemman streets were uncommon, public shootings even less so. Near her, a gaping guy was trying to record the scene with his ego. Mae fixed him with a hard look. "Call the police."

Things moved quickly after that. Johansson, the lieutenant they'd spoken to earlier, was among the responding officers and wasn't thrilled about the disruptive spectacle. There was little she could do against a prætorian, especially with a hostage situation.

Now that they were safe again, the crowd was vying to get a look at the aftermath. Mae tried to ignore them and the flashing egos. "I'm really curious to see what you'll turn up when you check her chip."

Johansson had been studying their surroundings with narrowed eyes but suddenly turned to Mae in surprise. "You think she's Nordic?"

"Of course she was. What else would she be?"

"Don't take this personally, prætorian, but you've been away for a long time." That leathery face smiled. "She wasn't Nordic. Even with what you did to her face, I could tell that."

Johansson clearly didn't want her around as her people dealt with the follow-up, and Mae retreated back to the casino, wondering if the lieutenant was right. Away from the heat of battle, Mae could think more clearly. The implant had metabolized most of its handiwork, and the telltale trembling was nearly gone.

She took a walk around the casino and basement, and then returned to the lobby in time to find Justin finishing his statement. She watched him unseen for long moments, wishing she could bury the hurt of his rejection. It was a stupid, girlish sentiment to have, considering she'd just shot someone in the face.

"Thank you, Dr. March," said the officer, slipping his ego

into his pocket. "We'll file your statement with the official report and then . . ." He glanced nervously over as Mae joined them. "Should we have it sent to your office, ma'am?"

"Yes," Justin answered for her. "And SCI too."

When the officer was gone, Mae sat down, unflinchingly meeting the gazes of those who stared. Word had spread that she was a prætorian, and they all looked away when they realized they'd caught her attention.

"My avenging Valkyrie," said Justin by way of greeting.

There was a familiarity in the endearment that she didn't like, in light of what had happened between them. "I heard what you said in your statement. That the woman attacked you when you went downstairs to use the bathroom."

"That's right."

"Then why was her underwear in the women's bathroom?"

Justin took a few moments to answer. "How would I know? I wasn't in there. And how do you even know it was hers?"

"If you were looking for someone novel, I guess you found her. Lucky for you, I hid the evidence for you," she said, trying not to grimace. "I threw them away." It was destruction of evidence, yes, but there was already going to be a huge uproar about a public shooting. Mae didn't want a sordid sex tale worked in, even if it didn't have anything to do with her.

"Well, thanks," he said. "I guess."

Her next words were very level. "Justin . . . that's not the evidence I'm really worried about. I don't suppose you mentioned the jaguar in your statement?"

"What jaguar?" he asked innocently.

"Oh, stop," she hissed. "I know you saw it! *She turned into a fucking jaguar.*"

"Of course I saw it. But I'm also a delusional zealot, remember?"

Mae looked away. "It couldn't have been real."

"Mae," he said patiently. "If you have another explanation, I'm all ears. Believe me, it would make my life easier."

She had none, and she knew he knew that. "There are no gods. There can't be. It's all make-believe." But her voice trembled as she spoke. She'd seen what she'd seen. It was real life, not a movie. And although she believed in the wonders technology could create, even she knew that transformation was beyond the workings of mankind. She also hadn't forgotten the sense of the dark power swirling within her—and its hesitation in the face of the jaguar woman.

"Gods are following us," he said. "Gods who may be responsible for murder and genetic work. Gods who put ravens in my head."

"Oh, yeah. I saw one."

He turned to her in surprise. "A god?"

"No . . . one of your ravens, I think. It flew at me upstairs and somehow showed me how to find you."

His jaw nearly hit the floor. "You saw Magnus?"

"I don't know which one it was."

"He left me briefly. That's why my head hurts so much." Justin actually looked delighted. "No one's ever seen him. Or them. Do you know what that's like? To finally not be the only one to see them?"

"You said you believed in them, though."

"Yeah. Mostly. But it's still a relief."

"I don't know how to handle what's happening," she said bluntly. "This. What my mom said. In one day, everything I've accepted about my life is gone. I kind of wish I was crazy."

"Yeah, I've wished that a lot too."

"How do you handle it?"

"One moment at a time."

"You told me your dream . . . but what do you really know about all of this? The bigger picture?"

He shook his head. "I've been trying to figure that out for almost five years. Cope. Lead a normal life. Learn as much as possible. Unfortunately, there's no real authority to go to for this. Callista's helped a little, but there are still so many questions."

Slightly calmer, Mae was able to focus more on him and noticed his shoulder, where long bloody lines cut through the shirt. "She . . . she scratched you with her, um, claws."

"Got my back too," he said with a wince. "And she did that even before the transformation."

"You should see a doctor."

He scoffed. "No way. I'm glad you and I had this break-through, but there's no way I'm talking to a professional. It's not that deep. You can do a field-medic job on me back in the room." The mention of his room brought back the memories of their brief moment of passion. "Mae—" he began.

She didn't want to hear whatever was coming and quickly pushed another topic. "That . . . thing that seizes me had a weird reaction to the jaguar. Almost as though they didn't want to fight each other."

Justin wisely followed her lead, though he looked reluctant. "Competing gods, maybe. I want to know what the police get on her. I want to know who sent her."

"It's obvious, isn't it? The group behind the murders."

"I don't know . . . jaguars and obsidian. That's not their style. Why didn't she use a silver dagger on you?"

"Maybe they only save them for special occasions."

He gave her a long, level look. "You do realize now that this is all tied together? You, the victims, your goddess. You're con-nected, no matter what Leo's tests say."

Mae started to protest when she noticed Tessa coming toward them. The girl caught the tail end. "Are you talking about god-desses?"

"SCI talk," Justin said quickly.

Tessa looked skeptical, but she put that aside as concern seized her. "Are you guys okay? I saw what happened from the roof . . . in the park. . . ." She looked more surprised than ap-palled, probably because of the common nature of Panamanian shootings. "I heard a policeman saying that woman attacked Justin."

"Kind of," said Mae. "It's a long story." Suddenly, she re-membered the beginning of her earlier conversation with Tessa. "What happened to you? And being accosted?"

Justin's head jerked up. "Accosted?"

"Bad word choice," said Tessa. No one was nearby, but she still looked around nervously. "I think we should go upstairs. I've got something kind of important to show you."

CHAPTER 32

DESPERATE TIMES AND ALL THAT

"Something important" was kind of an understatement.

Justin never would've believed Mae's genetic past and subsequent fight with a shape-shifting woman could be trumped by anything. Apparently, it was one of the rare times he was wrong. Equally incredible was listening to Tessa put together facts in the interview with the old man. Justin had known she was smart, but even he was amazed at her ability to ask the right questions. She'd had no idea how it all worked together, but her gut had told her to just keep gathering information.

Even prodigies needed sleep, however, and in the middle of her video's third viewing, he saw that Tessa was exhausted. He sent her off to bed while he and Mae held a war council in his room, both of them pointedly not sitting on the bed. Exerzol had given Justin a second wind, though he was so wired by the flood of data tonight that he couldn't have slept anyway. Mae, although not technically tired, had a weary look on her face, the expression of someone who was mentally drained.

Justin paced the room. "It's here, Mae. There's always a pattern, and we've almost got it."

"I feel like we just kind of have a mess."

"That too. But look. There are genetically superior patricians being engineered—magically or otherwise—with the assistance of some religious group. Said group sacrifices a plebeian to do it and demands a hefty price tag, as well as devotion from the designer baby." He thought back to his conversation with Callista and how she'd mused that a god might like "perfect" followers, though she hadn't understood why that god would kill said creations off. Now he knew. "But if they aren't loyal, they're sacrificed too and 'returned' to their goddess. Ilias Sandberg openly refused. None of the other victims mentioned being approached, but they were all antireligion, which suggests they weren't on board with some war or death goddess—hence they had to be dealt with."

"The video is real, then," she said. He could tell it took her a lot of effort to admit that. "We were seeing some supernatural assassin."

"It would appear so. Mae . . ." For a few moments, he couldn't go forward. Studying her and all those lovely features, he desperately wished he didn't have to bring up a subject that would only worsen their troubled relationship. But too much was on the line. "Please hear me out. Let me finish what I'm about to say."

The wary look on her face said she knew what was coming. "Okay."

"We know now that you were engineered too. You're the right age and have the right score. You have some 'dark' goddess following and possessing you, one that usually shows up when you're fighting. I'm not exactly saying that's a direct link to war and death, but it's pretty close. You have to see that."

To his relief, she didn't blow up at him. She simply clung to her safety blanket. "I'm not a match."

"I know, but is there anything else you can tell me about this goddess that seizes you? The ravens only get impressions off her. They aren't all-knowing, no matter how much they like to put on airs. You're the most direct connection we have. Please. Is there any other attribute you can think of to help us find these people before the next murder?"

Part of him wanted to go back and interrogate Astrid Koskinen. She *had* to know more about this cult than she'd let on. And yet . . . she'd been so convincing when she denied any knowledge.

She could just be better than you, Horatio said.

I know. I could easily bring her in as a person of interest, but that'd unearth a lot about Mae, not to mention implicate her mother in illegal activity.

They didn't really seem to get along, the raven reminded him.

It was true, but if there was some other way he could get what he needed to know, he'd try that first—if there was enough time. An internal struggle obviously raged through Mae. She was probably starting to accept that there were too many coincidences surrounding her life, but getting on board with this still had to be a shock to her system. She swallowed.

"There might be. There's this man who—"

Justin's ego rang. Irritated at the interruption, he started to silence the call when he saw the display showing a blocked number in Mexico. "Send call to the screen," he told it. He answered and found Callista Xie glaring at Mae and him.

"Where," she demanded, "did you get it?"

"Get what?" asked Mae. Seeing Callista snapped her out of her malaise and put her back in tough prætorian mode.

Justin already knew what Callista was referring to. Before his ill-fated trip to the casino, he'd sent the picture of Mae's necklace off to the authorities in the respective castes. On impulse, he'd also sent a copy to Callista.

"A couple of my genetically perfect castals had it," he said, leaving Mae's name out of this for now. "Does it mean anything to you?"

"It's the symbol of the servants of the Morrigan."

Immediately, Justin sifted through his mental files of gods and mythology. "Celtic," he said. He felt a sinking sensation in his stomach. "She fights with warriors in battle and appears to people before death. . . ."

Mae gave him an incredulous look. "You knew there was a goddess like that and didn't make the connection?"

"That applies to a hundred gods around the world," he shot back. "I didn't know which one it was. Death and battle are pervasive themes in the human experience." He turned back to a scowling Callista. "She's tied to other things too."

"Silver and moonlight?" suggested Mae wryly. "And crows?"

"Yes," he admitted. "And cows too, weirdly. Some also theorized she was a triple goddess and would've possessed other attributes through her different aspects."

"Not in the beliefs of her recent followers," said Callista. "They were—are—focused on her darker parts. They prefer power over enlightenment."

"How do you know so much?" asked Mae suspiciously.

"Because Amarantha is a warrior goddess, and I make it my business to know about rivals."

"I thought Amarantha was a goddess of magic."

"She's both." Impatient, Callista fixed her dark gaze on Justin. "You have to stop the Morrigan. Her people will kill again."

"I know they will! What do you think I'm trying to do here?" he asked. "If you know so much, where are they?"

Callista looked sheepish. "I don't know. On a Celtic grant probably."

"Very helpful," he grumbled.

One thing that made plebeians scornful of patricians was that at times it was really hard to define a genetic profile for an ethnic group. Sometimes the genes were telling. Often, castes went by phenotype, which could make things messy when a nationality could have any number of features. The Celtic castes were all over the place on their true ancestral appearances. Some argued for a light-haired, fair-skinned presence while others insisted the Celtic people had migrated from Iberia and had darker looks. The competing Irish castes—the Erinians and Hibernians—were particularly dysfunctional. Half the time, the traits a caste selected for seemed arbitrary. The Welsh caste had split the difference in accepted Celtic traits, and most citizens had pale skin, black hair, and dark blue or brown eyes. There were also two "meta" Celtic castes, which embraced multiple nationalities, much as the Nordics allowed all the Scandinavian regions and Finland.

The bottom line was that there were any number of Celtic grants this cult could be hiding in. Picking up his ego, Justin told it to bring up any servitor records of the Morrigan. It pulled up an investigation and subsequent license denial from twenty-six years ago—which made sense if that was when the genetically engineered castals had stopped being created. Their last location had been a plebeian city, which only complicated things.

"They didn't stay shut down," Callista told him. "They disappeared from my people too, but we get enough hints now and then to know they're still practicing."

"Yeah, it's been a little more extensive than 'hints.' We can probably assume it's a light-haired caste, based on the description of the guy who visited the victims." Inspiration suddenly struck Justin. "Hang on," he told Callista. He issued a series of commands to the screen.

It divided into two images, one of which was Callista's face. The other half displayed a map of the land grants in the Great Plains region of the country. Red dots in each grant marked the patrician victims, while green dots displayed the other living eights and nines in their respective castes. Yellow dots outside the borders indicated the plebeian deaths.

"You've got a lot more plebeians there than patricians," Callista observed. "Even counting the living ones."

"Because we're only looking at these five grants," he said. "The Morrigan's people probably worked on other castes. They just haven't had any deaths to catch our attention. I bet there's a perfect patrician for every plebeian there. And statistically, you'd expect some plebeian deaths to occur for nonsacrificial reasons."

Mae suddenly stood up. "There's a pattern."

"There's always a pattern."

"No, look." She pointed. "All the plebeian and patrician deaths make a circle around this grant. Is that the Pan-Celts?"

"Yes," said Justin, excitement racing through him. "One of the metas. Light haired, just like our guy."

"A lot of area for a group to hide out," said Callista with obvious dismay.

Justin shook his head in bitter amusement. "It'd be nice if your interest in stopping them was out of altruism for those poor victims, but something tells me you're more concerned with getting rid of a threat to your group."

"She should be," said Mae unexpectedly. "Because they want to kill her."

Both Justin and Callista stared. "How do you know that?" he asked.

"Because he asked me to. The, uh, guy who visited the others. He's come to me a couple of times."

Justin couldn't formulate any words right away. "*What?* And you only just now thought to mention it?"

"Don't take that tone," she snapped. "I didn't make the connection, any more than you did with a goddess who apparently fits all the criteria we've got! I thought he was trying to extort me for the Swedish mafia."

"What's going on?" asked Callista, angry at being left out.

"Oh, I must have forgotten to mention that the uncontrollable force that follows Mae is the Morrigan." Seeing Callista's mouth drop in shock, Justin quickly preempted any protests. "Don't question or make accusations. We're dealing with it." He turned to Mae. "He seriously asked you to kill her?"

Mae nodded. "Wasn't specific on the means. No mention of a silver dagger."

A troubling thought occurred to Justin. "Did he threaten you?" Even when he'd first suspected Mae might have a connection, he'd never considered she might be in real danger. After all, she wasn't like the others. She was unstoppable . . . right?

"What he said isn't important," Mae said.

"It is if your life's on the line!"

"It's not. No shadow creature's coming after me. Worry about these other patricians."

"And worry about the fact that they're eliminating their rivals too." Callista's face darkened with outrage. "Now do you see that they need to be stopped? For me, for her, for the others! They need to be disbanded and destroyed!"

Justin was growing frustrated, still shaken by the idea of something happening to Mae. "Yes, yes, I know! But we can't do anything until we find them."

She fixed him with a cold look. "Then I suggest you start looking. And *you* . . ." She turned to Mae. "You start taking this seriously if you don't want to be next. I told you before. If you want to be free, you need to break them. You could save yourself and the others. I . . . might be able to help you."

"I don't need your help," said Mae.

"Yeah, you're doing great on your own," said Callista dryly. "Fix this. Immediately." She disconnected.

Mae glared at the screen. "I really don't like her."

"Yeah, well, she helped us out with the name. We know a lot about the group now. We know a lot about *you*, whether you like it or not." He raked a hand through his hair with a sigh. The Exerzol was crashing down on him. "Everything except where they are. I wish you'd told me about that guy."

"So you could nobly throw yourself in front of me?" A glint in those eyes told him the ramifications of his earlier refusal weren't going away any time soon. "It was my business, not yours. And I certainly never could've guessed the bigger picture. I thought he was blackmailing me about my niece." She gave him a brief rundown of her encounters with Emil. It left Justin reeling.

"Well, at least it's still—" His ego rang again. "Fuck, doesn't anyone sleep?" It was still synced to the screen, which identified the caller as Leo. At least he had the excuse of an earlier time zone.

Leo appeared when Justin answered, not looking tired in the least. In fact, there was a light in his face that Justin knew well: the light of a breakthrough.

"I've got it," he said. "I know how your video could've been faked."

It was a blow to Justin's finely tuned theories. He'd grown comfortable with the idea of the shadowy assassin being some supernatural manifestation. If the video was proven to be a fake, then that meant the murderers had resorted to practical means, which still didn't rule out the Morrigan's involvement. It just meant they were using smoke and mirrors to scare others.

Still, Justin was anxious enough to find out the results that he changed their travel plans to go straight to Portland from the Nordic grant. He considered bringing Tessa but ended up sending her home on the original flight. She'd already been involved in too much.

When he and Mae stepped into Leo's house, they found a makeshift movie studio. Cameras and equipment Justin couldn't identify had been arranged around the living room, and a transparent plastic screen sat near one of the walls. He stared around in amazement.

"What's all this?"

"Your answer," said Leo excitedly. His worse half came strolling in, looking as unpleasant as usual.

"Saw a news story about a shooting on the Nordic land grant," Dominic remarked casually. "They say a prætorian was involved."

"Must have been a lucky break for them," Mae replied evenly. "Having one on hand."

Meanwhile, Leo could barely contain himself. "Let's do this." He put on a skintight black suit and hood, similar to what scuba divers wore, except shinier. He flipped on some of the equipment and shifted the clear screen so that it was between him and them. And then, just like that, his form became translucent and smoky and shot across the living room. He took off his head covering and grinned, looking at all of them expectantly.

"It's not fast enough," said Mae, speaking at last.

"And there's no way someone could set all this up without the victim noticing," added Justin. He didn't know whether he should be relieved or disappointed that they hadn't proven the fraud. "It's a good effort, Leo. Really. But I don't think it's a match."

"Good effort?" Leo's eyes bugged. "Do you know how long it took me to set this up? To get ahold of this kind of light-refraction equipment? I've looked at that video's code a million times! It wasn't tampered with. Whatever we're seeing was done on site, and this is a match. If it's not this, then it really is some kind of mystical apparition!"

Justin and Mae exchanged glances. "That's becoming more and more of a possibility," he muttered. "I'm sorry, but this isn't it."

Leo still looked a little put out that his brilliance wasn't being lauded, but he made no more protests. "I can keep trying."

"I don't know that it's needed," said Justin. "What we really need is to find an unlicensed cult serving a Celtic death goddess."

"Isn't that what you do all the time?" asked Dominic, a challenge in his voice.

"A little harder when they're not licensed," Justin retorted.

Leo didn't seem so sure. "Didn't you used to be tight with some groups in the underground?"

"Very tight," murmured Mae.

"My best source couldn't help," Justin said.

She suddenly frowned. "What about your other one? Geraki?"

"I—no." The suggestion momentarily stunned Justin; then he shook his head adamantly. "No. Definitely not. He's not a source. He's a stalker at best."

"I don't like him either, but he's wired into that stuff, right? And he claims he wants to help you. He even *did* kind of help you."

"He's crazy," Justin told her. That, and Geraki wasn't like Callista. Superficially, they shared a lot of the same traits. Both were cunning and charismatic. Both were smart enough to command others without calling attention to it. But there was something about Geraki that made Justin's skin crawl.

Because you're connected, said Magnus. *And he knows things about you.*

He could help if you'd give him a chance, added Horatio. *Probably with this. Most certainly with your calling. You need to start learning the craft.*

"Justin?" Mae leaned toward him, eyes concerned. He realized he'd spaced out. With a feeling of dread, he made his decision. He had only a few days left. Desperate times and all that.

He sighed. "Excuse me a moment."

He went outside, leaving the rest of them looking confused. "Call Demetrius Devereaux," he told his ego. "Voice only."

"Justin," boomed Geraki when he answered. "Look at that. And here I thought I was going to have a boring day." Even without seeing him, Justin could imagine the smug look.

"You claimed you wanted to help me last time. Is that still true?"

"No small talk, huh? What kind of help could a megalomaniac like me offer?"

Justin gritted his teeth. "I'd like to know if there's an unlicensed religion in the Pan-Celt grant. One serving the Morrigan."

"Haven't heard that name in a while. Why would I know anything about unlicensed religions? You've made some mistake—a rarity, I know."

"Goddamn it! We all know you're lying. I'm not asking you to give up anything on yourself and whatever nonsense you're running." Justin paused to take a deep breath. "I won't say anything to SCI. But I need to know about this group. They're killing innocents, and even if you're crazy, I don't think you want death on your hands."

" 'Crazy' is an arbitrary term. And someone like you isn't in a position to judge sanity." But Geraki didn't outright refuse. "If I could do this—and I'm not saying I can—what would you give me in return?"

"What do you want? And don't ask for something illegal."

"All I want is for you to do what I asked the last time we met."

"You asked for a lot of things. Most of which I didn't understand. Because they made no sense."

"You understood what I meant by yielding your stars and flowers." Geraki's voice was low and dangerous. "That doesn't sound too bad to me. A good bargain for information about a group you claim is killing people. If I can even find out such things, of course."

Something in Justin's chest tightened as Geraki's previous words rang in his head. *Yield your stars and flowers and accept the clever compromise.*

"I know what the stars and flowers mean but not the rest. I can't do what I don't understand."

"I'm sure our master will make it clear. When he does, promise you'll do it."

"Fine," said Justin, wondering just how much he'd regret this. "I'll do it—*if* you can even find out anything."

"Swear you'll do it," said Geraki. "And that this isn't being used as entrapment."

"I swear it," said Justin promptly.

"What do you swear by?"

"Does it matter?"

He could tell Geraki was smiling. "No. Your word will hold you, so don't try to break it. Hang on, and I'll call you back."

The call disconnected, and Justin wondered exactly how long he was supposed to "hang on."

He got his answer a few minutes later, one that was surprisingly detailed, if slightly ridiculous. But Justin made note of all the information Geraki gave him, promised to make good on the enigmatic deal, and then returned to his friends inside.

"Well," he declared. "I may have our hit. Turns out there's a grain warehouse in the Pan-Celt grant we might be interested in."

"Classy. Are you going to call in a raid?" asked Leo.

"I don't know." Justin leaned against the wall and passed his ego from hand to hand. "I could, but if nothing shows up, I'm going to face a lot of heat for sending military to a grant based on circumstantial evidence—especially if I really do keep Geraki out of it. I had a pissed-off voice mail this morning from Cornelia about what happened last night with the Nordics. Public shootings don't go over well. If I do something else spectacular that doesn't pan out, I could be in a lot of trouble."

Mae met his eyes, knowing what was on the line, despite how angry she was with him. "What if we did a preliminary visit?" she asked. "Unofficial. It can't be that hard getting into a warehouse. We look, and if you get your proof, then you go in for the kill. If nothing's there, we quietly leave."

Leo gave a harsh laugh. "Bold, but how exactly do you plan on breaking in? Do you have some technical expertise we don't know about, prætorian? Even a grain warehouse has a security system."

"One that'd be easy for a technical genius like yourself to crack," said Justin. It was a crazy plan, no question, but they'd passed the point of sanity a long time ago.

"You and I have different definitions of 'easy,'" said Leo.

"Leo . . ." Justin's voice cracked a little. "I don't want to sound melodramatic, but getting to the bottom of this might be essen—beneficial to my job. I wouldn't be suggesting something this drastic otherwise."

"*She* suggested it." But everyone could tell Leo was considering it.

Dominic nearly choked. "You're *all* crazy! Do you hear what you're saying?"

"We're saying we potentially have the chance to crack open this case and bust a cult that's killing people and conducting illegal genetic procedures." Justin shifted into sales mode. "All we need is one hint of that. Hell, if we just find evidence of an unlicensed religion, it'll be a good day's work. That video becomes irrelevant. We'll see what schematics we can get in advance about the place. It should give you an idea of what we need to get in, Leo."

Dominic still looked dumbfounded. "If you're going, then I'm going. Not that you should be going."

He and his husband locked eyes for several tense seconds. "Okay," said Leo at last. "We'll take a car. Dom doesn't like public transportation."

All of Justin's dislike for Dominic returned. "A car will take forever!"

"Just twenty-four hours," said Leo. "We'll sleep along the way."

Justin tried to size Dominic up. "What do you have to offer in this zany adventure? Drinks for the road?"

"Dom's a good person to have your back. Let Mae do the heavy lifting, and keep him around just in case." Leo smiled, but there was a nervous edge to it. "Besides, I'd like the company."

Once the fateful decision was made, the four of them huddled together to hash out plans. They spent the rest of the day analyzing what satellite and land records they could get ahold of on short notice, as well as planning the logistics of such a feat. When evening fell, they had as solid a plan as they were going to get. Unfortunately, it was going to take Leo nearly two days to get some necessary equipment—putting them in the grant the day before the full moon.

Cutting it close, said Horatio as Justin and Mae rode the train back to Vancouver.

Nothing to be done but wait and see how it unfolds, Justin told him.

You're the one who'll be waiting, said Magnus. *She's going to be doing all the work. She's risking herself for you.*

Justin glanced at Mae out of the corner of his eye. She sat

next to him, reading on her ego, her hair hanging around her face in a golden wave.

"Mae . . ." She glanced up too quickly, making him think she hadn't been reading. "Thank you for this. I know what a big risk you're taking for me."

Her face was carved of marble. "It's for my country." She looked back down again, and his stomach sank.

I guess I have to take what I can get, he thought.

You can help her, said Horatio.

How? I'm no prætorian. I'm not even a tank like Dominic.

You have the potential for power beyond physical strength, said Magnus. *If you'd just open yourself to it.*

I'm not interested in your mystical training. I'm not serving any god.

What harm is one spell? Horatio paused for impact. *One that could keep her safe.*

The only way she'd be safe is if she stayed at home. But Justin was intrigued, and he dared another covert look at her. *What would I have to do?*

He could feel the ravens' excitement. *Close your eyes,* said Magnus. *And concentrate on the symbol we're about to show you. . . .*

CHAPTER 33

MORTAL WEAPONS

"Honestly, who doesn't take public transportation?" asked Justin for what had to be the fifth time during his and Mae's journey two days later. "How does he get around?"

"He doesn't," she reminded him as they rode to their hotel. Two flights had just delivered them to Sioux Falls, the largest plebeian city outside of the Pan-Celt grant. "He stays at home and grows grapes."

Justin shook his head. "It's the sex, right? That has to be the only reason Leo would put up with that—though Dominic doesn't really strike me as the creative type."

Leo and Dominic had left by car last night and were due to rendezvous at the hotel in a few more hours. They couldn't have pulled off this escapade before nightfall anyway, but Justin was still incredulous over what he saw as a waste of time. Mae was weary of hearing about it but had a feeling it had become a way for him to cope with the stress of their upcoming task. Complaining about Dominic saved Justin from agonizing about the possible fallout if they failed. Tomorrow was the full moon, and neither knew what would happen to him if another murder slipped by.

They scanned their egos at their hotel's front desk, and moments later, an attendant returned with two room keys and a box. She split the keys and gave the box to Mae. "It arrived for you this afternoon."

Mae thanked her and studied the package as she and Justin walked to the elevators. A printed label clearly identified her name and the hotel, and the postage tracking code said it had been shipped express. The return address was for a bulk shipping facility, with no sender's name.

"What is this?" she asked Justin.

"How should I know? I didn't send it."

"Who else knows we're here?"

"Callista," he admitted. "Don't look at me like that. She wants them taken out as much as we do, so I've kept in touch. Now open it."

Inside, Mae found a knife. Or rather, a dagger. The handle was wrapped in three bands of yellow amber, and the guard was embellished with an inlay of multicolored stones. Carefully, she lifted the weapon out and found it had a good weight and solid craftsmanship.

"No silver here," she said, running her finger over the sharp steel blade. This was a recently constructed item, no ancient artifact, despite the embellishment. "The Morrigan's servants would have an easier time with one of these."

"They seem to be doing okay," he reminded her. "Any note or explanation?"

She checked the box. "Nope. Maybe Callista felt bad about keeping my other knife. I never got it back after I threw it into Raoul Menari."

Although Mae didn't want to accept any gift from Callista, she was struck by the weapon's beauty and strength. It also fit easily in the sheath she'd had sewn into the inside of her boot, almost as well as her old one had. Mae decided to keep it, much to Justin's amusement. As Tessa would say, you could never have too much protection.

"You want to get dinner once the luggage is settled?" They lingered out in the hall by their rooms, which were next door to each other. "Still a couple of hours before Leo and Dominic show up."

Mae deliberated for a long time. "Okay."

Later, she wished she'd refused. She couldn't muster any of the easy banter they used to share, not after what had passed, and Justin's constant attempts at conversation grated on her. All she kept thinking about was that Nordic hotel room. *Once I've been with a woman, there's no mystery. No novelty. There's no reason to go back once I know what it's like. And . . . I know what it's like with you.*

It was a relief when Leo and Dominic showed up. After checking in, the two left for their room, promising they'd be right back down. Justin looked forlorn.

"Do you see how tired Leo is? No one can get any real sleep in a car."

"Dominic looks okay."

"Yeah, but we don't need *his* technical genius sharp and alert."

The foursome ended up taking Leo and Dominic's rented car out to the grant and used Mae's credentials to get them in. As a fellow patrician, she had short-term access for herself and up to four guests. Justin could've obviously gotten them in as well, but he was afraid identifying himself as a servitor would attract too much attention—not that an armed prætorian was exactly low-profile either.

Once they were finally inside the borders, they ended up at another bar and simply waited for the clock to tick down. Leo had some of the satellite images of the warehouse that he went over with Mae, pointing out the most likely surveillance areas. Although she had more respect for his skills now, the "most likely" part unnerved her a little.

The appointed departure time came just before the bar closed, when most people were winding down and going to bed. Mae and the others drove to the warehouse, which was situated outside of town, and parked in a spot that kept the building in sight but was too far away to show up on any cameras. The thick trees and lack of lights on the road also kept their car well concealed.

"I should come with you," growled Dominic.

"I'll keep pinging you." Leo, sitting beside him in the front seat, rested his hand on Dominic's. "The fewer people here, the better. If we're caught, I don't want you taken out with the rest of us."

"You won't be caught," said Justin in what Mae recognized as his *I've got your back* voice. "As long as you don't get picked up on surveillance, you're good. Get in, get our evidence, and get out."

Mae looked at him and saw that although his words were glib, his face was drawn and tense. Noticing her scrutiny, he started to automatically smile but then faltered.

"Be careful," he told her. "I wish you didn't have to do my work for me."

"It's what I'm here for. We don't want to get you dirty." When he didn't smile, she added, "It'll be okay." She wasn't sure it would be okay but needed him to think it would. Seeing Leo and Dominic engaged in their good-byes, she lowered her voice. "Maybe you can get to know Dom better."

The look of distaste on his face was far more in line with the Justin she knew. "Don't count on it," he said. "And, Mae . . ." He started to reach out his hand to her and then stopped. After several moments of contemplation, he astonished her by snaking forward and kissing her on the cheek.

She had no chance to be outraged. She was too awestruck by the kiss itself. It had been light, but her skin literally burned where he'd touched her—and not with desire. There'd been actual heat in his lips. A fiery image flashed into her mind of a strange symbol, like a *Y* with an extra vertical line running through the top. Even after that flash, the afterimage of the symbol occasionally appeared in her vision as she blinked. She stared at him, aghast.

"What did you just do?" she exclaimed.

He had no time to answer because Leo was already getting out of the car. "You coming?"

Mae gave Justin one last questioning look and then opened the door. Her cheek was still warm, and that symbol kept popping in and out of her mind. *What did he do?* she wondered frantically. There'd been power in that kiss, but she didn't understand it. When had he started using supernatural means instead of just documenting them? That unsolicited show of power was just as unwelcome as the Morrigan.

The almost-full moon peeked through the clouds as Mae and Leo trekked across the field. She saw no signs of life anywhere, and all the building's windows were dark. One light shone near the entrance, lighting up the door. She'd worn all black tonight as the obvious camouflage choice, though it made her feel strange, like she had on a parody of her uniform.

"How does it feel to be a soldier of the Republic who's breaking its laws?" Leo whispered. He shifted a bag on his shoulder. Allegedly, he had a whole technological arsenal with him.

"Bigger laws say murder and runaway cults are worse," she replied. She didn't give voice to her fears about Justin. Her whole purpose in suggesting this break-in, aside from the obvious, was to help him. Cornelia's threats still hung heavy in Mae's mind, though she never would admit it.

Leo laughed softly. "Picking and choosing what you follow, huh?"

"Is your problem that I'm a prætorian, or is there just something about me you don't like?"

"I like you just fine," he said, growing sober. "I've just been around a lot of prætorians in my life. They're unpredictable, that's all. Stop."

They had nearly reached the back of the building. Here, the wall was shorter than the other sides and had no windows. He pointed at it.

"There's going to be minimal coverage there. You sure you can get up it?"

Mae assessed the wall, noting the corners and building's texture. A window would've made a better handhold, but that would've defeated the purpose of choosing this side. "Of course."

"Of course," he repeated. She suspected he was rolling his eyes. "Here." He showed her a square metal object that fit in the palm of her hand. "Once you're on the roof, see if you can get a view of the security panel above the door. It'll probably have five red lights on it—that's the most common system for a building like this. Hold this out and push the silver button here. It'll send a signal to switch the system into daytime mode. The cameras will still be on, but they won't trigger an alarm. We'll wipe them once we're in."

"Wouldn't an unauthorized religion that's involved with sacrificial murders use something a little more serious than a common system?"

He laughed again. "Theoretically, but a grain warehouse wouldn't. Having something 'serious' would attract attention."

"You have some pretty serious security on your house."

He handed over the device. "Because I know stuff like this exists. If you don't see five red lights, come back to me. It'll make this harder but probably not impossible."

"'Probably'?"

"I can't work miracles. Good luck."

She went to the short side of the building and hoped she could make good on her claim that she could get up it. The implant responded to her tension, and she felt all her abilities intensify. She could do this. With a running start, she leapt up toward the wall, propelling herself higher when her foot made contact. One hand caught the corner of the building, giving her a brief moment of stabilization that let her other hand reach toward the roof. Her fingers nearly didn't make it, and she braced herself for a fall. But she soon got enough of a grip to grasp higher with the other hand, and one more swing allowed her to catapult onto the roof.

She landed gracefully on all fours, her heart racing. The roof was large, with triangular peaks, but balance was no problem after what she'd just done. She hurried across to the opposite side, settled onto her stomach, and peered over the edge. Five red lights shone up at her. Reaching her arm down, she lowered the device Leo had given her and pushed the button. The lights turned green, and a click sounded.

As she jumped back to the ground, she tried not to think too hard about the kind of technology required to trip a system like this. This wasn't off-the-rack stuff, and Leo had most likely carried it off from his time in Internal Security, either physically or mentally. The laws and rules being violated on this trip were already numerous enough without her adding on more. The front door opened for her without resistance, and she ran back to retrieve Leo.

"Did you even break a sweat?" he asked.

"Did you want me to?"

They entered the warehouse, and Leo paused to send a signal back to Dominic on his ego. Mae uneasily surveyed her surroundings, not liking the lack of visibility. The high, narrow windows offered faint lighting, but most of the space was swathed in pitch-darkness. Even the small high-powered flashlights they'd brought wouldn't be able to light up the whole place, and that provided too many opportunities for attackers to hide.

She barely made out Leo pointing toward another panel near the inside of the door. "I'm going to cut the cameras and blank out some of their footage."

Meanwhile, Mae began a search of the facility. Justin had given them a wide range of evidence to look for, from obvious signs like silver daggers to more difficult ones like screens. Mostly all she found were neatly stacked and organized bags of grain. If there really was a cult hiding out here, it was an efficient one when it came to storage. A small office off to the side looked promising, but getting into the desk computer was beyond her abilities. Another light joined hers as she searched the room, and Leo stepped inside. He turned on the screen and looked disappointed.

"More basic security. Probably means there isn't anything groundbreaking in it." Still, he sat down at the desk and began working whatever magic he had to look into the system. "See if there's anything on the catwalk."

There wasn't. The only thing it provided was a good vantage to shine her light down on the main room. Nothing of consequence presented itself, but at least it reassured her they truly were alone. When she returned to the main floor, Leo was just walking out of the office.

"Nothing except fascinating records on corn hybrids," he said.

The final examination turned up nothing, and she didn't realize how many hopes she'd pinned on this trip until failure looked her in the eye. With a heavy heart, she joined Leo at the entrance and made one last desperate scan of the room. As she did, a strange feeling welled up in her. Some memory tickled her brain, nearly within her grasp—but not quite. It kept slipping through. There was something here she should recognize, but she didn't know what it was. Images flashed briefly through her mind, but they were only indistinct shadows.

"What's wrong?" Leo asked her.

"This isn't the kind of place a death goddess would have her temple in."

He snorted. "A warehouse with bags of grain? Yeah, I can see how that would detract from some of her magnificence. Justin's guy may have played him."

Mae still couldn't shake the sensation that she should know more. "Her temple would be darker . . . no windows." An idea clicked. "Is there a basement here?"

That got Leo's interest. "There could be."

"That would be a better fit than this place. More secrecy too. Plus, a death goddess would have more power within the earth."

In the dim light, she could see him staring. "How much time have you spent with Justin? Is he teaching religious-symbolism classes again?"

"It just feels right, that's all."

"If it's true, then that's where we'll find our real security system." He'd switched into problem-solving mode and actually sounded excited. "I know the kind of hardware I'd use to hide my deadly underground temple, and something like that'll have a strong electromagnetic field around it. We can find that."

He took out another device from his bag of tricks and plunged back into the warehouse without another word. Mae again recognized her limitations at this stage of the search and simply followed him around. Fifteen minutes later, he came to a halt in front of a large machine that appeared to be some kind of grain sorter.

"Here we are." He knelt down. "Help me move it."

The machine was heavy, but casters aided in getting it out of the way. Below it, Mae saw neither a security system nor an underground lair. "Shine the light down," he ordered. He ran his hands over the floor several times and then made a grunt of approval. "Nicely laid. I don't suppose you have a knife, do you?"

Mae handed him the one from her boot and heard him mutter, "Goddamned prætorians." But after a little prying with the blade, he lifted up a large section of the floor that had blended seamlessly with the concrete. A metal door showed itself, glowing with all sorts of lights. "Oh, baby," he breathed. Mae had a feeling that as far as he was concerned, this was a brush with divinity. He handed her his ego. "Send something to Dom, and make yourself comfortable."

One look at the tools he produced from his bag, and Mae was quick to comply. She sat cross-legged nearby and took out her own ego, once she'd sent Leo's message. To Justin, she tapped out: *Leo really is a genius.*

When no response came, she asked Leo, "Do you think they're all right? Justin isn't taking advantage of a chance to flout his superiority."

"Dom'll look after him," said Leo, eyes on the panel. "They're not the ones in danger of tripping an alarm."

She jerked her head around, nearly expecting attackers to come swooping in. "What happened to your amazing prowess?"

"I told you, I'm not a miracle worker." He sat back with a frown. "But I think we're okay." He took hold of two handles on the door and lifted it up. Both of them froze. No wailing sounded; no one rushed at them. "If I set it off, it'd be silent," he said, which didn't reassure her. He shined his light downward, illuminating a chute with a narrow, spiraling staircase. "How quaint. Let's make this fast."

Mae took the lead, gun out, trying her best to see ahead of her. Her fight-or-flight mode continued ramping up, burning nearly as strongly as it would have in active combat. The implant could sustain this state for a long time, but that just meant she'd experience a big crash later. She reached the ground unharmed, and after a quick survey with the light, she allowed Leo to join her.

"No windows. We can do an overhead light," he said. "It'll get us out of here faster."

The control switch was near the bottom of the stairs. He found it, and within seconds, light flooded the space, revealing a wide doorway that opened to an enormous room.

And Mae came face-to-face with her nightmares.

The walls of the vast room were painted with murals predominately in black and red, depicting people dying in gruesome ways. Entrails, skulls, expressions of terror. Around her, the smell of dampness and decay filled the air. A stone altar sat at one end of the room, stained with some dark substance and surrounded by piles of bones. The picture behind it depicted a monstrous woman, larger than life, whose form took up the entire wall. Her face managed to be human, reptilian, and aquiline all at the same time. Black robes clothed her body, the sleeves stretching down like bat wings. A high crown sat on her head, displaying a twisted pattern of thirteen tormented faces—and a crow made of knot work in the center. The sky painted behind her was the color of blood. That horrific face was mirrored in thirteen black masks hanging around the room—and they all were watching Mae.

"Fucked-up," said Leo. Mae couldn't speak. She could barely even breathe, and he turned to her in surprise when he noticed her reaction. "What's wrong?"

"I've been here," she said, her voice very small. The air felt oppressive, a heavy weight bearing down on her. "A long time ago."

It was the place her mother had taken her so many years ago, the place that had continued to haunt her dreams in shadows and half-formed faces. All this time, she'd thought her childhood imagination had twisted the memories into something greater than what they were. But here they were, exactly the same.

My mother lied, she realized fleetingly. *She had to have known about all this.*

Mae hadn't been truly afraid of anything in a very long time, but she wanted to run out of this place as quickly as she could.

"Are you going to be okay?" Leo asked.

I have to be, she thought. Her personal experiences were irrelevant and could be dealt with later. For now, they had to complete their task. This was what they'd been looking for. Even if they found no evidence linking the murders, it still contained an unlicensed church that SCI could shut down, possibly preventing tomorrow's murder. Justin would be completely justified in requesting a raid by local law enforcement or even the military right now. Maybe it wouldn't be enough to redeem himself in Cornelia's eyes, but it might very well keep him from Panama.

"I'm okay." Mae took a deep breath. "Let's take a quick look and get out of here. I'm going to tell Justin to call in his cavalry."

She sent the message and joined Leo in his survey of the room, despite her instincts' screaming against it. She felt choked and sluggish. That goddess, with her eyes everywhere, wanted to trap Mae. Claustrophobia had never been a problem for her, but now the walls seemed to be closing in. What was noticeable, however, was that Mae felt no invasion of her body—no sense of the Morrigan taking control. She still felt a pressure, like the air was heavy, pressing down with the weight of the Morrigan's *wanting* to penetrate Mae and take control . . . but she couldn't.

"Hello, hello," said Leo, crouching near the altar. She joined him but refused to kneel. Carefully, he pulled out a wooden tray covered in velvet that had been concealed inside a hidden compartment in the back. Three silver daggers portraying the stylized crow lay on it. "How much do you want to bet forensics can match this to what killed the victims?"

A surge of triumph shot through Mae. He was right. They'd connect this group to the murders, and even if they couldn't find the actual fanatics right away, the owners of this warehouse had to know what was happening. SCI could start with them and eventually take down the rest.

Leo started to stand when Mae caught sight of something in her periphery. She spun around instantly, aiming her gun. Her breath caught as black smoke billowed in from the wide doorway, filling up the other half of the room. It moved far more quickly than the laws of nature said it should and began to coalesce into distinct shapes. The panic she'd felt increased tenfold. "Get back," she told Leo. She advanced forward, not entirely sure what she was walking into, only that she had to confront it.

The shadows settled into seven humanoid forms—humanoid forms carrying silver blades. And they were *fast*. They practically flew toward Mae, and although every piece of reason told her she couldn't fight them, she fired anyway. She was an excellent shot, as proven at the Nordic concert, but the shadow warriors' rapid and erratic movements made them hard to target. She finally hit two of them, and rather than go right through as she expected, the bullets made contact with a seemingly solid surface. As the bullets hit their victims, the smoky black shapes transformed into very human ones. A man and a woman, blond and red haired respectively, materialized and fell to the ground, one wounded in the shoulder and the other with a lethal hit through the chest. Whatever they were, they were mortal. The implant refused to let her contemplate the matter further because the other five forms were swarming her. Only life and death mattered now.

The attackers also felt solid when they hit her, which made sense after the killing blow from the video. She elbowed and kicked them, slipping away when the shadow people swung their daggers toward her. Just like the bullets, her kicks made contact with solid substances. In fact, each strike that connected made the dark figures shift briefly to human form. In those fleeting moments of transformation, the attackers moved at regular speeds. She caught hold of one and slammed it hard against the stone floor, revealing a red-haired man who didn't move. The last attacker's dagger swiped her arm but didn't get through the fabric of her shirt. She spun around and shot him in the leg, making him cry out and fall to the ground. Ready to finish the job, she aimed her gun down at him—and heard a *snick* sound. She felt a biting pain in her chest and saw a small dart poking out of her shirt. She dismissed it. As scarce as guns were in the RUNA, domestic attackers often attempted poisonous hits on prætorians. There was usually some initial discomfort, but the implant was too good at identifying and metabolizing toxins. It wouldn't take long for it to work on whatever this was. Her concern was on who had actually fired the dart. Lifting her eyes, she saw a familiar person standing at the doorway beside the staircase: Emil. Five others stood behind him.

"Such ingratitude," he said. "For all you've received."

Mae had no time for soliloquies. All she knew was that her targets were standing still. She fixed her gun on Emil but hesitated to pull the trigger as a swirling feeling stirred in her stomach. That would be the toxin, she supposed. A lightness spread through her limbs, but she took her shot anyway—and missed. Scowling, she tried to fire again, but her shaking hands couldn't get a grip anymore. The gun slipped from her hands. It was like the recovery phase that followed implant activation, only far more violent than anything she'd ever experienced. Her knees buckled as that swirling in her stomach increased and spread to her chest. She was vaguely aware of Leo catching hold of her as she fell.

"A prætorian is only as good as her weapons," Emil said, a smug smile on his face. "And your mortal ones mean nothing."

"Yeah?" Mae gasped. She barely managed a nod at the man she'd killed. Her body shook fiercely now, and her vision was blurring. "Ask him if that's true."

"He's just one man," said Emil. She had the sense he was moving toward her. "His sacrifice will strengthen our mistress—as will yours. You wouldn't serve, and now your time is up. It's time for you to return to her and serve in death."

Mae tried to speak but couldn't. Her tongue seemed to fill up her mouth. Beside her, she heard Leo say, "The full moon isn't until tomorrow."

Emil chuckled. "Depends on your definition. It's after midnight. It *is* tomorrow."

That was the last thing Mae heard before her heart exploded.

NO ONE EVER
EXPECTS THE KNIFE

"Have you heard anything?" Justin asked.

"No," growled Dominic from the front seat. "Just like I hadn't thirty seconds ago."

Justin could forgive the gruff attitude for once because he knew Dominic was just as agitated as he was about the sudden silence. Leo had sent messages every few minutes until recently. Now ten minutes had gone past without communication. Concerned, Dominic had queried Leo a couple minutes ago but heard nothing.

"They probably found something and got distracted," said Justin. He was trying to reassure himself more than Dominic. As it was, Justin was fighting every instinct to go inside after them. "Leo's too smart to set off an alarm. And Mae's a prætorian for fuck's sake. They're fine."

"You put a lot of faith in prætorians," remarked Dominic.

"Of course I do. They're lethal—I mean, aside from when they're drinking heavily and acting ridiculous."

"It's how they cope," Dominic said. "You have to if you're going to survive that kind of lifestyle. They flip back and forth, but it's always extreme—even if they're off duty. They play hard, fuck hard, and fight hard and can switch into that 'on' mode in the space of a heartbeat. You ever seen Mae switch on?"

"Of course."

"With a few rowdy zealots? That's nothing. You see her now,

with that pretty face and all those manners, and you think, 'Oh, she's a castal who happens to be a prætorian.' But the truth is, she's a prætorian first who happens to be a castal. When she switches on, when she's really in that moment . . . she'll be something else. Something whose purpose is to fight and kill with single-minded focus. And it's not just the implant and the training. They don't just choose prætorians on physical ability. There's a psychological profile they screen for too, one that works very well with being pumped full of all those chemicals— and don't think those don't eventually take their toll."

"You don't like prætorians," said Justin, knowing what an understatement that was.

"I don't trust them," he corrected. "They're dangerous to others. They're dangerous to themselves."

Justin said nothing more, not wanting to provoke his paranoid companion. It was true that Mae was scary sometimes, but Justin had faith in her. He wasn't sure he had faith in the alleged charm he'd given her, though. The ravens had spent the last two days trying to teach him a symbol they claimed was one of their god's greatest mysteries. They called the symbol *algiz* and had been drilling its meaning into his head over and over. The problem was, they kept giving it all sorts of definitions. Initially, it had represented protection, which Justin thought was a reasonable concept to send a warrior into battle with. But then the ravens kept elaborating. It was an elk, a yew tree, life. When he showed them that he'd memorized everything, they condescendingly said he didn't truly *know* it, that it took a lifetime to understand. They did finally decide, however, that he had enough of a grasp to perform a rudimentary protection blessing on Mae. Whether it would do anything remained to be seen.

Do you feel that? Horatio suddenly asked, snapping Justin out of his thoughts.

Feel what—

Justin *could* feel something, just the slightest prickling along his skin. He would've ignored it if the raven hadn't pointed it out. It was the same sensation he occasionally got around strong practitioners.

Where's it coming from? he asked.

Where do you think? asked Magnus. *Dominic certainly hasn't found religion.*

Justin didn't wait to hear more. He opened the car door and swung his legs out, earning a cry of surprise from Dominic. "What are you doing?"

"Something's wrong." Justin took off at a sprint across the grassy field, and Dominic closed the distance easily. He grabbed Justin's shoulder.

"You're just going to go right in? You don't know what you're walking into."

Justin glared in the darkness. "I know it's one of two things. Either nothing's wrong, and there's no harm done, or something is wrong, and we can help."

"I think it's a little more complicated than that."

"You were the one who thought this was too dangerous in the first place." Justin turned back toward the warehouse. "Are you coming along or not?"

Dominic came along.

They immediately found signs of Mae and Leo's passing. The front door was ajar, and the inside security panel had been set to daytime mode. Other than that, the huge building was dark and silent. Dominic led the way, scanning the space and keeping protectively near Justin in a manner almost identical to the way Mae moved. Suddenly, Dominic stopped and pulled Justin behind a stack of crates with him. Justin's eyes had adjusted to the poor lighting, and he saw Dominic point ahead. Peering around the boxes, Justin could discern a spot of light shining on the floor near the far side of the warehouse and the dark shape of a man standing nearby who clearly wasn't Leo. He was pacing, standing guard, but hadn't seen them yet.

Justin was about to whisper and ask Dominic what they should do when Dominic surged forward without warning. The man by the hole in the floor spun around in surprise but was too slow. Dominic threw him to the floor and cut off the man's oxygen until he passed out.

"Holy shit," said Justin, hurrying over to look. The unconscious man wore a crow pendant. "What was that?"

"Quiet," whispered Dominic. "There could be more."

As Justin peered down at the staircase in the floor, he felt that prickling sensation increase. "Yeah. And they're down there."

Dominic did a quick check of his ego, as though hoping Leo might have sent a last-minute message that would fix all of this. His glower said no such message had arrived. "Wait here," he told Justin, who promptly followed him down the stairs. Dominic shook his head in exasperation but said nothing more.

They crept down, winding around the spiral stairs. Dominic slowed even more as they neared the bottom. A doorway came into sight, and he quickly gestured Justin over to the side so that they wouldn't be seen by those inside. Dominic stiffened, fists clenching.

Although the majority of his work really did consist of interviews and paperwork, Justin had still seen his fair share of deranged religious hideouts. And as he'd told Mae, he'd witnessed other incredible things that defied explanation. None of them compared to the shrine to death and blood that stretched before him. It was the kind of thing movies portrayed when trying to create the most terrifying images of religions they could.

But the décor paled beside the actual activity within. Two Pan-Celt men stood near a stone altar, while a woman in the room's corner pointed a gun that looked suspiciously like Mae's at Leo. Three other Pan-Celts tended some wounded, though one looked like he was past help. Most horrible of all, Mae herself was sprawled out on the altar, eyes staring blankly upward as her body shook. Dominic took a deep breath, forcing control.

"Fucking epinephrine," he muttered.

"What?"

"Epinephrine. They shot her full of it."

"Epinephrine's adrenaline," said Justin. "Not a poison."

"Might as well be for a prætorian," Dominic explained. "It's the main neurotransmitter in fight-or-flight. The implant shoots up production if it senses even the slightest increase in the body. Can you see that dart in her chest?" He pointed. "That is not a slight increase. It's a major dose that's sent the implant into overdrive. Not even her body can handle the amounts that are churning out."

Justin stared in horror, unable to believe he was seeing invincible Mae so debilitated. "Will it kill her?"

"No, but it'd give you a heart attack. Eventually, her implant's going to realize it doesn't need the body to make any more and will start eating it up." He grimaced. "It's a very neat way to incapacitate a prætorian with an easily obtainable substance. Actually more effective than using a true poison."

"How do you even know all of that?"

Dominic ignored him. "I think you've got more than enough evidence to request assistance."

He was right. Justin pulled out his ego and entered the quick code that would send local law enforcement to his location. Slipping it back into his pocket, he turned once more to the grisly scene ahead. The two Pan-Celt men by the altar were deep in conversation. Below them, Mae was still clearly out of action, but her spasms had slowed and were growing more irregular.

"I wonder why they've kept her alive," mused Dominic.

"So they can kill her," said Justin, seeing a flash of silver in the taller man's hands. "But they have to do it in a ritualistic way." The pieces fell together. Ordinary enemies of the Morrigan—like Callista—could be killed in whatever manner was most efficient. But these wayward creations . . . they required something special, he realized. Silver through the heart, on the day of the full moon, by one of the other prized servants. Those whom the Morrigan had created couldn't be killed haphazardly, even if it meant a slow rate of one a month. "They seem to be taking their time, though."

"They probably think they've got her put down for a while."

"Don't they?"

Dominic shrugged. "Probably not as long as they think. That's what I meant about prætorians being so dangerous. Even when you find a way to stop them, they don't stay stopped for long." His eyes flicked to Leo with concern, but mostly he still seemed to be a hostage. "As long as they don't try to kill anyone soon, we should just be able to wait for the police."

Don't wait, said Magnus.

The raven had barely finished speaking when the tall man

suddenly turned to the mural in the back of the room and raised his arms up high. "Great queen, we do your bidding and return to you one who has betrayed you."

And with a speed that caught both Justin and Leo by surprise, he spun around and turned the silver dagger, point down, toward Mae. He raised his arms in a killing blow and thrust downward—but then froze. It was as though he'd hit an invisible wall that he couldn't penetrate. Clearly astonished, he removed one of his hands from the dagger and lightly touched Mae's chest with no problem. But when he tried to bring the dagger to her again, he couldn't touch her.

I guess you aren't worthless after all, said Horatio.

"There's some spell on her," said the tall man incredulously. His brow furrowed in thought as he turned to his companions. "Do you have another blade?"

Someone else handed him an ordinary hunting knife. The man tentatively touched Mae's cheek with its tip, finding no resistance. He nodded in satisfaction.

"A charm that protects her from the divine. Won't last for long. We can wait it out." He studied the knife's blade in the light. "Or our mistress might still take her through an unblessed weapon."

"We can't wait around for them to decide," Justin hissed. "Or for the police, apparently."

Dominic nodded, a grim look on his face. "Six of them. One long-range weapon. That's the real bitch if we try to cover the distance to them."

"Mae always carries two guns," Justin told him. "So they probably have another one too."

"Let's just hope they aren't fast enough to get to it. If I can just take out the one with Leo, the rest'll be easy."

"That'll be easy?" asked Justin in disbelief.

"We need to distract her without getting us killed in the process."

Justin thought about that. "I might have a way. . . ."

How much do you guys hate crows? he asked.

Horatio knew what he was thinking. *If we do it, it's going to hurt. More than last time.*

I'll deal, Justin said, trying not to grimace. *Just make sure the woman with the gun isn't looking this way.*

To Dominic, he said, "Get ready to take her out."

And like that, the two ravens manifested before them, darker than the night outside. They flew into the room, swooping toward the two men who stood near Mae, scratching them with their claws and beaks. All of the Morrigan's people gaped in astonishment, and the woman with the gun turned to watch, wide-eyed. For a moment, Dominic seemed equally stunned. Then Justin, trying not to scream at the pain of having his supernatural companions ripped away, nudged him.

"Go! Now's your chance!"

Dominic shot across the room toward the armed woman and threw her down with remarkable force. He deftly wrestled the gun away from her, and when she lunged after him, he shot her with the skill and aim of someone who'd been using a gun his entire life. This dragged the others' attention away from the ravens—except for the tall man, whom the ravens were still attacking. Dominic met the Morrigan's people unflinchingly—only to face a situation he was completely unprepared for: their ability to shape-shift into fast, smoky shadow forms. After a few false starts, Dominic began to understand when he could make contact and soon gained ground, either shooting them or incapacitating them with incredible hand-to-hand feats.

Mae, Justin thought. *I have to get her out of here.*

He started into the room just as Leo reached him, having used the commotion to escape. "What are you doing?" Leo asked. "Get out. Let Dom handle it."

"I have to go to Mae!"

"You need to call the police."

"I did."

Leo shook his head. "I heard them talking. There's a signal blocker in here. It's why none of our messages were getting to you. Go back to the car and call them from there."

Justin took out his ego and, his vision swimming from the pain, punched in the code that allowed it to be used away from his identity chip. He shoved it into Leo's hand before taking off inside. "You call them."

"Wait—"

Dominic had astonishingly taken out four of the six active Pan-Celts and was advancing on a fifth. The tall man with the silver dagger was preoccupied trying to fend off Magnus and Horatio. At one point, his blade clipped Horatio's wing, and Justin staggered as excruciating pain—far more violent than when the ravens had departed—ripped through him. Like that, the birds vanished from sight, and he felt their presence settle back into his mind, though the pain remained.

Sorry, said Horatio. *The Morrigan blessed the blade.*

You did a good job, Justin assured him.

Justin's initial intent had been to grab Mae in the fray and carry her away from all of this, but with the ravens gone, the tall man was advancing on Dominic. Without further thought, Justin threw himself against the man's back, making him stumble and mess up his attack. Justin hadn't seen any makeshift weapons and had no idea how one really attempted an unarmed attack. He'd just figured his body weight would be enough to throw the man off balance. And it was—but not for long.

The man spun around and gave Justin a glancing blow with the dagger, which cut his cheek. More searing pain shot through him, stronger than what he would've expected.

See? asked Magnus.

The man recognized Justin and strode forward. "The servitor. How unexpected."

"Why? Did you think your assassin would take me out?" Behind his adversary, Justin saw that the man Dominic fought held the second gun. Dominic was still doing fine, but keeping clear of it meant this wasn't as easy a fight as the others. Justin was on his own.

"Assassin?" The Morrigan's servant looked comically clueless.

"The fake Nordic jaguar one."

The man shook his head. "I wouldn't waste my time sending an assassin after you. Your god, whoever he is, is too weak for my mistress to care about. Maybe some other god hates you."

"Yeah? Then how come—"

Justin's words died as Mae suddenly leapt up from the altar.

With no hesitation, she threw herself on the tall man, destruction in her eyes. He fell but shifted to smoke and darted away before she could pin him down. He reappeared in his human form, standing opposite her. The mockery he'd shown to Justin was gone. Only anger was there now, as he circled around with Mae. Each watched every move, no matter how small, of the other. Justin had the sense of something monumental happening. Even the divine force in the room seemed to be holding its breath.

Dominic's words about Mae's recovery had proven true. She showed no signs of her earlier distress. Her eyes narrowed as she assessed the man, and then, unexpectedly, she moved backward—throwing her weight into the altar. It was composed of a large piece of stone resting on two others, and she hit it in just the right way to make the whole thing topple over. A tremor went through the air, and the Morrigan's man gasped.

"Is that a problem, Emil?" Mae asked. She backed up farther, almost to the wall. Eyes still on him, she grabbed one of the masks and hurled it to the floor. It shattered. "What about this?"

The man—Emil—flushed an angry red. "You'll die for this desecration."

"I'm not dying today," she replied evenly. "And even if I did, I wouldn't go to your goddess."

"She created you! You belong to her."

"She doesn't have a claim on me anymore." She destroyed another mask. "Or any of the others. Enough blood's been paid."

Until now, everything Emil had done had been very calculated and controlled, but his emotions were obviously getting the best of him. He attacked, turning to smoke—only it was short-lived. He looked surprised to rematerialize so quickly but still managed to come dangerously close to her with the Morrigan-blessed dagger.

Dominic had finally finished with the others and had his confiscated gun pointing at Emil. Justin hurried over. "No, let her finish him."

"She's unarmed," said Dominic.

Mae was leading Emil on a merry chase, destroying things as

she went. It should've given him more openings, but with each part of the temple she took out, he seemed to falter even more. He also no longer shifted form. He was still fast and sharp but not in a superhuman way. Certainly not in a prætorian way.

"Just wait," Justin told Dominic. "She needs to do it."

Mae was moving toward the middle of the room now, with Emil in hot pursuit. Too late, Justin saw what she didn't catch in her periphery: One of the Pan-Celts who'd been incapacitated had come to. The woman managed to sit up and grabbed hold of Mae's leg when the deadly dance was close enough. Mae stumbled, and Emil made his big move, throwing himself at Mae with the dagger aimed right for her heart. Justin had no idea whether the charm that had protected her earlier was still in effect—nor did he have need to find out.

Mae rolled in a way that let her break free of the grasping woman while simultaneously pulling the amber dagger from its boot sheath. Emil was so fixated on his attack that he never saw Mae's dagger—not even when he threw himself onto her. The weight of his body knocked her down, but it was too late. Her dagger pierced his thigh, causing him to scream and recoil in pain. He dropped his own blade and actually tried to move off of her. She was more than accommodating, rolling him over onto his back so that she could hover over him and drive the amber dagger down for a second strike—into his heart. Justin saw the man's eyes widen in shock, no scream coming out of his mouth this time. Mae waited a few moments and then jerked her dagger out and got to her feet, standing and watching without expression as her victim twitched and bled. After several horrific seconds passed, Emil stilled. A crackle of power rippled through the air, and then the tingling Justin had felt against his skin vanished.

"No one ever expects the knife," Mae said flatly. She studied Emil's body a few moments more and then suddenly looked up in surprise. "The Morrigan's gone." She caught Justin's arm in excitement. "Can't you feel it? The air . . . it's lighter. She was here earlier, pressing down, trying to get into me. But she couldn't. That was because of you, wasn't it? What you did to me earlier?"

"I . . . don't know," he admitted, somewhat enchanted with the joy and light in her eyes. "It's just something I learned."

"Keep learning it," she said. "Maybe we can continue to keep her out."

No need, said Horatio. *Mae is free. The Morrigan has been undone. She may gather strength again and return someday, but all her old ties have been broken. You felt her being cut loose from the world. The destruction of the temple and her followers struck her hard, and that guy in particular was probably one of her highest servants.*

Using that dagger was extra devastating, added Magnus.

What makes you say that? asked Justin. *The part where it pierced his heart and killed him?*

The amber dagger is empowered by a deity, just like the silver ones were, explained Magnus. *Probably by the god—or goddess—of the person who gave it to her.*

Callista's god?

No.

Justin told Mae what the ravens said about the Morrigan's leaving and decided to edit out the part about how that pretty dagger was sacred to some deity.

The police arrived soon thereafter, astonished at the grisly scene before them. Leo had waited outside until they arrived, and only then did Justin notice that Dominic was gone. "Where is he?"

Leo's face was bland. "He was never here."

"The hell he wasn't! Half of those bodies are his. I saw it."

"So did I," said Mae, a small frown appearing on her face. "Part of it, at least. He was . . . good."

"We didn't think he'd get involved in anything like that when he came along," said Leo. He cast an anxious glance over at the officers organizing the scene and dropped his voice. "If you have any respect for our friendship, you won't say a word to anyone about him being here. All the casualties are Mae's. I'll swear to whatever story you want—that there really were smoke people or that we didn't see them. Just do *not* mention Dominic."

The earnestness in his voice caught Justin off guard. Out of habit, he exchanged glances with Mae, who looked just as surprised. Justin didn't like Dominic, but he'd saved their lives tonight, and many years of friendship with Leo carried a lot of weight.

"Okay," Justin said slowly. "Dominic was never here."

Mae opened her mouth to protest, but Justin shot her a warning look that kept her silent. Leo grasped his hand, nearly sagging in relief. "Thank you. I owe you."

Justin shook his head. "I don't know. I think I owe you for getting us here."

When Leo left to get some air, Mae immediately approached Justin. "Was that a good idea? You're going to lie about Dominic."

"I'm going to lie about you too," he said in a low voice. "When I say you had no choice but to stab that guy in the heart—after giving him a debilitating thigh wound."

Mae's face darkened. "I had to. He would've kept coming after me and others. *She* wouldn't have been banished. I'd never be free—"

Justin put an arm around her and led her to the stairs. "You don't have to convince me. I'm just saying, we've all got our reasons tonight. Once Internal Security matches those daggers and gets witnesses to verify Emil was stalking victims, no one's going to care how this case was closed."

The night was warm and breezy, the air thick and humid. The earlier clouds had passed, revealing a night brilliant with moon and stars. Being outside felt good and eased a little of Justin's throbbing headache and other pains, though he was still counting the moments until he could hunt down a real painkiller. He'd had good intentions to lay off some of his vices, but then, he'd never expected to be part of a supernatural battle.

Mae, for her part, appeared to be in peak condition. In fact, he thought she looked exceptionally beautiful as she gazed upward. Radiant, even.

It's the freedom, said Magnus. *No god weighs her down. She may embrace any other—and others will come after her.*

If you had any sense, added Horatio, *you could even win her over to our side.*

I'm *not even on your side,* Justin snapped.

"And what are you going to say for yourself in the official report?" Mae asked, her eyes as dark as the night. "As far as gods and supernatural warriors go?" Her words were a reminder of that monumental report from four years ago.

"I'm going to say whatever it takes to keep me here," he replied.

"Which is?"

"That's the thing. I'm not really sure yet."

CHAPTER 35

A RECLUSE AND A
TECHNICAL GENIUS

It took the wheels of SCI's bureaucracy a while to wrap up the case. The military was much more efficient, and within two days, Mae had a summons to General Gan's office.

This is it, she thought, approaching the base's entrance. *What I've been waiting for.*

Even though matters weren't officially closed, she'd been in touch with Justin and heard that all the damning evidence they'd hoped for was coming to light. No one could deny that it was an overwhelming success. She could hold her head up high with Gan and the prætorians again and return to where she belonged.

"A death temple and a genetic scandal." Gan chuckled at the absurdity of what had gone down on the Pan-Celt land grant. "When I was asked to put you with March, I had no idea what madness was coming."

His word choice caught her attention. She'd been spending too much time with Justin. "Asked? I thought you assigned me to him as a punishment. Sir."

"Did you?" He shook his head adamantly. "Oh, no. It was a bizarre set of circumstances, actually. SCI had asked us for a prætorian to retrieve Dr. March, and we had one assigned. I don't recall who. A Celadon, I believe. Anyway, Francis Kyle was on base for a meeting with the research department. He apparently got lost and received directions from some man who claimed to work here but didn't meet any description I knew."

"What did he look like, sir?" Mae had no reason to ask, and Gan had no reason to tell her. It wasn't relevant to the story, but some part of her needed to know what twist of fate had led her to this point.

Gan thought back. "I don't recall the exact details. Older man. No uniform. He had a glass eye, so maybe that was why his directions were so bad." He seemed very amused at the joke. "Anyway, he somehow sent Kyle over to our department, which was all abuzz over what to do with the prætorian who'd started a fight at a funeral."

She nearly pointed out that she hadn't started the fight but then thought better of it.

"Kyle heard you were Nordic and got worked up about it. He's a very excitable man, if you haven't noticed." "Excitable" was one way to put it, Mae thought, recalling how the director had salivated over Justin. "He requested you for SCI because he thought your background would help with all the patrician visits. And so, off you went."

"What would've happened to me otherwise, sir?"

"Slap on the wrist. Two weeks' suspension. And still banned from the uniform—which ended up being your only punishment, really. But we would've had you back in the field before long."

Mae was dumbfounded. Two weeks was nothing. Double that time had passed already. Two weeks, and she could've worn the black uniform again and been off fighting as she was intended to do. Instead, a set of bad directions and even worse timing had landed her an assignment that had ripped her world out from underneath her.

"We're all very pleased with how you handled things with those fanatics," Gan continued, oblivious to her churning thoughts. "You'll have a nice commendation to outweigh your reprimand." He looked at her expectantly, awaiting an appropriate response.

"Thank you, sir."

"And you've been granted your uniform again."

Mae caught her breath as joy rushed through her. The uniform! Being deprived of it had become a bigger burden than she'd ever expected. Even though few knew about the punishment, she'd felt as though she were walking around in a disgrace that was obvious to everyone.

"However," continued Gan, "I'm afraid you won't actually be wearing it for a while."

She snapped out of her daydreams. "Sir?"

A look of distaste crossed his features. "I was ready to have you back in regular duties once those patrician murders wrapped up, but Internal Security has requested that we allow you to stay with him—with March. Believe me, I argued against it, but . . . well, I lost." Mae wondered if Gan had ever admitted to losing anything. "To be fair, after what you faced, I can see why they want enhanced protection for their servitors. I offered to give them someone else, but Director Kyle insisted on you. It's an honorable mission," Gan added, watching her closely. "All prætorian missions are."

She swallowed. "Yes, sir. Of course. I'm just surprised, that's all. Do you know how long I'll be doing this?"

"No idea. Maybe if you're lucky, March'll do something to get himself exiled again." Gan laughed at his own joke, and Mae mustered a smile she didn't feel. "Regardless, I know you'll excel. You always do."

"Thank you, sir. May I ask you something? Something unrelated?"

"Of course." Sometimes it almost seemed as though he was simply curious to hear what came to her mind.

"Have any prætorians ever gone AWOL?"

He certainly hadn't expected that question. After a moment, his surprise turned to amusement. "Is this assignment going to drive you away?"

"No, sir," she said, unable to hold back a laugh of her own. "It'd take something a lot worse for that to happen. I just overheard some drunk prætorians talking about it at a bar, and I'd never even thought about it before. It doesn't seem believable."

"That's because you're too loyal, and, forgive me, that loyalty blinds you to those who are less noble. Yes, prætorians do try to disappear—usually because they don't want to give up their implant when they retire." He gazed past her, his thoughts elsewhere as he absentmindedly touched the black trim around his collar. "I remember when it happened to me. There are ways to ease the transition, drugs that can help . . . but it's still difficult. Losing it is like losing some intrinsic part of you. But it's necessary—remember that when you're forty. It's a gift from our country that must be returned."

"Yes, sir." Forty seemed like a lifetime away. "But they must get caught, right? None of them can get very far."

"Not if they stay in the country." He tapped something into a panel on his desk, and a screen on the wall behind him powered up. "Bring up the Donovan file."

Instantly, five head shots appeared. Text under them listed names and dates. Three names were in black, two were in red. Gan tapped the first picture.

"The file's named after Virgil Donovan, the first prætorian to ever try to flee with an implant. He was caught, as were these other two. But the last two . . ." He scowled. "They fled to the provinces. If they're ever found, they'll be executed for treason and stealing military technology."

"Have they been spotted in the provinces, sir?" She was surprised the RUNA wouldn't have sent anyone to retrieve the traitor prætorians.

"No, but there's really nowhere else they could be. If they were here, their identity chips would trigger a warrant."

Mae stared at the ex-prætorians at large. One was a man; one was a woman. She recognized neither. "Counterfeit chips exist, sir."

He nodded. "Yes, but they would only fool localized sensors. Any chip reader linked to the registry would immediately identify the fraudulent chip. And with the way the technology's always updated, it would be nearly impossible to keep up maintenance on a counterfeit chip, even for localized readers. You'd need to either have a full-time technical genius on hand or become a recluse who never goes near a reader to avoid detection."

"So they must be in the provinces," she murmured in agreement. She glanced back at the pictures, focusing on the man, Alexander Srisai. He still didn't look familiar.

Gan scrutinized her. "Are you sure you aren't going to run out on me?"

She realized then what a suspicious question it was. "No, sir. Thank you for humoring me."

It was noon when she was dismissed, later in the day than she'd intended. A look at train schedules told her she had time to make the trip she wanted, and after a quick call ahead, she soon found herself on a train to Portland. She reached Leo and Dominic's house in the late afternoon. Leo opened the door, more comfortable around her than he'd initially been but still not looking entirely thrilled to see her.

"Is Dominic out?" she asked, glancing around as she entered.

"He's at a wine-making seminar in California. It's examining the way soil components interact with some of the newer Chardonnay hybrids." There was a precision in the way he spoke that reminded her of the story he'd told her about how he'd met Dominic—the one Justin said was contrived.

"When's he coming back?"

Leo looked wary. "Why?"

"Just curious. I just wanted to say hello."

She made no mention of what had happened at the Morrigan's temple, and after a few moments, Leo seemed to realize he was being hostile. He forcibly relaxed. "About a month. Be sure to tell Justin that. I'm sure he'll have all sorts of witty commentary about how he hopes Dom'll learn something."

Mae smiled. "Maybe I should bring him back a bottle. It looks like we aren't getting rid of each other anytime soon."

"Oh?" Leo gave her a searching look. "How do you feel about that?"

"That it's my job."

"Yeah, but it's not exactly ideal for someone like you. I know how prætorians work."

Yes, she thought. *I'm sure you do.*

"Prætorians do what they're supposed to," she said.

"They certainly do," he said, a bit of bitterness in his voice.

After a little more small talk, Leo moved on to the reason she'd asked to come over today. If she'd learned anything about him, it was that his curiosity could trump a lot of his other more cautious feelings. Justin shared the same trait.

"So," Leo said, ushering her into his lab. "I'm happy to run your blood. I just don't get why you want me to do it."

"Just a hunch," she said.

The room looked completely chaotic, but Leo had no difficulty finding a box of new syringes among all the metal and glass. "It's going to take a few hours to process," he said once the blood was drawn. He suddenly looked very uncomfortable. "I'll have to check on it occasionally . . . but if you want to, I don't know . . . get something to eat . . ."

"Don't worry about it," she said, saving him from entertaining her. "I have some work to do, and I wouldn't mind taking a walk in your fields. I'll check back later."

In truth, Mae had no work to do. There was a call she wanted to make, but she couldn't do it yet and wanted to be in her own home for it anyway. She'd been telling the truth about the fields and set off into them, admiring the neat rows of grapes that were starting to climb their posts. Wine making was a mystery to her, but Dominic had clearly put in a lot of work, and maintaining this land would certainly be a very good excuse not to get out much.

Justin thinks he's just paranoid and antisocial, she thought. *He thinks that's why Leo wanted him left out of the official report.* Maybe it really was that simple. After all, Justin was the allegedly brilliant master of deduction. Mae, though she believed herself intelligent, would never claim to have his powers of reading other people. She did, however, put a lot of faith in her instincts. Following them was how she'd survived, and they were now telling her something very different from what Justin believed about Dominic.

Thinking of Justin turned her mind toward other areas. She hadn't had a chance to have much more than written contact with him, but he'd been in her thoughts a lot. Once again, he'd managed to confuse her perceptions of him. The man whose face had been filled with fierceness and affection as he risked his life with Emil bore little resemblance to the callous one who told her she was no longer interesting in bed. And always, always, the memory of the lover in Panama refused to leave her. All of those images had struck her deeply. She couldn't forget any of them. And she couldn't forgive one.

Her hardened heart's resolve was made slightly more complicated by continued calls and messages from Lucian. His latest request had been that she and Justin come as "honored guests" to a fund-raiser. Lucian had written: *We could have a dance or two, and no one would blink an eye.* Mae had yet to respond.

She eventually pushed all these considerations aside and returned to the house as the sky was turning purple. When she saw Leo's shocked face, her alarms went off. Maybe he'd guessed her conclusions about Dominic.

"What is it?" she asked.

He shook his head, amazement all over him. "Something you won't believe."

"You might be surprised at what I'd believe these days."

He led her to side-by-side screens. Each held what she recognized as DNA sequencing, along with numbers that made no sense to her. "This is what you sent a couple weeks ago, your full genetic analysis from the military," he said, pointing to one. "And here's the one I just ran on you now. They're not the same." He glanced over at her when she made no response. "You're not surprised."

"I am . . . ," she said slowly. "Well, I don't know. Obviously I wouldn't have had you do it if I didn't think there was something weird about it, but I didn't really know what to expect. Maybe the military sent you someone else's records."

"I'd believe that if the results they sent were completely different from these. But theirs is *almost* like this one. When you compare theirs to the real thing, it's obvious theirs has been altered. It's been altered in a way to make it look more . . . real."

"What else would it be?" she asked.

"It would look like this." He tapped the screen on the right. "You've got a genetic makeup exactly like the patrician victims. Indescribably perfect. Beautifully crafted genes. Someone did a very good job of putting believable flaws into the one the military has. I never would've guessed it was fake if I didn't have obvious proof here that *this* is you."

He almost sounded embarrassed at his oversight, but she supposed a technical genius would consider this a big failing.

As for her, she couldn't take her eyes off the screen or still the racing of her heart.

"The last crazy piece," she said in a voice that didn't sound like her own. "This makes it official."

"After everything that's happened, 'crazy' is kind of becoming the status quo. I mean, you're a designer baby created through either breakthrough genetic manipulation or the intervention of a goddess. And after what I saw that night . . ." No more swagger from Leo. "Well, I don't know what I believe. I'm still on the side of science, but I'd be lying if I said I wasn't unnerved that you and Justin haven't been nearly as shocked by this stuff as you should be. That kind of freaks me out."

"Speaking from the side of science, can you think of a reason for why the military would have altered genetic information on me?" she asked.

Leo lost his philosophical air and turned wry. "I learned a long time ago that there's nothing the military won't do. They have secrets within secrets. . . ." He hesitated. "Especially with prætorians."

She held his gaze. "You really do know a lot about prætorians."

"I'm not up-to-date on them anymore." He gave her a smile they both knew was faked. "I'm just a guy who works on birth control."

After they finished up, she declined his offer to stay the night. Neither would've enjoyed it. There was a late train going back to Vancouver, and sleep didn't matter to her. It did matter for a phone call she wanted to make, and the night passed slowly as she waited for the world to wake up. She tried reading and watching movies, but her mind couldn't focus on any of it. At last, morning approached, and she decided it was a reasonable enough hour in New Stockholm to call her mother.

Astrid Koskinen answered, groomed to her usual state of perfection. Mae hadn't woken her up, which hopefully meant she'd be in a cooperative mood.

"Maj, what a surprise. We've had more contact this month than we have in a year. I'm surprised you can take time from your fame and glory to check in on your family. *Everyone's* talking about the little scene you made during your visit."

Only her mother could call shooting someone in public a "little scene." Mae wasn't surprised the locals had discovered she was the prætorian involved. It was enough to have just stayed out of the national media.

"You lied to me," Mae said. "You told me you just made a genetic deal, that there wasn't any connection to a religion. But that's not true. I remember! I was in her temple. You took me. My story matches a dozen others. We were all given those crow pendants. How could you do that? How could you pay that kind of price for a perfect baby?"

Her mother's lack of shock was answer enough. "There you go again with using 'perfect' all the time. You certainly have a high opinion of yourself."

"Someone else died for me. You bound me to a death goddess. You wiped out the family's finances."

"No," spat her mother. "You wiped them out when you chose duty to a uniform over duty to us. We're one of the few families with more Finnish in our blood than Swedish. Do you know how rare that is?"

"Duty to you? You had a loan you couldn't repay. You gambled that you could sell me off for a profit, and your plan failed."

"I failed at a lot of things, Maj. I should never have allowed your father the liberties I did. When he confronted me about your conception, I panicked. I never would've let him have the influence he did if I'd known it would ruin you."

"His influence was the only thing that saved me!" Hearing her father belittled hurt Mae as much as the slight against the military. As she spoke, her childhood flashed through her mind—and more important, the way it had differed from Cyrus and Claudia's. Always, always, their mother had controlled every aspect of Mae's siblings' lives. But not Mae's. Her mother had glared and grumbled, but she'd stepped aside as Mae's father encouraged her in *canne* and let her skip so many of the grueling teas and etiquette lessons customary in the Nordic upper classes. It wasn't until her father's death that her mother had finally taken over with a vengeance.

"Was that the deal you made with him?" Mae asked. "He

kept quiet about what you'd done, so long as he could raise me? Was that why I didn't have to join that deranged cult?"

Mae's mother closed her eyes, finally letting pain show in her face. She took a deep breath and opened her eyes. "You didn't have to join because whenever I brought you to them, you made a scene. After a while, they asked me to stop and simply instruct you at home, through lessons and occasional visits from their priests. You didn't react well to that either. You woke the whole household with your screaming."

Mae reeled. All the nightmares that had tormented her before she joined the prætorians were the result of this unholy deal, her subconscious way of coping with something so twisted. "Dad stopped it, didn't he? The home instruction, the visits. He couldn't stand to see me go through that torment."

Her mother scowled. "*I* couldn't stand it. I'm not as heartless as you think I am, Maj, but it was a little too late. You slept somewhat better, but those nightmares never entirely went away."

"Because *she* never went away," Mae murmured, unable to believe how casually she was discussing the Morrigan. "You promised me to her, and she wouldn't let me go."

"There are a lot of rumors going around," her mother said lightly. "Rumors that aren't in the news. I heard the Morrigan's temple was dismantled, and that prætorians and SCI were involved. Seems like her power might not be what it used to be." Her mother's eyes narrowed. "How are your dreams now?"

"I don't dream. I don't sleep." Mae fell silent for a few moments. "How do *you* sleep knowing you put my life at risk? They must have told you the consequences if I didn't follow their path."

"I figured it was a problem we'd deal with later." So typical. "Besides, you seem alive and well to me."

What Mae felt was numbed. "How could you so casually sign on with a death cult, Mother? And which did you—do you—believe: that they used illicit technology or that they used unholy powers to create me?"

Her mother shrugged. "It made no difference. I'd heard

about their results, and after your disappointing siblings, I had to do something. Desperate times call for desperate actions, but our last, best hope ended up being a bad investment."

Mae had always resented the thought of being a commodity, but there was something even worse about being an investment. "I'm your daughter," she said simply.

"And you're a bad one of those too." Her mother glanced at her ego and sighed impatiently. "I'm meeting Dorothy Olsen for mimosas. If you have nothing else to complain about, then I'll be on my way, and you can return to playing soldier or whatever it is you like to do."

"I serve the most powerful force in the country, Mother."

"Do you, Maj?" Her mother's smile managed to be both condescending and wistful at the same time. "The next time you look at that 'perfect' face or do some incredible physical feat, ask yourself where the real power is these days."

CHAPTER 36

THE OTHER PATTERN

Justin wrote out two versions of his official report on the events at the Morrigan's temple. He knew both Mae and Leo would back up whichever version got sent. The decision now rested on him, and he put it off for as long as possible, which was easy to do since SCI left him hanging for almost a week after the raid. Finally, a passive-aggressive message came in from Cornelia, telling him she wanted a meeting and that it would be "useful" to have the report beforehand, so that she knew what the meeting was actually about.

That was an exaggeration, of course. The police had a broad picture of what had happened that night, and he knew Internal Security had hit the jackpot with evidence linking the cult to the murders. Nonetheless, his words, describing the specifics, would put the final stamp on this case—and possibly on his life.

So, he went back and forth, taking no action and vowing that when he did, he'd do it sober—which was easier said than done in these long, empty days waiting for SCI to get its act together. One thing both versions of the report shared was a harrowing tale of Mae's heroics, how she took out impossible numbers of attackers and finally was forced to kill Emil in self-defense. It was Justin's favor to both her and Leo and would also go a long way toward getting Mae back to the regular prætorian duty she longed for. Sure, she'd still have to cope with the mental fallout of the supernatural proceedings she'd witnessed, not to mention the earth-shattering revelations about her birth, but she was strong. She would survive and move on, eventually forgetting him.

I thought the self-pity and melodrama would end after Panama, said Magnus one evening as Justin mulled over his fate. *But you've managed to take it to new heights.*

I'm not being melodramatic, just stating a fact. She's hardly returned my calls, and it's better for both of us that way. She's getting on with her life, and I'm going to do the same. No point in sitting around.

Actually, that's kind of what you've been doing for the last week, Horatio retorted. *Unless you consider those roommates you went out with last night a worthy use of your time.*

Very worthy, Justin assured him.

You've gone through so much and seen so much, yet here you are, back to drinking, dice, and women, scolded Magnus. *At the very least, you should work on your runes in your downtime.*

No. One was enough.

Justin didn't want to do any more embracing of higher powers quite yet. He'd grown comfortable in exile with the ravens and the idea of a nebulous godly patron keeping track of him. Being face-to-face with powers of the magnitude he'd seen recently had been staggering, however, enough to make him seriously uneasy about his own future. Even the small charm he'd performed for Mae had left him unsettled, as was acknowledging that she was one of the elect. Seeing exactly what a deity could do made him want to avoid serving one more than ever. Mae was unquestionably off-limits, and her distance this week had made it easier to strengthen his resolve against future entanglements.

No, he told the ravens. *No Mae, no magic. I'm going to make a call on this goddamned report now and send it off. Then I'm going barhopping in the hopes of finding more creative roommates. Or maybe twins.*

No, you aren't, said Horatio. *You're going to Tessa's expo.*

Justin had nearly forgotten about tonight. Tessa had finally been readmitted to school, and her film class was having a viewing of all of the students' short documentaries, open to friends and family. The idea of watching two hours of student films made Justin want to gouge his eyes out, but Cynthia had threatened to gouge a lot more if he didn't go.

And so, a couple of hours later, he went to the high school with Cynthia and Quentin and made himself comfortable in one of the auditorium's seats. Most of the films were as inane as he'd expected, but thankfully, none was more than ten minutes. It gave his mind a chance to wander over the report dilemma. He'd almost convinced himself of what he'd do when Tessa's turn came.

She walked out onstage, wearing one of the dresses they'd bought that first week. Her hair was still as long as ever, but at least she no longer wore it in an obviously provincial way. He thought she looked adorable and dared anyone to say otherwise. She gave a small, succinct introduction about her film and how it was inspired by being an immigrant. Her speech was delivered in a loud, clear voice, but he heard a few people around him grumble about the accent. No wonder she always seemed so irate after school.

Her film was brilliant—and he was certain it wasn't just because of his bias. Her observations gave the Gemman audience a mirror for some of its odder idiosyncrasies, though he suspected most of tonight's viewers didn't find them odd at all. There was a poignancy to it that struck him deeply, and most of all, it was honest. Gemmans liked to act as though their world was out in the open, what with all the shows and documentaries peering into people's lives. But they were all edited and dressed up to create an image. Reporters and directors defined the truth—even he did in his job, according to Tessa. She did none of that, though. She didn't spin or sensationalize or grasp for things that weren't there. She simply told the truth. It was a talent—no, a gift, that she didn't even realize she possessed.

"Was it as bad as you thought?" Cynthia asked him later as they walked along a downtown sidewalk. They'd decided to take the family out to dinner, and Poppy—who Justin was sure really would be in a miscreant girls camp someday—had come along. Quentin and the two girls walked ahead, and he was attempting eight-year-old flirting, which Justin took as a promising sign.

"No."

Cynthia gave Justin an expectant look. "This is the part where you say, 'It was worse.' "

He smiled and shook his head. "It wasn't."

"What's the matter with you tonight?" she asked when he said nothing else.

"Cyn, what do you think was ultimately wrong with Mom as a parent?"

Cynthia nearly tripped, and he caught hold of her arm. "Are you seriously asking me that?"

"I don't mean the obvious stuff. I mean, I do, but . . . I don't know. There's something more basic to her personality, something I'm trying to figure out, that had such an impact on the way she raised us."

"There's nothing secret or mystical about it, Justin. She's an addict. Addicts have a dependence on certain substances and behaviors that become more important than everything else—even people. Even their children."

"Have you been taking psych classes?"

"Every day of my life," she retorted.

He stared ahead, barely seeing the crowds and endlessly flashing advertisements. "You know, when they came to offer me admission to the Hart School, they gave Mom a chance for you too."

"Yes," said Cynthia quietly. "I found out about that later."

It was something they rarely spoke about but that always lay between them. Justin had been "discovered" one day in the Anchorage Summer Market by a woman who taught at a private school on the other side of the city, in a much more affluent neighborhood. She'd been dazzled by his and Cynthia's guessing-game performance and questioned them extensively about it. He'd realized immediately that her interest was legitimate and had eagerly explained the way he watched people, turning on all the charisma he'd already learned at eleven. Cynthia, younger and warier, had thought they were going to get into trouble and had been reluctant to speak.

Although both siblings had impressed the woman, her power to get a charity scholarship could only initially extend to one student, and she'd chosen Justin. That switch had changed his life. Being put among students from affluent and well-educated tiers of society had propelled Justin toward one himself, opening doors he never could have had in his old life. His benefactor had later found a workaround way to get Cynthia in, but it required more government hoops than their mother was willing to jump through. Cynthia had been left behind.

"Why wouldn't she do it?" Justin asked Cynthia. "She loved us. In her way. All she would've had to do was fill out some paperwork and get a job—any job, even a part-time one—and they would've processed you through too. She could've even managed a subsidy to move across town!"

"It was too risky," Cynthia said. "She would've lost her rations and federal allowance."

"But she's a gambler. And between the subsidy and job, she would've ended up making more. She could've gotten high more often. She should've liked that."

"Too risky. Her life wasn't ideal, but it was comfortable and familiar. If she'd gone to all that trouble to get me transferred too, and something went wrong—like I hated the school or she lost her job—it would've been a bitch to go through all the social-aid procedure again."

"Yeah, but shouldn't it have been worth the risk that you might achieve greatness?"

"I'll ignore the subtext there—that I obviously haven't achieved greatness. But the point remains: Even though she liked to gamble, there were some risks Mom wouldn't take, not when her comfort was on the line. She went with the sure thing." Cynthia eyed him carefully. "Why do I have a feeling this isn't really about Mom?"

"It's about Tessa," he said in a rare moment of transparency. "I'm trying to make a decision that'll affect her future."

It took Cynthia several moments to process that, and when she did, her face was full of incredulity. "Why did you even use the word 'trying'? There's nothing to decide. Just do what's best for her."

"Doing it involves a risk," he said.

"Then you'd better decide how important her 'greatness' is to you."

Justin pondered her words over dinner and said little to the others. When they got back home later, he went straight to his office and finally sent one of the reports off to Cornelia. As he did, he noticed he had an unread message from Lucian.

> *Justin,*
> *Word's gotten around about the brilliant servitor and valiant prætorian responsible for busting open the patrician murders. Don't worry, I'll let them keep thinking you're a genius—because that's the kind of friend I am. In return, a good friend like you should come to an upcoming fund-raiser the party's having for me, and you should bring your valiant prætorian. It's black-tie, and I'll make sure you're seated with some of the prettier donors. No one will think twice about heroes coming to an event like that, even patrician ones. Think about it, and convince her too. I already asked her and haven't heard anything back. It's a pretty clever compromise, though, one that'll finally give me the semblance of an evening out with her that won't end up on the national news.*

Whatever satisfaction Justin felt at learning Mae was ignoring Lucian was immediately killed when he got to "clever compromise." The world came grinding to a halt, and Justin gripped the arms of his chair. *Clever compromise.* Those were the words Geraki had used in the Internal Security holding cell when he'd claimed the god he served had a message for Justin. *Yield your stars and flowers and accept the clever compromise.*

That was what this god wanted? For Justin to help set Mae up on a faux date with Lucian? It was ridiculous.

You promised Geraki you would, Horatio warned him. *When he helped you find the Morrigan. You said you'd do what our boss asked.*

That was before I knew what it was! No way am I going to help set Mae up with Lucian, even for something like this. He just wants her because he can't have her. He knows nothing about her except that the pants she had on when they met made her ass look great.

I thought you weren't interested in her, jabbed Horatio.

It's not interest. I'm stating a fact. Why aren't you chiming in, Magnus?

The other raven sounded forlorn. *Because I don't know what to do. We have to obey our god. But I don't want to give her to him. I just can't trust him.*

But one thing that came out of this was Justin's acceptance that he needed to do something very unwelcome and very unpleasant: talk to Geraki. This time, with no cameras and no pretenses from either of them. Justin had to go in with as much out in the open as he could. He called Geraki—who was irritatingly gleeful—and set up a meeting for the following day, just before Cornelia's debriefing.

When Justin showed up at the designated restaurant, Geraki was already there, sitting at a dark corner table that seemed to have been designed for him.

"You can't imagine how delighted I was by your call last night." Geraki grinned as Justin took a chair. "Is it a breach of the restraining order if you seek me out?"

"Depends on what you do." Justin brought up the menu screen and ordered bourbon. After a moment's consideration, he made it a double.

"I miss that, you know," said Geraki. "I used to love a good Pinot Noir."

"I know a guy who makes some, but it's not actually any good. Still, you could probably get a discount on it."

Geraki nodded to the glass of water on the table. "I have to keep my body pure now, in order to hear my master's voice."

"Are we going to finally talk about your god? The one whose name no one will tell me?"

"We're here to talk about anything you like. You're the one who contacted me."

Justin took a deep breath. It was now or never. "I finally figured out that message you gave me—about yielding my stars and flowers. I know what it means."

"I don't." Geraki sipped his water with as much reverence as he'd give a fine wine. "It made no sense to me then or now. I just relayed the message. Are you going to fulfill its terms? You promised, you know. I helped you, and you gave your word to him."

"Your master."

"Our master," corrected Geraki.

"Great. Are we back to us being brothers? My master is a woman with terrible hair who hates me."

"Why are you asking me questions if you don't believe the answers?" asked Geraki. "And what answer do you actually expect me to give that you would believe?"

"I don't know," Justin admitted. He felt weary and wished he'd taken more Exerzol.

"Then why are you here?"

"Because I've seen things—wondrous and terrible things that have no human explanation. And I accept—I had to a long time ago—that there are powerful forces in our world. The thing is, I know there's something bigger going on. I can feel it. It's more than a jumble of gods and supernatural feats. There's a pattern, but I can't find this one—or where I fit in."

Geraki laughed softly. "That's maddening for you, isn't it? Not being in on the master plan."

Justin's response was interrupted when a waitress came by with his bourbon. She had cropped brown hair and no bra on under her white tank top. A silver tongue piercing glittered when she spoke, reminding him of a girl he'd gone out with in college. After blatantly checking him out, she smiled and sauntered away.

Geraki grimaced. "You don't waste time, do you?"

"Or opportunities."

"You're wasting a woman who's worth ten of that one."

"Who, Mae?" Justin shook his head. "No. There's nothing like that going on between us."

"Then you must be an idiot." The ravens loved that. "She's a powerful elect who can't help but attract the divine."

"Yeah, we kind of noticed, seeing as she finally broke free from a death goddess that's stalked her since birth."

"There'll be more trying to woo her." Geraki got an eerie gleam in his eye, making him look very much like the prophet he claimed to be. Justin suddenly had a flashback to Mae burning with light and life in Claude's temple, when the ravens said another god had made a move on her. "It'll be interesting to see who gains her services. She's a remarkable woman. Magnificent."

"Well, if you're so interested in her, she's available."

The self-righteous look on Geraki's face told Justin what was coming. "I no longer engage in carnal activity. I told you, a prophet's body must be pure to hear the god's voice. A priest, on the other hand . . ." He shrugged. "You have a different role. You have no restrictions with a woman like that."

"And I told you I don't want her."

"Then you must be an idiot," Geraki repeated. "Which makes it stranger that you were chosen by our god. But we'll put aside the glorious woman you allegedly don't want. Obviously, you've seen something else of note, if not her."

"I've seen lots of things. I've seen the servants of a death goddess turn to smoke and gain supernatural strength and speed. I've seen genetically perfect people created from sacrifices to that same goddess. I fought a woman who turned into a jaguar. I've watched your 'prophecies' come true. I saw two ravens appear out of thin air and save my life, and now they won't leave me alone." Justin had no idea why he was spilling all of this. At least no one would believe Geraki anyway if he repeated it.

Geraki smiled and nodded along. "Ah, yes. Your thought and memory. Are you used to them yet? I had trouble with the wolves at first, but now I enjoy them. But then, I spend so much time alone in meditation that it's actually nice having the company."

Justin had once kind of wanted to find someone else who heard voices, but this wasn't what he'd imagined. "You obviously think you have some insight into the big picture here. Are you going to keep dangling it in front of me or finally come clean?"

The smugness and cynicism vanished from Geraki's face, and he leaned across the table. "You want the truth, Servant of Truth? The truth is, when you banish the gods from the world, they eventually come back—with a vengeance. Humans can't stay away from gods, and gods can't stay away from humans. It's the natural order of things. Our country's treatment of the divine was too harsh after the Decline. Our people have pushed the gods away for too long, and now the divine is pushing back. That's why these forces are stirring around us. There's a vacuum here, and entities we haven't seen for a very long time are rushing in, seeking followers. Belief is what powers the gods, and they're picking out their elect to conduct their earthly business."

His words chilled Justin because in some part of him, he knew it was all true. "How are the elect chosen?"

"All sorts of reasons. Sometimes it's shared blood and heritage. Sometimes it's about strength and usefulness—or alleged cleverness. Whatever's a match to that god's attributes and agenda. We're pieces on a gameboard, Dr. March, and some of us are more powerful than others. You. Me. Her. We're the ones the gods want. We're the ones they're fighting over. Of course, my allegiance is already sealed."

"And I suppose you consider yourself the king on this board?"

"You must not have played chess in a while. The king is the weakest piece in the game." He gave Justin a level look. "The queen's the strongest."

"What is it you and your master expect from me in this game? To use my alleged cleverness to convert new followers?"

Geraki shrugged. "That'd be a start. More followers means more belief, which means more power. Others will be doing the same for their gods. We're not the only ones who know what's happening. Your human masters know. So do powerful people you don't even suspect. This won't stay contained, and everyone will fight for the gods they've sworn to serve. Don't you want to be on the winning side? We need to fight for ours."

"I haven't 'sworn' to anyone or anything," Justin said.

"No." Geraki sighed. "Which is a shame. You won't be able to learn the full extent of his wisdom or grasp your power until you accept him. He's already accepted you. You even have his mark."

Geraki pushed up his sleeve, and Justin's heart nearly stopped. There, tattooed in blue, was a symbol identical to the scar Justin had received in the fire, that same odd F-shape.

"Where," Justin breathed, "did you get that?"

"From a tattooist on Brooks Street. Oh. The idea? Our god sent it to me."

The room swayed a little, but Justin's bourbon was only half-gone. "This is impossible."

"Is it?" Geraki's eyes seemed to see right into Justin's heart. "He's marked us both. I hear his voice, and you will deliver it. Everything I've said about the powers returning to the world . . . you know it's all true. I know you feel it. You can feel you have a role to play. So why won't you choose a side? How did you even reach this point with the ravens and a divine mark if you haven't sworn fealty?"

"Because your master slipped up and gave me the goods before I had to pay for them."

Geraki leaned across the table, face speculative. "You must be clever if you outwitted him. But you're not in the clear, are you? He wouldn't still be interested in you if you were. The ravens would have left. Instead, he's biding his time . . . waiting for the inevitable. What is it? What line are you dancing on that'll eventually bring you to his service?"

A woman among women.

"One I'm not going to cross."

Geraki slumped back. "Why are you fighting it?"

"Because gods do terrible things to people."

"And incredible things. You must know that. Haven't the ravens taught you wonders?"

Justin thought back on the past four years. "You mean their constant nagging about my choices and personal life?"

I think you mean advice, not nagging, said Horatio.

"I mean the runes and spells and other knowledge key to your path." At Justin's silence, Geraki looked uncharacteristically dumbfounded. "How . . . What kind of deal did you make? Didn't you promise to learn his ways?"

"Only if I swore myself to him."

Seeing Geraki stumped was almost making this trip worthwhile. "Someone as egotistical as you isn't interested in learning the secrets of one of the wisest, cleverest gods? If you had even a taste of his power, you'd want to follow him."

"A god whose name I don't know."

"You have to learn that for yourself. It's part of a wise man's path."

"Convenient. And I don't suppose he'll come talk to me himself?"

"I thought he already did." Geraki looked legitimately surprised. "In a dream?"

"A dream doesn't mean anything. I dreamed the other night that I went riding on a dinosaur."

"He doesn't just appear in the physical world at a man's whim," said Geraki, echoing what the ravens had once said. "To simply hear his voice alone, I have to fast and meditate and endure all sorts of torments."

"Right. No alcohol. No sex." Justin brought up the bill. "This is no different than any of the other religions I've looked at over the years. Maybe there really are gods in the world, maybe there's one who thinks I'm his elect. But for beings that want worship, they sure do make things hard for their followers. Not much in the way of concrete answers or guidance. It's just left for mortals to figure it all out."

"Wise men don't need concrete answers. By definition, they need wisdom, which you're lacking in." It was exactly the same kind of nonsensical commentary Justin had heard before, and he was surprised to find he was disappointed.

"Wise men thrive on concrete answers! I'm not going to learn from—let alone swear myself to—someone so nebulous. Someone whose face I haven't seen. Someone whose name I don't even know."

Geraki looked exasperated. Justin might have broken him. "Really? He spoke to you in a dream, sent you the ravens, and put an extraordinary woman in your path. But that's still not good enough? You need a face and a name before you'll start learning his ways? That's what it'll take?"

"You bet," said Justin, feeling triumphant at seeing Geraki squirm. "Think you can make it happen?"

"I have limits," he admitted. "So does our god."

"That's exactly what I thought." Justin swiped his ego and stood up in disgust.

"Wait." Geraki had gotten control of himself again. "Maybe

you can dodge everything else, but there's one thing that's unquestionable. Yielding the stars and flowers for the clever compromise. You promised, and even if you won't follow him, I know you believe in him and his power. Breaking your word is a grave thing."

Justin stilled. "If I do it, it'll be going against something else he wants. It's a contradiction."

"The plans of a god aren't for you to understand."

"That's the problem, isn't it?" Justin turned away. "Your water's on me. See you for your next inspection."

But as he walked out of the restaurant, he knew what he had to do.

CHAPTER 37

STEPHANOTIS

There were protesters outside Internal Security again when Justin showed up for his afternoon meeting. They shouted about religious freedom, and as security helped him push past, Justin uneasily wondered whether the fact that they kept popping up more frequently had anything to do with Geraki's game.

He reached Cornelia's reception area on the twentieth floor and found Mae sitting and reading her ego. Her presence lit up the room. A flicker of amusement flashed in her eyes at his unabashed surprise. "You didn't expect me here, did you?"

"No," he admitted. "When I didn't hear much, I figured my superstar prætorian had gotten her uniform back and was off fighting in an epic battle."

"I've been busy—but I did get the uniform back. There's just not much reason to wear it while running around with a servitor."

He hadn't really thought she'd stay on, and from that cool look on her face, she probably wasn't thrilled that she had. "Well, congratulations. I'm glad to have you, but I know it's not as action packed as you'd like."

She shot him a sidelong look. "Not action packed? Did you somehow miss this last month?"

An intern came to escort them to Cornelia's office. The girl's face brightened when she saw Justin. "Hey, I wondered what happened to you when you didn't call me."

Justin vaguely remembered a night out with her. "You know how it goes. Just been busy, Flora."

She looked hurt. "Flavia."

"Right." He smiled as winningly as he could. "We'll have to get together again sometime." Mae moved past him with no expression.

"Please be seated," said Cornelia as they stepped into her office. "We have a lot to discuss. And although it must be a disappointment, we actually aren't here to laud your brilliance and bravery. We need to talk about what really happened with the Pan-Celts."

"It was outstanding," piped Francis.

"It was a breach of a dozen policies," said Cornelia.

Justin leaned back in his chair, projecting more confidence than he felt. "I thought our policy was to dismantle dangerous religions. Seemed like we pulled that off pretty well *and* solved a national murder mystery."

"We thrive on order, Justin. You aren't a vigilante bringing justice to a lawless land. You should've notified us first and had an actual military team seize the compound. We'd have a few more suspects to question if you did." Cornelia had no jurisdiction over military personnel, but it was clear that last remark was a rebuke for Mae's killing spree.

"Do you know how fast word of a military raid would have spread?" Justin asked. "You'd have *no* suspects because they would've taken off beforehand, along with all the evidence." As it was, Justin was still puzzled over how Emil and friends had learned they were there. His best guess was that word of a prætorian's presence had leaked from border security.

That, or someone betrayed you, mused Magnus.

The tight line of Cornelia's lips showed her thoughts on that. "That's still not the reason we're here." She held up a reader. "Let's talk about your report."

Here it is, Justin thought, though he didn't even blink under Cornelia's scrutiny. "It's very detailed."

"Indeed it is," she said in agreement. "Far more detailed than I would like. It's even worse than your last one. Do you realize what you've signed off on? The idea that an ancient Celtic deity is responsible for repairing Cain in patricians through sacrificial magic?"

In his peripheral vision, Justin saw Mae taken aback. She hadn't believed he'd go through with it. After what had happened in his last report, she'd thought he'd lie about the events in the temple. Maybe he should have, but there was no going back on his gamble now.

"I didn't say that *definitely* happened. Just that it couldn't be ruled out. Maybe it was magic. Maybe it was some geneticist in her service. They were certainly a high-tech group to get those numbers."

"You weren't so vague about these alleged supernatural attackers. The people who turn into shadows and have superhuman powers?"

"They weren't alleged," he said. "I saw them. Prætorian Koskinen and Leo Chan did too."

Cornelia pretended not to hear. "It's all absurd."

"It's the truth!" exclaimed Francis. And for the first time, he didn't come across as a bedazzled fan. "Cornelia, it's happening everywhere, and you know it. We can't pretend it's not. We need to find it and control it before it controls us."

And like that, Justin knew his gamble had paid off. Cornelia had always had neutral responses when he'd brought his secret, off-the-record observations to her about mysterious phenomena. She hadn't accused him of insanity, but she'd certainly never once hinted that there might be something unusual going on in the world. Now her eyes told a different story. *We're not the only ones who know what's happening,* Geraki had said. *Your human masters know. So do powerful people you don't even suspect.*

Francis pointed at the reader and then fixed Justin with a penetrating look. "This isn't the first time we've seen phenomena like this. And you've seen it too. Other servitors are finding similar, inexplicable things, but most won't admit to it. They blur the details in the reports because they fear for their jobs. You're one of the few brave enough to tell the truth."

Or stupid enough, thought Justin. "What would you like me to do?"

"To keep doing what you do," said Francis. "We have a list of cases that require more than routine interviews and paperwork. Not just here, but in the provinces."

"Why would we care about that?" But it was the same thing Lucian had told Mae when he'd looked into servitor hiring.

"Because we need to know everything we can." Francis leaned across the table. "It doesn't matter where it is. The world is changing. There are powers hiding right in front of our eyes, and you'll be our lead in uncovering it all."

"Even though you have no idea what 'it' is," sneered Cornelia. "All we're going to find is a bunch of zealots fabricating 'miracles' we simply haven't been smart enough to crack."

"If that's true, then we'll get our proof, and that will be that," said Francis. But his voice showed he didn't believe that, and Cornelia picked up on it.

"You're insinuating ideas that go against every principle our country was founded on," she said. "If people start thinking there's a mystical force out there, we'll fall into chaos and have another Decline."

"Our country is founded on the truth," said Francis staunchly.

Cornelia faced him down and seemed to have momentarily forgotten Justin and Mae. "And what if that truth is dangerous?"

"Then learning about it will allow us to cover it up," said Francis, as though it were that simple. "We're very good at that, and I'm sure Dr. March will have no trouble keeping what he finds a secret. And regardless, we will take custody of those who truly seem to have some access to these powers. Pity we lost Emil Fitzpatrick."

"We're bounty hunters now?" asked Justin. That wasn't something he'd foreseen.

Francis's voice was stern. "I wouldn't say that. You're a servant of the truth, one who will do what it takes to uncover that truth. We need to know what's happening, and you, Dr. March, will find out. You will have increased access and influence, as well as whatever other powers you need. You don't have a new title, but, well . . ." He stood up and shook Justin's hand. "Congratulations. I'd say you've received a promotion. The likes of which none of us have ever seen. I hope you're ready for what's to come."

"Me too," murmured Justin.

There it was, his jackpot. Since returning from Panama, he'd lived in fear of what would happen to him. He'd been pretty sure no one would have any use for him if he didn't solve the murders, but even his future if he was successful had been unclear. After all, he was a servitor who believed in gods and the supernatural. That didn't happen. It *couldn't* happen. But the more he'd thought about it, especially after the temple, the more he'd realized his past meant something to them. Francis had been especially obsessed with it, and as Justin began to see more and more signs of forces stirring in the world, he'd come to believe a few different things.

One was that SCI wasn't going to get rid of him, not once he solved that case. It didn't matter how tainted his past was. Enough people knew of his involvement, and they couldn't make someone so high-profile disappear again. Justin had realized that if he turned in a proper report, with no mention of supernatural powers, no one would question it. He would have his old job back and return to comfortable run-of-the-mill licenses and inspections.

But even before Geraki's news, it had occurred to Justin that SCI had a problem that wasn't going to go away. They were going to have to deal with it, and who better than someone who was open-minded about what was truly happening in the world and who had an excellent track record? They needed someone like him, but they probably would've left him alone if he'd turned a blind eye to the supernatural in his report. In committing to what he'd seen, he had opened himself up for new opportunities—opportunities out of the public eye that would come along with the power and influence he'd indeed been offered.

Did he want to get involved with more of this stuff? That was the big question. He wouldn't have minded an ordinary life, but in taking on this one, he could create extraordinary lives for his family. A man who wielded the power Internal Security had given him could get a provincial girl into a private school that could appreciate her talents. He could do what someone had done for him. He could do equally monumental things for Cynthia and Quentin, when the time came. The only problem was that Justin didn't know what this would mean for *him*.

They sent Mae away after that in order to go over the logistics and bureaucracy of the new position. Although she'd be tied to it, she was still technically on loan from the military and not directly involved with Internal Security's inner workings. Justin was acutely aware of her absence, particularly since she was now in the very small circle of people who could really understand what he was going through.

He sent her a message afterward, asking to talk, and she sent one back saying she was busy with some friendly *canne* sparring, but that he was welcome to join her afterward. She sent him directions to the facility she was playing at, a large operation that offered training and competition for various martial arts. The front desk directed him to the small practice court she was on. He'd never been in any place like it and felt conspicuous in his suit among the handful of other spectators.

But it was worth it to see this bizarre sport. It was very much like what Val and Dag had described: stick fencing, with a few acrobatic moves thrown in. Mae and her opponent wore regulation clothing, rather than the party wear she and Porfirio had apparently fought in. Even in the lightly padded clothing and face mask, she was easy to spot, not just from the shape of her body but also the way she moved, with grace and speed born from natural and implant-induced abilities. It was mesmerizing, and most important, there was no divine glamour trailing her.

She won each of her matches, and when she and her opponent unmasked, Justin saw she'd fought against a chagrined-looking man. They shook hands, and as Mae turned to leave and allow the next combatants to take the ring, she spotted Justin and joined him on his bench. Her hair was pulled into a sloppy ponytail, and the T-shirt she revealed underneath her jacket was damp with sweat. Still, she looked happy and bright.

"The only people I can get to play these days are men who think they can take out a woman, even one who's a prætorian." She grinned. "They never do."

"You want to celebrate your victory with a drink?" he asked.

Her eyes weighed him a few moments, the smile fading into her neutral expression. "There's a divey little place around the corner that serves food too—if you can bring yourself to step inside."

"Hey, I've been in my share of dives."

Although, when they entered, he saw his clothing was even more out of place than it had been in the arena. This was very much a blue-collar establishment, and casually dressed people drank cheap liquor and played darts and pool. They found a corner table, and Mae ordered half the menu, needing to refuel after the frantic way the implant drove her body.

"What's up?" she asked. "New developments after I left?"

"New developments before then."

He told her about his bizarre meeting with Geraki, tying some of it to the SCI debriefing. Naturally, Justin was careful to edit out the parts pertaining to her, like how the two of them were supposed to run off together in some divine union and his own particular wheelings and dealings with Geraki's god. Here, in a bar full of laughter and clinking glasses, mystical forces seemed far away.

"Do you think it's true?" she asked between bites of her hamburger. "That there really is some great godly showdown coming?" She wasn't at ease with the idea of gods in the world, but she accepted them now. Not being possessed by one probably helped a little.

Justin tapped his glass of bourbon. "I kind of do. I don't know how or why, but I do. I just wish I knew what to expect."

She nodded. It was a rare side of her, this unkempt Mae, eating junk food. She was still dazzling, and it was hard not to remember how her lips and skin felt. He had to remind himself of the danger she represented. Another night with her would thrust him squarely into this game. That, and he was having difficulty forgetting the way she'd killed Emil. He recalled Dominic's words, that she was a prætorian first and a patrician second—more than that, she was the predator he'd been warned about. Justin could see it in the way she tensed at the breaking of a glass at the bar and the way her eyes assessed every single person who entered, even as she smiled and bantered.

And yet . . . in that moment, there was peace between them. A rapport and naturalness he couldn't remember sharing with a woman. Most conversations with his last serious girlfriend from five years ago had degenerated into "Where is this relationship going?" He knew he had to push that aside and do what he'd come to do.

"Mae . . . there's something I wanted to talk to you about."

She instantly grew wary.

"I . . . wasn't entirely honest about Lucian. There are old rivalries between us, and I kind of exaggerated things." Each word was agonizing. "He's actually a really good guy, and you should give him a chance." It wasn't entirely a lie. Lucian wasn't that bad. Justin just didn't want to give her up.

Clearly, this was the last thing she'd expected. "You . . . you want me to go out with Lucian?"

"Maybe not go out with, exactly," he said. "But, you know, at least talk to him. That fund-raiser thing he wrote about is actually a pretty good idea. Just get to know him in a way that isn't going to attract a media circus. Besides, how often do you get to go to black-tie political fund-raisers?" Justin smiled so that he wouldn't grit his teeth. "Hell, I'll even go like he asked and help deliver you to him."

Too late, Justin realized that was the worst thing he could have said to a woman who'd spent her life feeling like she was someone's possession. *Deliver you to him.* Her face confirmed it. There was no more shock. There was nothing at all—except, perhaps, a fleeting gleam of disappointment in her eyes.

He was taken aback. Was it possible that somewhere, after everything he'd put her through, she still wanted him? Justin ignored that and focused on what mattered: He'd fulfilled his promise to Geraki.

"Well, thanks for the advice," she said stiffly. "Maybe I'll go. Maybe I can salvage that mauve dress."

He couldn't tell whether she knew what a blow that was to him. Instead, he tried to recover his faltering smile. "Great. I'm sure he'll be thrilled. You want another round?" He didn't expect her to stop hating him. But maybe he could get her to hate him a little less.

"I have things I should do." They both knew she was lying.

"One drink," he beseeched. "I didn't give you all my insight on what SCI's doing."

After several agonizing moments, she nodded, not looking that enthused. "Sure."

Justin scooped up the empty glasses. As he waited at the bar for his refills, he looked up at a screen showing—of course—Lucian giving some speech in San Francisco, going on about his great unknown age. Justin had felt a headache coming on since they arrived at the bar, and this only made it worse.

"Goddamned politicians," a voice said. "You can't trust any of those government types."

Justin glanced over and saw a steel-haired businessman sitting at the bar with a glass of wine. With all the emphasis on national security and loyalty that surrounded Justin, he kind of liked the occasional conspiracy theorist. "I *am* a government type."

The man studied Justin, and the light just barely reflected off of what was a very, very good artificial eye. It was nearly indistinguishable from the real one, and judging from the guy's expensive suit, he had money to throw around. He even had a cluster of little white flowers on his lapel. Aside from Justin, he was the best-dressed person in the bar.

"Is that so?" The man chuckled. "Should I be worried, then, about what we aren't being told? What this Age of X is really going to entail for humankind?"

It was a good question. "Well, Senator Darling says it's going to be bright and wonderful. He seems to know."

"Of course he does," the man said with a snort. "Guys your age always think you know everything. Believe me, there's always more to learn."

"Not true. I'm a big believer in the pursuit of knowledge."

The man looked over to where Mae sat alone. "I'd like to get to know more about *her*. You're with her, right? Girlfriend? Wife?"

"Neither. In fact . . . she doesn't really like me right now."

"Lucky for me." The man knocked back his wine and stood up. "I'm going to go talk to her."

Incredibly, the guy made good on his word and walked over to Mae. Strangers' advances were second nature to her, and she looked up at him with a polite smile. She even seemed to thank him when he brazenly took the flowers from his jacket and tucked them behind her ear. He gave her a nod of farewell and walked away.

Justin returned with the drinks. "Did he ask you out?"

"Him?" She laughed, which was nice after the earlier animosity. "No, but he laid it on kind of thick. He could be you in thirty years. Started waxing poetic about how my beauty will live forever in thought and memory and how these were a paltry offering." She pulled the star-shaped white flowers out of her hair and examined them. "They smell good."

"Stephanotis," he said, pulling up his mental encyclopedia without thinking. "From the Greek word for 'crown' . . ."

Her eyebrows rose. "Stephanotis? Wasn't that the flower you told me about in Windsor?"

Justin nearly dropped his glass. He scanned the room frantically, searching for the man. No luck. "Be right back." He hurried up to the bar and waved to get the cute young bartender's attention. She was knocking back what looked like aspirin, something Justin wouldn't have minded since his own headache still pulsed at the back of his skull.

"You probably can't tell me this . . . but do you know that guy's name? When he scanned his ego?"

She hesitated about the breach of privacy and then groaned. "He didn't scan it. I asked him, but he started asking me if I played chess, and I forgot. My boss'll kill me. That was our most expensive wine!"

But Justin was already walking away. "I have to leave," he told Mae.

"Why?" She looked him over, and her concern for him was real. "What's wrong?"

Justin swallowed. "Nothing's wrong. It's just . . . well, the bartender's getting off her shift soon and asked me to go out. I can't turn that down." He put on what he hoped was a smug, bastardly smile.

This time, Mae's thoughts were perfectly obvious. She was

floored that after asking her for another drink, he was about to ditch her for a woman he'd just met.

"I see. Well, far be it from me to stand in your way." She stood up, rigid and formal. "Thanks for the drink. I'll meet you at SCI tomorrow." And without a backward glance, she strode out of the bar, the air freezing around her.

Justin stared after her, feeling forlorn.

Wallow later, said Horatio. *Do you want your answers or not?*

Justin did. He had to know. He had to finally know. He scooped up the flowers and headed out. Back at the house, he found the usual buzz of activity as his family welcomed him home. He ignored them all and went straight to his office, slamming the door behind him.

"I need a search," Justin said to his screen before he even reached his chair. "I need all references to the phrase 'thought and memory.'"

The screen complied with frustrating detail, far too many hits to begin to parse. He drummed his fingers against the desk.

"Filter the search by religious and mythological contexts."

That narrowed the list considerably. In fact, the only results left pertained to one subject. He brought up the first hit, which was a basic encyclopedic entry:

> *In Norse mythology, the god Odin (Wodan in German contexts) is accompanied by two ravens, Huginn (Thought) and Muninn (Memory), who advise him and report what they learn about the world.*

Justin felt mildly ill. He was familiar with stories of Odin, who frequently appeared with other Norse gods when Nordic and Scandinavian castes decided to attempt some revivalist religion. Odin was a major enough god that every servitor had a working knowledge of him. Justin had always thought he did as well, but apparently, he'd been lacking a particularly important detail about the god's choice of companions, a detail that certain invisible birds could've helpfully enlightened him about.

"Give me a full compilation about the Norse god Odin," ordered Justin. "Attributes, primary sources, and general folk-lore."

The screen complied, and with every line he read, Justin felt as though the world was starting to crumble beneath him.

> *Odin, or "All Father," is a Norse god of the Æsir associated with wisdom, cunning, knowledge, war and battle, magic, and death. He is usually accepted as the king of the Norse gods.*
>
> *Odin made many sacrifices for his wisdom. He gave up his eye in order to drink from Mimisbrunnr, the well of wisdom. He also hung himself from the world tree Yggdrasil in order to master the runes, which impart insight into the present and future.*

"I need an image of the runes." Justin already knew what he'd see.

The screen displayed a set of symbols, each labeled with a name. Most were nonsensical, save for one he knew very well since he saw it on his own skin every day. He asked the screen to identify it: *Ansuz—a rune with disputed meanings that is generally associated with the Æsir gods, particularly Odin.* Near it, Justin saw *algiz,* the protective rune the ravens had taught him.

On and on it went, and Justin saw pieces of his life play out before him. He read everything he could find, and after a while, he started reading the same information over and over. His eyesight grew bleary, and he was about to finally call it a day when one line caught his eye:

Odin is also accompanied by two wolves, Geri and Freki.

"Clear the search," he told the screen. "And call Demetrius Devereaux."

Geraki answered after only a couple of seconds, and Justin wondered if he'd been waiting for the call like some eager teenage girl.

"Did you get a guy with a glass eye to come mess with me and start dropping flowers and hints about the ravens?"

"I have absolutely no idea what you're talking about. I must not be smart enough to keep up with your razor-sharp brain."

Throwing something at the screen wasn't going to improve this situation, so Justin took a deep breath and tried to backtrack. "A man talked to me at a bar today. He had one eye and went off about the pursuit of knowledge. He gave me the same crap you do about Mae being so awesome, and then he went and talked to her about 'thought and memory' and gave her something only I knew about. Did you set it up?" Justin demanded. "Did you get someone to do this?"

Geraki looked completely dumbfounded, which would have been enjoyable under different circumstances. Understanding suddenly hit. His eyes widened in awe, and his cheeks flushed.

"He appeared to you! How? Why? You've done nothing but show disrespect, while I serve faithfully, but *you're* the one he comes to in the flesh?" A moment later, Geraki closed his eyes and looked pained. "I shouldn't have said that. I have no right to question my god's actions. I'm only here to listen to his voice."

"You can say his name now," said Justin bitterly. "Odin."

Geraki opened his eyes. "You know his name?"

"Yeah, it took, like, five seconds with a stream search. Why would a Norse god come after me? Why not someone like Mae? You said they gravitate to people with the same heritage."

"You have the blood of a dozen cultures in you, and one of them is probably from that region." Religious rambling was Geraki's specialty, and he seemed to be at ease back in familiar territory. "That, and I told you—a wise and clever god needs a priest with those same qualities."

"I'm not his priest. I'm not even a follower."

Geraki smiled in a way that reminded Justin of those frustrating yearly investigations. "No, but you're about to become his student. I asked what it'd take to make you learn. A name and a face, you said. You got those things. You shouldn't have gotten them, but you did."

Justin faltered. He *had* kind of said that.

"Learning isn't the same as serving or swearing devotion," he told Geraki.

"No, but it's an important step along the way—and don't try to dodge this time."

Justin had, of course, been trying to think of how to dodge it.

How could he be so stupid? He'd been so, so careful with Mae, only to stumble into some sort of divine apprenticeship.

"You remember everything," Geraki added. "Think back to exactly what you said. I asked if those things would get you to begin to train in our god's wisdom and magic. You said yes."

"No," said Justin, still hoping he could get out of this. "My exact words were 'you bet.'" *But it's not going to be good enough this time,* he realized.

"Those words are binding. You made your bargain, and now you'll learn what it means to embrace your calling." Geraki's eyes were alight with the kind of zealous fire that should have made Justin call the authorities. "Welcome to the service of Odin, brother. I look forward to working with you."

ACKNOWLEDGMENTS

This story has been a long time in coming, and many people helped bring it to light. Thank you to my husband for putting up with the late nights and religious speculation; my agent, Jim McCarthy, for his constant support and therapy; and editor Jessica Horvath for letting me do "just one more revision." Thank you also to the readers brave enough to join me on this new and very different adventure. You keep me writing, and I hope you love this series. My father, a great philosopher of religion and spirituality, passed away while I was writing this, and I hope he loves it too.

GLOSSARY

Arcadia—Post-Decline country formed from part of the southern and southeastern former United States. It possesses moderate technology and a religion-centric government. There's a lot of tension between it and the RUNA, both because of current border disputes and Arcadia's feeling as though it was abandoned after the Decline.

Age of Decline—Official name for the fifty years between Mephistopheles and the discovery of its vaccine.

Age of Renewal—Official name for the period of time following the discovery of the Mephistopheles vaccine and the rapid rebuilding of Gemman society that followed.

Age of X—Tongue-in-cheek political term for the RUNA's next age, its "unknown age" to come.

annexed lands—New territory recently conquered by the RUNA, usually in a state of unrest as they adopt Gemman policies and uniform culture.

Cain—A hereditary set of genetic defects created from Mephistopheles. It often involves damaged skin and hair, poor fertility, and asthma. It usually shows up only in those without mixed genetic backgrounds, such as the patricians or those from the provinces.

castal, castals—Slang term for those who belong to the castes.

castes—Slang term for patrician groups, those who clung to their ethnic heritage and were exempted from genetic mandates after the Decline because of financial contributions to the early government. Patricians identify with a particular culture (Irish, Egyptian, etc.) and select features associated with that culture. Many patricians still live off that early wealth and have established aristocratic mini-societies on special regions allocated to them called land grants.

Church of Humanity—A "secular religion." The only religion officially endorsed by the government. Although it has temples and priests, there is no deity involved. It is meant to encourage decent, humanitarian ways of living that are synced up with the RUNA's laws and philosophies.

consul—One of two leaders of the RUNA's senate. Consuls are elected from currently serving senators by other senators. A very powerful position.

contraceptive implants—Mandatory devices all Gemman women get upon puberty and are required to keep until they're twenty years old.

Decline—Name for the years immediately following Mephistopheles' devastation.

Division of Sect and Cult Investigation—The subdepartment within Internal Security that the servitors work out of. Sometimes called SCI.

Eastern Alliance—Called EA. The RUNA's sister country, formed from parts of what used to be China and Russia. It shares many genetic policies with the RUNA, including population swapping, but has a looser stance on religion. It nearly matches the RUNA in technology and order. Its primary language is Mandarin, followed by Russian.

ego—A small handheld device that functions much like a smartphone. It controls communications and is synced to the media stream as well as to the owner's identity chip. Unless a special code is entered, egos will not function if they're too far away from the owner's chip.

Gemman, Gemmans—Citizens of the RUNA. The term comes from the country's motto, *Gemma mundi*, which means "jewel of the world."

genetic mandates—A set of laws that the RUNA employed to create a diverse population resistant to Mephistopheles. Part of this included forcibly swapping parts of the population with others from the EA. For much of the RUNA's history, citizens were not allowed to reproduce with those who wouldn't produce genetically diverse offspring. Later, the law was amended to allow freedom of reproduction, but with monetary penalties to those who didn't reproduce optimally. In the current-day RUNA, there are no penalties, but those who still seek genetically diverse mates receive stipends from the government.

genetic resistance—A numeric score from 1 to 10 that identifies how resistant an individual is to Mephistopheles and Cain. The more mixed the person's background, the higher their score tends to be. Most plebeians now score between 8 and 10. Patricians average around 5.

identity chips—A small chip in the left hand of each Gemman citizen. The chip is keyed to the person's DNA and an entry in the National Registry that contains all their basic information. Chip readers scattered throughout the country regulate who enters secure areas and also help locate criminals and outsiders.

Internal Security—The ministry within the RUNA that handles threats and security inside the country's borders. The Division of Sect and Cult Investigation, which the servitors work out of, is part of it.

land grants—Exclusive regions of the country that patrician groups are allowed to live on. Most are in the middle of the country. Although the land grants have a caste's cultural slant, Gemman loyalty is still strongly enforced and borders are kept open to Gemman officials.

media stream—The RUNA's equivalent of the Internet, containing access to the country's data, resources, and entertainment channels (there is no separate television service). The media stream is a public resource, accessible to all citizens through egos and home screens. Called "the stream" for short.

Mephistopheles—Common name for a virus released into the world in the early twenty-first century that killed half of the earth's population. Those of diverse genetic backgrounds have greater resistance to it and the hereditary disease it created, Cain. A vaccine created in the RUNA fifty years after the virus's release has mostly wiped it out.

National Registry—Database of all Gemman citizens, containing their basic and genetic information. Identity chips are synced to the Registry, and all citizens must have names of Greek or Latin origin.

patriarchy, patrician, patricians—Those who clung to their ethnic heritage and were exempted from genetic mandates after the Decline because of financial contributions to the early government. Patricians identify with a particular culture (Irish, Egyptian, etc.) and select features associated with that culture. Many patricians still live off that early wealth and have established aristocratic mini-societies on special regions allocated to them called land grants. "Caste" and "castal" are slang terms for patricians used by the rest of the country.

plebeian, plebeians—Term for most of the RUNA's population, those created from its genetic mixing programs. Most plebeians have dark hair and eyes, with tanned skin.

population limits—Gemman women are allowed to have only two children unless they can provide proof of financial and social stability to care for more; if they can't, they are sterilized. Those qualifying may have up to four children total, with no exceptions.

prætorian, prætorians—The RUNA's "supersoldiers." Prætorians have a small positive feedback implant in their arms that will increase whatever neurotransmitters are being actively produced in their bodies. For example, when adrenaline is naturally produced in a fight, the implant will increase the body's production, enhancing the prætorian's abilities. Prætorians are divided into color-coded cohorts and serve for eighteen years, from age twenty-two to forty.

primary schooling—Elementary school in the RUNA.

provinces—The generic term used by Gemmans for any part of the world that isn't the RUNA or EA. It isn't an official designation in those regions, which range from semiorganized countries to completely unregulated regions.

Republic of United North America—Commonly called the RUNA. A country formed during the Decline from Canada and parts of what was fomerly the United States. It is the most stable and technologically advanced country in the world. Its primary language is English, followed by Spanish. Its official colors are maroon and dark purple.

RUNA—Pronounced "roo-na." See *Republic of United North America*.

secondary schooling—Collective term for middle school and high school in the RUNA.

servitor—From the Latin "*servitor veritatis*" or "servant of the truth." Government employees of Internal Security who license and investigate religious groups. Although much of the job consists of paperwork and interviews, some situations become volatile, and servitors have quick access to law enforcement and military resources. Their subdepartment is the Division of Sect and Cult Investigation.

stream—See *media stream*.

tertiary schooling—A required two-year degree that all Gemman citizens must complete, starting when they're eighteen. Unlike primary and secondary education, which is fairly standardized, tertiary education is more specialized to the person's interests, with the hope of encouraging a four-year college degree. Those starting college by a certain age have their education paid for by the government.

Read on for a look at the next book
in Richelle Mead's Age of X series,

THE IMMORTAL CROWN

Available in hardcover and e-book from Dutton

ELECTI

Mae Koskinen was one of her country's most elite soldiers. She'd excelled enough in her early training to be hand selected for the Prætorian Guard, a regiment of warriors whose lethal training was enhanced by small, high-tech arm implants that used natural endorphins to increase speed and strength. From that distinguished tier, she'd gone on to join a secret government mission involving the improbable—yet alarmingly real—return of supernatural forces to the world, putting her face-to-face with atrocities and wonders her fellow countrymen would never have believed. There was no one else in a position quite like Mae's, no one who'd seen the things she had. She was feared by ordinary people. She was feared by her own military.

"So why," she muttered to herself, "am I always breaking up bar fights?"

The well-dressed answer, she knew, stood a few steps behind her, staying out of the way as she swung a barstool at a furious man who was charging her with more emotion than skill. The stool broke into pieces as it made contact, knocking him backward to land on the dirt-packed floor with a *thump*. He lay there, momentarily dazed, and Mae used the opportunity to quickly scan the rest of the room. Thankfully, none of his cronies seemed too eager to join the fray in their fallen comrade's place. The implant had Mae churning with fight-or-flight chemicals, and as much as she might have actually enjoyed further altercation, she knew the smart thing to do was to get out of there while they still could. Their mission parameters always advised discretion, and they'd kind of blown it this time.

She tossed the splintered barstool leg on the floor and turned to the man standing behind her. "Come on—let's go."

Dr. Justin March—her partner and the cause of this fight—hesitated. After a moment of deliberation, he pulled some local currency out of his pocket and set it on a nearby table. "Sorry," he called to the bartender, who was watching them in a stunned state of disbelief. Mae grabbed Justin's arm and led him out, moving at a brisk pace, before someone thought to come after them.

"Really?" she snapped, once they were outside. "Is it possible for you to go one day without hitting on someone?"

"That girl?" He sounded legitimately offended. "I wasn't hitting on her. I was just making conversation while I waited for my drink. How was I to know her boyfriend would flip out?"

Mae said nothing as they hurried through the busy, dusty streets. Part of her was too angry to respond to his excuses. The rest of her was too focused on their surroundings, as she scouted around them for any signs of danger. No matter how many times she left her homeland in the Republic of United North America, she never quite got used to the shocking and often primitive differences found in the provinces. Nassau was no exception. It was like something out of a movie, with dirt-filled streets crowded with pedestrians, horses, and bicycle taxis. Street vendors hawked their wares, and many sets of eyes followed Mae and Justin. She knew they stood out, not just because of their lighter complexions but also because of their clothing and general healthy appearances. The Bahamas had had a mostly African-descended population when religious extremists unleashed the Mephistopheles virus on the world a century ago. Countries with diverse genetic backgrounds had shown greater resistance to the virus, but being on an island had cut the Bahamians off from the chance of mixing with other gene pools. As a result, many had died from the virus, and those who'd survived had passed on Cain, Mephistopheles's hereditary parting gift, which marked its victims with hair and skin damage, infertility, and asthma.

The region was poor too, and Justin and Mae appeared wealthy to many of the locals. They'd already dodged two attempted robberies on this trip. Usually, the sight of her gun dissuaded would-be thieves, but many thought a foreign woman was an easy target. Mae was always quick to correct them.

"Come on, Mae," said Justin, when he realized she wasn't

going to answer him. "I wasn't hitting on her. You know I have higher standards than that."

Mae wondered if she should feel flattered. Working with Justin these past couple of months had certainly given her a lot of insight into his preferences for flings—particularly since she'd been one of them. Things had ended abruptly when, after their one night together, he'd tersely informed her that a second time with her held no appeal. His subsequent cycling through other women had only driven home how meaningless she was on his list of conquests. What infuriated her the most was that she herself was no stranger to casting aside lovers. The problem was that, until Justin, she had never been the one cast aside. Her pride didn't handle injuries well, but she supposed she should be grateful Justin had walked away so easily, unlike her previous boyfriend, who'd wandered into dangerous obsession after their relationship had ended.

Justin sighed in frustration. "Fine. Be that way. We might as well head straight to Mama Orane's anyway. Maybe if we're there early, I can get a drink."

Mae certainly didn't mind staying away from their cramped hotel room, which had an unscreened window as air-conditioning and only one flyswatter as pest control. Justin's readiness to turn to drinking, though not unexpected, was more of a concern.

"Don't you think you should keep a clear head for this?" she asked. "You need to see what this woman's up to."

He seemed pleased to have drawn Mae out, and a little of his former professor mode took over. "I'd be very surprised if she turns out to be real. Fortune-tellers have been around since the dawn of time, no supernatural powers needed. It's easy to pick up on cues from people and make them believe what they want to hear."

Mae nearly said, "That sounds like what you do." She refused to be petty, though, and instead remarked, "Like Geraki?"

Justin grimaced at the reference to a would-be prophet back home. "Fortune-telling isn't the same as prophecy, and unfortunately for all of us, he's the real thing."

The weirdness of their conversation wasn't lost on Mae. Three months ago, she would've thought it was crazy. Their society denounced religion and the paranormal as blind superstition. The RUNA was so cautious of that kind of influence corrupting its citizens that it went to great pains to rein in those who worshipped higher powers. Anyone deemed dangerous was stamped out. The rest were cautiously allowed to continue but watched very closely. Justin, and the other servitors like him, were the ones who investigated and passed judgment.

That system had proved sound for most of the RUNA's history until their government—covertly—acknowledged that there actually were unexplained forces stirring in the world. Justin had the unique and rather obscure position of being both a star servitor and a believer, which had landed him—depending on one's view—the enviable or unenviable position of their lead investigator into such matters. And Mae, who had reluctantly seen enough to make her believe too, had been made his bodyguard. Most of their missions kept them safely within their comfortable and technologically advanced homeland . . . but every so often, they found themselves out in the wider world, in places like this.

After ten minutes of walking, the two of them reached their destination: the home of a woman whom the RUNA's intelligence had scouted as potentially being involved with supernatural forces. Mama Orane's barebones house was guarded by two hulking, armed men who looked Mae and Justin over with hard eyes. The small metal implant in her arm already had her on edge, and the sight of this new threat spun her up even more, triggering a greater flood of adrenaline and other neurotransmitters of battle. One wrong look from these guys, and she'd be on them instantly.

But once they saw the snake-engraved wooden charm Justin had bought that morning as a ticket to today's show, the guards waved them through, barely acknowledging the guns. Inside the house, a young woman collected the rest of the admission fee, which Justin paid in local currency. Mae didn't know the exact exchange rate but winced at what she saw as her tax dollars being handed over.

They were ushered through a beaded curtain, into a spacious living room filled with old velvet furniture and lit only by candles. At first, she thought that was simply for effect, until she realized there were no electric lights anywhere. For the price this place was charging, it seemed like they could've gotten on the island's grid, fledgling though it was. Everything in the room was cast in flickering shadows, and incense smoked in the air. Considering the lack of flies here, maybe the incense was as much repellent as ceremonial. Mae put a hand on Justin's arm to stop him from going farther as she scanned for hiding spots and points of entry. He leaned toward her and spoke softly.

"Look over there," he said. "We're not the only visitors from the RUNA."

He was right. Across the room, occupying two couches, were five loud, laughing individuals, two women and three men. They were passing two bottles of wine between them. Their clothing and mostly healthy features marked them as fellow Gemmans, the term their country's citizens went by. This group's red hair and pale skin in particular identified them as patricians: Gemmans whose ancestors hadn't been part of the RUNA's early forced genetic mixing program. That program had resulted in a diverse ethnic population that had better resisted Mephistopheles until a vaccine was developed and had allowed the RUNA to become the dominant country it was today. Most Gemmans born of this mixed heritage—nicknamed "plebeians"—had tanned skin, with dark hair and eyes, like Justin did. Patricians, in not being part of that breeding, had kept their recessive traits but faced greater health issues. Many had either died out or passed on Cain. Mae herself was of Finnish ancestry and a rare patrician who was born in perfect health.

Her safety assessment complete, Mae waved Justin toward a love seat in the corner that afforded a full view of the room and its two doors. She sat down beside him, and they were immediately noticed by one of the Gemman men. He had shocking red hair and too-smooth skin that suggested cosmetic surgery to clear up Cain acne scars.

"Hey," he called, holding up his glass in a toast. *"Gemma Mundi!"*

Justin nodded back, instantly putting on that charm that never seemed to dim. "Hope you brought your own," he called. "That stuff they sell here's one step away from vinegar."

The redheads whooped. "We got it from a guy over on Augusta," said one of the women. "It's EA rice wine. Not bad. You can have some." She glanced around, apparently searching for a glass. Seeing none, she simply took the bottle in its entirety from the other woman and offered it toward him. "Come on, Roisin. We can share with our countrymen."

"Got my own." Justin pulled out a flask from his coat and held it up. "Rum—which they don't mess up."

After a little more friendly banter, the other Gemmans returned to their revelry. More guests began to trickle in, many of whom were from neighboring areas in Central and South America. A couple of businessmen entered together, greeting the Gemmans with Eastern Alliance accents.

Justin was smiling like he was at a high-class party as he watched everything, but as Mae studied the way the candlelight made shadows play over his face, with its chiseled profile and dark, thoughtful eyes, she knew there was more going on beneath the surface. His sharp and cunning mind was always in motion, something others rarely realized beneath that friendly smile. Mae's upbringing in the Nordic patriarchy had taught her to conceal her feelings. Justin had simply picked up the habit along the way and used it to full advantage.

His words were quiet when he spoke to her. "About what I'd expect for tourists around here—except for those other Gemmans. Nassau's bargain beach resorts wouldn't be enough for them to leave the comforts of home, not when they could find safer escapes in Mazatlán."

"Dubiously safer," Mae corrected, recalling a trip they'd made there that had resulted in abduction and her fighting for her life. "Maybe they're here for the novelty. Maybe they want the risk."

"Maybe," agreed Justin. "Bored rich kids have certainly done stupider things. They'll be lucky if they make it back to their inn, though." His sharp eyes soon focused back on their surroundings, and she could see him taking in all the expressions and fragments of conversation that drifted their way. And more than that. Clothing, hair, posture, mannerisms . . . all of it was fodder for him. It was why, despite his many flaws, he excelled at a job that required him to use tiny clues to find dangerous influences.

"These latecomers are locals," he continued as a group of mixed ages and genders began filtering in. Most of the chairs and couches were gone now, but the newcomers happily took spots on the floor, laughing and chatting among themselves. "Friends or family. I'm guessing this is regular entertainment for them. And that must be the local beauty queen."

A young woman entered, maybe eighteen at most. Although her braided hair had the brittle quality often seen with Cain, her dark brown skin was lovely and smooth, free of any flaws. She raised her hands, and the room fell silent.

"Welcome, friends," she said. Although she spoke with an accent, at least to Mae's ears, the girl's English was clear, her voice high and sweet. "Welcome to Mama Orane's house. She is honored to have such guests grace her home."

"Well-paying guests," muttered Mae.

"Mama Orane is special," the girl continued. As she spoke, two young boys brought in a small, low table. "Mama Orane has been chosen by the spirits and powerful ones who move unseen in the world to be their vessel, so that we may hear their wisdom."

A chill ran down Mae's back at those words. A sidelong look at Justin's face showed he'd had a similar reaction. Although the world of gods and the supernatural was still largely mysterious to her, one thing Mae had learned was that gods rarely spoke directly to humans. Usually they used dreams or intermediaries. Was Mama Orane possibly one of the latter? Life as they knew it would certainly be a lot easier if they had a direct line to the divine.

The girl tilted her head back. "Prepare yourselves. Prepare yourselves for wondrous, powerful things. Even Mama Orane never knows what to expect. She places herself in the hands of those forces beyond." The girl swept a flourish-filled bow toward one of the doorways, and a short, curvaceous middle-aged woman entered. Her skin was as dark as that of the girl who'd introduced her but showed many of the acne scars typical of Cain. Mae couldn't make out the woman's hair because it was concealed under a bright red head scarf embroidered with gold.

The locals on the floor showed their approval by rhythmically patting their legs and murmuring, "Ma-ma, ma-ma. . . ."

Justin leaned forward, his elbows on his knees and his chin resting on clasped hands as he scrutinized her. The earlier banter was gone. This was serious, the reason they'd traveled out to the provinces.

Mama Orane stood in the middle of the room and hung her head so that she stared at the floor. Her assistant picked up a small drum from the table and began tapping out a steady beat as she murmured in what sounded like French. Although English was the island's main language, Haitian refugees had been coming to it both before and since the Decline.

The locals joined in with the girl, and Mama Orane began to shake. At first, she could have simply been dancing to the beat, but as her movements grew increasingly erratic, it was obvious she was having—or faking—some kind of fit. Despite all she'd witnessed in the past, Mae still entered these situations with a healthy dose of skepticism. She knew Justin, who was barely blinking, did too.

Mama Orane shook for several more moments and suddenly froze. Everyone in the room fell silent, and there was a collective intake of breath. Slowly, she lifted her head, her dark eyes looking around the room. Then a sly smile crept across her face. *"Bonsoir, mes petits."*

The tension broke as the locals cheered. "Josephine! It's Josephine!"

Mama Orane, who'd entered in a slow and stately way, suddenly sauntered forward, swaying her hips with the sass of a girl half her age. She circled the room, still with that sly smile, taking the measure of her guests as her assistant trailed a respectful distance behind. At last, Mama Orane stopped in front of one of the EA men. Her expression went from sassy to outright flirtatious, and she completely caught him off guard when she sat down in his lap, much to the delight of the onlookers.

She spoke in French, but her hovering assistant quickly translated. "Why are you so sad, sweetie? You still miss her?" Mama Orane gently stroked his face. "Don't be sad. She's not the one for you."

Amazingly, the man's earlier amused expression immediately began to crumple. "No, she *is*."

The assistant performed two-way translation, and Mama Orane shook her head. "No. You were better off when she left. Just you wait—someone else will come along."

"Really?" he asked, a flicker of hope in his eyes.

"Really. And until then, I'll be happy to keep you company." She darted in with a quick kiss on his cheek that actually made him blush, and then she moved on with a wink.

"Well?" Mae whispered to Justin, who looked unimpressed.

"Easy to guess at a recent separation," he responded quietly. "You can tell from his finger he used to wear a wedding ring. And he tipped her off early that he was the rejected party."

Mama Orane—or Josephine—continued visiting with other members of the audience, all men. She flirted shamelessly and dispensed various tidbits of romantic advice and predictions. Justin didn't break down any more of them for her, but Mae could tell from his face that he wasn't buying in yet.

As it turned out, Mama Orane made him her last visit. She looked down upon him from her demure height, hands on her hips, as she tsked. "I won't even bother with you, love. Not many women can catch you."

He smiled back gallantly. "I've been waiting for you."

She laughed in delight and patted his shoulder before returning to her central position. Her assistant took up the drum again, and there was another bout of shaking and chanting. When she came out of this spell and looked up, she spoke in English, in a much flatter tone than Josephine had: "Where's my rum?"

Those on the floor were overjoyed. "Reynard!"

Mama Orane's Reynard guise moved with a stride that was simply laid-back, rather than attempting any sex appeal. He or she—Mae wasn't entirely sure which was accurate—told fortunes on a variety of topics. One of Reynard's targets included the Gemman woman who'd offered Justin the wine.

"What's your name?"

"Elspeth," she said meekly.

"You can't stay away, you know. You've eventually gotta go back home."

Elspeth stuck her chin out defiantly and tried to stare down the small woman standing before her. "I'm not! I'm done with them. No one can make me go."

"No," agreed Mama Orane–as–Reynard. "Only you can. You going to keep breaking your parents' hearts?"

Elspeth's lip quivered, and she looked away, refusing to make eye contact. Mama Orane left it at that and returned to the room's center, where another round of chanting and drumming began.

"What was that one?" Mae asked, her voice covered by the din.

Justin was silent as he studied the red-haired group. "Elspeth," he said after several moments. "She's a Scottish castal." He used the slang term for "patrician" without thought. "One of the others was named Roisin. Irish. She's fraternizing outside her caste. That's what she's dreading going home to."

"They could be from a meta-caste," Mae reminded him. "One with lots of Celtic varieties."

"The only two out there select for recessive-colored eyes. Hers are brown, which the Caledonians allow." Justin shook his head. "She's good. Really good."

Mama Orane's third transformation was into a man the others called El Diable.

"The Devil," said Justin. "Subtle."

This guise elicited none of the joy in the onlookers that Josephine and Reynard had. A hush fell over the room as those gathered sat tensely. Mama Orane's face was cold and devoid of emotion as she surveyed the room. Then, astonishingly, she strode straight toward Mae and Justin. The woman herself posed no physical threat, but the look in her eyes made Mae's implant ramp up. There was something so eerie in that gaze, something inhuman that Mae couldn't quite put her finger on.

But even that was less shocking than what happened next. Mama Orane leaned forward so that she was at their eye level. When she spoke as El Diable, it was barely a whisper, like a snake's voice.

"*Electi . . .*"

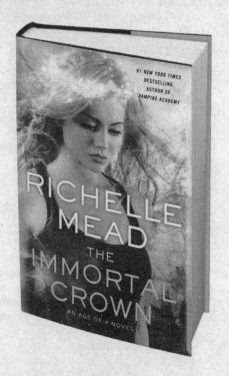

The *New York Times* bestselling Morganville Vampires series

by Rachel Caine

College student Claire Danvers has her share of challenges—like being a genius in a school that favors beauty over brains, battling homicidal girls in her dorm, and finding out that her college town is overrun with the living dead.

rachelcaine.com

Available wherever books are sold or at penguin.com

R0036